VESPERTINE VEIL

ALISHA KORVANE

Three Pines & Ink Publishing

Vespertine Veil

ISBN: 979-8-9938691-0-0

Cover by Cass @ Opulent Designs

Editing by Editing4Indies

Map by Simplefantasymaps

*To the ones who never fit in, but instead colored
outside the lines, and were labeled weird.
The old souls and the individuals who marched
to the beat of their own drum.*

I saved a seat for you.

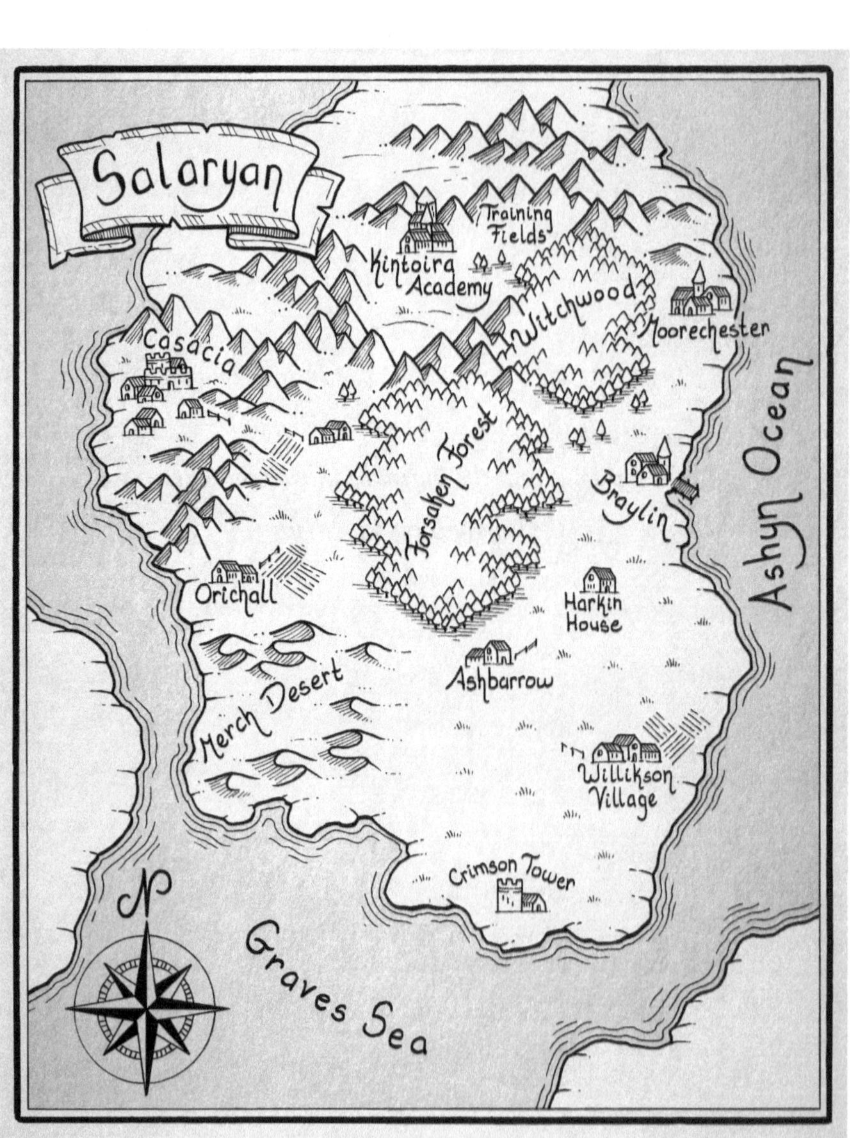

Salaryan
Training Fields
Kintoira Academy
Witchwood
Moorechester
Casacia
Forsaken Forest
Braylin
Ashyn Ocean
Orichall
Harkin House
Merch Desert
Ashbarrow
Willikson Village
Crimson Tower
N
Graves Sea

CONTENTS

If the Veils stand for everything light, honest, and worthy,
then the Noctryns are the antithesis of that. Immoral, vicious, and corrupt.
The only thing the two have in common is that both are weaponized

Chapter One

I've come to realize that solitude isn't a weakness. It's a delicate strength. And if you aren't careful, it can become highly addictive.

The second thing I've recognized is that when you're alone, it's harder to hide from what you're becoming. Which is why I'm currently sitting in this darkened, run-down pub brimming to the rafters with people. The very same individuals who make my brain feel like it's dying. Gasping for that last sliver of breath.

All the while, death sits in the corner, and impatiently waits to claw its way down my throat.

But I'm not the one death will ultimately claim.

The stench of stale ale permeates my nostrils as I let my eyes roam over the dimly lit room, filled with too many bodies and not enough air. They just sit in here laughing and hiding behind their cups, pretending their world isn't one fragile stone away from crumbling.

They're naive.

And they'll die for it.

Civilians of Salaryan, the same ones who don't care if their abilities are allowed to manifest. You can bet your ass they will be the first ones screaming for help, though. If I don't get away from this place soon, my biggest fear is that I'll become just like them. Content to bury my head in the sand and stay complacent. To never reclaim what should never have been taken in the first place.

Sweat builds on the palms of my hands, and my cloak feels like it's too heavy. I feel like I'm suffocating. I rub the moisture on my lap and look around for the nearest exit. It dawns on me this probably wasn't one of my best ideas as the door I came in swings open, and a handful of loud men who can't seem to hold their ale or their loud opinions burl through.

This dingy establishment leaves a lot to be desired, and not just in the clientele. The once claret-colored paint on the walls is so faded it now resembles chipping rust. Warped wooden planks protrude from the ground in various places, and the booth beneath me wobbles every time I so much as breathe, as if it's fighting for its life. The wooden beams holding up the ceiling sag and look as if they might crumble in defeat at any moment.

Candlelight flickers against the warped glass windows, throwing eerie shadows across the faces of patrons eager to forget. This was the kind of crowd that lingered because they had nowhere else to go.

Some would go as far as to call this place a complete and utter shit-hole.

My lips pull up in a faint smile, half guilt and half defiance. I knew coming here was a mistake, but I did it anyway.

Voracious laughter from my left causes me to duck my head slightly lower than normal.

It's obvious he's not coming, and I was an idiot for believing he could get out of the academy and back without anyone noticing. Even after picking the nearest city, which was small enough not to be on the academy's radar but large enough to be discreet, it was a long shot that he could sneak away and meet up.

I tuck my hair behind my ear and make sure my hood is securely in place before sliding out of the worn-down booth, the wood creaking beneath my weight. Head down and chin tucked, I avoid making eye contact with anyone. I don't want to give them a reason to remember me being here.

I head toward the back, silently disappearing through the crowd. At nineteen years old, and not exactly the type to frequent shady company, I've never been here before. I kind of planned on just leaving the way I came in, but the crowd has doubled since I arrived. I don't feel like trying to elbow my way through.

I slip into the long hallway tucked to the side. The candles sitting in the tarnished brass holders flicker, casting shadows on the peeling walls. It really adds a nice touch of *I'm about to die* to the putrid ambience.

Walking quickly and tossing glances behind me sporadically, I head toward the end of the hallway before cutting a sharp left and breathe in a deep sigh of relief.

There's a door.

Thank fuck there's a door.

It's partially hanging off its hinges, but it's there.

It takes everything in me not to run toward it to just be able to take a full breath of fresh air again. One that's not filled with alcohol and body odor.

The moment I step outside, the cool night air slaps me in the face, reminding me I'm alive, and for the moment, it's a blessing. Tomorrow might change that opinion, but tonight, I have things worth living for.

Without a backward glance I make my escape. "This was a dumb idea," I mumble, kicking a pebble as I walk down the dark, cobbled street, shadows following in my wake. Each step is heavy with disappointment. Of all the nights for one of our plans not to come together, the night before the start of Asylamation would be the absolute worst-case scenario.

Welcome to the worst-case scenario.

This little excursion should have given me a nice edge over my competition. Something that someone like me, adequate to the core, desperately needs. I'm not too proud to admit that, thus far in my short life, I haven't really excelled at anything. I've just been sufficient. An abundance of mediocrity. To finally be able to take part in the initiation period is all I've been able to think about. To be able to manifest what has been mine since birth but withheld. I'd love nothing more than to show those who always doubted me that they can choke on it.

A quick motion to my right catches my eye, but too late, I realize my mistake as a hand lands over my mouth, blocking any scream. The attacker's other hand rests right below my rib cage, effectively trapping me.

"Leaving so soon, brat?" a deep voice purrs into my ear.

A sharp breath escapes from my lungs, half laugh, half growl.

This asshole.

I utter every colorful curse word that comes to mind. Unfortunately, it's muffled behind the firm grip pressing into my lips.

I know that voice almost as well as I know my own.

Ambrose Ballard.

He hesitates before lowering his hand from my mouth, like he's not sure my creative vocabulary won't continue the moment he does.

"You could have just said hello like a normal person," I huff, rubbing my lips with the back of my hand.

His masculine chuckle wraps around me before he grabs my shoulders, turning me to face him. The first thing I focus on is the smirk resting on his stubbornly handsome face. It's like a punch straight to the gut. It's been so long since I've seen that smirk.

I've missed it. Desperately.

"You know how much I love to make an entrance, and what better way to make one than ending up with a pretty girl in my arms?" he asks in a playful tone, his eyes raking me from head to toe like he's missed me too.

Too bad for me that I know he's just playing. Best friend privileges also come with a big, fat off-limits sign plastered to my forehead. Regrettably, I think it's the only thing he sees when looking at me. It's a far cry from what I see every time I look at him. Like the way his easy smile shows off his perfectly straight teeth, or the way his glacial-blue eyes crinkle at the sides when he laughs. The fact that he towers over me with his impressive height, and how, somehow, I always instantly feel safe by his side.

The glow of the torchlight along the wall makes his dark brown waves, which sit on his shoulders, appear almost auburn. He's the most beautiful person I know and the most unattainable, especially for me.

You sound pathetic, Nori.

I clear my throat because I do sound pathetic. Even to myself. "You may be well on your way to becoming one of the best soldiers in the regiment, but you're not there yet," I warn as I poke him in the chest. His very solid, defined chest. A year at the academy has brought about some changes for him. "What held you up? I figured you'd bailed on me," I say, craning my neck back to peer into his amused eyes.

"What took me so long? I'll tell you what took me so long," he says with a saccharine grin. "I was stealing *this* for you."

I watch with growing anticipation as his hand disappears in his pocket before withdrawing a small piece of parchment. "Is that what I think it is? Please tell me that's what I think it is," I plead, reaching for it.

His smug grin is slowly replaced with an uneasy one.

"Yeah, Nori, it's exactly what you think it is," he replies, holding it out of my reach. "A death sentence for both of us if you get caught with it. Also known as a copy of this year's written portion of the Asylamation."

I don't know whether I want to punch him or kiss him. Neither is highly recommended for different reasons.

When he got word to me last month, explaining that he might be able to give me an advantage and obtain a copy of the exam, I was hesitant for about three seconds. I'm not above lying, cheating, or stealing at this point in my life to get into Kintoira Academy. The academy that trains all of the realm's future soldiers. Also, it just happens to be Ambrose's current residence. I'd do anything to become a student. Even enroll and commit to Asylamation week. The week that tests the prospects by trial of blood through written and physical assessments.

He and I both know what's at stake if either of us gets caught with this document. I want to be a student, but I never said I have any qualms about how I get there. It was, however, very stupid of me to agree to let Ambrose be a part of this. Not that anyone really *lets* him do anything, but he put himself in danger for me, and that's not something I take lightly.

If I were caught, there would be a swift punishment of execution. No questions asked, no jury or second chances. Not many people would notice or care. But Ambrose Ballard's execution would certainly be noticed.

And a tragedy.

There are two portions to the test—a written and a physical. The academy weighs each answer given in the written portion and watches every move and decision made during the physical portion. Not only are the prospects trying to just stay alive but they're also being judged for every choice they make. What lies within their core? Are they dark wielders or light wielders? It's not just about capabilities but also about who we are at our very essence.

As if anything is ever really that simple.

Kintoira Academy is the birthplace of the fiercest fighters in all of the Domains. That much is pretty simple. It's not even up for debate. It's also the one place you must attend in Salaryan if you want to manifest your birth-given abilities. Which is absolute bullshit if you ask me, but to voice this out loud is heresy. So, I'll keep my mouth shut and my head firmly attached to my shoulders, thank you very much.

Their motto is that they withhold our powers from us to protect us. According to them, we can't control our abilities unless we're taught how to. To prevent our powers from manifesting, all newborns are given blockers at birth. I know the truth, though, even if I can't say it out loud.

It's just an excuse for them to control us.

To keep us on a tight leash.

I'm done letting them hold the reins.

I gingerly run my fingers over the brittle parchment. It's surreal that something so small and inconspicuous could hold so much weight in the direction my life is about to take.

I can't help but grin as I look up at him, my chest feeling lighter than it has in days. "Thank you, Ambrose. I know what this could have cost you. I'm sorry I even agreed to this when you mentioned it, but I don't regret it. Not if it means we'll finally be together again."

Growing up with someone whom you see every day and then being suddenly ripped apart is the absolute worst. Being a year younger than him, I had to stay behind, wandering aimlessly through each day until I could join him at Kintoira. I never realized just how long a day can feel until he wasn't a part of them anymore. I have to land in his regiment, it's nonnegotiable.

I curl my fingers around the parchment. This is my ticket to being by his side.

His blue eyes are full of concern as he trails a long, slender finger down my cheek, causing my body to lean forward on its own accord.

Traitor.

I'm as touch-starved as I am suicidal. First by thinking I can cheat my way into the academy, and now by leaning into my best friend's touch.

Oh, how the mighty have fallen.

"I knew what was at stake, Nori. I didn't just do it for you. I selfishly did it for me too," he softly whispers. His deep baritone wraps around me like a security blanket, offering a fleeting feeling of warmth and safety. Slowly, he drops his hand, causing me to step back.

I pull my sleeve down and adjust the front of my cloak. I know better than to allow myself to fall into the false sense of security his presence always brings. In the end, I'm his best friend, and that's the role I'll play. The line has all but been drawn in the sand. I'm not willing to try to blur it.

The consequences could be too great.

The damp cobbled streets are quiet tonight. Most of the patrons are indoors drinking their worries away or by their hearths. They're doing their best to try to stay warm from the bitter cold that descends on us like an unwelcome guest that never leaves. This region is always frigid, being so far north, but lately, it's been particularly unbearable.

Moving from foot to foot to keep my blood flowing, I carefully tuck the parchment in my deep pocket. I should feel bad for cheating, but I don't.

Desperation has robbed me of a lot of my emotions.

Leaning back against the brick wall, Ambrose runs his hand through his thick waves, a telltale sign he's got things on his mind. When he catches me watching him, he drops his hand and rubs the sharp line of his jaw instead.

"I'm going to be there on the sidelines watching. I'll see every single move you make."

I arch a brow. Not what I was expecting, but okay. I'll take it. It shouldn't make my stomach feel weird and tingly, but it does.

"You've always been on the sidelines for me," I acknowledge. "I remember the nights I would sneak out and hide in the sawgrass, lying up and looking at the stars, wishing I could become one of them. Even if for just a moment, before I burned out. You'd always find me."

His eyes soften at the memories as he pushes off the wall. "Try to review as much as you can tonight. You don't have much time before you sit for the exam, but it's more than any other prospect could hope for." His brows lower, and his eyes take on a hard edge. "The last thing you want to do is end up in the wrong regiment."

I nod in understanding.

He runs his palms down his face in obvious agitation at not being able to control the outcome tomorrow and the entire week following. He's always been a control freak. "They would use everything good about you and bend it until there was nothing left but broken fragments. Don't give them that satisfaction," he continues in a gruff voice, barely more than a whisper.

I nod again in clear understanding and more than enough agreement.

I don't want to end up in the *other* regiment. The infamous dark regiment. Whereas the light regiment has Veils, the dark regiment has Noctryns, and they couldn't be more different. Unfortunately, Kintoira Academy trains both. They tolerate each other out of necessity, but they certainly don't like each other.

In other words, it's kind of like a shitty marriage.

The only thing they have in common is that both are prisons in the shape of armor.

I swear I can feel my brows hit my hairline when he removes a dagger from a sheath at his waist and firmly puts it in my hand. I've never really held a dagger before. I've never needed a weapon, not only because of who my mother is but also because I had Ambrose.

I hold it up closer to my face, inspecting the intricate details of the hilt, and carefully run my finger along the blade.

"Take it, keep it hidden, and do not under any circumstances leave without it strapped somewhere to your person," he orders in the stern tone he usually uses on everyone but me.

The dagger is light with a small blade that appears to be made of black steel. It's small enough to conceal. Tossing it from hand to hand, I test its weight and feel.

I immediately drop it.

I quickly pick it up before bringing my attention back to Ambrose.

He raises an eyebrow at me.

I give him a slow, deliberate blink.

Obviously, I have some work to do on the weaponry aspect.

"Try not to stab yourself. Remember this is to hurt *other* people, Nori."

I purse my lips at him. "Your faith in me is inspiring."

He continues like he didn't hear me, "Also, it's technically frowned upon for first-years to have weapons. Keep it hidden and only use it if necessary."

I give him a mock salute.

He narrows his eyes. "Funny. She's got jokes."

"Better be careful there. You're starting to sound like you're kind of fond of me," I tease him, my lips pulling into a big toothy grin.

"I always have been," he replies, his tone soft but firm.

The breeze blows down the alleyway, causing my hood to billow around my hollow cheeks, making it easy to discreetly tuck my head and hide the false hope in my eyes that his words cause. I take a deep breath before finding my backbone and raising my head to find his glacier-blue eyes still watching me.

One minute, I'm standing there in all my awkward glory, and the next, I'm being pulled into one of his signature bear hugs.

"Even though I know you won't need it. Good luck, Nori."

I squeeze him tightly.

I hate goodbyes, but especially this goodbye, because it feels like everything is about to change.

Chapter Two

I've made a mistake.

It appears that sheer desire and fortitude of the mind aren't enough to prevent me from keeling over and emptying the contents of my stomach. In fact, I'm not the only one. We all look like we're on the verge of puking or passing out, and let's be honest, it's not a good look for any of us.

I wipe my mouth with the back of my hand and stare at the ground, hunched over and half broken.

Kintoira Academy sits at the very top of a steep mountain. To get there, we have to make our way through a dense forest of pines and evergreens at a sharp incline. The foliage is so thick that it blocks out any hint of the gloomy sky above. I now understand why it's widely known that you can easily get lost if you don't know your way around these woods. That's also why it's called The Forsaken Forest.

This place makes you feel fucking forsaken.

Today is going to suck.

All four thousand and forty-seven steps.

I did my research. It sucked when I discovered it, and that sentiment hasn't deviated. Salaryan may be known for her beauty, but she's also a fickle bitch. Between her deserts, snowcapped mountains, and turbulent oceans, she can't decide if she wants you to admire her or if she wants to kill you. This mountain wants to kill us if the feeling in my lungs is any indication.

Wincing, I stand and push the pine branches out of my face. Each breath becomes more painful than the last. I hurt in places I didn't even think I could hurt.

I lean up against the bark of a nearby evergreen and let my pack slide off my shoulder.

We're almost there. I quit counting the steps a while back because, frankly, it was becoming depressing, but I know we're close. The bitter taste of self-doubt coats my tongue, leaving a residual taste of failure. I've worked way too hard to fail before I even get a chance to try.

A shoulder knocks into mine from behind, causing my arm to scrape against the rough bark. "We're all tired. Keep moving," an irritated voice growls as she passes by before stopping to turn and stare at me.

Uh, excuse you.

I let my gaze rake her from head to toe and back up again. A clear fuck-you gesture if there ever was one.

She's almost twice my height, and without a doubt, has more muscle mass than I do. The silver lip ring adds a desperate flare of wanting to be a badass, but sadly for her, it falls short. I watch with casual disinterest as she tucks her shoulder-length bleached hair behind her ear. Her makeup is smeared on the left side of her deep-set eyes. The same eyes that are currently daring me to make the next move.

I can feel the irritation bubbling below my skin. The need to bite back. To give what I'm being given. I push it deep down like I've been doing for years. I'm way too tired for this, but if I don't stand my ground now, I'll lose all credibility among my peers.

I blow out a big breath and push off the tree. "I'm going to assume you're just fatigued and not normally this much of a bitch," I casually throw in her direction. Inside, I'm dreading this going any further, but on the outside, I'm as cool as a cucumber.

Her nostrils flare.

Yep. She wants to hit me.

Instead, she balls her fists and gives me a tight-lipped smile before roughly turning on her heel and pushing forward. Guess she's too tired for this shit too. Thank the gods. I know without a doubt I would have gotten my ass handed to me.

"I'm off to a great start," I reply under my breath, shaking my head.

A few prospective students walk around me, our little quarrel not fazing them in the least. When I bend down to pick up my pack from the damp, moss-covered floor, a pair of black combat boots, shoelaces untied and hanging haphazardly at the side, come into view.

"She's pleasant," a male voice drawls. "Maybe we'll get lucky and room in the same hall as her."

"I'd better sleep with one eye open, then," I mutter, still staring at his boots as I tighten the strap of my pack.

I would rather roll all the way back down this mountain than share a hall with her. I know luck hasn't been on my side lately, but that would be just unreasonable.

I fling the strap over my shoulder and rise, my eyes falling on the man who joined me. A hint of amusement swims in his hazel eyes. Ash-blond curls spring up all over his head, the ringlets perfectly in place, with not even one misbehaving. Meanwhile, I look like I frolicked in a bog. Probably smell like it too.

"How are you not dying out here like the rest of us?" I genuinely ask.

"My brother graduated from the academy last year," he says, grinning. "But before that, he was a pain in the ass who didn't cut me any slack. He had me running laps and hiking shitty trails with him until he left for the academy a few years ago. I just continued doing it after he was already gone."

I tuck that little tidbit of information away for a rainy day. I bet he has quite a bit of knowledge that could be useful to a prospect. I would think his brother gave him some tips on what to expect heading into this. Unfortunately, I didn't have time to get much information from Ambrose last night, and his letters were always vague and few and far between.

"Where's he stationed now?" I ask as we start to walk, keeping my eyes on the terrain in front of me.

"He's stationed at Crimson Tower near the Southern border. He's tasked with maintaining our walls just past the little trading village of *Willikson*. I haven't heard from him in a few weeks, though." His mouth moves around a small piece of pine straw that he picked up along the way. "Which isn't uncommon. It's hard to pen letters back home when you're out on patrol."

Being on patrol instead of locked in battle is a good sign that the walls are holding up against the bane of our existence.

Wraiths.

Their main goal in life is ending ours.

He extends his hand for me to take. "The name's Finnley," he says, moving the pine needle around from one side of his mouth to the other.

Without breaking stride, I reach out and take his hand. "Norissa, but everyone calls me Nori."

It's dusk by the time we arrive at the top of the mountain. Shivering and exhausted, I pull my hood tighter around my face to protect it from the wind. It's fierce this high up, and the temperatures are dropping significantly, numbing my fingers and causing them to take on an indigo hue. It feels as if a thousand little needles have buried themselves in my fingertips.

I shift my pack from one shoulder to the other, trying to balance the weight. Both shoulders throb at this point, so I have just been bouncing it back and forth between the two for the past hour. I don't even have much in it, but with the incline and length of the hike, it feels like it's filled with bricks.

Not one of us looks better than death. Except for Finnley. He looks like this is just another day for him. It's completely abnormal and slightly terrifying.

We all stand around and stare at the large iron gate that stands between us and our destination, unsure of what to do next. It looks formidable and very uninviting. Finally, a girl with curly black hair falling over her shoulder opens the gate from the other side, the hinges creaking loudly as they swing. She runs her sharp eyes over the large group, about a hundred of us in total.

Whatever she sees doesn't impress her much.

Her lips pull into a tight sneer. "There are fewer of you than expected." Given her solid-black attire, she's definitely a Noctryn. She walks toward us with the intimidation factor that they wear like a second skin.

I wonder if it's standard-issue by the academy.

I'm startled when I realize she's looking directly at me, causing me to stand a little straighter. My shoulders are protesting, screaming at me that slouching is allowed right now, but I won't. I meet her glare with an unflinching stare. I might be here on a whim and a prayer, but I will not cower.

She raises her right eyebrow slightly, seemingly surprised by my small act of defiance, before shifting her attention back to the group. Her voice rises so the people in the back can hear her over the howling wind. "You'll follow me to the top. Stay in a single file line." Her glare pins us to the spot, like she's speaking directly to each one of us, challenging us to disobey. "Or don't. You'll fall, and your bones will join the others who also couldn't follow directions." She gestures to the deep drop-off to the right of the narrow pathway leading upward. I'm assuming that's where said bones lie. She doesn't ask whether everyone heard or if they understood before briskly turning and stalking back through the gates she had opened.

The fact that she mentioned falling makes my skin crawl. There's only one thing I hate worse than most people, and it's heights. I try not to let the fear show on my face as Finnley joins me.

The other candidates whisper among themselves, either questioning their sanity or trying to build themselves up for the remaining climb. Our limbs protest and beg for a respite, but there isn't one to give.

I wring my hands together to try to expel some of the nervous energy flowing through my body. This is going to suck on so many levels.

Finnley's gaze passes over me. He can clearly see my discomfort at the situation. "I'll go first. You follow."

With a bow of my head, I don't argue and follow him. Pride has no place in trying to stay alive. I realize this is it, the point of no return. Once I'm at the top, I'm fully committed.

No turning back.

Following his lead, I grab onto the rope that's anchored into the side of the mountain and start the treacherous climb up. The pathway is so narrow that the only option is to put one foot in front of the other and hold on to the rope for dear life.

The wind batters us with its brutal intensity. I tuck my chin, trying to escape the onslaught, and make the mistake of looking down. My vision starts to blur, and my stomach feels like it just fell out.

Why would I look down? Everyone knows not to look down.

"Don't look down," Finnley yells over the wind in front of me.

Pulling myself together, I keep putting one foot in front of the other and stare straight ahead. I've got this.

A raindrop lands soundly on the tip of my nose. Thunder cracks against the sky like a whip, causing me to jump and slip on the cold, damp stone. My left knee twists during the quick motion before slamming into the ground with enormous force. I panic and let go of the rope with my right hand, trying to find balance as my leg dangles precariously over the side of the mountain.

Pain shoots across my palm as the skin tears, the rope burrowing into my flesh as my full body weight is now being supported by one hand. Regardless of your size, it doesn't matter when you're hanging by one arm. It's all dead weight at that point.

The rain is getting heavier, making everything more difficult. I try to pull myself back up, but I can't find any leverage on the slippery stone. It doesn't help that my upper body strength is severely lacking.

I probably should have worked on that sooner.

My leg keeps slipping every time I try to get a steady grip on my boot. If I wasn't looking down before, I'm definitely looking down now.

The person behind me makes no move to help me—and why would they?

They'd be just as likely to join me in slipping off this damn mountain and have their bones added to the collection below us. What does it matter if I live or die to them?

In short, it doesn't.

Out of nowhere, a hand reaches out and grabs my flailing arm, pulling me slowly and steadily back onto the path. After my heart stops trying to beat out of my chest, I wipe the hair and rain from my eyes as the downpour continues in a steady torrent.

I'm not dead.

A borderline hysterical laugh escapes as I look myself over. Blood drips from my palm where the rope dug in, and my knee is going to have a nasty bruise come tomorrow, but I'm alive.

A low whistle escapes Finnley's mouth. "We're going to really have to work on your self-preservation skills," he yells over the wind and rain.

It appears I'm going to have to work on a lot of things.

I nod my head in thanks. "That was a close one," I acknowledge, even though he can't hear me. The shock and adrenaline are wearing off, and exhaustion is settling in. I want a hot shower, a warm bed, and the promise of nothingness.

Not necessarily in that order.

An hour later, we reach the top, and my night goes from bad to worse.

Chapter Three

We barely make it to the landing before we find ourselves standing at attention facing a horde of Noctryn. They immediately start separating us into groups.

I can scarcely see past my nose due to the rain, but make no mistake, these upperclassmen don't even seem to notice it. One might even go so far as to say they even enjoy it.

There isn't a Veil in sight.

With a grim face, Finnley and I, who were thankfully placed in the same group, stand together waiting for an order to be issued. Right now, it's just a sea of black staring down a group of tired, wet, timid prospects. I had just assumed there would be representatives from both regiments to greet us. Although I'm not sure I would actually call this a greeting party.

What I wouldn't give to see Ambrose right now. I push the stinging feeling of disappointment away. I'm sure there's a reason the Veils aren't here.

If the Veils stand for everything light, honest, and worthy, then the Noctryns are the antithesis of that. Immoral, vicious, and corrupt. The only thing the two have in common is that both are weaponized.

I wipe wet strands of hair from my face, trying to make the movement minimal. I don't want any attention directed toward me. We have no idea why they separated us, and we're soaked, cold, and tired. The last thing I want is to be singled out for any reason. Fly under the radar and get through this week in one piece.

That's the only plan I have.

The dark regiment just stands and stares at us through their blackened helms, their eyes completely shielded behind obsidian visors. Armor covers every inch of their frames, the flexible metal pulling tightly over their chests and fitting snugly to their abdomens, almost outlining the ridges hidden beneath. It's unlike any kind of armor I've seen before, protection crafted to conceal, but more whisper than weight. More like a living thing formed for obedience than something merely worn. An extra layer doubly covers their forearms. Most have various weapons attached, and some even have swords strapped to their backs.

They came to *greet* us in full battle gear.

"We will be calling one member from each of your groups to act as your bracket's temporary lieutenant." The Noctryn who spoke swivels his helmet in the direction of the three groups. "When I call your name, you are to come to the front to obtain further directions."

I quickly avert my eyes, hoping that if I don't make eye contact, perhaps I'll just blend in with the others. I step back quickly and discreetly, pushing through the prospects. The ground is completely saturated, causing my boots to sink into the mud and rainwater to seep through the sides. I whisper apologies as I slip past people, bumping into them along the way.

"Aksel Penton, Maylin Zhou, and Norissa Caderyn," the gravelly voice echoes across the open courtyard. Even with his visor down, standing in the pouring rain, you can hear him say my name so damn clear.

Grinding my teeth, I push back through the throng of people I just came through, passing by Finnley and his knowing smile. He gives me a small nod of encouragement.

Please let this be a mistake. Why would they choose me? I'm not leadership material. I'm barely not falling off the mountain material.

I stop before the Noctryn who issued the order, with my shoulders back and chin up. Wet copper strands hang limp across my forehead, but I can't be bothered to swipe them away again. My entire focus is on maintaining my fearless facade, which I'm trying so hard to keep in place. It takes everything in me to maintain eye contact with the direct, unnerving focus of someone whose eyes I can't even see. His entire being commands obedience, and for some reason, I just know it would be unwise to portray weakness.

The very air crackles with expectation.

When I don't think I can maintain the facade much longer, he finally decides to show a sliver of mercy and breaks the tension. "You three will each act as lieutenant. This title was not given out carelessly or without thought. You are responsible for your entire group. Their wins as well as their losses." He folds his arms across his armored chest. "Their compliance as well as their defiance."

I glance at the girl standing next to me, who's in charge of leading one of the other groups. Mayline, I believe he said her name was. Her mink-brown eyes widen at him as she mutters something under her breath. Possibly a prayer, but more likely a curse word.

The academic leaders are ranked as in a military unit. I knew this coming in, but I just didn't realize they assigned team leads on day one. The hierarchy among the classes is: first-year leaders are lieutenants, the second-years are captains, third-years are majors, and the graduating class is our generals.

"What if we don't make good leaders? What happens then?" I ask quickly before I lose my nerve.

His blackened helm slowly turns to face me before tilting slightly. "I suggest you do your very best not to find out."

Okay, well, that settles that. Failure isn't an option in the leadership department. Got it. I do my best not to fold in on myself and to keep my shoulders back and eyes up.

The tall, lanky boy on the other side of Mayline, who was also named lieutenant, removes his glasses before feebly attempting to wipe the rain off. He cuts a quick glance sideways in our direction. His floppy brown hair is plastered to his head. I watch as he gives it a good shake to expel some of the water, but it's useless. It's just beating down on us.

The Noctryn gestures to himself and the other two fully armored upperclassmen flanking him. "We're a few of the captains within the dark regiment, and as such, we were instructed to give you your ranks, orders, and show you to your quarters." He states all of this in a no-nonsense sort of way. "Group one is assigned to Nori. Aksel, you're group two, and that leaves you, Mayline, with group three." The other two captains stand stoic at his side but remain silent.

Captain Surly, which is how I will refer to him since he hasn't offered up a name, gives us instructions to round up our group and get them in order before casually turning his back on us to talk with his comrades.

I spin on my heels and head back over to the other prospects watching me expectantly.

Dread fills every fiber of my being, knowing I have to pretend to know how to be authoritative and get this group not only to listen to me but also to take me seriously.

"It went as well as you would expect," I reply in answer to Finnley's questioning look.

Wringing his cloak out with both hands, he tilts his head in the direction of the captains. "What's the verdict? Are they planning on making us swim tonight, or do we get to go inside?"

I wouldn't take anything off the table at this point.

"We're about to be taken to our rooms. I think. Hopefully, we can all get out of these wet clothes and into something more comfortable," I answer, blinking through the rain.

His eyebrows shoot up before proceeding to wiggle in a sexual way.

"Not a chance."

"Ouch, straight to the chest," he cries out, appearing wounded, his hand clutching his heart, full of mock hurt.

I quirk my eyebrow, unimpressed with his theatrics.

Those curls alone could get him company tonight. Girls love curls. But add in those big hazel eyes and that lazy smile that never seems to leave, and yeah, he won't have any trouble finding someone to warm his bed.

Grabbing Finnley's elbow, I pull him forward.

The surly captain and his comrades have started moving in the direction of the academy. They must assume we're not complete idiots and will figure out they want us to follow them. Best not to prove them wrong this early on.

I can feel my heart beating so hard. This is it. We're about to enter the infamous Kintoira Academy. Home sweet home. We either place in a bracket and live within these walls for the next four years, or we die.

Pretty cut-and-dried, honestly.

After crossing through the barbican, we enter the inside of the academy through a set of huge steel doors. My eyes dart around, trying to take in everything at once. It's surreal to be standing inside. I've dreamed about this moment for so long, and it's finally here.

The first thing I notice is that it's exactly as I would expect it to be—dark, mysterious, and forbidding, cloaked in a Gothic vibe. The second thing that I notice is the warmth of the fire that's burning in the overside grate. It wraps around me like a warm cup of tea, thawing the blood in my limbs and bringing feeling back to my fingertips. It feels glorious.

I rub my hands together furiously, trying to warm them up as quickly as possible to dampen the sting of needles shooting through them. I still can't believe I'm here. I made it into the trials. I'm so proud of myself for having the courage to try. Even if I fail, I freakin' tried.

I'm also scared I'm going to wake up tomorrow and this will all have been a dream.

I let my eyes continue to roam around the entryway, afraid I'm going to miss something as we wait for the rest of the group to work their way in.

Almost immediately, my mouth drops open upon spotting the intricate tapestry hanging above the hearth. Kintoira's crest displayed in all its triumph. I've read all about the tapestry at my prior school. A golden goblet filled with dark blood, accompanied by a blackened serpent wrapped around the stem, is woven into the threads. The black serpent for cunning, the golden goblet for wealth in knowledge, and last but certainly not least, the blood spilled for sacrifices made.

The weaver did an incredible job of bringing it to life. The goblet of muted gold looks tangible enough to grab onto, filled with dark crimson liquid that appears realistic enough to slosh over the brim. An onyx snake wraps itself around the stem, with a penetrating and genuine stare of dissent.

Tearing my eyes away from the lifelike image, I sidestep through a few prospects to where Finnley is talking with a petite girl who's sporting a platinum asymmetrical cut. It's different but really suits her. He must have heard me approaching because he looks up and waves me over.

"Hi again," he says with his signature lopsided smile. "I was just telling Mallory how this place was built over seven hundred years ago as a place of sanctuary and refuge, around the time the wraiths started descending on Salaryan and making our lives hell."

She watches every move his mouth makes. I see it, but I'm pretty sure he is completely oblivious. When she pulls her stare away from him, her large, catlike eyes land on me. She leans closer, extending her delicate hand for an introduction.

"Nice to meet you, Nori. Finnley was telling me a bit about how you two became quick friends on the journey here," she says. "Although I have to admit, I'm not sure it's a great idea to make friends just yet."

At my confused expression, she continues, "You know, until we figure out our respective regiments. It just doesn't make sense to start a friendship that isn't going to remain past the end of the week."

She's not wrong.

Truth be told, there are various reasons making a friend this early on is a bad idea. But that's a big one. Veils and Noctryns will never be on friendly terms.

"Solid point," I agree, leaning up against the wall. The throbbing in my knee has intensified. As soon as we get to the privacy of our rooms, I'll have to assess the damage. It feels sore just to stretch it out in front of me, and that doesn't bode well for the upcoming week.

Finnley's eyes track my movement, catching on quickly.

"Well, ladies, it looks like the last straggler just made their way in. We should head to the front. I'm sure the *lieutenant* will be needed," he says with a corny wink my way and a heavy emphasis on the word lieutenant. I appreciate him providing the distraction, though.

Grimacing, I push off the wall and follow him and Mallory.

Two of the captains head in different directions, taking the other two groups with them, and one walks ahead of us. It's impossible to tell whether it's the same person who was talking to us earlier. They all look identical except for their weapons, but I wasn't paying close enough attention to know who had what.

Mallory drops back, weaving her arm through mine. I glance down at our now joined arms. What happened to not making friends this early on?

"I'm so excited for tomorrow. I'm pretty sure I know where I'm going to place," she singsongs as we push forward, following the captain.

I'm pretty sure I know where *I'm* going to place, also. There isn't another option for me. My mother was a Veil, and her mother before her. So I either place accordingly, die trying, or she may very likely kill me herself.

Wet boots smack against the stone floors as we follow our silent, fuck-with-me-and-I'll-gut-you guide. I, for one, would not fuck with him, seeing as I don't have a death wish. I'm also suddenly very aware of the sheer magnitude of the academy. It would be so easy to get lost in the maze of hallways and dark passageways, and while he may not be pleasant, he knows his way around.

We clearly do not.

We pass a couple of classrooms and lecture halls before climbing a few staircases until we arrive on the third level. Annoyance seems to just drip from our dark guide as he stops and has to wait for the entire group to crest the stairs. I wonder if he lost a bet or pissed off some higher-up and got stuck with tour duty.

The corridors on each side stretch endlessly, long and dimly lit, with cathedral ceilings. The smell of candle wax and damp air lingers around us.

Shivering, I peel off my wet cloak as we wait. I still have about two more layers of soggy material on, but there's nothing I can do about those. It doesn't help that the academy walls are stone throughout, causing the cold to permeate straight through my bones, especially in the long hallway where we're standing. The numerous windows do absolutely nothing to keep the draft out.

I try to distract myself and trace my finger through the condensation coating the nearest arched pane. It's cold to the touch and recondenses almost instantly. There are mounted candelabras on each side of the window that flicker with warm light, creating shadows that look like things that aren't really there. The exhaustion from today is causing my mind to play tricks on me.

A deep, familiar voice echoes throughout the hall and pulls me out of creeping myself out. Seems like luck just isn't on my side tonight. They may all look identical, but I'm betting they don't sound it. "You'll bunk with a teammate for the first week of Asylamation in one of the rooms in this hall." He looks left, then right, as if we might not be able to come to the assumption on our own that there are rooms on both sides. "Once you survive and place into either dark or light, Veil or Noctryn, whatever you'd like to call it, you'll be moved to the quarters associated with that regiment," he says. "You'll then be assigned to your final roommate for the remainder of the academic year," he drawls in a bored tone like he wants to be anywhere but here.

It's still incredibly frustrating that I can't see who's behind the visor. Everything is covered, even his hands. Speaking of hands, the gloves covering his look as if they're specially crafted or something. I've seen him have way too much flexibility within them while cracking his knuckles more than once on this little tour. I bet he's still able to have a solid grip on his weapon during fighting without them being overly cumbersome.

I want a pair.

Pulling my gaze away from his gloved hands before he thinks I'm some kind of weirdo, I look around at the people surrounding me, wondering who I am going to be bunked with this week. I have no idea if it's coed or not, so if we can pick, I'm picking Finnley without a doubt. The worst thing that could happen is for him to get a glimpse of my backside while I'm changing. Honestly, the least of my concerns.

I nudge Finnley in the side. "If we can pick, are you game to share?" I ask under my breath.

"Yeah, just don't try to make any moves on me in my sleep," he retorts out of the side of his mouth.

I snort. "You wish."

A sullen expression passes over Mallory's face as she watches our exchange. There's no need for it. I'm rooting for her to bag her man, just not tonight. Tonight, I want a solid sleep with no visitors in my roomie's bed. He doesn't strike me as the quiet type.

The captain points and curls a gloved finger in my direction.

Shit.

I bet he saw me staring at his hands.

Sighing, I do my best not to limp as I walk toward him.

"Lieutenant, there are thirty-three prospects in your bracket. There will be two in each room, leaving someone to bunk alone."

Crisis averted, he didn't see me ogling him.

Also, I should jump at the chance to have my own room. I make a mental note to examine why exactly I am not doing that at a later time.

He does that eerie head tilt again, as if he's waiting for me to say something.

"Okay, sounds like a plan," I respond. Lamely.

I don't know what it is about these Noctryns, but they make it hard to think clearly. They're intimidation personified. I really hope the Veils are just as formidable when we see them tomorrow. I've only ever witnessed them in the military passing through, but never as students. I'd be disappointed if the regiment I'm destined for isn't just as foreboding.

It would have never occurred to me for one second that Noctryns could be so dangerous before even *leaving* the academy.

"Assign pairs gender specific," he orders while crossing his arms and widening his stance. "Now is as good a time as any to mention a fun little rule here at Kintoira," he says while leaning forward to get closer to me before whispering through his helmet. "No fornication for the first-years."

I can't see it, but I swear I can feel the satisfied smirk on his face.

"The academy doesn't like distractions for the prospects. Focus on not dying and being good enough that the academy deems you *worthy* enough to place."

Is it just me, or was there an edge of bitterness to his voice during that last little remark?

This will be fun to break to my bracket. He's definitely making it easy for them to hate me early on.

An upperclassman in full black gear, matching my new surly friend here, walks up on our right. I didn't even hear him coming up the steps, which is kind of disconcerting. "Makon, they're ready for us," he says to our guide.

So he does have a name. Makon. For some reason, it's fitting.

He gives a curt nod in response before advancing toward me. "Good luck, Nori, you're going to need it. You all are."

Chapter Four

Pulling my long red waves over my shoulder, I quickly and efficiently braid them into a fishtail. It's been too long since I last cut it, resulting in my hair now falling to mid-back.

Sleep was elusive last night, and boy, am I feeling the ramifications of it this morning. Between staying up late the night before last to study the exam Ambrose gave me and last night's nerves, I'm dragging ass this morning. I have exactly one hour before I have to be seated in the orientation hall for the Asylamation written portion, and I still have to get dressed before trying to find my way there.

I wish I could say the sun is shining through the window of my temporary room, offering some kind of reprieve from the gloom-and-doom feeling sitting in my gut, but that would be a lie. Dense fog settles over Kintoira, enveloping us in her embrace. You can't see shit out of the windows. It's as if the academy is in a constant state of a Cimmerian atmosphere.

I'm pretty sure this is my new norm.

The days of running around in the sun, with my feet in the surf and toes in the sand are over. The afternoons of collecting just as many freckles across the bridge of my nose as seashells in my hands have come to an end.

Honestly, if all goes according to plan, it's going to be a bit before I see Brylan again. I'll miss the turf and the warm weather of home, but that's about it.

I glance one more time at my little bed, wishing I could just hide under the covers a little longer. Our current room is the bare minimum with two twin beds, a small wooden dresser that leans slightly to the left, and a simple standing mirror. But after the day I had yesterday, it was paradise to walk in and see.

Walking over to the mirror, I study my reflection. Wide, bright-green eyes stare back at me, taking in the ivory-colored prospect uniform that hangs loosely on my lithe, borderline skinny frame. Something I've always been self-conscious about. I glide my fingers over the buttons lining my shirt before tugging on the high collar that rests just below my chin. It's slightly suffocating, but I'm going to have to just grin and bear it.

I'll only have to wear it the first week until I place, and then I'll be given my regiment attire. Unfortunately, I won't get my badass battle gear until next year, when we become captains, but putting on that Veil first-year uniform will be enough.

For now.

I asked Finnley where he wanted to place, and he said he didn't care as long as he got to kill some wraiths. I'd be sad to see him end up on the other side, but it's not up to us.

There was an announcement this morning over the intercoms that another attack had taken place, this time on the western border. They're getting bolder. The little village of *Orichall,* which sits along the border beside the Merch Desert, suffered heavy civilian casualties. As I was walking back from the community showers this morning, I heard the whispers. They're saying it was a massacre. The military is still trying to locate all the pieces of some of the residents.

Those people didn't stand a chance. Being a small village that sells spices and fabrics, they weren't even on the radar for an attack. It doesn't make any sense. It's not spices they're after. It also doesn't add up that they would attack a small village with such a low population.

We're missing something.

A good number of our forces have been stationed along the eastern and southern borders, where the wealthy towns rich in trade and bartering are located. *Brylan*, where Ambrose and I grew up on the eastern coast, is heavily guarded to protect the popular trading port. However, the majority of our force lies along the northwestern coast in *Casacia*, the wealthiest city in Salaryan. Rich in all things trade, but her specialty lies in her rich mineral-infused soil. Incredibly sought after and very, very expensive.

Also, heavily populated.

I doubt I'll get to see it anytime soon, though, especially if I place as a Veil. That particular city demands the most ruthless guard for her walls. The ones with low morals and even lower scruples. They certainly don't make it a secret that they favor dark magic in their soldiers, and for dark magic to be used, you need Noctryns. As far back as our history takes us, the black regiment has stood guard for that city. The Noctryns aren't guarding against just one enemy though, but against *anything* that crosses into their territory.

The wraiths have tried numerous times to overthrow the Casacians but have failed due to the black regiments' tenacity and callousness. And the fact that there isn't a line they won't cross to protect what they deem theirs. The city has been a main target for the wraith strikes for over a century, but the attacks are becoming more frequent. I'm assuming the growing population has a lot to do with it. That's a lot of energy to feed on. They have to eat, after all.

Unfortunately for us, their food is our very essence.

The fiber that makes us who we are.

Our souls.

And they aren't picky about the flavor.

Veils may be known for their intelligence and ability to wield once they are allowed to manifest, which is just a fancy way of saying reclaiming what should have been theirs to begin with, but the Noctryns are dark in nature. They fight with their own moral code and without regret. They control the shadows and dark magic. But like most things, it doesn't come without a heavy price.

They sacrifice their manifestations to be able to do so.

There are also a few elites every generation who can fabricate any illusion they dream up. In other words, they can put you in your own living nightmare.

Where the Veils practice light magic to fight evil, the Noctryns specialize in dark magic to fight it. But in the Realms' eye, better the devil you know than the one you don't. Conveniently, they don't have a problem with dark magic used by a soldier under their control.

They keep a heavy hand and an even shorter leash on the Noctryns.

The two entities might coexist, but there certainly isn't any love lost between them. In fact, it's a constant power struggle.

Of course, none of us will know what abilities we were born with or if we're forfeiting them until we finish the trials and place. Then we'll know if we're casting the powers we manifest or if we're offering the ultimate sacrifice and giving it all up to be able to wield darkness.

That doesn't stop some of us from hoping for one or the other, though.

The very fact that a person wishes to wield light magic or dark magic is a pretty clear indication of where they're going to end up. It's a reflection of what lies within us.

Pulling the braid over my shoulder, I walk to the edge of my bed and carefully sit, drawing up my pants leg. An angry-looking cerulean-blue bruise covers my entire left knee.

I've had my fair share of scrapes and bruises. It comes with the territory of living in a port town. New people are always arriving and leaving, and more often than not, they bring their families. Ambrose and I had a never-ending supply of new kids to play with every month, and we would always get into some kind of adventure or trouble. Especially Ambrose, who was always determined to establish who was in charge.

That boy was always out to prove something and couldn't walk away from a dare if he wanted to, which landed us in some precarious situations.

I straighten my knee, trying to stretch out the stiffness. The bone feels like it's locked in place, and I'm almost positive I just heard a popping noise.

"Pretty sure that's not good," a chipper tone comments from behind me. "Looks like a torn meniscus to me."

I have no idea what a meniscus is, let alone a torn one, but I'm assuming that it is, in fact, *not good*. I school my features to try to hide that I have no idea what she's talking about. The physical portion of the trial is in two days, and last I checked, I need two working knees to get through it.

Nonchalantly, I push my pants leg back down and turn to look over my shoulder at Mallory, my new temporary roommate. She's standing behind me, arranging her hair into a fauxhawk. The girl really can pull off any look.

"What's a, um, torn meniscus?" I ask, pushing my pride aside.

"Basically, it means you tore your knee joint," she replies, as if this isn't catastrophic news to me. "You should be fine if it's small. Try to ice it tonight and rest when you can."

I make a mental note to look up information on torn joints during our free time, after we finish the first portion of the trials. Then the next stop is finding the medical wing. I'm going out on a limb here, no pun intended, but I'm thinking a wrap or something might be needed.

"How did you know?" I question.

Her brows pull together in confusion.

"How'd you know all that just from looking at my knee?"

She puts the last remaining touches on her hair and walks over to me, propping her hip against the dresser. "Dad's a healer for the regiments. He brought a lot of his work home with him, whether it be theories he was testing or actual patients who needed extra monitoring." She does a quick eye roll. "He's extremely gifted. His ability is to feel his patient's pain. It certainly makes it easy to pinpoint the issue, but I don't want to follow in his footsteps."

Understandable. I'm not sure many people would.

I bite my lip as I try to imagine actually feeling another person's pain.

It sounds awful.

"How did it work? Did he have to be in the same room as his patient or like actually touch them?" I ask curiously.

She laughs at the expression of intrigue on my face. "Yeah, he has to have a connection to their energy, by touch," she says. "I was lucky enough as a kid that he occasionally let me watch him work, so I learned a lot about battle injuries and whatnot."

A loud knock on the door causes us to stop talking. Lifting a quizzical brow at me, Mallory walks over, tucking in her prospect shirt as she goes, and slowly opens it. I can hear a muffled voice on the other side but can't quite make out what they're saying.

Pushing off the bed, I walk over to the dresser to finish putting my things away from my pack that I didn't get to last night. My hands still when I hear the mention of my name.

"Yes, I'm Nori's roommate," Mallory replies in an enthralled tone to whoever she's speaking with. "Give me a second, and I'll let her know you're asking for her."

Shutting the door slightly, she spins around, looking at me with her delicate eyebrows almost raised to her hairline and her mouth hanging open. Nodding her head in the direction of the door, and fanning herself as if she's overheated, she mouths, *"He's beautiful."*

My face breaks out in a huge grin. I only know one beautiful person who would be looking for me. "Ambrose Ballard, get your ass in here!" I yell, clapping my hands together in excitement.

Mallory jumps out of the way just in time before the door crashes open, and I'm greeted with the sight of my favorite person.

And what a fucking devastating sight it is.

His brown hair falls in thick waves to his shoulders, and his arctic-blue eyes lock on mine, magnetic and unrelenting. His bronze skin has lightened a little from being away from home, something I couldn't see in the dark the other night. But it's the easy smile that reaches his eyes that really does me in.

It's only been a little over a day since I last saw him, but it was rushed and forbidden. I didn't get to really bask in it.

He reaches me in a few short strides, lifting me off the ground like I weigh nothing, and spins me around. "Nori," he whispers in my ear. "You're really here."

As if I would have changed my mind and not come.

I burrow my nose in his neck, inhaling his familiar scent of salt and soap, like he just stepped off the beach. It just feels right to be wrapped up in his embrace, like it was made just for me. I don't want to let go, but the choice is taken from me when he cuts the hug entirely too short and gently lowers me to the floor.

It doesn't go unnoticed that he doesn't remove his hands from around my waist. He can keep them there all day if he wants. Fuck the assessment. I'd give up everything for this man. He just doesn't know it.

And I'll be taking that secret to my grave.

Tilting my head back, I look up into his glacial stare, ironically full of nothing but warmth. People say blue eyes can be cold and distant, but all I see when I look at his are kept promises, infinite loyalty, and everything worth breathing for.

I run my hands over his arms, so happy he's here, but also kind of not believing he's real either. Besides our quick meeting the other night, we haven't seen each other for a little over a year. With him at the academy and me finishing up my primary studies, it wasn't possible. Especially since leaving the grounds of Kintoira without approval is grounds for dismissal or worse, and it's almost impossible to get approval. A soldier doesn't have a life outside of these stone walls.

The minute they set foot into the academy, their freedom is forfeit.

"I was wondering if I would see you before Asylamation begins," I say, keeping my tone light. But I certainly don't feel light inside. I feel weighed down with uncertainties and nerves. I need him to ground me and give me that edge of motivation before I put quill to parchment. Sometimes I think I depend on him too much.

His lips move into that reassuring smile I always come to expect from him. It's one of the things I love about him. He's always so patient and tolerant with me. I never feel less than or a hindrance.

Something foreign in my home life.

Except for him.

He drops one of his hands from my waist and brings it up to my face, rubbing his thumb along my jaw. Goose bumps break out along my arms. This is new territory, and I'm not sure what the hell I'm supposed to be doing with my hands right now. They're just kind of hanging awkwardly at my sides because I'm afraid of reading this wrong and messing it all up.

"I've been trying to find where they stationed you all morning. Makon wasn't so forthcoming with the information, though, being the usual bastard he is," he says in annoyance. "He made me really work for it. I've been knocking on doors all morning."

Makon, the surly guide from last night. Figures he'd make things difficult for me even when not around. His demeanor didn't exactly scream helpful. Although the thought of Ambrose knocking on doors all morning to find me does bring me more than a small amount of happiness.

His eyes dart to a movement behind me, dropping his hand from my face.

I snap my fingers together. Shit, I forgot all about Mallory being here. He just kind of stole my entire focus the moment he walked through the door.

"Ambrose, meet Mallory," I say as he reaches over my shoulder to shake her hand. "Mallory, this is Ambrose. A friend of mine."

The word friend tastes like lead on my tongue.

He clears his throat, moving his entire focus back down to me. "Best friend, actually," he corrects.

The lead tastes slightly more bearable.

"Well, as nice as it was to meet you, and trust me, it was nice," she says, her eyes twinkling with mischief, "we'd better get going or they're going to start the test without us." Grabbing her set of quills from her bed, she heads toward the door. "I'll just wait for you out here, Nori. We can walk down together when you two are finished."

I nod in her direction, giving an encouraging smile that I'll be right out before she silently shuts the door. She's definitely doing me a solid by giving us a little privacy to say our goodbyes. Who knows when we'll see each other again, let alone actually be alone together, and as mentioned, I hate goodbyes.

I always have.

The only thing worse is when someone leaves without one.

Make it make sense.

His eyes search mine like he's looking for all the answers before settling on one question. "Do you still have the dagger I gave you?" he asks in a hushed voice.

My shoulders slightly drop. Not the question I was hoping for.

"I do," I reassure him. "Although I'm not sure what you think is going to happen. I promised you I would carry it on me at all times, and I don't break my promises."

I instinctively touch the thigh sheath hidden under my loose-fitting pants. The material is soft and not form-fitting, making it easy to pull up and remove my dagger quickly if need be.

"You can never be too careful." He looks away, like he's hesitating to say more. Ambrose has never been one to shy away from the truth with me, and he's not going to start now. "Just remember your promise and keep it hidden."

"I know you're hiding something, Ambrose, so spill it," I demand, planting my hands on my hips.

He rubs the back of his neck, his perfect teeth biting down on his lip before coming to a decision. It'd better be to tell me the truth, or dammit, we're going to have problems. We don't hide things from each other, ever, and we aren't starting now. "Don't trust people here, Nori. Not everyone has good intentions," he finally warns. His voice has taken on a deeper edge than he's ever really used with me, and I'm starting to wonder what exactly I have gotten myself into.

Chapter Five

I was right. The goodbye sucked just as much as I thought it would. It also didn't end with a heart-stopping kiss like I daydream about an unhealthy amount of times per day, but it still felt good seeing him.

I press my lips together tightly.

Get it together, woman.

Maybe if I keep reminding myself I'm deep in friend territory, it will sink in. At the moment, I need to focus on other things, though. Like passing this trial and not meeting my untimely demise.

I'm too young to die—I haven't even experienced life yet.

Not only do I have to successfully place to stay the hand of the executioner, but I also have to place specifically as a Veil or face the very real possibility of being repudiated by my own mother. No one hates Noctryns quite like her. In fact, I think the only thing she hates more is my father.

No pressure or anything.

Taking a deep breath, I calm myself with the hopes that if I was meant to be in that regiment, I would have felt something by now. Some sinister force flowing through my veins just waiting to be released. But I don't. I feel light and valiant, like I'm a good person who only wants to make a difference in this world.

At least that's what I keep reiterating to myself.

Mallory and I make it just in time for the test. The professor is already standing at the podium in his dark robes and looks up when we enter. We quickly make our way to Finnley and take the two seats he saved for us while trying to be as discreet as possible.

I get situated, assure myself that not everyone is staring at me for almost being late and let my eyes roam across the sea of ivory-colored prospects already in their seats. It's a sobering thought that most of us won't make it to the commencement ceremony. I think statistically only like 40 percent, or something like that, complete Asylamation.

Frowning, I pull myself from the macabre thoughts and focus on my other surroundings. The large lecture hall is so quiet that you could hear a quill drop, which is astonishing, considering almost every seat is filled with students. All one hundred and three of us. The stadium-style seats are divided into three sections, with the three of us seated in the upper-left, back row.

The only sound that slightly reaches my ears is Finnley, softly steepling his fingers on the old wooden desk. I notice the Gothic vibe carries over into this particular room as well. Dark stone walls blend into a nebulous vaulted ceiling that appears to have stars shimmering throughout it. It's actually quite mesmerizing.

"They're not really stars, but thousands of tiny glowworms," Mallory whispers from my left, as if she read my mind before turning her attention back to the professor. It seems her dad gave her more insight into the academy than my parent did. Or maybe my mother deemed it too trivial and not worth mentioning.

Either way, it's a sight to behold.

Bending down, I reach into my pack and pull out a quill. I'll never be more ready than I am right now, especially after reviewing the questions.

Thank you very much, Ambrose.

The professor clears his throat and begins. "You are all here today because you think you have what it takes to place in a regiment of Salaryan's army. I commend you for your bravery, or stupidity, depending on how you want to look at it." He pauses dramatically, letting his gaze roam around the lecture hall. "My name is Professor Moravek, and if you place in the black regiment, I will be your professor for blood magic."

His face is completely blank as he folds his bony hands in front of him, patiently waiting for the hushed whispers to die down.

I hear Finnley blow out the breath from his cheeks. I guess we're really in it now. What's next, a class on necromancy? This is why some of us just aren't made to be anything but Veils. The very idea of dark magic is just repulsive to some of us.

"Today, however, I am your proctor. There will be no tolerance for talking or cheating, and under absolutely no condition will there be any tapping of quills." I straighten in my chair, immediately setting my quill down.

With a flick of his wrist, a piece of parchment appears in front of each of us.

The written portion.

The aged-looking parchment is covered in gold writing that shimmers throughout, basically reading us our last rites before we begin. I quickly scan my eyes over the verbiage, essentially telling us we can't back out once we begin, and we will be placed in one of the two regiments or face execution by choice of the academy. Also, an additional reminder that it's a lifetime commitment. There is no such thing as retiring from our assigned regiment.

I pick up the quill, gripping it tightly in my hand and sign my name next to the red X at the bottom. All the words disappear, and the most important questions of my life take their place.

Chapter Six

"That was intense," Mallory exclaims, sounding dejected. Makeup is smudged along her eyes and around her palms.

"You can say that again. I feel like I'm going to puke or cry. Maybe both," Finnley half-whispers, farther down the table. A long, slow exhale slips between his lips.

I just stare straight ahead, mentally tapped.

A nagging ache works its way around my knee, and a defeated war cry is brewing in my chest. I'll save it for later when I can scream alone.

Best not to show them all your crazy at once.

Everyone is focused on their own inner turmoil, so we eat in silence for a while. The quiet is beyond welcome, and I bask in it. I tuck everything away, compartmentalize it, and burrow into the comfort of silence.

A few other prospects join us, each looking as defeated, if not more so, than the prior. We went into that test so cocky, like it was going to be easy for us to just jot down some answers. Boom. Done. Onto the next.

I thought I had it in the bag. I was supposed to know what was going to be on the test!

Wrong.

So very wrong.

It was a completely different test from what I studied. The questions were changed to be more difficult, almost as if the answers were impossible. The subjects ranged from ethics to alchemy to poisons. It was so broad that, honestly, I'm not sure anyone could study for it. I mean, fuck, I couldn't even cheat properly on it.

It was humbling, to say the least.

"I'm so doomed," someone at the table moans.

We're all doomed.

I don't know what I expected coming into this, but I guess I thought I'd just find my footing and it'd be simple. If the written portion was this tough, I dread even thinking about the physical portion. This portion was supposed to be where I excelled.

I mindlessly chew on a mushy turnip.

"At least we get the rest of the day off," someone who I don't recognize asks. "What's everyone doing with it?"

I close my eyes.

Hiding.

Hiding is what I'll be doing.

A sinister chuckle causes me to open one eye. "I know what I'm doing. I'm going to check out the merchandise and see where I land this evening," Mallory replies with a shit-eating grin on her face. Guess she's moved her sights from Finnley. She proceeds to scan the lunch hall, letting her gaze fall over the crowd of prospects.

"No fornication, remember," I mumble through the fingers holding my head up off the table. Emory, another prospect, sits back in her chair, looking deep in thought, her hands folded together on the table. She hasn't taken her eyes off one of the far corner tables.

"They never said anything about looking," Mallory chides.

Finnley doesn't answer. He just continues shoveling food into his mouth.

A hushed whisper falls over the dining hall as some of the upperclassmen start trickling in. All conversation at our table ceases entirely. Between being completely deflated and the newcomers acquiring our attention, it's enough to effectively shut us up.

Thank the gods.

Interestingly enough, the Veils tend to enter in larger groups, laughing and talking among themselves, whereas the Noctryns come in alone or just a few at a time. They're also no longer in battle gear, allowing me to finally see their faces.

I was correct in my assumption. They're just as terrifying out of the armor as they are in it. It appears they traded their battle attire for dark fighting leathers. I also notice that each one of them is still fully armed with various weapons.

They sure don't let their guard down.

Even to eat.

The Veils are also in their academic-issued fighting leathers, but unlike the black ones, theirs are dark brown. Only a few have weapons. A bow here or there, maybe a throwing spear. It makes sense, really, since Veils aren't known for their hand-to-hand combat skills. Their weapon of choice is their manifestations. It would be a mistake to underestimate them. Their abilities are formidable, far more than a piece of steel.

My appraisal is cut short as Ambrose walks in with his head thrown back in laughter at whatever the woman attached to his arm just said. Of course, he couldn't be in a large group like the rest. Instead, he's attached to a random, adoring female.

A lump forms in my throat, and I quickly avert my gaze. I know he isn't a virgin or anything. I was there the night that bitch Lynda dragged him off during one of our shore parties and effectively removed that label. I hated her then, and I still hate her now. I may be kindhearted, but I can hold a grudge with the best of them. If it's fuck you now, it's fuck you until the day I die. I'll see you in the afterlife and hate you there too.

A swift kick to my shin causes me to grunt and look across the table. A sympathetic smile lines Mallory's face. "You got it bad, huh?" she asks softly.

No, but my shin is now throbbing.

Thanks for asking.

I shake my head in denial. "Me? No"—I laugh nervously—"it's not like that. We're just friends," I assure her. The fake smile plastered to my face is a dead giveaway, I'm sure. I probably look like I'm snarling instead of smiling at her.

I'm a terrible liar. Always have been. Probably always will be.

She reaches across the table, giving my hand a soft pat. "It's okay. Your secret is safe with me. Just remember, Nori, he may be pretty to look at, but no boy is worth having your heart willingly stomped on."

Trust me, it's not willingly.

"I know the score, and besides, my focus is on this place right now, not my love life." Or lack thereof. But whether I say it for her benefit or mine is anyone's guess.

I remove my hand from under hers and go back to moving the food around on my plate. I didn't have much of an appetite before he walked in, but I certainly don't have any now.

I force myself to look in their direction again.

I never thought of myself as a masochist, but look at me now. A full-blown masochist. Glutton for punishment. Pity party for one, please.

The leggy brunette has her arms draped all over him, but he's just staring down at the food selection like he doesn't notice. He probably doesn't.

It's just another Monday for him. He may only be one year older than me, but it feels like he has decades of experience on me when it comes to the opposite sex.

Whenever a boy showed the slightest notion of interest in me, I would say the wrong thing, or awkwardness would become my entire personality. And that's if Ambrose didn't catch a whiff of it first. If he did, he would ruin it before anything could even potentially come to fruition. He said it was in my best interest, looking out for me and all.

I eventually just kind of gave up and accepted that I'm going to die alone while watching my best friend sleep his way through the realm.

Fun times.

After picking out his food, they start walking in our direction.

Shit.

I quickly duck my head and become very invested in the potatoes on my plate. I do not want to have to bear witness to Ambrose getting his face sucked off the rest of lunch.

Gods, please, anything but that.

It's one thing to know about it. It's another to have to sit there and witness it. Knowing it's hardly unlikely that he won't spot my unruly red hair, it's impossible to miss after all, I slouch down further, trying to make myself as small as possible.

I can be quite good at that.

Making myself small for other people.

"Yo, Nori, you good? You look like a cooked shrimp down there," Finnley calls down the table.

My eyes shoot up from the plate I'm currently hunched over just in time to see Ambrose's gaze fall on me. His brow lifts in confusion, and he starts heading our way.

Dammit, Finnley.

"Hey brat, didn't think you would be done yet," Ambrose says as he reaches me. He sets his tray down and takes the seat next to me. "How'd it go?" he asks, genuine interest reflected in his eyes.

The brunette who was so shamelessly hanging on him mere minutes ago now stands next to him, her hand resting on his shoulder like a mark of possession as her unblinking eyes land on me. I give a slight eye roll and pull my gaze from her glare. Instead, I can now feel it burning into the side of my head.

"Honestly, I think it chewed me up and spit me out," I admit.

Pushing my tray away, I turn and give him my full attention. "I was too confident going in, way more than I should have been. Nothing I studied for prepared me for anything that was on that parchment." He narrows his eyes, the underlying insinuation hitting home. All the risk we'd taken wasn't worth it in the end. It wasn't even the same test.

"She's not giving herself enough credit. She was one of the first ones done," Mallory says, pointing her fork at me.

"That doesn't surprise me. She always was the smartest," Ambrose responds to her while winking at me.

My cheeks warm at the compliment.

"Or maybe," the leggy brunette sneers down her nose, "she's right and finished quickly because she got them all wrong." She's obviously not liking the attention I'm getting.

Trust me, I'd rather be in your shoes.

Before I can respond, Mallory beats me to it. "I'm sorry, who are you?"

"Who am I? I'm the girl who—"

"That's enough, Yaretta." Ambrose's words come out soft but stern, leaving no room for argument and effectively cutting off anything she was about to say.

I pick the apple off Ambrose's tray and take a big bite, wiggling my eyebrows at her before shrugging at his amused expression. Sometimes the best thing you can say to hurt someone is just not to say anything at all.

Make them feel insignificant.

Conversation picks back up around us, and Mallory and Finnley start bickering about what fresh hell is going to be on the agility portion of the trials. I pretend not to see Ambrose pull his new flavor of the week down on his lap. Or the feline grin that she throws my way. Apparently, all is forgiven on his part.

His deep laughter and her shrill giggles are making me contemplate driving this fork right through my eye. Which means it's as good of time as any to admit lunch is over.

Just as I'm about to stand up, the energy shifts around the table.

A familiar gravelly voice comes from behind me. "Tell me something, Ambrose," he drawls. "*How do I taste?*"

It's said just loud enough that classmen from other tables stop eating and chatting among themselves to watch what's about to transpire.

Ambrose's head whips around, a look of pure malice lining his face. "What the fuck did you just say?" he demands.

"Oh boy," Mallory whispers. Her head is moving quickly from one man to the other, almost comically.

Slowly, I twist my upper body to look behind me as well. The first thing that hits me is how very correct I was in the images I had conjured in my head. He's exactly what I expected him to be.

A walking menace to society.

Offering zero apologies for it, as well.

"I said, how. Do. I. Taste," he repeats, with an emphasis on each individual word.

Dressed in all black, a Damascus dagger sticking out of a tactical sheath that's draped across his chest, he oozes fuck-off vibes. He looks the same size, if not larger, than he did in full armor. How is that even possible? His stern lips are pulled into a threatening sneer, and a challenging look fills his eyes. Deep brown eyes that never even look in my direction.

I shrug to myself.

Fine by me.

I openly stare at him, though.

Long, thick black hair, with war braids woven throughout, falls down his back, with the top half being partially pulled up. An almost perfectly straight scar runs down one temple to the corner of his mouth, adding an even more ominous edge to his appearance.

Apparently, it was the wrong thing for him to say to Ambrose, though.

He stands, causing me to jump to my feet as well. I choose to ignore the fact that Yaretta just landed on her ass and quickly grab onto his arm.

"It's not worth it. Just let it go," I plead. There's a time and place, and this is not it. If he heard me, he doesn't show it. Or maybe he just doesn't care. He's vibrating with anger, and I'm getting a feeling this isn't something that just developed today between the two. This is anger that's had time to fester.

Ambrose gets right in Makon's face, grabbing a fistful of his shirt. "What the fuck is that supposed to mean, Makon?" he snarls.

They're almost nose to nose, and I'm pretty sure I'm going to have to pick my jaw up off the floor. I'm stuck between horror and fascination at how quickly things have transpired.

"Are you trying to get a firsthand experience, Ballard?" Makon retorts in that mocking tone that I've come to associate with him. "You should have just asked. Although I have to be honest, men aren't my thing," he says. "I prefer something a little sweeter."

It's like he wants to get punched.

"Fuck you." Ambrose's jaw ticks with barely contained fury. "If you have something to say, then say it or piss off," he replies through clenched teeth. Releasing Makon's shirt from his grasp, he shoves him away like touching his clothing will taint him.

There's so much testosterone surrounding us that you could choke on it.

Their little altercation has drawn the attention of a few more Noctryns, who are making their way over to stand behind Makon. If there was anyone in this room who probably didn't need backup, my guess is it would be him.

I'm going to keep that little opinion to myself, though.

The Veils seem content to watch from a distance. Which is fine. I'm not worried. Ambrose has everything under control.

Smoothing down the front of his shirt, Makon lets out a soft chuckle as if this is all just some big joke.

He's not fooling me, though. I see the cruel glint in his eye and know this is just who he is. He likes to make people uncomfortable and watch them squirm.

I know his type all too well.

I can hear Finnley behind me crunching down and chewing as he's watching the events unfold. Seemingly and completely unbothered. Here I am, having trouble even swallowing the saliva in my mouth, and he's enjoying his carrots.

Makon's attention falls to the woman still sitting on the floor. She's watching the two men with wide, fearful eyes. A rabbit caught in the crosshairs of two wolves. The moment his lips lift in a sinister smile, I know shit's about to go down. She seems to know as well if her sudden pale complexion is any indication.

"Why don't you ask the current object sitting so prettily at your feet," he all but purrs. Yaretta gulps and looks around before slightly whimpering. I wouldn't want to be the one pinned beneath that penetrating glare either. Having Makon's full attention does not sound like a good time. "Better yet, let me," Makon suggests in a lethal whisper.

He walks around Ambrose and kneels to the level of the whimpering female crumpled on the floor. He rubs his thumb slowly over her bottom lip, his touch more condescending than gentle. "Yaretta, darling, why don't you share with the class what you were doing with those lovely lips last night?" He tilts his head, waiting for her to respond. "No? Not in the mood to disclose?" he asks. "Allow me then."

He pushes off the floor, rising to his full height, slowly circling Ambrose before walking back to his comrades. "You see, Ambrose," he says, turning his hard eyes toward us, "those devious lips you were kissing in the hall just moments ago? Those very same lips were fit snugly around me last night." His smile widens as he lets the words hit their mark. "*All of me.*"

A soft gasp escapes Yaretta's lips before she throws her hand over her mouth, trying to cover it.

Makon's brown eyes are literally glowing with triumph.

"So I'll ask you one more time, for curiosity's sake and all. How do I taste, Ballard?" he asks darkly.

I actually feel bad for her.

I no longer desire to be in her shoes.

I feel even worse for Ambrose.

He's never cared about sharing his toys before, but I doubt he'll appreciate being taunted with it so publicly, especially in front of an entire dining hall. If he protects one thing viciously, it's his pride.

I've seen him throw haymakers for less.

Judging by the way he's opening and closing his fists, this is about to go from bad to worse. Very fast. His shoulders are tense, and his jaw is clenched.

The entire dining hall is now watching. I can tell my best friend is fighting for control and losing. I can't stand to see him be humiliated like this. I reach out to gently grab his hand. A shriek escapes my mouth as my palm connects with his, and it immediately feels like molten embers embed into my skin. Tears well in my eyes from the pain, and the skin is red and charred-looking by the time I pull it away.

I wasn't here to see him manifest, and I haven't witnessed it yet, but I've heard through mutual friends what his ability is.

Fire.

He looks down at me. His entire demeanor is wound tight, and his eyes are blank. Void. It's as if no one's home, but he's looking right at me.

I step back a little, unease sinking into my stomach.

This is new.

"Nori, get over here," Makon growls under his breath. His words are directed at me, but his eyes never leave Ambrose. I hesitate, because why would I leave the person's side I've known my entire life and trust to go stand by him? His gaze swings from me to Ambrose and back again, full of irritation and hostility. "It wasn't a suggestion but an order. Unless you'd like to see what happens when he loses the internal battle he's currently fighting."

Ambrose stands eerily still now, watching Makon with an empty stare. His fingernails dig into his palms. The veins in his forearms protrude due to the exertion he's placing on keeping the fire suppressed. His control is slipping, and it's evident to anyone within standing distance.

"You might want to listen, just this one time," Finnley suggests in a whisper-shout across the table. "He's starting to flame."

Sure enough, there are small flickers of flames in both hands.

He's losing control.

I slowly walk to Makon's side, careful not to make any sudden movements. The moment I reach him, he shoves me behind him into another Noctryn's waiting arms. I grab at them, trying to pry myself out of their restraint, but the soldier's grip is unbreakable.

What is even happening right now?

I'm furious at Ambrose for letting himself get this worked up. Why would he give this asshole that much power over him? Fire ability is hard to control at best and unpredictable at worst. And that's to someone who didn't just manifest within the last year.

I lean forward, trying to see what's happening, and stop breathing as dark shadows emerge from Makon's fingertips. They are like a living, breathing entity as they move toward Ambrose, wrapping themselves around both men, completely obscuring them from our view.

It's beautiful and terrifying.

Desperately, I claw at the rigid arms holding me in place, but it's no use. I'm stuck. It's as if the entire dining hall and everyone in it is collectively holding their breath.

What happens if one captain kills another captain?

Ambrose's anger fueled his fire, but a captain is expected to be able to control their abilities at all times. Will he lose the C insignia he wears so proudly on his shoulder?

I force myself to calm down. Hysteria won't get me anywhere. Biting down on my lips, I think of a hundred different outcomes. At least one of them has to be positive, right?

The obsidian shadows move around the two men like a lover's caress, coaxing yet determined. When I don't think I can stand another second of watching helplessly on the sidelines, Makon's darkness starts to recede.

The shadows act like an extension of him, completely and utterly at his disposal.

The outline of the two men slowly becomes visible again.

Kicking backward, I land a solid boot to my captive's shin and push forward with all my weight. A harsh grunt leaves him. "Not only was that unwise, but it also hurt. Stop," the Noctryn hisses in my ear.

Sorry to burst your bubble, pal, but I don't give one flying shit if it hurt or not.

That was kind of the goal.

I wiggle and throw myself around unsuccessfully.

At this point, the shadows are fully reclaimed by Makon, as if they were never there. Both men square off against one another, the eye contact making me uncomfortable, and I'm not even a part of it.

The hatred in both of their eyes is positively blinding.

I know the two separate regiments aren't a fan of each other, but something deeper is at play here. Something more than the crude insults and innuendos thrown around today. Something I don't know about because Ambrose decided to be a sellout and not fill me in.

Some best friend he is.

Ambrose's laughter comes out gentle but devious. I've never heard him laugh in such a threatening way. "You're just like him, aren't you? Desperate to be noticed. Determined to make a name for yourself." His dark hair falls over his brow as he taunts Makon. "You've already failed, though, haven't you? You couldn't even place as a Veil. All you'll ever be good at is dirty magic," he says with a smug smile.

Repulsion sweeps across Makon's face. "I'd slit my own throat before accepting the signia of a Veil." His gaze turns cold, unforgiving. "One day, Ballard, I'll stare down at your lifeless body and golden morals both bleeding out on the battlefield."

He looks like the type who wouldn't just look down at Ambrose's lifeless body but would smile upon it. This man is downright terrifying. What I really want to know is how his shadows snuffed out Ambrose's flames. Are they more powerful than certain manifestations?

Ambrose, being Ambrose, just has to get the last word in, though.

"It makes perfect sense, you know." He laughs, rubbing the corners of his mouth. "You two are cut from the exact same cloth after all."

Who is cut from what cloth? Why am I so in the dark here?

The fire may have fully subsided in his hands, but apparently not in his anger toward Makon. Now there's just residual ash encased around his fingernails. A stark reminder he lost control today, and a Noctryn gained it.

Whether, I like him or not, which I most definitely do not, Makon just saved us from all becoming tinder for the academy. My favorite part of all of this, though, is when my buddy, who's pretty high up on my shit list at the moment, turns toward me, remembering I'm still here.

Ambrose's eyes widen in surprise, like he actually did forget I was here.

I tilt my chin and let out a quiet huff, not bothering to hide it.

It takes a second before his eyes fall to the pair of arms holding me hostage, causing his lips to lift in a snarl. "Remove your fucking hands," he warns the Noctryn holding me.

Makon examines his fingernails, like this is all incredibly boring to him at this point.

"He wouldn't have to restrain her if you could control yourself, *Veil*." He says the last word as if it's filthy. "If we had left her in your very incapable hands, figuratively and literally, she'd be embers at this point."

If looks could kill, Makon would be dead on the spot. Fury and hatred pour out of Ambrose, and I'd bet anything he's dismembering him in his head.

Slowly.

A chill works its way down my spine at the murderous glint in his eye.

Makon says something to the man restraining me, but it's in a language I don't recognize. I'm immediately released and rush over to Ambrose. He tucks me under his arm, not even looking at me. It's okay, though. I'm sure he's just out of sorts right now and trying to keep me safe.

Makon cuts a glance toward me before his brown eyes narrow on Ambrose. Without another word, he turns on his heel, leaving with his horde of dark comrades following closely behind.

The rest of us are left standing here, wondering what just happened.

Yaretta is nowhere to be seen.

Chapter Seven

I spit dirt from my mouth.

The granules are stuck between my teeth, and my tongue feels like sandpaper against the roof of my mouth. I can only imagine how much is in my hair after being unceremoniously shoved into the arena and landing on my face.

First, we were crammed into the dark, cavernous tunnels, our eyesight taken from us, and had to rely on touch to find our way through. Then, without warning, once we reached the end of the very long underpass, we were shoved into daylight, our eyes not having time to adjust.

This is how my face ended up breaking my fall into the dirt.

So far, being a lieutenant for the prospects has come with zero rewards, only setbacks. I'm at the front of the group because of the leader signia on my shoulder, which means I have no time to regain my composure before being instructed to climb to the first agility assessment.

Craning my neck back, I shield my eyes and look up the rope ladder. It looks flimsy and unreliable. There's also the main issue at play here. I absolutely loathe heights. The tingly feeling is already starting in my legs, and I know I'm about to lose all authority over their actions.

"Up you go. It won't get easier the longer you stare at it," a Veil standing at the foot of the ladder orders. She shakes the rope for added emphasis.

I swallow down my fear.

Here goes nothing.

I grip the first rung and bite the inside of my cheek to keep from pleading for mercy. The taste of copper floods my mouth from how hard I am biting down, but I don't let up. I can do this. *I can do this.* I'm the daughter of Maeve Caderyn, one of the greatest Veils to ever grace the halls of Kintoira Academy.

I start my ascent and pray to Lansointh, the god of fortitude, that I have the strength to keep going. If there was one god who's been present in my life without fail, it's him.

The climb up the rope ladder to the grass-covered podium is slow and steady. Honestly, though, the fact that my legs are moving at all is progress. The chill from the mountainous winds bites through my bones, but regardless of how frigid the air is, beads of sweat still fall over my brow. I'm sweating and freezing at the same time, and my legs feel like jelly.

It's time to face the *Death Giver* as it's been so kindly named by the prospects before us. The agility portion of Asylamation. The part I've been dreading. And apparently for very good reason. I knew I was going to hate this. I *knew* it. And here I am, being all right and stuff, hating this.

It couldn't be the last portion of it that ended with us in the sky. No, it had to be the very first. I think I'm almost halfway up. I've kept my face forward, or rather upward, and haven't made the dire mistake of looking down again, so I can't be sure, but it feels like I've made a fair amount of progress.

After what feels like forever, I finally crest the top and release my cheek from the painful bite. The taste of blood washes over my tongue. The coppery tang surrounds my taste buds. Upperclassmen sit in the stadium seating that surrounds us, throwing taunts and jeers our way, but I go to that place in my head where I can block them all out. There's only me and the distance it will take to get from this podium to the next.

I grind my teeth and wipe my hands on my shirt, the buttons now askew. I think a few might even be missing.

Cracking my knuckles, I focus on the task ahead of me.

Wooden spikes, sharpened to a lethal point, line the entire floor between the two podiums. A dark substance stains the tips of many. It isn't hard to imagine what made those stains. It's at least an eighty-four-foot drop to reach the spikes.

I will not contribute to those stains.

Head up, chin up.

I can do this.

I gulp down any remaining moisture and blood that's left in my mouth and count the rings between the podiums. There are twenty in total. It would be hard enough on its own, but add in the frigid temperatures and the fact that I had to remove my cheap gloves to prevent my grip from slipping on the rings, and I'm starting to feel like it's a lost cause.

I'll need to jump high enough to grip the first ring firmly with both hands and then swing myself with enough momentum to grab the next. That's the part that makes me nervous—the momentum. Too little and I won't make it, falling to my death. Too much and my hand will slip, again, falling to my death.

I step from foot to foot, trying to expel some of this nervous energy as I wait for my turn, watching the other lieutenant cross the rings. I met him on the first night of Asylamation. He's the one with floppy brown hair and thick, large, rimmed glasses that appear just a little too big for his face. Aksel, I think his name was. He's more than halfway across and has a steady rhythm to his swinging. He's making it look so easy.

I chew on my nails, the black polish chipped and faded.

As a child, this would have been cake. As an adult, my arms are more like limp noodles. They serve a purpose but are also useless in most situations.

He effortlessly swings himself to the next ring. His brows are drawn tight in concentration, but his eyes aren't holding any tension. He's confident in his ability. The veins in his hand flex with the assertion of holding on for so long, but he's almost to the end. There are only a few rings left.

Maybe this won't be so hard after all.

As long as I keep looking forward and not down.

He rocks his hips back and forth, chasing the last bit of vigor needed to land on the opposite podium. His hand reaches out and grabs the next ring, but I don't miss the way he flexes his finger over the top. If I were to guess, I'd say he's trying to work the cold out and get the blood flowing, but there's just no escaping it. It's a mind-numbing kind of cold.

I'm sure it was intended this way, to host Asylamation during the most bitter months of the year, just to add another layer of agony to the already treacherous task. We don't even get winter gear, just our standard-issued prospect uniforms.

I rub my arms vigorously as my veins chase a sliver of warmth.

My eyes follow his movements as his entire body is thrown into the next transition, eager to be finished. I can't blame him. He's so close he can probably taste it. The sweet taste of escaping death and being one step closer to his goal.

I do my best not to blink or take my eyes off Aksel as I shove the wayward hairs out of my face. The ferocious winds are blowing them all over the place, escaping the severe bun I put them in, causing them to smack me directly in the mouth and eyes. Eyes that currently narrow in on Aksel, watching his facial expressions.

If I weren't staring at him at exactly the right moment, I would miss the way his eyes widen, and fear overtakes his features right after he lets go of the ring with his left hand. He knows immediately he overcompensated and doesn't have the precise control needed to grab onto the next ring. His arm catches his glasses mid-swing, knocking them off into the pit below. I watch in horror as his hand frantically grabs air, searching for the ring.

A pulse of dread ripples beneath my skin.

All I can do is watch helplessly.

Lines form between his brows as he slams his eyes shut. Panic is etched into every crevice of his face, and it looks like he's just trying to block out the noise of the crowd to focus on one disaster at a time. I can only imagine what he's hearing and feeling.

The ringing in my ears blocked out the screams and jeers some time ago, but it looks like every syllable muttered is landing like a heavy blow upon him.

Watching someone struggle, fighting for their life with all dignity left at the door, is such a depleting feeling. Everything in me feels hollow and too full at the same time. It's as if I am the one hanging between the podiums, entertainment for the masses, as I blindly reach for my saving grace, only to come up empty-handed time and time again.

When I'm about to close my eyes because it just feels like too much, by some miracle, he grabs the ring. I close my eyes in relief, and I send up a silent prayer.

How am I going to make it through these trials when I feel this drained from just spectating the first one? Death is inevitable this week. It's expected. But that doesn't make it any easier.

If I don't die in the process of participating, just watching might kill me.

He makes no move to grab onto the next ring. The muscles in his arms strain under his weight, but he's just hanging in place. I can see his chest rising and falling with deep breaths as he works up the courage to keep going. I'm assuming by the thickness of the glasses he wore that he's practically blind without them.

My shoulders tense.

I think I'm going to puke.

He finally lets go of the ring and reaches toward one of the last remaining. His fingers miss it by the smallest fraction, causing him to swing backward by one arm, his body spinning uncontrollably. His arm flails recklessly again, looking for the next ring to grab, but he misses it each time. The momentum of the swing is too much for him to remain holding with one arm. His fingers are slipping.

"It's to your right," I shout through my hands. "REACH TO YOUR RIGHT!"

He frantically grabs the air to the right of him, continuing to miss.

A scream lodges in my throat, refusing to come out as I watch his fingers slip off, and he falls.

And falls.

He keeps reaching for the ring even in his descent.

He never even makes a noise going down.

I shake my head in denial.

Carefully getting down on my hands and knees, I crawl to the edge. I close my eyes, willing strength into my heart because I know this is going to hurt, but I have to look. There has to be some kind of closure, even if it tears another small fragment of my soul out and casts it to these damn winds.

Dread and reluctance line my spine, but I force myself to open my eyes and peer over the ledge. His body now rests in the cavern between the two podiums, multiple wooden spikes penetrating him. The broken glasses rest mere inches from his head.

I flinch as *Aksel Penton deceased. Ashlyn Yvaine, promoted to lieutenant, group two,* is broadcast across the speakers. Screams and taunts surround me, as if the voices are amplified with some kind of magic.

I can't do this.

I dig my hands into the cold grass, grounding myself before scooting backward and finding the resilience to stand. I wanted to be something other than adequate, and here's my chance to prove to myself that I'm capable of more than I ever thought possible. But maybe adequate isn't so bad after all. Adequate and alive sure sounds better than extraordinary and dead.

"You're up," the candidate behind me, hanging on the ladder with one hand, declares. Like I didn't already know this. As if I didn't watch a young man fall to his death, opening up the spot for the next prospect to attempt the same damn suicidal mission.

There's only enough room for one person at a time to be up here and get the running start needed, so until I jump, he has to continue hanging on the ropes. The permanent-looking scowl on his upturned face doesn't exactly scream team spirit, so I just nod and make my way over to him, allowing plenty of space for my running start.

I shiver and shake out my arms. The fact that Ambrose is in the stands watching, and Finnley and Mallory are somewhere in line to do this reckless trial, makes me feel like heaving. I have to just block it out for now and pretend it's just me here. Just me and these rings, and I'm going to crush it.

I will not die a senseless death.

I won't fucking fail.

I'm sure there's some self-encouragement speech out there that's better, but this is all I've got.

Screw it. I'm just going to go with it.

Dirt and grass crunch beneath my feet as I move them into position. I push my stubborn hair back out of my face, my chest rising and falling with rapid breaths, and count to three.

Grass flies up from beneath my feet as I sprint across the large podium, my eyes set only on the first ring. This is it. I just have to wrap my hand around that first ring. I can feel the wind whip across my cheeks, the icy air biting into my skin. Red waves break free from their bindings and fly in a symphony of chaos behind me.

The bones in my injured knee protest at the speed I'm forcing it into, but when my feet leave the ground, and nothingness sits underneath me, I'm thankful for the exertion and painful massages I put it through. Although my palms are past the point of sweaty, by some miracle, the grip that I land on the first ring is solid and true. My body swings in a heavy momentum back and forth as I just hang on for dear life.

Thank fuck I ran as hard as I did, or I would already be dead.

The first ring is set farther back than it looks from the podium, almost as if it's an illusion. Pain radiates across my shoulders as I hang from the ring and try to get my bearings.

One down, only nineteen more to go.

Fuck me sideways.

Squinting, I look in the direction of the next ring. It's overcast, but snow from the surrounding mountains still makes it hell on the eyes. If I misjudge even a fraction, it could be fatal. I rock my hips back and forth, needing more momentum to swing one arm to the next ring. This is the hardest part in this particular trial, in my opinion, moving from a two-handed grip to a one-handed grip.

I push back against the self-doubt and fear. There isn't room for it.

Once I've gained enough momentum, I shoot my left hand forward, grabbing onto the next ring. My head falls back in relief. I close my eyes for a moment and thank whoever is watching over me today.

Apparently, death doesn't want me just yet.

If I can just keep up this cadence, I might make it to the end. Confidence that I didn't necessarily have a few minutes ago blooms in my chest, and I keep swinging my hips, releasing my right hand and grabbing onto the third ring. The bitter cold is actually working in my favor right now, drying up the sweat on my palms and keeping me cool despite my rising body temperature. Very carefully, I flex my fingers around the rings, keeping the blood flowing, and adjust the weight in each hand.

I continue to swing my hips and move onto ring after ring.

After a while, I forget I'm hanging eighty-four feet in the air and pretend it's just like when I was a kid. We would swing from clotheslines, windows, trees, basically anything a kid shouldn't be hanging from.

It's just me and four remaining rings by the time my arms start screaming in defiance. For having weak upper-body strength, I lasted longer than I thought I would. Every muscle and tendon in them is currently fighting for its life, and it feels like they're going to war against one another. I'm so close. I just have to hang on a little bit longer, and it'll all be over.

I will not die a senseless death.

I won't fucking fail.

I just have to keep repeating it to myself.

A scream of fury tears through my throat, and I force my arm to reach out for the next ring. Fluid trickles between my fingers, running down my wrist before landing right below my eye. It's as if I am crying tears of pus at this point. The padding at the base of my fingers is absolutely shredded. Between the fall off the side of the mountain and hanging from the rope to dangling from these rings, my hands have been to hell and back.

The tears are making my grip less stable, and I know I need to get my ass on that next podium sooner rather than later. I rotate my head in a small circle to ease some of the tension in my shoulders.

The prospect going after me is now standing on the grass, scrutinizing my every move. He's smart, trying to figure out what works and what doesn't, just like I did. "Here's to hoping the outcome is a little bit different from the one before me," I whisper to myself.

I put everything I have into my next few swings. My body has been pushed to its limit, the soft muscles screaming at me and begging for mercy. To give them the smallest reprieve from the abuse I'm putting them through.

The minute my feet land on the grass, I immediately collapse on all fours. For a second, I just stay in this position. My forehead pressed into the grass and my ass in the air. Once I feel like I'm not going to pass out, I roll over onto my back, the grass sticking to my sweaty neck, and allow my gaze to float across the open sky.

I sigh out a breath of relief.

Ominous gray skies hover above me, but I find beauty in their somber desolation. Right now, I would find beauty in just about anything. It's funny, how when faced with your own mortality, everything suddenly becomes more precious.

The intense pain in my palms reminds me that my heart is still beating. The burning in my arms implies they can still come out swinging. My short breaths are proof that my lungs are still working.

I did it.

I punch the air.

I fucking did it.

Chapter Eight

The death toll continues to climb throughout the physical trials.

At this point, they no longer announce it over the intercoms. Rather, they just list names on delicate scrolls lined throughout the gloomy stone hallways. Amber flames from the wall candelabras splash warm colors over the names of the dead. The only warmth they'll ever feel again. This is what they've become. A hollow name on a meaningless piece of parchment. These young men and women with big dreams and hopes of achievement are now just a bunch of useless letters.

Death and tribulations hold our hand each day, beckoning us.

Tempting us.

The trials have become increasingly harder with messier ways to die, and the fact that today is the last couldn't be more welcome. I'm haunted by the things I've seen and endured. I feel like I've lived countless lives this week alone.

The dull ache in my knee is just starting to subside, but my shoulders still burn like hell from hanging on the rings in the first trial. Both of my hands are bandaged from the flesh being torn repeatedly. The treacherous climb up the rocks on trial two didn't help matters. A swift and brutal kick to the jaw from a falling prospect climbing up those same rocks also didn't make things easier on me.

I wiggle my jaw back and forth.

It still hurts like a bitch.

It would be unfair to forget the gash across my abdomen that the Alkinean bear gave me during our forge through the Forsaken Forest during trial three. That will be a nice souvenir after this is all said and done. Alkinean bears are four to five times the size of a normal bear, and they are ferocious. Also, funny enough, very territorial.

They feasted that day.

The professors were kind enough to give us friendly advice before leaving us in the dense trees—don't die.

That's it.

That was the lifeline they tossed us.

Not all of us listened.

They also forgot to mention the forest dwellers that live and breathe to kill, or the fact that we would have to make it past them to get to the green base. The base was our ticket out of the forest. We found it and succeeded, or we tried until we didn't.

Conveniently, it was the same color as every damn tree surrounding us.

This place is more than just an academy.

It's a damn battlefield.

Had it not been for the dagger that Ambrose gave me, I would have been a morsel for the taking. The only reason I wasn't is sheer luck. I ducked and rolled after the first strike of its paw to my stomach and hid in an abandoned burrow. By some weird stroke of fortune, the burrow was covered in Braxton berries, which I used my dagger to cut open and rub all over myself. If it wasn't for the sharp blade, I'd never have been able to penetrate the hard outer shell. The smell is so repulsive that it even deters bears from eating you.

I hold my arm up to my nose.

I still stink.

Gravel crunches under my boots as I make my way outside to the court-yard where we've been instructed to meet. I've barely made it a few steps before a pair of hands falls over my eyes.

"Guess who?" a deep voice whispers softly in my ear.

A defeated sigh escapes before I can rein it back in, and disappointment curdles in my stomach. I thought it was Ambrose. I was hoping it was him.

I press my hands over the back of the ones covering my eyes and pull them away. "Don't you have anything better to do, Finnley?"

He drops his hands to his sides as I turn to face him. A roguish smile plays across his face, and he looks like he doesn't, in fact, have anything better to do. Other than pestering me. "You know better than that. Besides, you're my partner today," he states before rubbing the top of my head like an annoying brother might.

I push his hands off the top of my head, my braid now thoroughly messed up.

"What are you talking about?" I ask in a cautious tone, patting my hair down and trying to subdue it into submission.

Today is the last trial. I've heard the last is the worst, but I don't know how they can top the previous ones.

"A leprechaun-looking professor just came by telling us to partner up," he explains, jerking his chin in the direction of the battlement. "So are you ready, partner?" He emphasizes the 'P' in partner extra hard.

I look around the open courtyard. Prospects line the area, chatting among themselves, and it appears they are looking to pair up. There are so few of us now—maybe forty-five or so from the original one hundred and three. Quite a few have already teamed up, while others are testing the waters and approaching potential teammates.

A petite girl with elfin features makes eye contact with me, but I quickly glance away. It appears I already have my partner, and I don't feel like having to turn anyone down. We've been through enough.

A few Veils and Noctryns stand off to the side, watching like vultures waiting for a meal.

I notice Makon and Corrine, another of his kind, standing together. Her long, dark hair is piled high on top of her head, and the usual bored expression graces her features. She was the one who opened the gate for us the first night we arrived. She seems as unimpressed with us now as she was then.

Glad to see we're staying consistent in her eyes.

Makon leans over and whispers something in her ear, and her eyes rise and fall on me. They're both watching me with an uncomfortable intensity.

My nostrils flare, and I openly stare back at them.

I feel like Makon is always watching. Observing. Almost as if documenting everything for someone else.

Creep.

"Ready as I'll ever be," I answer, pulling my gaze away from the dark duo.

I give my full attention to Finnley, my eyes roaming over his pristine uniform and lack of wounds. There isn't one scratch on him. At least not from what I can see.

"Like what you see?" he asks, wiggling his eyebrows suggestively.

"How do you not have any battle wounds or stains?" I demand in a high-pitched voice, my hands turning him in circles to look for hidden marks. He's as polished as he was on the day I met him. Every curl perfectly in place with not one wrinkle on his issued outfit. You can hardly tell that the rest of the prospects' uniforms were once cream-colored, mine included. His is spotless.

"I have plenty," he corrects, wincing in my grip. "Just not any in places you can see. Unless you want to. Do you want to see, Nori?" he asks, his words filled with amusement and something darker.

I snort.

The hopeful look falls from his face, but I know it's all a ploy. He has about as much interest in me as I do in him. Somehow, along the way, we fell into a sibling rivalry kind of friendship, and I actually kind of love it.

I drop my hands, releasing him from my inspection, and take a step back.

His upper body leans back, arms extended behind him, stretching. "I don't know what they have lined up for us today, but if I had to die with anyone by my side, I'm happy it's you."

"Aw, Finnley, are you going and getting sentimental on me?" I bat my eyelashes in his direction.

"You know me, just a big ole sap." He laughs, then rubs a hand down the front of his shirt, smoothing out invisible wrinkles. But I don't miss the serious undertone in his voice, his fake laugh not entirely covering it. Regardless of his joking exterior, right now, he really does mean he's happy to die at my side if it comes to that.

It might be the nicest thing anyone has ever said to me.

I won't let it come to that, though. We've come too far to fail when we're so freakin close. "We aren't going to die, Finnley. One day, yes, but that day is not today," I counter in a confident tone.

Our conversation is cut short when a professor who does indeed look like a little leprechaun walks along the battlement. His beady eyes sweep down over us, and I don't know how it's possible, but his small, upturned nose rises even higher in the air.

Another young professor rushes out with a small stool and helps him step up on it. "Allow me to introduce myself," the leprechaun-looking one says. "I am one of the professors here at Kintoira Academy, Professor Lyric, and I will be judge, jury, and arbiter today," he declares in a pompous tone. "Any other day, you can find me teaching alchemy to both Veils and Noctryns alike."

He stands silently as if he's waiting for applause that never comes.

We all just continue to stare at him, curious and nervous to get to the most important part. The part where he tells us what we're facing today. He fidgets with his sleeve then adjusts the neckline of his professor's robe, before huffing and finally continuing. "You have been instructed to pair up. I assume you can all follow simple directions and have done so," he says while simultaneously wrinkling his nose.

Finnley and I make eye contact before both rolling our eyes.

How bad do I need alchemy classes? If it isn't mandatory, I'm out.

There must be an even number of prospects left because no one raises their hands or admits they don't have a partner. If there is someone, I don't blame them for remaining quiet. I would rather do whatever it is alone than be the object under his scrutiny.

A shuffling sound draws my attention to the right, where Mallory is squeezing between people and making her way toward us. Her hand is gripped around the wrist of a fellow lieutenant, whose being dragged behind her. Mayline offers me a weak smile and a shrug as if she had no say in the matter of being pulled our way.

"Glad to see you're still here," I admit in a hushed tone.

"Glad to be here," Mayline responds.

I give Mallory a quick hug before she moves to stand next to Finnley, and our attention is back on Professor Lyric.

He pulls out a parchment from the sleeve of his robe and proceeds to read from it. "Today, you will face your biggest obstacle of Asylamation. You've made it thus far, and for that, congratulations." He raises his squinty gaze from the words and lets it fall over us before continuing. "The winning streak for many will end here. You'll no longer depend on just yourself for victory, but your partner as well. Rather, you place as a Veil or Noctryn, you must know how to work as a unit, or you won't survive the atrocities that wait for you outside of the academy," he advises. "You must have eyes in front of you, to the sides, and behind you. To do this, you need team members. You need to be able to trust your fellow soldiers with your life."

I'm not sure I trust anyone with my life, let alone people I barely know. But if I wanted anyone in this courtyard at my back, it's the man beside me. Things are about to get messy, and he's the definition of composure and confidence.

Regardless of what we face, this will, without a doubt, be the hardest challenge because we must depend on our teammate and not just ourselves. Almost every prospect standing in this courtyard is self-reliant and headstrong, or they wouldn't even be here in the first place. They would have joined the healers or the librarians in their academies. They certainly wouldn't have enrolled at Kintoira to become soldiers. Or they would have simply remained civilians, not working for the realm at all. Complacent to let others take care of them and protect them from the enemies chomping at the gates.

And there are many.

Mayline stiffens at my side, rolling her shoulders back as if she is about to go to war. I don't know if this is going to be more of an internal war or an outright physical one, but it certainly feels like warfare, nonetheless.

"You must cross the finish line together, or you forfeit, and you'll be forced to try again until you cross as a pair." The corners of his mouth pull up in a sinister smile. "Also, I should not fail to mention, before you enter, you will have a malediction placed upon you that dictates if your partner perishes during the trial, then so too shall you," he finishes in a malicious tone that makes my skin crawl.

I slowly turn my head and look at Finnley.

His hazel eyes meet mine. "I've got you," he mouths.

After a curt nod, I turn back toward the battlements.

Professor Lyric hands the parchment off to the other professor before clapping his hands together in quick succession. I hope he claps hard enough that he falls off his little stool.

"And last, I will be watching to be sure there is no cheating. I will be your judge, and what I determine will be law. If I say you're cheating, you are cheating." He narrows his eyes into devious little slits. "You may not add marks or leave breadcrumbs. This trial will be accomplished through sheer intellect and problem-solving. If you cheat, you start over." Rubbing his hands together, he gleefully finishes his speech. "The walls never stop moving and the obstacles have teeth, so it would be unwise to start over," he adds. "Or get lost. Good luck!"

He hops off his stool, his head now barely taller than the battlement wall, and walks off with the other professor scrambling after him.

A sharp tug on my braid pulls my head back, and steely eyes meet mine.

"We got this, Nori," Finnley declares with determination oozing from every fiber of his being. "Remember, we'll die one day, but today is not that day," he echoes back to me.

I gulp and offer up a weak smile before he drops my braid, and my head falls forward.

The walls never stop moving.

Don't leave breadcrumbs... why would we try to leave a trail?

And why are the walls moving... what walls?

I bite my lip, trying to work out what it all means. Voices surround us, growing in volume as everyone else does the same.

It has walls. We can't leave breadcrumbs. And getting lost is a very real possibility.

Oh shit...

I smack myself in the forehead for being so daft.

It's a maze.

I spin around and grip Finnley's forearm. "Finnley, I think I know what it is," I breathe, my nails digging into the cords beneath my fingers. "It's a maze. We have to survive whatever is in the maze!"

I can see the moment the wheels start spinning in his head.

"That should be simple enough, except for the moving wall part. And the teeth part," Mallory jokes, coming to stand beside me.

"The teeth part is what I'm most looking forward to," Mayline sarcastically retorts. Her round facial features are relaxed, and her hooded eyes are closed while she gently massages her temples. Even when trying to be extremely relaxed, her lithe frame stands straight and disciplined.

Finnley starts walking in circles, chewing on his thumbnail, seemingly working out scenarios in his head, while I just internally panic.

It's gotten me this far, why change things up now?

"The part I don't understand is the partner aspect," he mutters to himself while he continues to pace, his brow furrowed.

A knot burrows in my chest. I have a feeling it has more to do with what we're going to face than actually needing each other to find the exit. It's about learning to depend on your squad during combat. A sinking feeling fills me as I think we're about to see a form of combat that we aren't ready for.

Mallory walks over and loops her arm in mine. Worry lines crease her forehead as she looks around the courtyard. There is so much uncertainty and fear in the air that it nearly chokes me.

This is my college experience.

Death and fear.

Loss and grief.

Today won't be the first time I've second-guessed my decision to become a soldier like my mother and her mother before her. There are plenty of days I think I should have just become a librarian and soaked up the knowledge and lore in books. I deviated from that plan because I want what I'm owed, what was stolen from me. I've had enough taken from me in this lifetime, and I'm not letting anything else be claimed.

Not if I have it in me to reclaim it.

I could have buried myself in the silence of old tomes, cataloging histories that didn't belong to me. It would have certainly been easier. But there's been something humming beneath my skin, something restless that doesn't quite understand peace. I told everyone I wanted to serve. To protect, to fight, and manifest what was stolen. But the truth is far more sinister than that.

I'm afraid.

I fear what lingers in me when things stay quiet for too long.

I needed to come here to prove to myself it's all in my head. There's nothing wrong with me, and I am a light wielder.

When the Conscriptor arrived on our doorstep and handed me the enrollment form, I couldn't sign my name fast enough. The same choice had to be made by every recent graduate in Salaryan. Even fewer signed up this year than the prior year.

The risk continues to increase. And the numbers enrolling continue to dwindle.

But every quadrant comes with its own risks, even the library branch. They've lost numerous librarians over the centuries to curses mistakenly read from pages or from portals that opened up and swallowed them, never to be seen again. I've even heard of instances when the spines of tomes were accidentally broken, and the caretakers followed suit.

But some, like the ones in this courtyard, do enroll. Especially those like me who think it's our right to manifest our abilities, and unfortunately, this is the only way.

Sell your soul to the realm.

"What do you think is in store for us?" Mallory asks, pulling me in closer. Her stare remains on the prospects gathered around us as if she's trying to memorize their faces.

I gently squeeze her hand, wishing I had a more positive answer, but I don't. "Death or ruin," I say simply. "I don't think we come out of that maze without one or the other."

We die, or the things we're about to witness will make us feel like we have.

She pulls her sleeves down, burrowing into me either from the cold or trepidation. At this point, it doesn't really matter. I'm not particularly the hugging type, but I don't push her away. She needs this right now, and maybe a small part of me does too.

"We'll be celebrating in our room before you know it," she whispers.

"Don't start without me," I reply, both of us just staring straight ahead.

I feel sick to my stomach, but I have no time to dwell on it because the crowd starts moving toward an archway on the other side of the courtyard. Thankfully, they didn't mention anything about the assigned lieutenants having to go first this time, so I stay in the back.

My pulse is vibrating in my ears. It takes a lot of effort to keep my face neutral and not give away what I'm feeling.

The four of us slowly follow the other students. Mallory reluctantly lets go of my arm to walk beside Mayline. The tips of her blonde fauxhawk are colored teal today, a stark contrast to the constant gray surrounding us. Between the stone walls, shadowy skies, and slate-colored mountains, she's a burst of color.

I blow into my hands, the warm air offering a small moment of comfort.

Finnley takes his place beside me. He shoulder bumps me and offers an encouraging smile. His presence is becoming reassuring, like hiding under a big blanket that keeps the monsters from getting you as a child.

I look up as we pass through an archway, ivy leaves hanging down above our heads as we climb down a set of stairs that lead to a small, pebbled trail. Pine trees surround us, the smell invigorating and peaceful. We don't have pine trees in Brylan, as they don't particularly thrive in ports. I could get used to being surrounded by their aroma, though. It's freedom without inhibitions and solidarity all rolled into one. A person could become addicted to that smell.

The trees open to the usual gloomy skies as we break through the end of the trail and come to an enormous field of sorts. In the dead center is the next test of how deep our will to survive goes. Three separate steel doors stand resolute like sentinels, weathered and scarred. On each side are thick rock walls stretching upward, thirty—no, thirty-six feet high. Walls that appear very thick and high enough not to be able to climb over. These walls were meant to keep things out.

Or keep something in.

The training field, vast and open, seems to shrink around it. I can feel the stillness pressing into my lungs. The kind that makes itself known right before a trial takes place. The kind that's designed to push the candidates to their breaking point.

We're one of the last to arrive, but we can still easily see the front.

Professor Lyric and the young professor I saw earlier are standing in front of the middle door, with Noctryns and Veils on either side.

The breath catches in my throat. Ambrose is among those Veils.

He stands tall with both hands behind his back, his athletic build at attention and ready for orders. His shoulder-length hair is pulled back from his face, allowing his arctic eyes to really stand out in contrast to his tan skin.

I stare unabashedly at him since he doesn't know where I am in the crowd. The man has always been beautiful, but his physique has changed so much over the past year that he no longer even looks like the boy I grew up with. He's harder and more sculpted in places where he was lean, and his entire demeanor is more polished and refined. He's becoming the epitome of a Salaryan soldier.

I lick my lips.

It looks fucking good on him.

His sharp gaze swings across the field, landing right on me. As if he could feel my stare.

I give him a meek little wave.

Ever so slightly, he lowers his chin, acknowledging me.

Ah, quite the little soldier aren't we, Ambrose? Not even breaking form to smile or wave.

Such a good boy.

I can't help the little smirk that plays across my face. This rigid version of him is so different from the reckless hellion I knew him to be. It's doing things to me.

Finnley bristles next to me as he takes in the sight before us. I know he's running a million different scenarios through his head, trying to figure out the best means of survival. I've learned that's how his mind works. Assess, dissect, and solve.

Like it or not, this is happening.

Our final trial in the Death Bringer.

I, for one, am just happy it's almost over.

The sound of a raven cawing overhead and the sun being completely obscured by dark clouds set a foreboding backdrop to the difficult task ahead. It's so unlike anything at home, where you're more likely to hear waves crashing upon the shore while searching for the perfect seashell or bawdy laughter from one of the many taverns in the busy port town.

Everything about Kintoira is ominous. It's like a constant warning to count your days. It's exhausting in a way. I haven't let my guard down since the night I arrived. To do so would be a colossal mistake and one I'm not willing to make.

I crack my neck and focus on the task at hand.

Professor Lyric claps his hands, and any chatter among us dies out quickly. The professor who's been following him around steps forward, his tall, slender frame the exact opposite of Professor Lyric's. A timid expression seems to be permanently painted on his face with sunken eyes that are always darting around like he's in constant fight-or-flight mode. "Good day, ladies and gentlemen. I trust we are all here and no one tried to sneak off?" he jokes in a nasally nervous tone. He's met with an awkward silence, much like the professor's introduction before him.

Tough crowd.

He breaks eye contact with us and looks down at the back of his hands, examining his fingernails in great detail. Without bringing his gaze back up, he continues talking but inspects the back of his hands while doing so. He's a bit odd, honestly. His twitchy movements give me anxiety, and I don't even have anxiety.

"As you can see, your next task awaits you behind these walls. These very walls were set up specifically for your last trial, and tomorrow, everything you see before you will be gone." He jerks his head to the side in a quick motion. "Back to our training field once again. However, don't let that fool you into thinking this was constructed quickly and without great thought to make this as difficult and trying as possible."

I laugh under my breath.

Of course, we wouldn't make the mistake of thinking that. The main objective here is to weed out anyone who doesn't want it enough or is too weak to survive the academy.

We get it. Everything this week is meant to kill us, maim us, or ruin us. Noted.

"In case you haven't figured it out yet, you and your teammate will be working your way through a carefully constructed maze." His eyes dart upward before flying back down to his hands. "But this isn't just any maze. No, don't fall into a false sense of safety. This one is filled with darkness and unlike anything you've come across this far in your short lives. It is filled with creations of dark magic that will strip you to the essence of your core."

The Noctryns alongside him throw us taunting grins.

Slowly, I sneak a peek at Ambrose to gauge his reaction to all of this. Is this what he went through? I wonder if the trials are replaced each year with new ones. I know his feelings on dark magic, and to say he hates everything Noctryn would be an understatement. He's way too self-righteous to ever think there is a valid reason to use any kind of magic except the one that manifests within us. The one that slumbers since birth, just waiting to be awakened.

A boy, a few inches taller than my five-foot-four frame, moves directly in front of me, making it difficult to even see Ambrose.

I shuffle a bit to the right to get a better view. When I spot him again, his eyes are already on me. The concern and frustration filling them are the only things that aren't rigid and battle-ready. He can mold everything into their demands except his eyes. Those will always tell me the truth.

It sucks, with him being there and me here. Opposite ends of the playing field but with the same objective. And with what feels like endless hoops to jump through until we can just be with each other again.

He was mine before theirs. Now I have to share him.

I curl my hands into tight fists.

I've never been very good at sharing.

I lower my eyes and move back to my spot in the crowd. There's no sense in torturing myself any more than I already do. The professor is speaking, and I missed some of it because my heart is on my sleeve, and I can't seem to keep my eyes or mind off Ambrose.

"You'll line up in pairs in front of one of the three sets of doors. After receiving your malediction, you will both enter at the same time," he informs us. "You can ask me any questions at any time before you enter. After that, sadly, you are on your own." He scratches the back of his hand while nodding his head in approval. "I'm Professor Tainey, by the way. Almost forgot to mention that!" he adds. His tongue comes out to quickly lick his lips as he raises his eyes to meet ours before swiftly lowering them again and moving to Professor Lyric's side.

It's all done in jerky motions, and just watching him is stressful.

"Everyone, line up. Hurry now," Professor Lyric demands urgently. He pushes a pair of timid-looking girls, hovering off to the side, toward the third maze with his small, chubby hands. The girls throw a cautious look over their shoulders as they quickly shuffle to the steel doors. They're probably scared he's going to throw them into the maze.

Mallory breaks my attention by grabbing my shoulders and pulling me into a strong hug. I've never really had girlfriends before. It's different but nice. They're a lot more affectionate, though, and I'm not sure how I feel about that yet.

The verdict is still out.

"Don't forget, we have a party in our room to attend tonight," she promises quietly before pulling back.

"I wouldn't miss it for the world," I say, offering her a bright smile that I don't necessarily feel inside. If my face reflected how I actually feel, it would come out more like a grimace.

Mayline approaches Mallory from behind, and you can see the resolution in her spine. She has her war face on, and I know Mallory is in good hands. They made Mayline a lieutenant for a reason. She exudes the leadership skills you read about.

Still not sure why they made me one.

"Good luck to you both," she says to Finnley and me in that stern way of hers.

Finnley, who's now leaning half his weight on my shoulder, blows her a kiss. "You too, babe."

With a roll of her eyes, she turns to walk toward the maze doors, pulling Mallory along.

"See you on the other side!" Mallory yells over her shoulder while simultaneously tripping over her feet. She keeps her eyes on Finnley and me as long as seemingly possible, almost as if she's scared this is the last time she'll be able to.

"Welp, just you and me now," he murmurs in my ear, watching them go. "Finally, alone."

There he is. For a second, I thought this trial might have robbed him of his jokes.

"You, me, and the monsters ahead of us," I retort, shaking my head.

"We'll just kick Mallory out of the little shindig tonight, and you and I can have our very own party. Nothing but alone time," he says in that thick drawl of his.

"Un-fucking-likely," a voice of steel responds directly behind us.

Spinning on my heel, I come face-to-face with the one person I need like my next breath of air. His hardened features take Finnley in from head to toe before turning to me and instantly softening. Warmth coats my cheeks just from being the focal point of his intense stare.

This is getting out of hand. I need to man up and make a move or stop pining for him. I can't live in this in-between for the rest of my life.

It's excruciating.

The thought of staying in this stagnant place of constant want, mixed with the fear of rejection, causes my heart to physically hurt. The only thing worse would be for me to confess my feelings only to find out it's all one-sided.

That would not be survivable.

He reaches out, tucking a loose strand of hair behind my ear. As he pulls his hand back, his thumb gently caresses the side of my face and the rough calluses on his palms scratch my cheek. Is he just as torn as I am, and the danger I'm about to face is bringing it all to the surface? Or am I reading too much into it and seeing what I want to see?

He grips my jaw, forcing my head to tilt back. "I miss seeing you under better circumstances," he says in a teasing tone.

I miss seeing him altogether, but I'll refrain from saying that. "Yeah, it tends to be more fun when one of us isn't fighting for our lives."

"Who's he?" he demands, turning his head and looking directly at Finnley.

"*He* is standing right here," Finnley drawls. His arms are folded across his chest, and his eyes move from me to Ambrose and back again. He lifts a brow, waiting for an introduction.

"This is Finnley. Finnley, meet Ambrose."

I keep it short and sweet. That's all we have time for.

Finnley throws a lazy smile toward Ambrose. It could be deemed innocent, but I know him well enough to know it's full of gloat and dripping with antagonization.

Ambrose's lips draw together in a thin line. Apparently, it's somewhat obvious after all.

He turns toward me, giving Finnley his back, and cranes his neck down to look into my eyes. "I'll do everything I can to be at the finish line when you cross—"

"When *we* cross," Finnley interjects over Ambrose's shoulder.

"—but if I'm not, just know that someone is filling me in the moment you step foot outside those walls."

It guts me to think he might not be there when I complete the last trial of Asylamation. I know it's not up to him, that we're expected not to ask questions when they say jump, just start fucking jumping. It still sucks, though. When I cross that line, it's the first time I'm on the same playing field as him, an actual student at the academy. He should be there to see it happen. To support me in not dying, at the very least.

Instead of saying all of this, I just give him a subtle nod.

Bury it deep down and keep going.

My insides feel like they're in knots, but I'm good at pretending everything is okay. "I'll see you on the other side," I say, grabbing his hand and squeezing.

A loud sigh comes from Finnley. "Well, if you two aren't going to kiss, then we'd better get a move on," he states matter-of-factly.

Ambrose turns slightly toward him, and I take the opportunity to shoot daggers at him with my eyes, promising a slow, torturous death. "You'd better take care of her in there, or I'll bring you back to life just to kill you again."

He doesn't acknowledge the kiss comment.

"You can't do that." Finnley laughs before stopping altogether at the look in Ambrose's eyes. He gulps and looks at me, slightly terrified. "Can he do that?"

"That would require dark magic, something you wouldn't catch a Veil touching," I answer evenly, although at the moment, murdering him and bringing him back to life sounds like a grand idea. I tuck that little dark tendency away with everything else and squeeze Ambrose's hand tightly. "I'll be fine. I promise. Pinky."

There's a strain in my voice, but I'm proud of myself for it not wobbling as I hold up my pinky finger on my other hand.

What if this is the last time I see him? The last time I get to stare into those clear blue eyes or at the wide smile that I've been on the receiving end of too many times to count.

"I'm going to hold you to that, Nori," he promises in an agonized tone.

I know it kills him that he's so helpless right now when it comes to me. He raises his hand, looping his much larger pinky with my smaller one, sealing our promise.

It can't be broken now.

I've never broken a pinky promise to him, and I don't intend to start today.

I reluctantly watch him turn and walk off to his comrades, his stride confident and full of authority. The brown fighting leathers accent every hard ridge his body has been honed into. A longbow hangs loosely over his back, a favored option for the Veils who don't particularly prefer hand-to-hand combat. That's one characteristic he didn't inherit, however. I've seen him take on three to four men at once and not only come out victorious but laughing.

It's all a game to him... or it was.

He looks pretty serious at the moment, though, speaking with his fellow captains. All business. His brows are pulled down in a tight line, with an unforgiving glare being directed at the captain across from him. If their body language is any indication, they're arguing about something. She looks just as pissed as he does. If I'm being honest, possibly more so.

Her finger jabs him in the chest, and her face is scrunched in fury.

Not wanting to get caught staring, I grab Finnley's elbow, and we make our way over to the first set of doors. Trepidation is heavy in every step we take. We both know it. We're just trying to do each other a solid and not let it show.

"Wow, they're even bigger up close."

I turn toward Finnley, who's staring at the steel doors, his eyes looking them up and down. "Yeah," I breathe. "They are."

The doors are huge.

I originally thought they were steel, but it looks to be something more malleable. Something more viable, as if it has a life and heartbeat of its own.

These aren't normal doors.

Two dark upperclassmen motion us forward. We're the last to enter maze one, and only a few are in line for the other two mazes. Finnley and I don't speak as they write something down on the clipboards in their hands. They opted for their fighting leathers today, just like the Veils did. There are slight differences, though, besides one being black and the other brown. The Noctryns have multiple sheaths for their daggers and various weapons strapped to their bodies. The Veil's brown leathers tend to have less weaponry in mind. Most don't need it since they manifest an ability and prefer it over steel.

It's as if the gods gifted the Veils these destructive powers for staying light and true, and they took back the powers gifted to the Noctryns, replacing them with nebulous shadows and dark magic for their cores being impure.

It's always a give-and-take, isn't it?

Also, I won't admit this out loud, but the latter really does look badass.

"You two know the rules. Finish together or repeat the trial. Stay alive, or both of you end up dead," the male Noctryn relays in a tone that lacks absolutely any empathy. He's just following orders to be here. It matters not who lives or dies to them, when, at this point, they don't even know which side we'll end up placing on if we survive.

Heavy emphasis on the if.

And to be perfectly honest, most Noctryn tend to think we'd be better off dead than placing Veil. Vice versa for the Veils.

The female at his side moves her head from side to side, cracking her neck. I take an involuntary step back when she makes a move toward me.

"Relax, I'm just issuing your malediction. No need to be so jumpy."

I watch her pull a metallic-looking pen out of her pocket, the end sharp and jagged. I make absolutely no move to step forward. If she wants to curse me, she's going to have to come to me.

Captain or not.

I've never had a curse placed on me, and I'm not exactly eager to check that off my bucket list. Especially when it comes at the end of a lethal-looking quill pen.

Her lips pull into an annoyed frown as she looks from me to Finnley.

I don't care. And from Finnley's expression, he doesn't appear to either.

"I'm going to ask you once and only once. Step forward for your malediction."

My fingers dig into my palms. It's like asking someone to jump off a cliff instead of just pushing them. She could at least offer a small mercy and come to me instead of asking my body to cooperate when it vehemently doesn't want to.

The male Noctryn has clearly reached his limit in the patience department and starts toward Finnley.

"Ok, ok, we're coming," I cry out before he can reach him.

I flinch at the look Finnley is directing toward the captain and reach out to grab his hand. At this point, besides Ambrose, he's my closest friend and ally and about to be my lifeline. I need him to be levelheaded. And not disintegrated by a pissed-off Noctryn captain.

The dark wielder may only be in his second year at the academy, but even at that level, he could incinerate us with his dark magic right where we stand. Or end us with the wicked-looking dagger hanging from his hip.

Either way, it would suck.

I doubt I'd even have time to reach for my hidden weapon before his would be at my throat. We're basically helpless newborns in our first year at the academy, let alone during trial week. I put on a brave face and step forward, pulling Finnley with me. He cooperates, thank the gods, and allows me to drag him forward. He makes absolutely zero effort to hide the distaste on his face, though.

I pinch the inside of his arm.

Hard.

He averts his focus to me instead. "You've got my attention, love. Was there something you needed?" he asks in a sarcastic tone.

Yes, I need you to fix your face.

Instead of replying, I stop directly in front of the female captain, openly ignoring the fact that Finnley is now staring at the side of my head.

"Extend your arm," she demands.

Hesitantly, I hold out my arm. The skin pinches as she grips it firmly, then turns it over and lifts my sleeve.

I wince.

goose bumps rise on the pale skin of my wrist.

The contents of my stomach are going to come up as she places the sharp tip of the pen on my exposed wrist while pressing down and drawing blood.

Her eyelids flutter closed, and she raises her face to the clouded sky. "Bound by trial, forged by trust, your lives are now combined. Thus, you now must stay alive, or both shall become blood dust," she mutters in a strange voice while smearing my blood in spiral shapes.

The drawing resembles what the inside of a maze might look like, with swirls and various circles. I've just had dirty blood magic performed on me, and all I can focus on is the abstract shapes now etched into my wrist.

She slowly lowers her face and opens her large feline-shaped eyes. Her pupils are completely blown, making her eyes appear black.

A sharp grunt from my left pulls my attention to Finnley and the now bleeding wrist he's holding as well. We have matching blood smears. Wonderful.

The deep baritone of the same curse washes over me again as it's recited over his wrist by the other captain.

Our lives are now truly combined. At least until we cross that finish line.

Both Noctryns pull open the metal doors, the hinges creaking and bellowing under the weight as their fully darkened eyes beckon us through.

A deep musky smell penetrates my nostrils immediately.

It smells like damp earth and long-buried secrets.

Chapter Nine

A little voice in the back of my head is telling me to turn around and run. Okay, maybe not so little. More like a bellow demanding I obey.

The only problem is I've never been good at being obedient.

Instead of listening, I pull my sleeve down to cover the wet blood on my wrist and take a deep breath of fresh air, expanding my lungs to absorb as much as possible. I have a feeling, after entering the twisted passageways within these musty walls, that as soon as the doors shut behind us, fresh air will be the first thing I crave.

Finnley's sharp gaze pulls away from the entrance of our next trial to look at me in question. "You ready?" he asks softly.

"As ready as I'll ever be," I whisper, nodding my head slowly.

I'm forcing myself to be numb. Emotions tangle everything up, and chaos ensues.

The moment we step through the doors, they immediately shut behind us, sealing us in with a resounding thud and effectively cutting off any means of escape. A feeling of immense claustrophobia washes over me. I force it down, along with my fear, and allow my eyes to adjust.

There are stairs that lead downward, spiraling in their descent. Cautiously, I step on the first one. The cracked stone covered in moss makes it slippery. The air is stale and still, as if nothing has stirred in quite some time.

Finnley's heavier footsteps follow behind.

The stairs wind down to another level, where there are east-and west-facing arches. Both are covered with intricate runes that appear ancient, as if this place has endured through centuries and withstood tribulations we could never understand.

The hairs on the back of my neck stand up, and every nerve ending in my body is on high alert.

It's too calm.

Too still.

Squinting up at the writings, Finnley rubs his hand across the runes. A few stone pieces crumble and fall beneath his touch. He jumps back before they have a chance to land on his head.

The walls may appear to be steadfast and still standing, but they're delicate from age. Or maybe it's not steadfast at all and is trying to lure us into a false sense of security.

I trust nothing here.

"What's it going to be, Lieutenant? Are we going left or right?" he asks over his shoulder.

Oh, so we're pulling the rank card. For a second, I forgot I had that responsibility. How kind of him to remind me.

I walk up beside him and let my eyes roam over the delicate arches. Both are identical in nature. The only difference is that they sit on opposite sides. Why can't one have like a giant snake rune or something to give us some kind of hint of which way not to go? I can't help but feel like either choice is the wrong choice. What if there isn't a right option and one is just the lesser of two evils? The question is which is the lesser evil.

"We go right."

"I would have gone left," he deadpans.

"Well, I can't change it now! They always say to go with your first choice and follow your gut, so now I'm obligated to go right." I would be pissed if I changed my mind and went left, only to die because of my indecisiveness.

He smiles at the look of horror on my face and the fact that I am indeed second-guessing my decision. "I'll go first. Follow me," he says, ruffling my hair again as he passes by.

I scurry after him. "That's not very lieutenant-like of me to let you go first."

"Tough, because you're not going in front of me," he states in a matter-of-fact tone, like it's the end of the discussion.

I grip his elbow, forcing him to turn back toward me. Indignation is plastered across my face, making it clear just what I think of his demands. "Listen, I'm going to pick my battles here, but just remember our lives are intertwined in this place. So regardless of you wanting to be a hero, by you going first, it only means if something is lying in wait for us, you'll just die first, and I'll be next."

"Fair point. But I'm still going first." He looks down at my hand on his elbow, raising a brow.

I sigh and drop his arm. I'll forfeit this one, but if he thinks I'm going to back down to every order he issues during this trial, he's wrong.

I follow him cautiously as we go through the east arch. I make my footsteps as light as possible. Who knows? Maybe we can just sneak our way through this without anything even knowing we're here. I haven't heard any screams or voices of other prospects. To be honest, I haven't heard anything except the soft sound of our boots on the stone floor.

I wonder if they incorporated some kind of magical weave within this space to block out any trace of the others participating in the trial. It would make sense. I can't imagine they would like groups of us working together. Or dying together, for that matter.

The army does need soldiers after all.

I keep close to Finnley. It's so quiet I can hear my heartbeat in my ears.

Thud.

Thud.

Thud.

He holds up a finger, cueing me to stop behind him.

I peer around his arm, the walls so close on each side of us that I can't make out much. The only thing I can see is that it gets very dark up ahead, and any light provided by the sky is about to be completely blocked.

I grab his arm with both hands and stand on my tippy-toes so I can whisper in his ear. "Should we turn around?"

"What happened to always going with your first choice?" he drawls.

My gaze keeps flitting back to the dark tunnel ahead of us. I'm not too proud to admit when I'm wrong.

I shake my head and angrily whisper, "Maybe we make an exception just this one time!"

"No, I think we stick with the original plan." He speaks in a calm tone, not a trace of self-doubt to be found. "I think you were right when you said we shouldn't second-guess our gut feeling. That may be very well what keeps us alive in here."

Let's hope so.

I admire that he can be authoritative yet also listen to my suggestions. Hopefully, that very same attribute doesn't bite us in the ass. I lower my heels back down and take my place behind him. "Oh, one more thing. How are we going to see in there?" I whisper-shout.

He glances over his shoulder, pressing his index finger to his mouth, indicating I should probably lower my voice. "We're not. We'll have to go by touch."

A sardonic chuckle slips free. It just gets better and better.

A part of me was scared he was going to say that. I grab the back of his shirt with one hand and pat my thigh to make sure my dagger is still in place with the other.

It takes us mere seconds to be fully submerged in darkness.

I hold Finnley's shirt in my hand with a death grip. He's not getting away from me. I'm following so closely that I've stepped on the back of his heels numerous times, but he hasn't said one word about it.

This kind of darkness is absolute. My eyes are fully adjusted at this point, and I still can't see anything. I can't even make out Finnley's form in front of me. It would be damn near impossible to find each other if we got separated.

The thought makes me want to jump out of my skin.

He reaches back and grabs the hand not tangled up in his shirt, giving it a reassuring squeeze. Neither one of us talks. It feels detrimental to our survival to make unnecessary noise when we can't even see what's coming at us.

Honestly, though, maybe this is it. Perhaps we just have to work our way through unfavorable circumstances when they rob us of each of our senses. That wouldn't be so bad. Especially with Finnley by my side.

His presence is the only thing making this bearable.

We continue through the passageway at a slow and steady pace. It feels like it goes on forever, but we've probably only been walking through it for a couple of minutes.

After a while, the path beneath our feet begins to curve upward, and eventually, small beams of light shine ahead. The light is subdued as the sun is completely blocked out by dark clouds, as usual, but it's enough that we have to shield our eyes with the back of our hands as we emerge.

We come to another fork in the path to choose from. This time, we have three arches to pick from. Each one is identical, but with more runes decorating the rims. The only difference is that one lets a bit more light through than the other two.

I blow out a breath and glance over at Finnley. His curls are messy and sticking up in different directions like he's been running a hand through them.

"Does any certain one call out to you?" he asks without taking his eyes off the archways.

Not even a little. In fact, they all scream at me not to enter. To tuck tail and run back the way we came. "Nope, and if we're playing this fair, it's your turn to pick."

Nodding like he's come to a decision, he finally looks at me. He bites his bottom lip like he's nervous to say his choice. "Rock, paper, scissors, it is," he suggests in a rushed tone. He's now fully facing me and holding a fist in the flat palm of his other hand.

You've got to be kidding me.

"Absolutely not," I respond.

"Worth a shot." He sighs, running a hand down his face. "Okay, let's go with this one," he counters, looking toward the archway that has some light coming through. "I don't know about you, but I'm over not being able to see shit."

"Agreed."

We step through the arch, and I move up to walk beside him as the pathway is much larger than the one we just came through.

There isn't a ceiling on this part of the maze like in the other corridors, but it's also colder here than it was inside. I pull my sleeves down to try to cover my hands as much as possible, and the fresh cut on my wrist stings as I do so.

Finnley blows small rings of air out of his mouth into the cold air. "Cold as a bear's ass in winter out here," he mutters while rubbing his hands together.

One of the many perks of finishing Asylamation is that upon completion, we're issued proper clothing for the harsh temperatures of the northern mountains. I never thought I'd say this, but I kind of miss home. I'd give anything to feel the rays of the sun warming my cheeks right now. I can almost taste the salt from the ocean on my tongue and hear the seagulls squawking overhead.

"I've never heard it put quite so eloquently before, but yeah, it certainly is," I breathe.

"Alright, let's go before our asses freeze off."

"Finnley, has anyone ever told you you've got a way with words?"

"All the time," he says in a serious tone. His eyes, however, are filled with humor.

Uneven, huge stone blocks line the path ahead, and after tripping multiple times, we learn to keep our eyes on the ground as much as possible. Thick bands of ivy coat the walls and portions of the walkway. Even in the frigid temperatures, it's spread like a disease, overtaking everything in its path. Dead brown leaves mix in with bright-green ones as if they couldn't decide whether they wanted to thrive and take over or wither away in final peace.

Opaque clouds move quickly overhead, the only reminder that life is carrying on outside of the confinement of these walls. It's easy to get wrapped up in the endless corridors and the quietude of this place as if nothing else exists.

I wonder if Mallory and Mayline have made it out yet. Are they still wandering through the winding pathways of their selection? Is Ambrose at the finish line patiently waiting for us to emerge? Is he worried about me? How about I be a little more wrapped up in someone I clearly shouldn't be?

It was so much easier when hormones weren't involved, and he was just my best friend. Not the man I think I'm in love with and constantly lusting over. I never imagined myself as the simpering female in someone else's story.

Yet here I am. Simpin'.

It's pathetic, really. I know this, truly I do, but I still can't turn it off.

The sound of water greets us as we turn around a sharp corner and come to a bridgehead. A Gothic bridge made of burnished stone, supported by medieval-looking arcs, sits directly in front of us. The entire thing is covered in an abundance of half-dead ivy that surrounds us, sprinkled with bits of moss. It could almost be described as beautiful in an ethereal kind of way. Entrancing even.

Finnley inches closer to the edge, peering down into the murky dark waters. "I don't even want to know what could be in that water."

"Let's not stick around to find out. Best to keep moving."

"Watch the overgrowth where you step. I'm fond of you and all, but I really don't want to have to jump in after you."

"Says the man who's tripped multiple times so far," I tease, grabbing onto his bicep and pulling him from the edge before I'm the one who has to jump in after him.

"Oh stop, you just want a reason to touch my muscles," he says through that permanent smirk he wears like armor.

"Finnley, your muscles are not the ones I think about touching," I shoot back while jumping up and rubbing the top of his head. I'd feel bad about messing up his beautiful curls if they weren't already in disarray from his own hands. At my transgression, his hair falls over his brow in curly chaos, giving him the look of a fallen angel. I can see why the ladies fawn over him. He definitely has that sensual appeal.

I just prefer the more deviant tendencies in my men as opposed to the divine ones.

I turn back toward the bridge, acknowledging we're going to have to cross it regardless of what's below. I step forward and quickly but carefully walk out onto it, not waiting for the argument that I know will come from behind me when he realizes I'm taking the initiative to go first. Ivy crunches under my boot, the only sound in the vast cavern.

And that's exactly what this is—a cavern of some sort. The ceiling is open to the sky, but aside from the intricate bridge and the water beneath, it's surrounded by stone walls. It is huge, though. The bridge itself will take some time to cross, especially with the added risk of the overgrowth.

Finnley catches up to me quicker than I anticipated and glares at me, narrowing his eyes in disapproval. I raise my shoulders and put my palms in the air. I don't apologize in the least.

We walk side by side, only stopping here and there to move a branch out of our way or to peer over the edge to confirm there isn't any movement in the murky green waters below us. So far, not even a ripple.

There's just us walking across the bridge, tension an unwelcome guest, sitting heavily on our shoulders, waiting for the other shoe to drop because thus far, it's been too fucking easy. If life has taught me one thing, it's that nothing is ever this easy.

I crouch down and duck through an archway that has crumbled through time. Finnley practically has to get on all fours and crawl to be able to fit. Slowly, I stand and wipe my hands together to remove as much of the dirt and dead leaves as possible.

Brushing the wayward hairs from my eyes, I look toward Finnley as he finally gets through the smallest portion of the collapse and can stand. He makes a quick effort to wipe the grit from his hands and knees and looks up to say something to me, but before he can utter the first syllable, he locks in on something behind me. His entire body goes stiff. His hands curl into fists at his side, and I can see his visible gulp from where I'm standing.

The hairs stand up on the back of my neck.

Slowly, not being able to hold off the inevitable, I turn my head and look in the same direction that he's looking. There's nothing there except the remainder of the bridge.

I turn back to face him. "Finnley..." I question.

He doesn't take his eyes off whatever he's looking at. "Do you see what I'm seeing right now?" he asks so low that I can barely hear him. His eyes are wide and panicked.

This is the first time in the entire Asylamation I've seen this expression on his face.

Fear.

I turn my head to look again, but I don't see anything. Just overgrowth and stone. I take careful steps back over to him, walking over broken fragments of rock and slippery moss. I pick up his hand, threading our fingers together.

"I don't see anything. Are you feeling alright?" I ask, using the back of my other hand to feel his forehead.

"It's looking right at us," he whispers, still staring at whatever it is he thinks he sees. I don't think he's blinked this entire time.

I squeeze his hand tighter. "There's nothing there, Finnley, it's just this place messing with you."

"Nori, get behind me, and whatever happens, protect your face."

Protect your face.

I can feel the color drain from the very face he's instructing me to protect.

I let my eyes roam over his, looking for any hint of a smile or indication he's messing with me. There's nothing. Not a single trace of his usual playful nature. It's as if I'm looking at a version of Finnley I haven't seen before. The one he hides under his mischievous guise. The one with secrets and suffering that he doesn't share. The *real* Finnley. And there's only one thing in this realm he would instruct me specifically to protect my face from. The only thing I'd have to shield my mouth from... the thing that devours souls.

Wraiths.

I swallow down the saliva coating the inside of my mouth, drop his hands, and turn to stare back at the spot his determined glare is pinned to.

Nothing. There's nothing there and certainly not a wraith.

A lump forms in my throat.

He's losing his mind. Delirious possibly.

We haven't had anything to drink or eat in I don't know how long. There's no sense of time in here. Maybe he's just dehydrated.

"There's nothing there, Finnley. I swear to you. You're just not yourself right now."

He moves his gaze toward me, his pale eyes narrowing. "I'm not crazy, Nori."

I squeeze his arm. "I never said you were."

He drags his eyes forward again, his mouth now pulled into a harsh line.

"I believe you," I promise. And I do. If he thinks he sees something, then I believe he does in his own mind.

"We're at a disadvantage without weapons, and fighting our way out on a narrow bridge isn't going to be easy," he warns.

I close my eyes and blow out a breath. Ambrose told me to hide the dagger and keep it a secret, but I can't not tell Finnley. Especially right now when he thinks we're in a dire situation about to fight for our lives. It feels wrong to keep it from him.

"Actually, we do have one weapon," I offer, lifting my shoulders in a shrug.

He glances at me, brows drawn. "The academy hasn't issued any yet. What are you talking about?"

"Well, yes, that's technically corre—"

"Nori, get behind me," he orders while grabbing onto my sleeve and shoving me roughly behind his back. "It's coming." He spreads his feet wide and raises his arms, fists clenched in a fighting stance.

Cautiously, I peer around him.

Yep. Still nothing. Finnley is about to fight *absolutely nothing*.

At this point, I'm doubting my bright idea of handing over a dagger to him. I'm not sure he's stable enough to be handling weapons at the moment.

He bends his knees slightly like he's about to throw his entire body into the attack. "Stay back," he orders.

I reach for his shirt to try to anchor him to reality, but he's already pushing forward. His steps are cautious but urgent. No longer watching the ground or sidestepping dead foliage, he walks forward with resolve. His steps are deliberate, and his body rigid. He doesn't even look back to see if I'm following his orders like a good little soldier.

I am, though.

I haven't moved a step.

I'm not sure if I should be more worried about this maze or the man who's currently in it with me. The only sound surrounding us is his footfall across the decrepit stones. The combination of eerie silence and Finnley's figure stalking across the bridge, ready to confront an illusory threat, paints an absurd image of insanity.

What is even happening right now?

Just when I think it can't get any more bizarre, his tall form bends down to pick up a particularly sharp-looking rock. It looks sizable and lethal even from this far back in his large hands. He abruptly stops and rolls his shoulders back, preparing for combat. His large frame relaxes as a fighter's does right before raising both fists again, the one holding the jagged rock toward the front.

I shuffle my feet forward, then stop. Uncertainty weighs me down. I falter slightly too long, as in the next moment Finnley quickly ducks before rising and swinging out with the hand holding the rock. He sidesteps to the right, leaning back to avoid what I can only imagine he sees as someone trying to punch him in the jaw. Both of his feet move forward again, and his arm swings upward to deliver what would be a mean uppercut to his opponent.

A splashing sound echoes throughout the cavern as pebbles and stone fragments are kicked into the chasm below. The shadowy water ripples, and I swear I see movement below the rings. I look up, quickly refocusing on Finnley. I can't even concentrate on anything else right now when my partner is mentally fighting for his life. Technically, in his mind, he's fighting for both of our lives.

An experienced soldier would have difficulty defeating a wraith on his own, let alone a prospect who hasn't even started his first year. He's fighting an impossible fight. I flinch when his head is thrown backward, his body following suit, pushing him toward the edge of the crossing.

What the fuck.

He brings the back of his hand to his mouth, wiping what I imagine he sees as blood.

His lips pull into a snarl before he darts up and forward, throwing his elbow out, followed by a swift punch from his other hand. "FUCK YOU!!!" he screams, his face scrunched in defiance. Spinning around, he sidesteps something but immediately falls to his knees, clutching at his chest. He grabs a fistful of his shirt, pulling at it, gasping for breath.

I've seen a boy punched in the diaphragm before, and he looked a lot like Finnley looks right now. The boy later told us it felt like his lungs had seized up and he would never breathe again. He described the pain as if his chest was on fire, but with the blue kind, not the red. The kind that burns so intensely there isn't any warmth, only unbearable pain.

Without thinking twice, I run toward him. My feet jump over broken pieces of the bridge and loose rocks, but I have to get to him. We're in this together, even if I know he'll be okay, and the only threat he's facing right now is himself.

Pain ripples across his face as he clutches at his chest with one hand and leans on the other for support. Slowly, his head raises, brows drawn as if even doing this small gesture is excruciating.

His eyes clash with mine.

They're filled with sorrow and defeat.

"I'M COMING!" I yell.

I'm so close I can see the different browns and greens immersed within his irises.

Gravel digs into my knees as I slide across the stone, grabbing onto his face and forcing him to look at me. "You're okay," I assure him, gripping the sides of his jaw, forcing his broken stare to meet mine.

I move one hand to his back, rubbing in small circles. Willing him to take a full breath. He hasn't taken his eyes off mine. They're filled with apologies and despair. I never want to see this defeated version of Finnley ever again. Give me the goofy, arrogant, flirty version back. The one he wears like a second skin.

I drop my hand from his face and let it settle into his clammy hand, grasping onto it tightly, offering reassurances the only way I know how. The moment our palms connect, it's as if a curtain is lifted.

And it's absolutely horrifying.

Standing directly behind him is the object of nightmares. Evil in a living, breathing form.

My blood runs cold, and the fight momentarily leaves my body.

Long fingers, covered with ash-colored rotting flesh, hold each of Finnley's cheeks within their grasp. The smell hits my nostrils almost immediately, and a gag works its way up my throat.

Vomiting would be so easy.

It's a combination of decaying flesh and burnt sulfur. Rancid enough to leave a residual taste in my mouth that I don't think will ever fully diminish. Tattered gray robes hang loosely over its tall, slightly bent form. A large hood obscures the face that lies beneath.

A face I've read about in countless history books.

A face that I've heard my mother describe to me with a haunted expression.

I drop Finnley's hand and reach for my dagger. The minute our palms no longer have the connection, the wraith disappears completely.

Abruptly, I grab his hand again. The wraith reappears directly behind him. A slimy hand raises to push back the hood concealing its face, the other still firmly holding onto Finnley's cheek. As the hood falls, an audible gasp leaves my mouth. Even being prepared for what I knew I was going to see, I wasn't ready.

The abomination that stares back at me can only be described as pulsating evil.

Where there were once eyes now sit empty caverns filled with decayed muscle. The nose is completely decomposed, and its mouth is lined with razor-sharp teeth, dripping a black-tarlike substance from their points. Slowly, as if it has all the time in the world, it tilts Finnley's face back and starts to lower its mouth toward his.

It's preparing to consume.

These atrocities devour every inch of a person's essence before moving on to flesh and bone. The more powerful their meal is, the stronger the wraith becomes. Unfortunately for this asshole, neither of us holds much power.

And even more unlucky is the fact that it's my friend's face he's holding on to.

Sharp nails dig into Finnley's cheeks, but his eyes remain on mine. It's as if my face is the last thing he wants to see before drawing his final breath. He's accepted his fate.

That's not going to work for me.

Carefully, without releasing his hand, I pull up my cloth pant leg and remove the dagger strapped to my thigh. The prick doesn't even pay me any mind, quickly deeming me a nonconsequential threat.

Their mouths are almost touching as I yank my dagger free and plunge it directly into the side of the monster's skull. An obnoxious scream rips from its mouth. Black blood oozes out over the hilt, dripping down my sleeve.

The only way to completely defeat a wraith is to fully remove the head from the body, but any kind of damage to the brain canal will severely slow them down until they can rejuvenate.

All I need is a few seconds.

The cloaked figure collapses, and without thinking twice, I yank my dagger out of the rotting flesh and pull Finnley up with all my strength.

And we run.

I don't wait for him to fully catch his breath. His color is returning, and honestly, even if it wasn't, we would still run because I have no idea how long a wraith stays down when its head is still attached. We don't even stop to contemplate which archway to go through at the next set. We just run through the nearest.

The moment we cross the threshold, our feet sink into obsidian sand. There's no longer stone surrounding us, but instead a thick hedge. Stems cut into my hand as I push into the branches, testing out how thick they are. Thick enough we can't climb through easily, but not sturdy enough to try to climb up.

"You had a dagger," he rasps in an incredulous tone, causing me to wince.

Here we go.

"Well, I was in the process of telling you that before you interrupted me."

"You thought I was crazy," he accuses, his voice slowly returning to normal and his hands resting on his hips like a pissed-off girlfriend.

"It might have crossed my mind."

He scoffs and rubs his eyes with the base of his palms. "This place is fucking with us."

Yes, it certainly is.

My chest rises and falls in uneven, shallow breaths. "I couldn't see anything you were seeing until our hands connected. I don't know what's real and what's not. Maybe it was some kind of hallucination, and we had to be connected for me to see." I throw my hands in the air. "Honestly, it doesn't matter at this point. I don't want to stick around and test out my theory."

I dig my heel into the sand. The feeling of it beneath my feet hits me with a crushing familiarity, reminding me of home. But this is far from home. In fact, it feels like hell.

"So we're basically going insane, and the only way someone can join our deranged party is by physical touch..." he whispers. "In other words, dark magic."

"It makes sense since the Noctryns are supposedly the ones responsible for setting up this little shindig," I mutter, kicking the sand. "But I think it has to be hand-to-hand contact. I didn't see anything when I touched your arms or back."

"It felt so real. I felt its breath on the back of my neck," he mutters, before closing his eyes. "Fuck."

"We don't necessarily know it wasn't. Not yet."

We can't make the mistake of underestimating the things in here.

I start walking again, ready to be out of this mind fuck and back into a place that makes sense. I'm also so tired of the absence of noise. No crickets, birds, not even the rustle of air movement. Just our heavy breathing.

I can see why people lose their minds in the padded asylum rooms of Harkin House. Each cell is created to block out all sound and sight, created specifically to torture someone into madness. If they weren't already to begin with. They say if you're not already mad when you enter that place, you will be within days.

We come to a small courtyard with a beautiful fountain standing in the middle. A phoenix rises from the center, water rushing out of its beak into the basin below. We don't stop to admire it. We just turn left and continue. We cross rows upon rows of thick hedges and pass random stone statues. Each more grand than the prior.

After what feels like hours, we come to another courtyard with another phoenix fountain. The water is beckoning us to drink, asking us if we're thirsty. Tempting us. How long has it been since we've had anything? Without thinking, I shove both hands in, cupping the water.

I yelp and yank my hands back out.

Both are covered in hundreds of little cuts, blood seeping from the abrasions. The water continues to shimmer in an invitation to quench our thirst. The shimmers aren't reflections, though—there's no sun for the water to reflect off.

If I weren't so bone-tired, I'd have noticed this before. I'm getting sloppy. The water is full of little shards of crystal. Sharp enough to tear flesh. The phoenix looks down on me, standing in the same stance as the previous one. The only difference is that I swear this one has a condescending look on its face.

"Uh, Nori… you may want to look at this," Finnley calls from an archway.

I flick off the phoenix before walking over.

He's hunched down looking at something in the sand, ashy curls falling over his scrunched brow.

I stop next to him, bending down to look at the dark sand. The arch's entrance has two sets of footprints.

Our footprints.

We've been here before.

"Son of a bitch…. The walls must have moved."

We've been walking in circles for hours. How many times have the walls moved and we haven't noticed? Have we been seeing the same stone statues over and over again? All the hedge looks the same, every part identical. It's impossible to tell how long we've been in here.

I open my mouth, then slam it shut. Bitching and complaining right now won't get us anywhere.

Life's not fair, Norissa. Caderyn women do not show weakness.

My mother's words come at me full force. I stand up, working out our next move in my head. We can't leave breadcrumbs or any kind of trail, per the professor. But he never said anything about going out of our way to prevent them from naturally occurring.

My nails dig into my palms.

Finnley stands to his full height, looking left and then right. He runs a hand down his stubbled jaw before turning his attention back to me.

I see the moment he decides.

"We wing it," he states as if it's the most obvious answer.

"Yeah, look how well that's worked out for us so far," I retort.

"Listen, we don't exactly have a choice," he says, his voice filled with patience that I'm not sure I deserve.

"I know that," I reply, pinching the bridge of my nose.

"Then let's go," he answers, his eyes blazing with determination.

I take a deep breath. "Then let's go."

We turn left and then right. Then left. We just keep picking random arches, hoping our luck changes, and we see something different, but it's just endless hedge and onyx sand.

We're almost to the point of feeling delirious when we walk through a small arch and come to a pathway filled with mirrors. Hedges still line both sides, same as all the other pathways, but this one has mirrors hanging from them in varying sizes. Some are simple in design, others are intricate and antique-looking.

My fingers trail down the bronze frame of a particularly old-looking mirror. The attention to detail is magnificent. The creator poured their love and creativity into it.

Finnley hasn't stepped forward yet and is looking at the mirrors through narrowed eyes, as if they're going to sprout legs and chase us.

"Got any tricks hidden up your sleeve to help with this one?" he tosses nonchalantly my way.

I look at him and roll my eyes.

"Well, just thought I'd ask," he says before proceeding to walk down the pathway.

"No, the only trick I had was saving your ass," I shoot back, using my middle finger to apply imaginary lipstick before blowing him a kiss.

He catches it and shoves it in his pocket. "For later," he says while giving me an exaggerated wink.

I bet he practiced that for hours while looking at himself.

I walk in front of the mirror I was admiring and peer at my reflection. Vibrant red hair sticks out in various places, my long braid almost entirely undone at this point. Black blood splatters are splashed across the right side of my face and the bridge of my nose. My usual vibrant green eyes appear tired and dull. Even my expression is muted and monotonous.

I look like a dim version of myself.

I shift to the side, and my reflection does the same. I stick out my tongue, and it follows suit. Long, slender fingers wiggle back at me as I raise my hands and move them. But then the subdued expression on my face slowly morphs into something else. Full lips pull up into a taunting sneer with one delicate brow arching sinisterly.

I instinctively touch my face.

The reflection in the mirror never raises her hands. She just continues to watch me with morbid satisfaction shining in her eyes. I glance over at Finnley, who is walking from mirror to mirror, investigating each of them.

"Why are you looking at him?" it mocks in a cynical tone. "Have you settled on the knight in shining armor since Ambrose will never love you the way you love him?"

I rear back as if I've been struck, refocusing on my likeness.

"Haven't you learned that no one will ever truly love you?" it hums, raking its eyes up and down my body. "You just keep being the good girl, the one who yearns for the approval and admiration of others, all the while putting on a brave front of not caring what anyone thinks."

I throw my head back and laugh. Or rather, it does.

I just go completely still.

Clutching its sides, it tampers down its maniacal laughter long enough to spit more poison in my direction. "You can't even make Mommy Dearest proud, can you? And how could you? It's because of you that the love of her life left," it delivers with dark pleasure.

Fatality.

She just killed me with a wound to the heart.

I'd love to just cover my ears like a small child and pretend nothing she said wasn't already festering inside me, but that would be a lie.

Instead, I retaliate.

"Shut your fucking mouth," I say with all the conviction I can muster.

Finnley's head whips toward me. "I didn't say anything."

The reflection laughs at me in pity. I step back, retreating from the merciless taunts. Quickly, I turn and flee toward Finnley, who's watching me with curiosity.

"You good?" he asks me, his eyes laced with concern.

I offer him a thumbs-up because I can't trust myself to talk and not cry simultaneously. Cautiously, while walking his way, I throw a peek sideways at the mirror next to me. It's just my normal reflection. An exhausted girl staring at me with trepidation in her eyes.

I hesitantly walk over to it.

I raise my brows, and the reflection does the same. I mimic pulling the string of a bow and releasing an arrow, and the reflection follows.

With a heavy sigh, I lower my head. I feel stripped raw and grossly vulnerable right now.

"You will never wear the signia of a Veil. You aren't pure enough, Norissa, and you know it."

I stiffen but don't look up.

"You may play pretend and act so pristine, but you can't lie to me. Yourself. *I know how very dark we truly are,*" it hisses full of malice. "And soon, so will everyone else. Oh, how Mommy will be so very disappointed."

I lift my head, heavy from the weight of the words thrown at me, and punch the mirror, causing glass to shatter all around.

Blood drips down my knuckles into the dark sand.

Drip, drip, drip.

"Finnley, let's go," I plead, staring at the broken shards of glass hanging from the mirror. I need out of this place.

But he doesn't answer me. Lifting my head toward him, I see him just standing and staring into a simple-looking mirror rimmed with a burnished gold frame.

Dammit. Not him, too.

"FINNLEY! DON'T LOOK IN IT," I shout, my feet already moving and flying across the sand. "LOOK AT ME!"

He continues gazing into the mirror, a look of agony tearing across his face. I'm close enough now that I can hear the words clear as day when he murmurs them.

"Don't go. Please don't go," he begs, gripping the edges of the mirror hard enough that his knuckles turn white.

I push myself even harder.

Almost there.

He places his palm on the mirror as if he can touch the person he's seeing. The next moment, he's pulled through.

Chapter Ten

Time is a fickle bitch.

Precious moments that you want to simmer in and relish are fleeting. Moments that test your resolve and push you to the brink seem to be eternal in their duration.

I stand in front of the mirror Finnley disappeared into for what feels like an eternity. I willed my reflection to come back and taunt me, shun me, anything as long as I could see something. Something other than the bloodshot eyes that stare hollowly back at me, appearing dark and sunken in.

I look more dead than alive at this point.

When that didn't work, I screamed and then resorted to crying tears of anger and frustration. Sand still lies under my fingernail from grabbing fistfuls of it and throwing it at the glass while cursing it with every colorful word I could think of.

The one thing I didn't do was break any more mirrors.

Perhaps this was my punishment for breaking the first one. Finnley being taken. He's still alive, that much I am sure of. Or I'd be dead too. At least in death, I would know where he was. As it is, I'm just wandering around aimlessly.

I'm starting to wonder if we'll spend the rest of our lives just wandering around this forsaken maze looking for one another.

After staring at myself for longer than is comfortable, I start blowing hot air onto the mirrors and drawing little sad faces in the condensation. Eventually, it gets too cold to remain idle, and I'm forced to move on. There's always the off chance he's not even in the blasted mirror anymore and just teleported to another section of this fucking never-ending maze.

I've come to realize through all of this that solitude is, in fact, dangerous. Just like I suspected. You can become addicted to it. Soak in your peace. No fear of loss or hurt. On the other hand, it can be a methodical form of self-torture. The walls close in on your carefully crafted world, and you bathe in the self-doubt and truths you've avoided. There is no noise or the chaos of others to block it out.

Granules of sand sink beneath my boots as I walk along a double set of footprints. The simple crown I've woven together of broken branches sits on top of my head, my long waves resting beneath the sharp twigs as they hang loosely down my back.

I rotate the hilt of my dagger between my fingers, the light weight offering a small source of comfort. My hand jabs outwards with it before striking sideways, battling an imaginary enemy.

A few strands of hair are blown out of my face when I release a large breath of air. I slightly stumble and stop walking, closing my eyes for a moment. They feel so heavy that the moment drags on longer than I anticipate. It's harder than it should be to open them and continue on this endless path. Are we the last ones in the maze? I bet everyone is in the great hall eating dinner and acknowledging us as the weakest link.

I let Finnley down. He should have chosen another partner. He could have easily vanquished this trial with an adept partner. I'm not sure when I became so delicate. I was a tough kid. I had to be. Now, I'm a softer, more unsure version of who I was. What would that little girl think if she saw me right this instant? Would she be disappointed at what she was to become?

Heavy clouds continue to move overhead, the sky taking on a darker hue. It will be nightfall soon. If this place is this hellish during the day, I don't want to see what it looks like at night. Leaves rustle up ahead, causing me to stop in my tracks. I listen for any further movement, but there's only silence.

"Finnley," I whisper. "Is that you?"

I take a cautious step forward, and the rustling starts again. I halt my steps immediately.

"Hello, is someone there?" My dagger sits securely in my hand, ready to be used at a moment's notice. I might be slightly unskilled with it, but I know how to stab something. The leaves rustle louder, causing fear and apprehension to dance along my spine. Although I have the dagger ready and poised, my feet are as well.

Ready to run at a moment's notice.

Whatever is coming through the hedge sounds big. Bigger than Finnley.

A thick, hairy leg extends from the foliage. That's only the start of what makes my eyes widen in fear. Soon, I bear witness to all the horror it has to offer. Long legs support an oblong body with too many eyes to count and long, lethal fangs protrude from its narrow face. I've never heard of anyone actually liking spiders, so I'm not unique in despising them. However, this one takes the cake. It looks as if it spins webs of nightmares and feeds off terror.

It's also currently looking at me as if it's starving and I'm the only dish on the menu. Yeah, this one's going to be a flight decision. There is no fight in this scenario.

I spin on my heel and run with everything in me.

The ground vibrates behind me with its heavy strides, hunger and malevolence fueling it. I'm running so hard that I fear my feet won't be able to maintain the rhythm, and I'm going to crash face-first into the ground, basically offering myself to it on a silver platter. The desire to look over my shoulder is so intense that I have to physically restrain myself. I know without a doubt that if I do, that would be the catalyst that ends this chase.

I whip around a corner, my breath coming in short, ragged gasps, and continue running with what little energy I have left. I can feel the atrocity breathing down my neck. One of the heavy legs touches the back of my calf, causing a whimper to escape my lips.

Shit. Come on, Nori. You have to push harder.

The problem is there's nothing left to pull from. I've given it my all. I'm exhausted, dehydrated, and weak. On the other hand, I may be a lot of things, but I'm not a quitter. Even when I should. Even when there's nothing left to take from. This time is different, though, as I'm not sure that my body will listen to my mind much longer.

I keep running, my heart physically hurting from the exertion, but the only other option is being eaten alive.

A sound vibrates from its throat, and I just know this is it. This is the morbid way I go.

I'm bracing for the pain I know is soon to follow, but it's not the puncture of teeth that causes a scream to be ripped from my throat. Leaves and bramble cut my face and hands as I'm yanked out of mid-run through the thick hedge. The fact that I am even being pulled through is miraculous. It's so dense, I have no idea how I'm making it through.

Whatever has me in their clutches must be extremely strong or very motivated.

Sand softens the blow my hands and knees take as I burst through to the other side. A shrill shriek comes from the opposite side of the hedge, followed by the sound of swift running.

It's not giving up.

I tentatively raise my head, expecting to be greeted with some new kind of hell.

Warm hazel eyes greet me.

"Hi again."

The cry that tears out of my throat doesn't sound human as I jump up and throw my arms around Finnley's neck. Sobs rack my entire body, and the exhaustion and fear from the day bleed out through them.

Without hesitating, he wraps me in his strong arms, whispering reassurances in my ear. Somehow, I know he's applying more pressure than he typically does in a hug. He knows I need the extra strength. I need to feel secure and know that everything is okay, that he's okay.

"Please, let's get out of this shit show," I beg, crying into his shoulder.

His touch, gentle yet firm, carefully tips my head back to peer up at him. I've always been an ugly crier, so I know I look like a hot mess right now, but you wouldn't know it by the way he's looking at me. He's looking at me the way someone does when they think they'll never see you again.

"You took the words right out of my mouth," he answers, his thumb wiping my tears away.

A loud wail echoes across the maze.

Time to get moving.

After all of the torment and mental fatigue, finding the end of the maze was pretty anticlimactic. We were so exhausted mentally and physically, that we didn't even register that we were stepping over the threshold back into reality.

We must have run for hours, evading the spider determined to feed on us.

The indigo night sky sparkles above us as if someone splashed moon dust across it. I take a deep breath, breathing in the smell of pine trees and freedom. And the noises! Actual sounds create a symphony of life around us. Students chatter among themselves, and fireflies twinkle and zip around. Even the wind creates its own unique clamor.

Finnley stays by my side as we make our way through the crowd.

Bruised, bloodied, and ragged.

A stoic reserve replaces his usual playfulness. He refuses to say what happened in the mirror or how he got out, and as much as I want to know, I also respect his wishes.

Prospects and upperclassmen alike mix and mingle with us. It looks like they've deemed us worthy of interaction now that we haven't died during Asylamation week. Now that we're technically no longer prospects but first-years.

I should feel exhilarated that I'm officially a student at Kintoira.

I survived.

What I should be doing is joining in on the celebration. Partaking in the free-flowing ale and camaraderie that's finally being extended our way. I shouldn't be standing off to the side searching the throng of classmates for a certain captain.

A certain nowhere-to-be-seen captain.

I've been casting myself in self-doubt this entire week, and when I finally succeed, I isolate myself by searching for someone who isn't even here. Someone who couldn't even make it a priority.

Finnley is pulled into conversation by a few other first years. It honestly feels a bit surreal. I take the opportunity of his distraction to push a little farther through the throng of students and get a better view of our surroundings.

Fire crackles in the air around me. Numerous firepits burn throughout the training field, casting students in their warm shadows. The sound is comforting in a way. It has a very peaceful ambience to it. A striking contrast to our weary and depleted forms. So many of us are streaked with dried blood and varying injuries.

In fact, a dark reddish-brown coats my knuckles. The sting has dulled, but it probably wouldn't hurt to visit the medical wing first thing tomorrow. *Again*. Various places on my face and neck also sting from being pulled through the hedge. My once pristine uniform, along with most of the other first-years', hangs in various states of disarray.

It's hard to tell how many we lost this trial, if any, as so many Veils and Noctryns are scattered among us. I try to let the warmth of the flames chase away the frigid sting of disappointment.

He isn't here.

I'd have seen him by now. He stands taller than most, and I'd have easily spotted him. Disappointment buries itself all the way to the bone, and I can feel the pressure of tears behind my eyes, but I refuse to let them fall.

I'm done crying over the people in my life.

He won't take my pride along with everything else he's stolen. My heart included. There had to be a valid reason he couldn't make it.

Sharp feminine laughter pulls my attention back to Finnley. He now has an arm slung over the shoulder of a petite brunette wearing a Noctryn uniform.

That's probably not going to end well.

She tucks her head and giggles at something he says, causing her short hair to partially conceal her face. He must really be laying on the charm.

My lips pull up into a small smile. It's good to see him thawing out and returning to his usual self.

I just hope he's not putting on a mask and burying his inner turmoil.

"Disgusting, isn't it?" a female voice asks out of nowhere, her tone instantly causing my smile to drop.

I turn my head slightly to face her.

The Veil captain Ambrose was arguing with before I entered the final trial is standing right beside me. She keeps her face forward, watching Finnley nuzzle the other student's neck.

"The affection part or the fact a Noctryn is fornicating with someone who might end up not being a dark wielder," I ask reluctantly, not really wanting to participate in this conversation.

"Both," she deadpans.

I shake my head. "Was there something you needed? I doubt you're here talking to me for the sheer pleasure of it."

She doesn't look like the type of person to do anything for the sheer pleasure of it. Her lips are still pulled down in a disapproving frown, and she has yet to remove her glare from the two cuddling across the field from us.

"I saw you looking for him. He isn't here, by the way," she delivers sharply. "Which is why I am."

"Thanks for the clarification."

Her eyes cut toward me and narrow.

"I'm here because he asked me to, in order to congratulate you when you completed the last trial. Congratulations." She offers the monotonic praise like some kind of accolade. "He also wanted to be informed of your success should you achieve it, so I'll be on my way now to do just that."

He knew he wasn't going to be here. That's why they were arguing before I even entered the last trial. He was asking her to come for him. Something she clearly didn't want to do.

I don't even reply. I'm mentally tapped out and just can't find a fuck to give.

Certainly not enough of one to give to her.

She turns and casts one more repulsed look in Finnley's direction before stalking off. Her mahogany ponytail swishes in rhythm with her angry strides. She's heading toward the Gothic structure that's to be my home for the next four years. That must be where Ambrose is. It looms in the distance, a colossal reminder of what has come between us within the last year.

The Veils must be having their own celebration.

I mentally shrug, burying the disappointment.

Seems I've been put in my place where I rank in the overall scheme of things. I'm sure the upperclassmen are glad to be done with babysitting duties this week. The professors rely heavily on them during Asylamation week, especially since they still have courses to instruct.

Laughter surrounds me in complete odds with my demeanor.

I rub the sting from my eyes and scan the faces surrounding me for Mallory and Mayline, but they could be anywhere. In fact, they're probably already celebrating somewhere.

As they should be.

I start walking toward the academy. Each step is deliberate but slower than normal.

A drunk Veil gives me a mock salute as he stumbles past me, almost landing face-first in one of the many firepits. There are going to be a lot of people hurting tomorrow morning from hangovers or injuries. It's a fifty-fifty shot, honestly.

I throw one more look over my shoulder to make sure Finnley is still being kept busy when I spot Mallory through the flames running up and hugging him tightly. She pulls back, raising her hands to his cheeks as if she's confirming he's real.

It looks like we all made it. Gratitude swells in my chest.

However, I'm going to skip out on our little soiree. Exhaustion and disappointment are my companions tonight, and I'd rather enjoy their company alone.

I tip my head back and stare at the stars one more time.

The only bright side to today is that it can't get any worse.

Chapter Eleven

The echo of my boots bounces off the stone walls as I make my way down the long hall. Shadows dance along the crevices from the constant burning candles that line the dim corridors. I'm not sure I'll ever get used to the perpetual grayness that lives and breathes within Kintoira. Even the skies have adopted the endless melancholy aesthetic.

The walk to breakfast is pretty isolated since most people are still in bed. The banter and vivacious laughter filled the dorm hallways most of the night. Mallory never made it back to the room. I know because I stayed up most of the night waiting for her.

Hopefully, once we're assigned to our designated regiments, our rooms will be a bit more private than our current ones.

I turn the corner and start down the stairs.

A smile spreads across my face. Today, we get our Asylamation results. The professors combine our written and physical portions to determine our placement. We also get our class schedule for our first year.

I nod my head at a pair of third-years as I pass by, evident by the three solid lines embroidered into the shoulder of their uniform. They're holding cups of something that smells deliciously like coffee. They tip their heads in my direction without pausing their conversation. They acknowledged me like I WAS one of them. It feels really good to find my place. Everyone has one. The place where you feel kinship, understood, and needed.

It's finding it that's the hard part.

Right now, the first mission of the day is to find out where the coffee is.

Taking the stairs two at a time, I make it down to the grand hall in record speed. There's still so much I need to learn about the academy as far as where things are located and shortcuts to get there, but one thing I can find without help is the dining hall. The smell of bacon and eggs hits my nose first. The overpowering aroma fills the room, but it's not what I'm desperately craving.

The usual boisterous area is eerily quiet, making the massive dining area seem even larger. A few students are scattered throughout, but even they are talking in hushed tones. I walk through the rows of large wooden tables, making my way to the food line, each step pronounced on the hard floor. I grab a flaky biscuit and follow the line, peeking at the other options. A plump woman with silver hair fills up the fruit trays, humming a cheerful tune under her breath.

I clear my throat, hesitant to disturb her.

She continues to hum and organize the fruit by color.

Okay, guess I'm grabbing a fruit. I reach out and select a shiny red apple. "Um, excuse me," I say softly, especially because it's so quiet in here, "can you tell me where the coffee is?"

Her robust form rocks back on her heels as she throws a hand over her heart. "Goodness, you've given me a fright. I didn't even see you there," she breathes out heavily.

"I apologize. I didn't mean to scare you."

"No, no, it was my own fault. So wrapped up in getting these fruits just right. If it's coffee you're wanting, head over to the room next door," she says. "There are all kinds of morning beverages for your selection." She's speaking in a normal tone, which sounds like it's amplified in the almost silent hall.

I quickly thank her before making my way out.

Directly next door is another dining area, large but smaller than the main one, and filled with anything you could possibly thirst for in the morning. I bypass the orange juice and various brewed concoctions and head straight to the coffee selection. The biscuit and apple are no longer appetizing with all the different flavors and options of this coffee bar. Honestly, just get me an IV and hook me up.

After getting the strongest option they offer, I head back into the hall, eager to explore. I have plenty of time to kill while I wait for the morning to start and the day to begin for everyone else. I'm usually never up this early, but I couldn't sleep anymore. My nerves are too distraught.

My stomach is a little queasy, and anxiety fills my veins. But I'm not focusing on that.

The coffee warms my hands as I make my way along the flickering halls. Tapestries adorn a few walls, depicting various battles between soldiers and multiple enemies. The largest of them is a vivid portrayal of the Battle of Eyonean, when Salaryan unleashed every able-bodied soldier onto the wraiths. They broke through our wards that day, and many civilian lives were lost before the soldiers could arrive. It was the first time the wraiths had ever penetrated our magic and attacked a heavily populated region. They were absolutely slaughtered for doing so.

Since then, most attacks have been on small villages on the outlying borders, where wards are thinner and the areas are sparsely populated. The borders are and have always been a violent place. The demons want more, though. They've always lusted after the larger cities, overflowing with souls for the taking.

I run my fingers over the tapestry.

The threads feel as if they vibrate beneath my fingertips. Their story screams to be told. The souls of those long dead begging not to be forgotten.

Loud talking and heavy footsteps pull my attention from the intricate weave.

Roughly seven or eight Noctryns in full battle gear are walking in my direction. A few of them still wear their helmets, completely blocking out their identities, while the others carry them in their hands or tucked under their arms. Regardless, each one exudes power and a deadly aura. It's hard not to respect them, even if you don't particularly like them and what they stand for.

A shudder makes its way down my spine at the picture they paint walking this way. For some reason, my gut screams at me not to draw their attention.

Blend in and shut up, Norissa.

I plaster my back to the cold stone wall, trying my best to bleed into it. Carefully, I bend down to set my coffee on the floor. There's a little alcove that partially hides me from their direction, and with any luck they won't even see me here. I'm pretty sure they can't see me at all, actually, but I can see them.

If the shape their armor is in is any indication, they've been fighting. Scuffs and debris adorn the flexible metal on multiple bodies, and those with exposed faces have the look of battle aftermath. It's impossible to hide the haunting hollowness that fills the eyes after bloodshed.

Even if you're trained for it.

Tiny hairs stand up on the back of my neck when a Noctryn from the back makes his way toward the front. By his sheer size, I immediately know it's a man, even with his helmet on and visor pulled down. He easily stands at least six-feet, four inches, if not taller. He also has the authoritative and masculine walk of a man.

But also, something *more*. Some people just have that something more about them, and he definitely has it.

His companions part almost instinctively to let him walk through.

They're headed my way.

My brain is telling me to become one with the wall. Disappear and don't look back.

But my nosy ass gut is telling me not to miss a single detail.

Two of them, with their helmets in their hands, are talking in hushed tones, low enough I can't make out what they're saying. The leaner one, with short blond hair that's buzzed all over, nods at what the other one is saying. The one talking is broader with beautiful braids.

But my attention keeps coming back to the lethal-looking one now in the front.

Footsteps from behind cause me to stiffen. I don't turn around, though. I just focus on staying hidden. I'm definitely more visible from that direction, and it's very obvious that I'm not only hiding but openly spying.

The Noctryn with the arrogant gait zeros in on whoever's approaching. His head dips, and his gloved hands clench into fists before visibly relaxing again.

"Nori, what are you doing?" a familiar voice asks from behind.

His voice drips with humor. A voice that instantly makes me want to punch something, particularly him. He really does have the worst timing. That's if and when he can actually make the time to show up.

Pain slices through my lip as my teeth sink into the bottom one. Slowly, while I try to rein in my annoyance, I turn and face him, giving the approaching dark wielders my back. Ambrose is gifted with nothing short of a look of pure disdain on my face.

He tilts his head back and blows out a large breath before bringing it back down to look at me. I'd like to think I'm seeing regret on his face, but who knows. The only thing I'm sure of is that he knows I'm pissed. If the crossed arms, defiant stance, and pursed lips didn't give it away, he would know by the fact that I haven't moved toward him.

The first thing I normally do when I see him is throw my arms around his neck or land a playful punch to his bicep, anything to just touch him. Right now, the only touching I want to do to him is to inflict pain, so I keep my distance.

"I'm sorry. You know I am. I wanted to be there, but I had other obligations that took precedence." He delivers this sentence like it didn't just punch a hole in my already bruised heart.

I uncross my arms and let them hang at my sides. I refuse to look vulnerable right now. Even if it's just a front to protect myself in the smallest way, it's something. "Yes, you're fellow captain kindly informed me," I answer sarcastically. They say not to hurt the messenger, but at the moment, I'd like to hurt them both.

"Then you know exactly how bad I wanted to be there."

"No, what I do know is that you weren't. I also know that you knew you wouldn't be there before I even entered the final trial. You lied to me." I know the hurt shines in my eyes, but regardless of how much I try to hide that vulnerability, I can't. He sees it, too, because he's doing his best now to look anywhere but directly at me.

"I didn't lie, Nori. I just slightly omitted."

"It's the same thing!" I snap, my hands curling into fists at my sides. I can feel the hurt turning to anger. I can feel the need to lash out and hurt him the way he hurt me.

The sounds of boots behind us draw closer.

"You know I would have done anything to be there, to see you not only succeed but achieve one of your biggest dreams, but I have responsibilities," he delivers in brutal honesty. "Something you should understand, given that you are the assigned lieutenant of your bracket. It will only become clearer if they allow you to keep that rank upon placement."

He leans forward like he's going to reach for my hand, causing me to step back even farther into the alcove. Disappointment washes over his features before he quickly masks it. "You can't be upset at me for doing what's required," he scolds, his jaw clenching the moment he closes his mouth.

The audacity of this man.

"I can and will be. You don't get to dictate what upsets me!" I dig my nails into my palms and do my best to keep the violent urges subdued. "I know that I would have been there for you, and I deserved the same. If disappointing you and being forced to lie are the benefits of having the rank they bestowed on me, then they can keep it."

I'm downright seething on the outside. But inside, I'm a complete ball of devastation. When did I become an afterthought to him? When did he become so cold and detached? And ambitious? I never thought I'd see the day that reckless Ambrose became ambitious.

"Still winning the hearts of ladies throughout the realm, I see," a husky voice calls out.

Shaking his head at me as if he's disappointed, Ambrose reluctantly turns to face the approaching Noctryns. "Fuck off, Griffin, this doesn't concern you," he bites out to the one with the shaved head.

"Touchy today, aren't we?" Griffin responds, his mouth pulled up in a smile. It seems to bring him great pleasure to see Ambrose upset.

"Don't you have some blood ritual to do or sacrifices to be made?" Ambrose asks in an exasperated tone as if this is the last thing he wants to deal with.

"Why do you want to know? Are you volunteering as tribute?" he counters back in a saccharine voice.

"He's not typically our type," the man with beautiful braids and mocha skin quips.

"Valid point, Koa. We need to dirty him up a little first."

"She looks to be more our type," Koa says, his russet-colored eyes turning in my direction and raking me from head to toe.

I swallow down anything I was going to say.

I'm so far in the alcove I can't go back any farther. So much for remaining unseen.

"I'll burn you where you stand," Ambrose growls as he reaches out and grabs the front of the man's armor, yanking him closer. They're nose to nose, staring at each other like they'd like nothing more than to eviscerate the other.

Koa's hand rests on his dagger, but he hasn't made a move to fully unsheathe it.

The veins in Ambrose's forehead protrude in anger, and his eyes spark with the inferno building beneath his skin. This is the boy who protected me from everything. The one I played with as a child, grew up with, and ultimately fell in love with. The one who would get between me and whatever was set on harming me, regardless of the circumstances. It used to drive me crazy. I just wanted to be seen as one of the boys. Currently, I appreciate it, but we are severely outnumbered, and my skill set for survival doesn't really exist. I won't be much help, and I'm not too proud to admit that.

I hold my breath, silently praying that he doesn't unleash his fire ability out of anger again. Fire wielders are notorious for their temper, and it's a constant internal battle for them to regulate it.

"I would advise against threatening my squad again, Captain," a deep, menacing voice orders.

It sounds like a threat and a promise rolled into one.

The one in the front that my eyes kept flittering back to steps forward toward the two men. He's silently stood back, letting the events unfold until now. I'd completely forgotten about him, so wrapped up in the dick measuring contest that was happening in front of me.

At the moment, he commands not only my attention but also the attention of everyone surrounding us.

His helmed head tilts down to look at Ambrose's hand gripping the top of Koa's armor. A silent question and threat rolled into the gesture.

Ambrose stares at the Noctryn, his nostrils flaring. After an incredibly long moment, he drops his grip on the armor and shoves Koa away.

Koa darts forward to retaliate, but the leader of the group extends his arm out, abruptly stopping him. Actually, I have no idea if he is the leader, but the way those around him respond to him makes it seem plausible.

"Back so soon, Kingston? I didn't even have a chance to properly miss you," Ambrose says snidely, his lip pulling up in distaste.

A tsking sound comes from Griffin. He holds up his index finger, moving it back and forth in a mocking form of scolding. "Pretty sure you forgot a teeny tiny tidbit there when you addressed him," he says with a smug grin. I'd love to smack it right off his face. "It's Major Adair to you," he warns.

Major... So he's a third-year.

Their solid black armor offers zero clues to their ranks. The Noctryns believe that offering up that information so clearly in battle is a disadvantage. The enemy targets those in charge first, creating chaos on the battlefield.

Of course, the Veils disagree.

Ambrose continues speaking like Griffin didn't just interrupt. "Already done murdering and maiming innocents," he asks the leader, his voice tight with what sounds a lot like hatred. "You really didn't waste any time this round, did you?"

"Already playing the avenging hero? I heard that worked out really well for you with the last one," Kingston responds from behind his helmet. His stance is relaxed but prepared. Two huge swords are strapped to his back, and various weapons are tucked and sheathed throughout his darkened armor. Most blend in so well that you have to really look closely to see them.

I'm definitely looking.

To take your eyes off this man seems risky.

Ambrose wears his standard-issued uniform, considering he didn't just come back from doing something shady. Dark brown slacks topped with an ivory shirt under an even darker brown hooded cloak. If he has weapons on him, they're discreetly hidden. Knowing Ambrose, he definitely has weapons somewhere on his body.

"Your brother is welcome to her. I was already done," Ambrose says with an arrogant smile. "But at least he had the guts to speak face-to-face and not hide behind a helmet."

Brother?

It takes me a second, but I put two and two together. Makon and Kingston are brothers.

Well, that certainly explains the hostility.

Immediately, I'm relieved that Ambrose and Yaretta weren't anything serious. However, after the relief hits, so does the revulsion at his words. *He was already done with her.* Exactly how many times has he done this sort of thing if he can speak so callously about it? About her. I mean, don't get me wrong, I'm not her number one fan, but she's still a human being.

And I'm not the only one who didn't take kindly to his words. The Noctryns shift among themselves, some grabbing the hilt of their daggers or swords, others dropping their helmets and stepping toward Ambrose. I have no doubt it's not because they are offended on Yaretta's behalf. They're moving forward out of respect for their leader.

Apparently, the closest person in the world to me has a death wish.

Could he take on a few of them by himself? Absolutely.

All eight of them? We're both dead.

I can feel the tension in the air.

It feels tangible enough that you could reach out and grab it.

The larger-than-life major reaches for his helmet. His large, gloved hands grip the sides and pull it off.

My eyes widen as they roam over his features.

I was not ready. I don't think there's a way to even be prepared.

His face is nothing less than masculine perfection.

The kind of perfection that demands your complete and whole attention.

A sharp jawline, strong nose, and full lips. His face is perfectly symmetrical. Black hair that's short on the sides and a little longer on top, and slightly messed up from his helmet.

Soldiers have different kinds of weapons in their arsenal that they wear throughout their life to protect themselves—some being obvious and others catching you by surprise. Kingston's caught me by surprise. He is covered in weapons, but his face is the main one.

Where Ambrose is warmth, safety, and everything beautiful in a man, Kingston is cold, diabolical, and unapproachable. Both stunning but in completely different ways.

He sucks all the oxygen out of the room, and I wouldn't be surprised if darkness started seeping from his pores. Gorgeous but in a "look don't touch" kind of way.

Beautiful.

Dangerous.

Very pissed off.

He steps closer to Ambrose, who doesn't back down. It's like watching two alpha wolves circle each other, looking for weaknesses. Where to strike to cause the most damage.

"I hide behind nothing, Ballard. Something you know better than most," he says, his eyes cutting to me as I've stepped unknowingly closer to Ambrose during the altercation.

His eyes are unique. Warm brown, the color of dark honey, but rimmed with black. He's staring at me derisively in a way that feels like it's licking its way up my spine, tasting me and finding me wholly unsatisfying.

It's not at all comfortable.

"Didn't your mother ever teach you it was rude to stare?" I ask, forcing myself to hold his gaze.

I swear his lip twitches, but it's gone so fast I could have imagined it.

"Didn't your mother teach you the same?" he answers back without missing a beat.

I wasn't as hidden as I thought while watching them.

Well, that's slightly embarrassing.

"Leave her out of this. She isn't one of your pawns to be used and discarded," Ambrose declares, moving to stand in front of me, blocking me completely from Kingston's view.

That's rich coming from him.

I step around his bigger frame, moving back to his side. He doesn't get to use the overprotective best friend card right now. Not when I'm still pissed off at him.

Kingston's lips pull into a half smile that borders on a sneer as his cold eyes slide over my body and back to my face. "She's not my type."

A sharp chuckle slips free from my lips.

This motherfucker.

Not that I care if I'm his type or not, but rude much?

"Well, now that we've established that much, we'll be on our way," I insist, grabbing Ambrose's hand and weaving through the armored men, careful not to touch any as I pass.

They make no move to step aside.

Ambrose allows me to pull him along, more than likely only because he knows I'm angry with him. The last thing he wants to do right now is add to the shit list he's already on.

I don't turn around to confirm it, but I swear I can feel the asshole Noctryn's eyes on my back as we work our way through his men. Pain radiates along my jawbone from clenching my teeth so hard. It's because I'm pissed off at the beautiful man next to me and not because the asshole behind me just insulted me and made me feel weird in my own skin all at the same time. He's not my type either. Everything I want is next to me, even if I haven't exactly told him that yet.

"I take it you two aren't particularly close," I say, stating the obvious.

We walk side by side down the main hall, turning corners and weaving through the endless passageways.

"Caught on to that, did you?" he replies coyly. His hands rest in the pockets of his trousers.

I'm not particularly a betting person, but if I were, I'd say it's to prevent himself from trying to touch me again. We typically never stay mad at each other for very long, but he knows I'm hurt. Regardless of whether he's adamant that it couldn't be helped.

"Kind of hard to miss with all the testosterone being thrown around," I acknowledge with a slight eye roll.

"There's certainly no love lost between us."

"Why do you hate him?"

"I don't hate him. I despise him. Slightly different."

"Okay," I reply, "so what's the backstory. Why all the animosity?" I need the tea like I need my next breath. It's been so long since Ambrose and I have exchanged juicy gossip like two old women with nothing better to do.

I've missed this. The least he can do is give me this.

He pulls both hands out of his pockets, using one to open a large wooden door to the right of us, and the other to gesture me through. The moment I enter, all my questions evaporate into thin air.

Books.

So. Many. Books.

I inhale deeply, the smell feeling like being welcomed home by an old friend. There's just something about the smell of books that is so comforting. The ink, parchment, and bindings all come together to create a blend of familiarity.

Thousands of books must fill the surrounding shelves from the floor to the top of the cathedral ceilings. They seem endless in their grandeur, and the massive stained glass window on the far wall only adds to the majestic feel of this place. I bet if Kintoira ever sees even the tiniest sliver of sunshine, colors would splash across every surface in here, making it look like somewhere in a fantasy.

My pulse speeds up, and my hands itch to start grabbing everything in my vicinity.

Six wooden tables, each with eight chairs, are placed on either side of the main walkway, with smaller tables scattered throughout the multitude of bookshelves. I've never seen this many books in one place before. There are sections on history, battle tactics, healing remedies and antidotes, all the way to folklore and popular fables.

It's endless.

It's beautiful.

This is the first room that I've been in since arriving that feels warm within this cold fortress. Small lamps with bulbs lit by fire magic sit atop the various tables, and warm-colored rugs line the floors.

I spin around.

I never want to leave this room.

"If I tell you, will you please forgive me?" he asks in a solemn tone.

"Tell me what?" I reply absent-mindedly.

I run my finger down the spine of a particularly worn-looking book, the spine slightly bent and the hardcover peeling back. *The Many Ways to Use Wolfsbane* is faded but still legible. Either a lot of people want to poison someone, or the healers favor this toxic plant for traditional medicine. It could honestly go either way.

His deep baritone laughter brings me out of my macabre thoughts. "I see you like the library. I thought you might." A grin spreads across his face.

It's unfair how beautiful this man is on any given day, but when he smiles? It's so easy to forget why I'm upset with him. Even the beauty of this library has nothing on him.

Sharp blue eyes watch me as I push the book back onto the shelf. His hair hangs loosely to his shoulders today, the thick waves pushed back from his face, highlighting the sharp line of his jaw.

I pull my gaze away.

We walk through a narrow aisle, taking a seat at the back of the library, being sure to keep our voices to a whisper.

"I'll tell you the backstory if you say you'll forgive me for letting you down. I promise, where I had to be couldn't be avoided."

"Ambrose, I'm upset. But that's something I need time to work through. I can't stuff my feelings in a little box and make them go away to suit you."

"Is there anything I can do to speed up the process?" he asks, his voice soft and low, but with a slight humorous tone.

"Where were you last night that was so important you couldn't be there for me?"

He shakes his head. "Anything but that."

I push my chair back from the table. "Back to square one. Secrets. Since when did we start keeping secrets from each other?"

"Since I have to," he says without an ounce of regret. "I can't tell you what you want to know about last night, but I can answer your first question. Kingston and I have bad blood because of who he is. What he stands for—" he presses his lips together, waiting for the small, frail-looking woman with an arm full of books to pass. She must be the librarian.

As soon as she passes, he continues, his beautiful blue eyes taking on a hardened edge. "—Kingston doesn't just practice dark magic. He *is* dark magic. Dark to the core and makes no apologies for it. He's one of the most talented in the academy at mind control." His lip curls in distaste. "Only a select few Noctryns can perform that level of dark magic. He will wedge himself into your thoughts, taking what he wants and leaving whatever he desires. And when he's done, if he doesn't eliminate you, he'll make you want to terminate yourself."

I don't say anything. I just listen.

His lips lift in a sneer, causing his straight white teeth to stand out against his tan skin. "As you know, we as Veils use the gifts we were bestowed upon at birth, our rightful abilities. They're different," he adds. "The Noctryns sacrifice their natural-born powers to wield darkness, both figuratively and literally. He's the worst of his kind here at Kintoira."

He sounds dangerous. Interesting—I'll give him that—but dangerous.

It's entirely up to us where we fall on the spectrum of good versus evil. Light versus dark. The academy assigns us to a regiment, but we play a big part in it all. How we test during the Asylamation will tell the academy exactly what they need to know. At least that's what they feed us.

Do we stay to the light and use our core powers to defend and fight for the realm, or do we sacrifice those for the dark powers of wielding shadows, mind control, and blood magic? They're both valuable and dangerous in their own right.

One is just naturally born, and the other is, in a way, stolen.

I steeple my hands on the table, staring intently at Ambrose. I raise both of my eyebrows at him, knowing there's more.

"Has anyone ever told you you're like a dog with a bone?" His words say one thing, but his eyes say something else. He's looking at me like he's impressed, not annoyed. "You don't give up."

"Don't evade, Mr. Ballard."

Sighing, he leans back in his chair and folds his arms across his chest. "Last year, when a certain object went missing—"

"A dark object?"

"And a professor—"

"A professor went missing?"

"The Noctryn leadership was tasked with finding out who took both. All of the first-year Veils were interrogated. I was lucky enough to be interrogated by Kingston," he says sarcastically, rocking back in his chair.

He has my full attention. I lean forward, resting my elbows on the table.

"It wasn't pleasant to say the least, and I was introduced up close and personal to his interrogation skills. For a first-year, he was proficient. I'll give him that." He chuckles darkly.

A first-year? That can't be right.

"I thought he was a major. How was he a first-year last year?"

Ambrose dips his chin in acknowledgment.

"He is a major. He's also a second-year now. He skipped the captain rank entirely because he excelled at the dark arts on a level that hasn't been seen in a long time." He uncrosses his arms, leaning onto the table to look me dead in the eye. "As a first-year, I had absolutely no training on how to block someone from entering my thoughts. He saw things I'm not particularly proud of and wouldn't willingly share with anyone. Let alone him," he states. "It was violating, and he hasn't let me forget the things he discovered since."

That sounds an awful lot like being assaulted. "Did you know something about the disappearances?"

"No. But I knew enough about other things to give him leverage over me that he keeps tucked away in his back pocket."

I rest my face in my hands as I stare at him. I know him like the back of my hand. I also know he's not being entirely honest. He's being evasive and giving me partial truths, but I'll let him have it.

This time.

"Thanks for sharing this information with me. I'm still pissed you're keeping other secrets, but thank you for trusting me with this much." I extend an arm out, holding up the pinky on my right hand as a symbol of a temporary truce.

His eyes roam over my face. "Some secrets have to be kept. To protect those who don't know they need it." He wraps his larger pinky around my smaller one.

Upperclassmen slowly trickle in, but I haven't seen any other first-years yet.

The dark skies outside are beginning to lighten. Slivers of light beam through the windowpanes, meaning the sun has risen and we're seeing the most of it we're going to.

The trial results will be posted soon. They get posted before the start of the first period.

We'll get our schedule later in the day. Around this time tomorrow, I'll be getting ready for my first class! Excitement bubbles in my chest. This is really happening.

Ambrose's strong hands wrap around mine, our pinkies still interlocked. His calloused palms rub against my softer ones. I've always loved his hands. The way they're so much bigger than mine, the veins that pop out on the back, and the hardened calluses from weaponry training. This man has seriously caused me to develop a hand fetish.

I envision those very same hands wrapped around my throat as he pins me to the nearest wall, finally devouring me in all the devious ways I've imagined. It would be rough, unapologetic, and years in the making.

I run my tongue along my upper lip, as my mouth suddenly feels very dry.

His icy-blue eyes follow the movement, falling to my lips.

A loud announcement over the speakers breaks the moment.

Results are being posted in the halls.

"You ready for this?" he asks, clearing his throat and pulling his hands away.

An emptiness settles over me.

Not at all.

Chapter Twelve

There's a small crowd gathered already.

The taller students read over the heads of others. Smaller first-years stand in the front, getting an up-close-and-personal view of the results.

I haven't worked up the courage to walk over. Instead, I just stand off to the side, my back pressed against the cold stone wall. Ambrose stands next to me, a silent pillar of strength. He talks with various Veils who stop and converse with him, but he never leaves my side or tries to drag me into the conversation. He just allows me to stand here and find my bearings.

To find my courage.

I watch as the other first-years read down the list, searching for their names. Some jump up and down, hugging the friends they've made this past week. Others shake their heads, disappointment written all over their faces.

All their emotions are understandable but pointless. It doesn't matter what we feel or want. The academy decides our future.

But the diverse display of emotions isn't what's causing anxiety to claw its way up my throat, digging deep into the tissue and drawing blood. No, that's saved for the students who cast looks in my direction with varying expressions of pity or confusion.

Please do not let me be a dark wielder.

I wring my hands in front of me.

Anything but that.

I swallow, forcing myself to calm down. Getting upset isn't going to accomplish anything.

Most of the surviving first-years know how badly I want that Veil title. Our numbers have dwindled to around forty over the past week, so we've gotten to know each other in a sense, even if only on a superficial level. Enough to know who's gunning for Veil and who has their eyes set on becoming a Noctryn.

"Nori!" a feminine voice yells, causing me to look over. Mallory is heading in my direction, her cheeks pink from running. They match her cherry-blossom fauxhawk. Her feet skid to a halt right in front of me as she grabs my shoulders for balance. "Have you looked yet?" she asks excitedly, a huge smile lighting up her face.

"Not yet. But I'm working on it," I reply, forcing myself to appear cool, calm, and collected.

But I know my nervousness is written all over my face. I've always been shit at hiding my emotions. The sympathetic look she's currently directing at me tells me she definitely picked up on it.

"What are you waiting for? You know exactly where your name is on that list. At this point, you're only confirming it," she states in a confident tone. Both hands propped on her hips.

"Yeah, that's kind of what I'm working up the courage for."

"What are we getting courage for?" Finnley asks, coming up beside her and giving my braid a playful tug.

"She's nervous about the results," Mallory explains, pulling my braid out of Finnley's grasp.

"She has nothing to be nervous about. She's a Veil through and through," Ambrose joins in, turning away from the upperclassmen he was talking to and wrapping his arm around my shoulders.

"Or... she's a Noctryn, which is okay as well," Finnley replies, but his sincere smile and understanding eyes are directed at me.

Ambrose cuts an annoyed look toward Finnley but doesn't say anything more.

He's working really hard to dig himself out of the trenches.

Mallory looks around at us all, both hands back to resting on her slim hips. "Well, I'm walking up and finding my name. Who's coming with me?"

"Right behind you," Finnley answers, turning his torso side to side and stretching his arms like he's preparing for war.

"Me too," I whisper.

"Nori, you got this," Ambrose says, grabbing my face gently with both hands and turning me to look at him. "You and me until the end. We always knew we would be Veils together. We've waited for this day since we were kids." His scent wraps around me, the familiar smell of ocean breeze and broken waves grounding me. Reminding me of who I am.

And that I'm not alone.

I nod, breaking eye contact and stepping back to follow my friends.

My steps falter slightly behind Finnley and Mallory, their excitement outweighing my trepidation. Ambrose stays back, allowing us to experience this together as first-years. It's better this way. For some reason, I'd be even more nervous with him reading the names with me.

The pressure would just be that much more intense.

A large parchment is pinned to the stone, with the Kintoira Academy crest pressed into black wax, dripping down the right corner. The names are written in Solarish, the most common language throughout the realm. Also mandated that everyone know how to read and write in it.

Bold letters in elegant gold writing clearly state "Noctryn" with a group of names beneath.

I take a deep breath and scan the names below, looking for mine. My eyes are reading almost quicker than I can decipher. Samason Nivinche, the quiet boy from Willikson, Mayline Zhou, Zackary Winchell. The fact that they aren't in alphabetical order just adds to the anticipation.

When I come to the last name and still haven't found mine, a sigh of relief escapes me.

I drop my head forward.

Thank the gods.

Mentally shaking myself, I raise my head and continue reading. The next section in bold, eloquent letters says "Veil," with more names listed below.

Mallory jumps up, punching the air next to me.

I pull my eyes from her and back to the list.

Emory Voss, Eryk Porter, Mallory Blaire... I continue reading through the names, the list getting shorter and shorter.

I come to the last name on the scroll, and it's not mine.

Finnley Stax.

What. The. Fuck.

Finnley goes still next to me, apparently reading at the same speed.

In bold letters at the bottom of the list is another header.

Inconclusive.

There's a singular name below it: *Norissa Caderyn.*

"It must be a mistake," Finnley says under his breath, looking from the parchment to me and back again.

The academy doesn't make mistakes.

I stare at my name like it betrayed me. I'm a Caderyn. We're Veils.

Quickly, I peek over my shoulder at Ambrose. He's watching me with an intense expression on his face. Both brows are drawn, and his sharp eyes are narrowed in on me.

I offer him a hollow smile and turn back to the list.

I blink at my name.

Still there.

"It's okay. We'll just head down to the headmistress's office, and she'll straighten it out," Mallory offers. Her wide eyes are full of false optimism.

The headmistress. A shiver crawls across my skin. No one wants to go to her office. You stay off her radar at all costs. I can't imagine crossing her threshold and not even belonging to one of the two regiments under her thumb.

Finnley squeezes my shoulder reassuringly. He doesn't offer any more words of encouragement or false hope. This is why he's one of my favorite people here. No bullshit, no making light of a bad situation, just there to walk through the misery with me.

This isn't how I expected to be inducted into the academy.

So many years of envisioning this moment. Some little girls daydream of the day they'll walk down the aisle and become a bride. Not me. I always dreamed of the day I'd see my name assigned to the Veils. Upholding my family legacy. Making my mother proud in the only way I'd ever be able to. Even when I proved to her time and time again that I wasn't cut out for it. It didn't matter. I had my sights set on wearing that uniform.

I turn on my heel and walk back toward my best friend. How do I even tell him? Everything we dreamed about while lying in those sawgrass fields staring at the midnight sky just evaporated into broken dreams. A wisp slipping through my fingers.

I stop in front of him, take a deep breath, and raise my head. Arctic eyes collide with my green ones.

He reaches for me, and I let him.

"What's wrong? What did it say?" His tone is urgent, but his touch is gentle as he grabs the back of my neck, pulling me into his solid chest.

"I don't know... I don't understand. It says I didn't place."

My words come out muffled as my face is buried in his rough embrace. He grips the back of my hair in his fist, gently pulling my head back and tilting my chin up with his other hand.

"You have to place, and there are only two options." His words are confident, but his eyes hold something else. Something that resembles hesitation. Possibly fear.

"Yeah, that's exactly what I said," Mallory chimes in as she walks up behind me, biting her fingernails.

"Same," Finnley agrees, coming up and standing at my other side.

"The results were clearly written," I reply, rubbing my exhausted eyes. Maybe if I rub hard enough, I'll wake up and this will all be a bad dream.

Every single answer was put forth with such careful consideration. I spoon-fed my written portion with Veil-inspired answers. Each showing empathy and fortitude. The physical portion was given the same formula. Perseverance and patience. Nothing that would even become close to triggering a Noctryn response. They're rash, unapologetic, and unmerciful—the opposite of my Asylamation approach.

"Something you did or wrote threw them for a loop," Mallory states, tapping her chin with her index finger.

Although not helpful, I agree.

Everyone stares at me like I have the answer hidden up my sleeve on how I got in this predicament.

Surprise.

I don't.

"It's okay. We'll figure it out. I got you," Ambrose says. "We've figured our way out of worse situations than this." His words tell me one thing, but his eyes tell me another. This is uncharted territory, and he knows it.

Finnley sighs dramatically.

I lift the corner of my lips in a defeated half-grin. Same page, buddy. Same fucking word.

"It's fine, guys, I'll handle it. Don't let this ruin your results. You guys are Veils!" I exclaim in an overly chipper tone. "You should be celebrating." I force a smile on my face. I won't let my disappointment ruin their elation. They worked their asses off for this and deserve to finally enjoy it.

"Nori, we're in this together. We started it together, and we'll finish it together," Mallory says, leaning toward me and wrapping her arms around my shoulders. "As Veils," she finishes softly in my ear.

I give her hand an encouraging pat and unravel myself from her embrace to fist pump Finnley and hug Ambrose. The latter places a small kiss on my forehead before pulling away with one last look of turmoil, before I usher him to his first class.

Finnley and Mallory invite me to breakfast, which I kindly decline. Instead, I head to the courtyard for some fresh air.

I turn down a long hallway that leads to a side exit on the southern side of the fortress. The air in this part of the academy is cold and damp. More so than usual. Regardless of how many hearths are burning, this portion is in a constant state of frigidity. The ceiling is crafted from intricate glass panes molded into a dome shape. It's beautiful but not a good heat conductor. Thick vines cover the outside glass, blocking any view of the sky.

A little farther up to the right is a small set of stairs that leads out to a partial balcony covered with the same delicate-looking ceiling. It's anything but fragile, though. Nothing in this fortress is, regardless of how it appears.

The academy and its occupants. Poised and ready to strike at any given moment. Regardless of the presentation, they're deadly.

I've done my research on this place. Those glass panes were crafted by the most talented glass blowers in the realm. They were created in the Merch Desert and can withstand the same force or trauma as the stones that make up these walls.

The moisture in the air is causing condensation to form on the glass, and the delicate baby hairs around my neck to coil up and become loose from my braid. I can feel them resting on my neck. Another grievance to add to the ever-growing list of annoyances from today. Some days, I think I should cut the long waves into something more manageable, but then moments like this remind me that I would hate anything touching my neck. If I can't pile it high on top of my head, it's just not happening.

It becomes something I can't control.

And that doesn't sit well with me.

The only thing that can soften the aggravation growing within my soul right now is solitude wrapped in fresh air. I need to get outside.

Chandeliers hang from the ceiling, filled with fire magic, lighting my way down the small passageway to the exit. I only know about this exit door because, unlike many of the rooms and passages in Kintoira, it was included in the research I conducted.

I just need to erase the chaos playing in my mind. Nothing erases the noise like isolation. Once I have a few moments to myself, I'll figure out how to approach the headmistress.

Lugworth is not someone you're in a hurry to chat with.

She's vicious and cutthroat.

And that's just to her friends.

The moment I pass through the door and into the courtyard, the dampness is erased by a slap of cold air. It's as uncomfortable as it is invigorating.

Slate-colored clouds move quickly overhead. It looks like snow is well on its way. Autumn is almost behind us. It's only a matter of time before this place is blanketed in white.

December will be harsh. And it's almost here.

The harmony of birds chirping in the distance causes my eyes to flutter closed. Their days begin with song. How peaceful and naive that must be. To think everything is going to be okay, at least long enough to lower your guard each and every morning to sing.

I stretch my neck, trying to alleviate the tension I'm holding in my shoulders. It's so easy to forget why I came here in the first place. So simple to not recall what lies in wait beyond our walls. Honestly, it's effortless to forget why I'm here altogether.

It started as a child, with me wanting to matter to someone. Anyone. To be a hero in someone's story. As I grew, it morphed into wanting to make the impossible-to-impress Maeve Caderyn proud. I wanted to prove her wrong. Show her I had what it took.

Then Ambrose became the sun in my orbit. I realized that all I really wanted was to remain by the side of the boy I had come to love. I wanted to fight, achieve, and flourish with him. And I'd do whatever it took to make that happen.

And there were always the subtle wisps of gray I tried to bury deep beneath the surface. To pretend they weren't there, biding their time.

Now that I'm actually here and I see what this place really is and the path I chose, I'm not so sure I made the right decision. I'm not as skilled as the other students. The deaths this week made me realize exactly how mortal I am. I'm honestly not sure if any of this was selfishly for me, or just to bend myself into what I thought others expected of me?

I sit on a small stone bench facing the eastern mountain range. If the sun were visible at all, I'd have a beautiful view of it from this spot. I bring my legs up and cross them under myself. I may have overestimated my ability to adapt. I feel sorely underqualified to be here.

Like an impostor.

I have impostor syndrome.

I'm pretending to belong and have what it takes. I've carefully crafted myself into who I think I should be. I exhale sharply, a humorless sound halfway between a sigh and a scoff. Look how well that worked out for me.

Inconclusive.

"Aren't you supposed to be celebrating?" a deep voice asks, shattering my moment of internal self-loathing, causing my eyes to fly open and my feet to shoot out from under me.

I look up at the imposing figure standing directly above me. The same one who challenged Ambrose in the hallway.

Kingston.

He moved so silently I didn't hear him approach. He's huge, I should have heard him. There's no way he should have been able to catch me unaware.

He moves like the shadows he controls and looks just as unapproachable.

His face is a cool mask of indifference. Dark penetrating eyes stare at me as if they want nothing more than to eviscerate my insides from where I sit. His black fighting leathers strain against his broad frame. He's leaner than Ambrose but slightly taller, and just as imposing. More so if you count the wrathful look that's been on his face both times I've seen him.

"Maybe it's because of you," he murmurs, staring at me with those distinctive ringed eyes.

"Excuse me?" I ask, rearing back.

"Maybe I look this *unapproachable* because of the person in my direct vicinity," he says slowly as if I'm an imbecile.

My nostrils flare, but I control my anger.

A fact that I'll pat myself on the back for later.

"You approached me, not the other way around," I snap. "And how did you know I thought you were unapproa—"

I slap a palm against my thigh, muttering a harsh curse under my breath.

He's one of the most talented in the academy at mind control.

Ambrose's words ring through my brain.

My eyes close as it clicks into place.

I slowly open them and glare at him.

His full lips turn up into a sinful smirk. No one should be allowed to look that wicked while smirking.

"Rude," I say in a level tone. "If I had wanted you to know my inner thoughts, I'd have spoken them out loud."

I stand to my full height. I still barely reach his collarbone.

"If I cared about being rude, I'd have asked instead of dipping into your shallow thoughts," he drawls, looking down his perfectly straight nose at me. "Turns out, I don't care."

The longer portion of his hair on top is no longer messy from his helmet but slicked back. The sides are closely shaved, accentuating the sharp angles of his face. I bet this is how he usually wears it.

Controlled. Restrained. No loose ends.

A low laugh comes from behind him.

I sidestep slightly, trying to look past the arrogant man blocking my view.

His brother leans against a birch tree with one leg propped up. The opposite of Kingston in so many ways. His long hair hangs loose over his shoulders with war braids woven randomly throughout. He's casually using a lethal-looking dagger to peel an apple as he eavesdrops on our conversation.

"I see it runs in the family," I say, the words dripping with condescension, nodding toward Makon. "Rudeness, in case it went over your head."

Kingston's smirk widens.

"A lot of things run in my family. Giving a shit isn't one of them."

"Aren't you supposed to be in some dark dungeon working with demons or something?" I ask, arching a delicate brow in his direction.

"Only on Tuesdays," he deadpans.

"How unfortunate for me that today isn't Tuesday," I answer, tilting my head back further to stare up at him. "What exactly does a person have to do to get some seclusion around here?"

"How about you tell me, since you intruded on ours," he replies in an icy tone.

"I don't see your name on this courtyard," I rebuke, crossing my arms over my chest and looking around.

He lifts one shoulder. "Now who's being rude?"

I scowl up at him. "I didn't see you out here, or I'd have turned right back around and headed inside. I'd like to say this has been a pleasure, but I'm rude, not a liar," I state. "Now, if you'll excuse me, I have some place to be with fewer interruptions."

His eyes flick up and down my body, cold with detachment, before slowly moving to the side. "It seems you do." His unnerving stare doesn't falter. "It's been a while since we've had a Liminal at the academy."

My shoulders tighten. "A Liminal?"

He tilts his head to the side slightly. "Someone who doesn't really fit here nor there," he answers cryptically, as his fingers trail along the hilt of the dagger hanging at his waist.

A short, sharp laugh comes from the side. "I have somewhere she'd fit," Makon suggests, pointing his chin in my direction.

Ugh. Gross.

Kingston slowly turns his head toward his brother, and whatever Makon sees causes him to laugh under his breath darkly, before taking a big bite out of his apple.

He doesn't say anything else, though.

"What are you talking about?" I ask Kingston, bringing the discussion back.

A smile, void of any warmth, ghosts over his lips. "Not a Veil but not quite a Noctryn either. Where does that leave you, Caderyn?" His eyes darken, gleaming with something I can't quite put my finger on. "Or perhaps you're looking at it all wrong. Maybe you're *both*."

I've heard a lot of crazy things in my short life, but this is top-tier.

You can't be Noctryn and Veil.

It's not possible to be good and evil. Light and dark. That's like saying the sun is part moon and vice versa.

Impossible.

And how does he even know I didn't place? He wasn't in the halls this morning. Not that I was looking for him or anything.

"Are you snooping on me?" I ask incredulously.

He gives me a slow, deliberate blink. "Don't flatter yourself. Every upperclassman will be looking at that list today. We want to know who we'll be training with over the next few years and who we'll be fighting beside afterward," he says, leaning in slightly, voice dropping low. "That includes all within Salaryan's combat force. Not just you," he adds.

My eyes go from him to Makon and back again.

"Well, it won't be me by your side. I can guarantee that," I say, a small, slightly hysterical laugh breaking free. "There's just been a mistake, that's all. I'm a Veil, through and through."

"Are you, though?" he asks with a polite smile that doesn't quite reach his eyes.

I'm not sure what comes over me, possibly fear, probably anger. I shove him in the chest with everything I have. He doesn't move an inch.

Of course, he doesn't move.

"I am not a Noctryn! I'm not like you or him," I shout, looking at him while pointing at his brother.

His face remains cold and detached, which makes me feel like I'm the crazy one here.

"I have a moral compass. There are lines that I refuse to cross to accomplish my objectives."

"I think you're wrong. I think that you are a little darker than you'd like to be. And it scares you." His lip curls. "The academy picked up on it, and you're now in panic mode. Perhaps you're a bit more *heathen* than you thought, after all," he says coldly, holding the intense eye contact just a little too long, with that damn smug smirk in place.

"Want to know what I think? I think you are an asshole!" I shout, my voice rising despite doing my absolute best to maintain my composure.

He shrugs. "That, among other things," he replies with calm indifference. His expression is unreadable. He has perfected the mask of apathy, and it's chilling.

I give him a curt nod. I'm done here. "Well, like I said, I have places to be."

"As do we," Makon answers, strolling over as he takes another big bite out of his apple. His eyes travel over me, assessing before turning to Kingston. "You ready?"

"Beyond," Kingston answers dryly.

Makon chucks the core onto the gravel.

Animal.

"Should have stayed off his radar, Norissa," he says under his breath as he walks past me and through the gate to the training field.

Kingston's gaze lingers on me for a moment longer before he tips his head slightly, the gesture more of a mocking farewell than an actual one. "Until next time, *Heathen*," he says, his lips curling into a half smile before he turns on his heel and walks away.

I stand there for a moment longer, staring after them.

Liminal.

Why have I never heard of this before?

I gather my wits, but mostly my courage, and head inside to find the headmistress's office and straighten this mess out.

It's time to get some answers.

Chapter Thirteen

"So let me get this straight," Finnley utters, "you literally didn't place in either but are part of both according to the headmistress."

"A Liminal," Mallory explains, echoing what I just told them.

"Yeah, I get that," he replies, folding his arms, "but where exactly does she go from here? Where does she train? What quarters does she sleep in? Will her powers come into play, or will she manipulate shadows? Why don't they execute her for not placing in one of the two categories?" he asks, kicking his feet up onto the small table.

I stare at him. He's voicing everything I've already thought of.

"I've heard about this happening once before, a few centuries ago. My grandfather used to tell me stories of the old warriors, and I remember this one he spoke about had a Liminal in it," Mayline chimes in, her feet tucked under her in the large armchair. She may have been assigned Noctryn, but she's still hanging out with us. For now.

We all stare at her, waiting for her to continue.

She leans back. "I don't know much just what was in the folklore he would recite to me. It's obviously very rare and unpredictable for this to occur." She drags a finger over her bottom lip, thinking. "I recall him explaining that each Liminal is unique in their abilities. They could have powers and shadows... or only one or the other. The last one documented was amazing at blood magic but couldn't control the shadows. He was lethal at manipulating people's emotions, though."

We all sit in silence, letting her words sink in, each of us lost in our own reflection of thoughts. The study hall is quiet right now, so we were able to snag a few armchairs in the corner without being bothered by anyone.

I rub the healing scab on the inside of my wrist. "Did he know how it occurred? Becoming a Liminal?" I'm not sure if I'm going to like the answer, but I want it all the same.

She shakes her head, her hooded eyes softening in understanding. "No, he wouldn't say anything more, and I couldn't find anything in our history books. It felt a bit taboo from the way he was speaking, like perhaps they don't want us to know much about the topic."

Mallory's mouth opens, then closes. She looks at me like she wants to ask something but isn't sure if she should.

I wave her on to ask. It can't get any worse at this point.

"Before you left, did she happen to mention what your curriculum is going to look like?"

Yes. The real kicker in this shit show.

I let out a sharp exhale through my nose. "She did. In very thorough details I might add."

Finnley drops his feet from the table and leans in toward me, his elbows resting on his knees. Concern marks his furrowed brow as he waits for me to continue.

"Apparently, I'm going to be training with both. Veils and Noctryns. I've been instructed that my class schedule will host both courses as well as combat training techniques equally," I groan, dragging a hand down my face.

Finnley runs his tongue along his teeth before speaking. "How exactly are you going to manage that kind of class load?" he asks.

I gather my hair in my hands, twisting it and securing it high on my head in a messy bun. "Reluctantly. That's how," I answer. "But because I actually did place, it just happened to be in both regiments, I get to live to see another day. So there's a bright side in all of this, I guess." I laugh hollowly.

By the time we leave the study hall, the sun has long since settled behind the mountains. Not that we were able to enjoy any of her warmth, but we knew she was there. Sometimes that's all that matters in the end.

Knowing something is there, even if you can't see it.

The thin chiffon drapes hanging in my room billow in the wind as I stare up at the vast indigo sky through my window. There are so many more stars in this region than back home. In Brylan, the streets are lined with orange flickering carriage lights, and the ports are full of structures and homes that block out any view of the stars worth seeing.

The only thing that could make the vibe more perfect is the sound of the waves crashing against the shore at night. It was my own personal lullaby.

One of the very few perks of being the daughter of a high-ranking Veil is the good housing with even better views. Other than that, the only thing you received was dinners eaten alone, holidays celebrated unaccompanied, and high expectations placed on your shoulders.

It would have been a lonely childhood without Ambrose.

My new room isn't anything to complain about either. The view is pretty spectacular. Thousands of evergreen pine trees crest the tops of various mountain peaks, their needles still a deep bluish-green color despite the dropping temperatures. Low-lying clouds drift over their highest points, creating an enigmatic feeling that settles into my soul just right.

Student housing decided that there was more room in the Noctryn quarters and placed me here for the remainder of the year. Not only am I forced to study with them, but I also have to live with them.

Let's not forget the fact that there's also a communal bathroom that we all get to bond over.

I'm being forced into their vicinity whether I like it or not. And just to clarify, I do not. The only perk in the room situation is that anyone who survives the first week as a prospect is assigned their own room.

No more sharing.

Speaking of sharing, we must have gone over a hundred scenarios this evening on how I ended up in this predicament. Each one we came up with was improbable and impossible to explain. Honestly, at this point, it doesn't even matter. We can't undo what has already been done.

I grab my steaming mug of tea and take a generous sip, the hot liquid warming my throat as it goes down. I'm nervous about the classes I'll be assigned to tomorrow, and I was having trouble falling asleep because of it. The kitchen steward recommended this brew when I asked for something calming to sip on before bed. I feel like perhaps Kintoira has bitten off more for me than I can chew. How does someone balance light and dark magic without it driving them completely mad?

Walking that kind of fine line is dangerous.

A coin cannot show both sides at once. It's either one side or the other.

Reading the results hurt. Like physically hurt. The sharp jab of pain from seeing my name at the bottom of the parchment causes the back of my throat to itch and my eyes to feel heavy. I tried so hard. I gave it my everything, and it still wasn't enough.

I still wasn't pure or righteous enough. And that scares me.

Correspondences aren't allowed during the first few weeks of learning so that we have time to acclimate to the social structure within these walls without outside influences. It seems I've been given a hiatus before my mother finds out. That's if someone here doesn't leak the information to her first.

Which let's be honest. She probably already knows.

I set my tea down and uncurl from the window seat, stretching my arms above my head. My eyes feel heavier than they did mere moments ago, and the urge to lie across my new bed to test it out is overwhelming.

The thick material of the comforter surrounds me as I jump into the blankets face-first.

I roll onto my back slowly and let out a big sigh.

The bed is so soft and cozy. That's the last thought I have before unnerving dreams take hold.

The next day starts in typical fashion.

Badly.

A curse leaves my lips as one of my books bounces off the stone floor, causing it to open and fall sideways, bending a few pages in the process.

"Watch it," a girl wearing all black barks at me.

"Sorry," I mutter to her retreating back.

I rearrange the pack hanging on my shoulder, all while trying to balance the multiple books in my other arm and bend down to pick it up. I have to carry around twice as many texts as everyone else because I have twice as many courses.

Most students have study periods or library sessions coordinated into their schedules, but not me. They filled those with additional classes. The only bright spot is that they took away my lieutenant rank due to my courseload, so I don't have to attend officer classes or shoulder that responsibility.

Ashlyn remains a lieutenant in the Veil squad, and Mayline kept her as well for the Noctryns. I have no idea who replaced me, if anyone. Apparently, there isn't a set number of officers who can be assigned each year. It just depends on how many individuals qualify.

I still haven't figured out the qualifications.

At the moment, it's pretty low on my fucks to give.

Class schedules were given out toward the end of last week, and I'm still struggling to find my way around. Typically, it results in me running from one end of the academy to another since the dark and light classes are separated.

I roll my eyes. They couldn't make it easy on me and schedule them accordingly.

The few courses the two regiments do take together aren't on my schedule until the end of the day. By then, I am a sweaty, exhausted mess.

A bell chimes, and my next class has already begun by the time I make it to the upper northwest corner of the academy and slip through the door. The professor is writing on the blackboard, her long blond hair twisted into an elegant style that falls down her back, swishing back and forth as she writes.

I slip into an empty desk a few rows from the back and set the *Shadowcraft: Fundamentals of Shadow Weaving* book on top. The guy to my right is bouncing his leg full of nervous energy as he scans the contents of page 43.

I quickly flip to the same page in my book.

The tapping of chalk on the board continues. Professor Rinkin is written in capital letters at the top, and below are rows of numbers with complex codes of letters and different wavelengths beneath them.

I already hate this class.

Students are quietly waiting at their desks for the professor to finish writing as my eyes dart around the room. I pull the edge of my long-sleeved gray shirt down and readjust myself in my seat. It's probably pointless for me to even attend Shadow Wielding. More than likely, I won't have anything to wield, but there's still a ball of nervous energy burning in my stomach. Especially from being in a room with so many dark wielders at once.

All levels of Noctryn attend this class, from first-years all the way through fourth. I stand out like a sore thumb in my gray-issued uniform against the sea of blackness surrounding me.

Neither light nor dark, I was assigned gray.

It's kind of perfect since it matches my mood these days.

I'm stuck in a constant state of in-between.

The majority of Veils don't trust me because, technically, I only tested partially light. Which means I tested partially dark, and any Veil worth their weight knows you don't trust Noctryns. The Noctryns don't respect me because I didn't test entirely dark. If you're not pitch black, you're not dark enough for them.

Hence, my state of in-between.

I don't really belong anywhere but everywhere. Surprisingly, having too much of everything is incredibly lonely. I feel hollow inside as I sit in this lecture hall surrounded by over a hundred other students, unable to relate to a single one of them.

I hate when people play the victim mentality game, I really do, and I'm trying my best not to land on that foundation, but damn, I feel like the universe is against me right now. I keep coming out swinging, but my arms are getting tired. I'm not sure how much more fight I have in me when it seems all I do is face-plant into a heaping pile of failure.

I grip my quill as my eyes dart around the room again. I usually feel the watchful weight of people looking at me, curious about the new Liminal, but everyone is actually otherwise occupied for once and not concentrating on me. Some are skimming their textbooks, others are watching the professor write, and some whisper among themselves.

It's the first time I haven't had multiple sets of eyes on me with rampant conspiracy theories being thrown about, whispered behind their hands. For someone who strives not to be the center of attention, I've somehow landed on the highest pedestal of public judgment.

I had the audacity to be *different.*

People don't like different.

It scares them.

And when they become fearful, they act rashly and judgmentally.

A prickling sensation burns its way up the back of my neck. As subtly as possible, I turn my head to the right, pretending to look out the window. Out of the corner of my eye, the only thing I see is a female student scribbling furiously into her notepad, not paying me a lick of attention.

The wooden chair groans slightly when I turn back around. The suffocating feeling of being dissected under a stare still wraps itself around me. One thing an introvert knows is when they are on someone's radar. Ninety-nine percent of the time, it's unwanted, and we'll do anything to prevent it.

Throwing away all pretenses at this point, I turn in the opposite direction from before and look directly behind me. An impassive face that could pass for stone for all its sharp angles and edges stares back at me. He doesn't even attempt to look away, just remains casually leaning back in his chair with his dumb, muscular arms folded across his chest. His glare is brazen as he looks at me without an ounce of self-doubt or apologies.

I wonder what it's like to be so self-assured all the time.

"You're late," he mouths.

I reply in the only logical way there is.

I lift my middle finger and top it off with a sardonic smirk.

His dark brow lifts in response.

"I hope everyone has their books out and open on their desks," the professor warns, still writing on the blackboard.

Kingston twirls his finger in the universal sign for "turn around."

With an exaggerated eye roll, I turn in my seat. Not because he told me to, but because the last thing I want to do is get on the professor's bad side on day one.

The guy next to me continues to bounce his knee. It's extremely distracting, but I try to focus on the stern-looking professor as she turns and faces the class. She doesn't make use of her podium. Instead, she walks back and forth as she speaks. Her inklike professor robes swish in a theatrical way each time she stops and turns to walk in the opposite direction.

"As you know, some of your peers are just being exposed to this class, while others have prior experience. This is what we call a mixed-level course, filled with students from first year all the way to fourth," she says while tapping the chalk in her hand.

I discreetly look around, and while some students are in their black fighting leathers, others are in their academy-issued standard uniforms. The one leniency Kintoira offers is that you can wear whichever assigned attire you want as long as it's assigned. The ones in uniform have varying grade levels embroidered on their shoulders, from one line to four lines.

I absentmindedly rub the singular line sewn into my right shoulder.

"As you've been told, this is a lecture course but leans heavily on the interactive side. Student engagement is a large portion of your grade as well as class participation."

Kill me now.

The overly friendly smile lingering on her pear-shaped face causes a sense of suspicion and dread to creep its way into my gut. A smile like that is never good news. I'm not the only one she's making nervous. Multiple classmates stir in their seats or make knowing eye contact with a friend.

She finally drops the smile and, without missing a beat, delivers the punch line. "Another thing you will be happy to know is that you won't suffer alone. As Noctryns, we tend to be self-efficient and loathe relying on others." Her arms sweep wide, and a faint dusting of chalk clings to her sleeve. "However, this is something that must be accepted to be victorious in battle. Which is why, this year in my class, we will be working in pairs," she says, her stern tone changing to an almost cheerful pitch.

Murmurs break out across the rows as people start claiming their prospective partner.

The loud rhythmic beat of clapping hands silences all noise. Professor Rinkin stands with both of her hands still pressed together in the air, looking at us like we're misbehaved children. "You will not be with someone of the same year. Upperclassmen have much to teach the lower classes, but do not sell yourself short, first and second-years. You can remind them that they don't know everything."

I'd rather run naked through a briar patch than be assigned to group work. I've always done better working on my own, and I don't see that changing anytime soon.

Fidgety guy next to me is already looking at a blond girl across the way, so there goes that chance. Shame.

He could have bounced the shadows right out of himself.

The professor slowly crosses her arms, waiting for the voices to die down. "I should also mention that not only do I have you working in pairs, but I also assign them."

A collective groan fills the room, causing her overly bright smile to reappear.

"Yes, I thought you might like that little tidbit, which is why I saved it for last. Now, for the fun part. Finding out who your partner is for the remainder of the year," she says, smiling coyly. "However, I should warn those who are new to the class, shadow welding is an exhausting process for those just starting and will bring forth character traits you didn't even know you possess." She walks to the podium, running a finger along the spine of a text. "To do this with a partner can be very intimate on so many levels. You will show your partner a vulnerability that not many, if any, will ever bear witness to. Once you perfect the craft, your vulnerabilities become your weaknesses, so you hold them close to your chest." Her eyes bore into us. "Noctryns do not submit. Ever."

Well, that should be easy to work with. I've been taught since birth that to show weakness is to show defeat.

Submission isn't even in my vocabulary.

The professor sets the chalk on the podium and stands there, her hands now steepled as she looks us over. "Row one, turn to the person sitting directly behind you in row two, and introduce yourself to your new partner. Row three all the way to row seven, follow suit."

I'm in row seven.

Fucking fantastic.

Everyone else is busy turning around or meeting the person sitting in front of them.

Not me.

Nope.

My eyes are glued to page 43 of my book. The words and images blur together because I'm not even focused on them, but I refuse to turn around.

I feel him reach forward and grab the tips of the hair hanging down my back. His long, deft fingers casually proceed to twirl them in circles.

"Looks like it's you and me, *Heathen*."

I spin quickly in my chair and come face-to-face with my new nemesis.

His lips are much closer than they should be. So close that if I leaned forward even an inch, mine would be pressed right up against his. His eyes are a contradiction. They're warm like burnt honey but cold and calculating. It's as if the gods messed up when they put him together, but in the most beautiful ways.

His beauty almost hides his cruelty. *Almost.*

He doesn't pull back, but to my credit, neither do I. We're at an impasse, a battle of wills neither of us wants to lose.

I honestly don't even know how we got here.

"My name is Nori," I say through my teeth.

"I like Heathen better. It suits you more," he replies. Elongated canines peek beneath the edges of his unkind smile.

I've heard stories about certain dark wielders who dug just a little too deep into the darkness and lost human aspects of themselves. It strips something from them. It tears away the tether that connects them to their humanity, piece by piece, until they're more animal than man.

It gives him an even more lethal edge to his already deviant, unapproachable appearance.

I click my tongue, trying to appear unimpressed. "You know," I say casually, "you feel familiar for some reason."

He raises an eyebrow, not rising to the bait.

"It's almost like I've hated you in more than just one lifetime," I say, my tone calm but just taunting enough to push for a reaction.

He doesn't give me one. The bastard is unflappable.

He smirks without saying a word, just enough to provoke me.

I narrow my eyes at him, imagining all the ways I want to cause him bodily harm, before slowly turning back around. How this man causes my ire to rise so effortlessly is beyond me. I'm usually better at letting the bullshit roll off my shoulders.

We don't even know each other for goodness sake.

I rub my temples and pray for patience. At least we don't have to partner up today.

We go over a few sections in the book before she proceeds to explain how shadow wielding comes from within the cortex of our being. Basically, the dark energy that we consist of creates vibrations through electromagnetic fields and gamma brainwaves, resulting in shadows. The formula of numbers and letters on the board is the supposed key to finding our footing and getting the process started.

In other words, I have absolutely no fucking idea what's going on.

Chapter Fourteen

The rest of the day is pretty uneventful.

Finnley and I sit through Runes and Wards together with matching thousand-yard stares. I wasn't able to join Mallory and Mayline in Apothecary, one of the few mixed classes where Veils and Noctryns attend together. There was a slight mix-up in my schedule that had to be adjusted.

I use the term *mixed* lightly, as the latter sits on one side and the Veils on the other.

The rest of our classes were canceled for the day due to the Blood Initiation Ceremony, which is the formal name for our commencement ceremony. The final step in pledging our lives and powers to Salaryan. No one but those who have already experienced it knows exactly what to expect during the ritual beyond the obvious. Blood will be taken from each first-year. It's a big event at Kintoira Academy, and all the upperclassmen are supposed to attend in full battle gear. I'm guessing that's some kind of way to dress formally for the event, but that hasn't been confirmed.

After we swear fealty by blood, we are fully locked in.

Forever indebted to the realm.

Servants for battle.

I glance down at myself. The gray uniform hangs loosely and unflattering on my frame. I look about as threatening as a midge, probably less dangerous. The woman staring back at me looks so young with her wide-angled eyes full of hesitation and hope. How can I look one way but feel an entirely different way?

I feel so much older than what my reflection offers.

My hands remain steady as I smooth down the front of my shirt before sliding my arms into the coal-colored robe. I carefully pull the hood up and over my head. The door shuts quietly behind me, and the only sound heard is the lock clicking into place.

Can't be too careful these days. They may not trust me, but I don't trust them either.

I make my way down the hall, flittering between passing students and keeping my eyes averted. I told Finnley and Mallory that I'd meet them in the main lobby, and we could walk to the ceremonial hall together. I was able to see Ambrose during lunch, but his attention was diverted in multiple directions by people in his bracket. It's like someone always needs him for something, a problem always needs to be resolved, and he's the only one who can do it. I won't be able to see him again before the ceremony.

He's in his officer's class now, and they never get released early. Ever.

I was hoping to have a little more time with him without distractions, but it doesn't seem to be on today's agenda.

Same story, different day.

The stairwell is tight as I squeeze through students coming and going. I keep my head down as I shuffle through them. As soon as my feet hit the landing, I make my way to the far corner of the foyer and sink into an antique-looking chair lined with awful green velvet fabric.

I lower my head into my hands and stare at the ground. Nerves dance in my stomach like butterflies taking flight. Once I give my blood, the remainder of my life is no longer mine. It belongs to the realm until the day my body becomes dirt. Probably even after that.

That's a heavy commitment.

Although, to be honest, it's too late in the game to change my mind now anyway. Not that I would, but to have the choice off the table is a little daunting.

The heavy steel doors to my left swing open, allowing students to step through, along with the breath of the bitter cold. A handful of Noctryns make their way over to the hearth to warm their hands, causing two Veils standing in front of the flames to turn up their noses and retreat down the hall. They must be coming in from field training to bear witness to our pledge.

I tuck my head back down and stare at my feet, tapping them in rhythm to the loud tempo of the heartbeat echoing in my ears. A dark pair of armored legs comes into view, followed by an exaggerated sigh.

"You'd make a shit spy, Caderyn," Makon mocks in a disappointed voice.

I don't even have to look up to know it's him. Only one person can sound that instigating with a simple sentence.

"And you make a shit mind reader. It should be blaringly obvious that I want to be left alone," I counter in an annoyed tone.

He taps his helmet against his leg, causing the metal to clink together. "Well, considering I can't read minds, it would make sense I didn't know," he says dryly. "And considering you're staring at the floor, I certainly can't read any social cues you might be giving off," he adds.

I lift my head and meet his amused expression.

"I guess I just assumed since your brother could, that you could as well," I answer sardonically. "Read minds that is."

He nods his head in a sympathetic gesture of understanding. It's clearly brimming with mockery. "Well, you know what they say about assumptions. Besides, there's a lot Kingston does that most of us cannot or will not do." At my confused expression, he continues, "The cost is too high."

Without another word, he turns to leave as if the conversation is done. I don't know why, but I don't want it to be finished. I want to know more about his brooding brother.

Color me surprised as well.

"So are you guys twins or something? Fraternal, possibly?" I ask.

He turns back around, tilting his head, a slight grin playing along his lips. "Yes and no."

"Care to explain?"

"No," he answers flatly. But his eyes don't match his tone. They're filled with mirth and mayhem.

It's odd how similar the brothers are to each other, but also strikingly different. Same dark hair, complexion, and menacing good looks, but that's about where the similarities end. Where Makon is feral, spontaneous, and impulsive, his brother is rigid, cold, and calculating. They certainly don't act like twins, but they are in the same year at the academy, so, they're close in age if not born on the same day.

My attention is diverted from Makon and directed toward the stairs where Finnley and Mallory are making their way down, arms waving in unison in my direction.

So much for remaining discreet.

The Noctryns idling by the hearth are suddenly invested as well, looking from my friends' flailing arms back to me. Their eyes are filled with contempt, but I don't miss the lingering curiosity as well.

"That's my cue. See you at the ceremony," Makon says as he tips his head in my direction, walking away, his helmet gripped loosely in his hand.

Mallory is all but dragging Finnley across the lobby toward me. He rolls his eyes but makes no move to stop her. I've noticed he humors her a lot. Her hair is in the usual style she favors, but bright blonde today, almost silver. Her delicate features are covered in heavy smoky makeup, giving her the appearance of a Gothic queen.

"We're about to be legit," she shrieks in a high-pitched tone, jumping up and down while hanging onto Finnley's arm. His body follows suit like a puppet on strings.

"I've never met anyone so excited to donate their blood," Finnley says in a dry tone.

I quirk a brow in her direction. "Especially when they have no idea just how much we're obligated to give."

She stops bouncing and drops his arm, staring at both of us. "Way to ruin the excitement," she states before a scowl settles over her face. Life is like a big celebration for her. She finds the positive in everything.

Leave it to me to disillusion her.

There is only black and white in life. No in-between. Which is rather ironic, I know, considering I'm fully clothed in shades of gray and labeled as a Liminal.

I stand up, securing my hood back in place, and follow a sulking Mallory.

Finnley gives me a wink before falling into step next to me. The atmosphere is thick with anticipation of the unknown. Students move in unison toward the ceremonial hall, setting the pace for what's to come.

The passageway stretches long, and the stone walls are lined with antique looking candelabras. The flames flicker restlessly, highlighting the soot-covered pictures of old families and long-forgotten professors that decorate the walls. Our footsteps echo against the rough stones, a steady rhythm made soft by being swallowed by vaulted ceilings.

The air is heavy. Scented wax, anxiety and something slightly metallic surround us. It feels as if the hallway itself is watching, waiting.

I keep my face forward. Every breath I take feels forced and full of tension, the kind that makes you feel like throwing up.

Voices and laughter echo off the walls as we enter through the double doors into a ginormous chamber. Mallory gasps, and I can't blame her. It is breathtaking. It's three times the size of the dining hall. If I could sum up the vibe in minimal words, it would be Gothic grandeur. The floor is made of polished onyx marble.

Rows upon rows of dark mahogany pews fill each side of the room. A large wooden dais sits in the center with a dramatic backdrop of dozens of lanterns hanging from the ceiling, amber flames flickering within. Forty bronze-trimmed armchairs fit across the dais with room to spare. That's how massive it is.

Another nice touch is the hundreds of candles scattered throughout, adding to the mysteriously romantic vibe. It's like a vampire's wet dream.

The pews are filling up fast as we make our way down the center aisle and head toward the armchairs. Multiple seats are already taken by the time we climb the few steps and choose three chairs next to each other.

Finley sits down heavily and begins tapping his fingers along the armrest. "Well, this is cozy," he drawls.

A soft laugh slips free. I'm thankful for him trying to break the tension we all feel.

"By all means, keep ruining the moment," Mallory says from her seat in a sarcastic quip, but even her eyes have taken on an apprehensive look.

Anxiety settles in as I gaze across the sea of students in the pews. One side is completely black—all the Noctryns are decked out in full battle gear, including helmets. You can't tell one from the other. The other side is filled with Veils, also fully clothed in their own variation of battle gear. Dark brown ballistic vests cover each wielder's chest, leather gauntlets cover their wrists and forearms, and sinister hoods obscure their faces. They look like lethal assassins.

Both sides are fully armed.

Almost as if he's reading my thoughts, Finnley leans over and whispers, "Do you find it somewhat alarming that everyone, besides us, is armed to the teeth?"

I nod slowly. "Slightly."

The left side of the room is stiff and silent. Their helmed faces point in our direction as if we're not the guests of honor but something not to be trusted. The right side sits just as rigid but whispers among themselves, adding a layer of humanity to their bracket.

I allow my eyes to roam over the figures, searching for the one who resembles Ambrose.

He's here, I know it.

I can feel him in this room.

I notice Finnley turning his head toward me out of my peripheral vision. I halt my desperate search and face him. His brows are furrowed, and he gives me a sad smile. "You think he's here?"

"I hope so," I say.

It's hard to pinpoint for sure, though, since everyone looks so uniform. If it wasn't blatantly obvious that this place doesn't favor individualism by the way I've been treated since my test came back inconclusive, the student's attire would be a dead giveaway. It could be a battle tactic, but something in me says it's a bit more to do with snuffing out anyone and anything that can't be controlled.

I'll save that for another day, though.

A few of the Veils in the middle rows are on the smaller side. Most likely the women. All of the others are roughly the same size, making any form of identification damn near impossible.

I pull the hem of my sleeve over my palm. The small gesture makes me feel safe. I feel like I'm being inspected under a microscope, sitting up here under the glare of my peers. It's not a great feeling.

Sitting rigidly in my chair, I curl my hands in my lap, the weight of the ceremonial hall pressing down on me. A few chairs are still waiting to be filled on the dais. The rest of us who are already here just wait and squirm in anticipation.

I glance over at the Noctryns. I know without a doubt that *asshole* is somewhere in the crowd. The one who seems to get his only enjoyment in life out of pestering me. I'm still not sure how I won that honorary position, but it's been bestowed upon me, nonetheless. Benefits of being friends with Ambrose, I guess.

There's no way Kingston would miss a chance to see people bleed. Or be uncomfortable.

The air feels expectant, charged with what is to come. I let my gaze continue to linger over the sea of black as the identical helmed bodies watch us from their seats. A unit of duplicated dark executioners.

A couple have twin swords strapped to their backs, so that isn't exactly telling when trying to pinpoint an identity with weapon choice. The only similarity between the two regiments in front of me is the sheer number of weapons.

Even the Veils are heavily armed today.

Something about the Noctryn sitting in the third row stands out from his cohorts. It's in the way he holds himself. Rigid like the rest, but an air of detachment clings to him, almost as if his guard isn't truly up because nothing in his vicinity is threatening enough for it.

Don't get me wrong, I'm all for a good game of cat and mouse, but I'm not sure I want to play that with him for the next three years. That's a game you play with someone who draws a line in the sand and has limits. I don't think either would pertain to him, and that's risky.

Even for me.

I pull my stare away and instead zone in on my foot tapping uncontrollably under the pressure of nerves. I'm so glad I skipped lunch, or it would be threatening to join us during this little bloodletting session. In all seriousness, they can't take too much of our blood, right? I mean, it's probably just a prick to the thumb for a drop.

Although from the importance placed on this ceremony and the fact that everyone is decked out in full body armor, I'm beginning to wonder exactly what they expect to happen.

The last of the first-years pass in front of us, taking their seats, followed swiftly by the professors walking in through the double doors, heads bowed. Their ceremonial mantels drag along the floor behind them. Not a single face isn't completely obscured by the decorative hoods, adding a layer of anonymity but also aligning nicely with the Gothic vibe of this entire scenario.

The heavy layer of secrecy this event is cloaked in makes it feel slightly ritualistic in a macabre sense.

I immediately force my leg still and casually look down the row at the other first-years. Even without being able to see their profiles, the tension is evident in their body gestures. Even Finnley, who is unflappable, is cracking his knuckles one by one.

Pain rests in my palms as my nails dig into the soft flesh. The discomfort helps ground me in the present and reminds me I've gotten this far and have survived worse. I hope in a few moments, I still believe this.

All of the professors take their seats in rows one and two. All except one. That professor walks to the side of the dais and picks up a small pillar that looks to be made of bloodstone. This particular stone is named for the dark rust hue it favors, and its many uses in the art of blood magic. He or she walks it to the center, almost directly in front of Mallory, and places it down before walking back to their seat.

We all stare at the pillar. I very much doubt any of us are breathing at this point.

The silence is deafening.

Footsteps break the tension, sounding somewhere down the hall, growing louder as they approach. Every person on the dais swivels toward the door, but not one person in the audience turns around. They remain as still as statues staring forward.

Any saliva or moisture that was in my mouth is now gone.

I'm nerve parched.

I gingerly move my tongue around, trying to create some lubricant, but it's just not happening. I'm also hyper-aware of everything right now in a way that's borderline uncomfortable. The fire crackling in the lanterns, the metal clinking as a sword shifts in its scabbard, and chairs wobbling on the dais.

When the steps are near enough that I know they will be turning the corner any moment, I scoot forward in my seat a little. It's as if my body knows it's about to have to decide between fight or flight. I'd like to think I'd be a fighter, but no one ever really knows until they're put in the situation.

Most don't like what they discover.

A looming figure rounds the corner dressed in iridescent robes, their face completely obscured by a matching hood. As beautiful as the attire is, that's not what holds my attention. The object in their hands is what captivates me. It's a sizable goblet that looks to be made of antique gold, with a black serpent wrapped around the stem. A very much alive serpent whose tongue keeps flickering in and out. They are carrying the crest of Kintoira Academy.

The very same crest that has been associated with the heaviest and most deadly black magic on the continent.

Holy shit.

I slide back in my seat, warily watching them approach.

The swishing of their robes can be heard throughout the vast hall as they climb the few stairs and make their way to the pillar. With the utmost care, they set the goblet on top before briskly turning around and leaving the way they came.

"That's a large cup. Looks like it can hold a lot of blood," Finnley whispers out of the side of his mouth.

I shoot him a look of incredulity. That is the last thing I want to hear right now. He's not wrong, but still. There's a time and place and this sure as shit is not it.

A different professor from the previous one stands in the front row and walks toward us. Once they reach the golden goblet, they caress the serpent's head, face the audience, and address them in a commanding voice.

The answering silence amplifies it.

"The day has come. The sacred blood initiation is upon us," the masculine voice states. "These cadets have fought their way through both mental and physical trials. Their worth has been measured in blood. Today, they will pledge their oath in that very same blood. They will be joined through their offering. Lifeblood and consent mix together to satisfy the union of the participant and Salaryan's military until the day they take their last breath." He threads his fingers together, head dipped low to maintain the anonymity. "Through every milestone in life, from marriage to births to old age, their duty to the realm will always come first."

There's that heavy commitment again.

I know all about it. Even at this very moment, my mother is on some covert mission. I haven't seen her in months, which, let's be honest, is probably a good thing. I've had fewer chances to do something disappointing in her eyes. But I've been ready to make this choice my entire life, regardless of what it costs me. I'll pay the price.

The professor holds his arms out to his sides in a grand gesture, slowly turning to address both units in the audience. "These cadets will become your brothers and sisters in arms. They will suffer alongside you as well as succeed by your side. Your loss is their loss. Their gain is your gain. This is the moment that they offer their sacrifice and loyalty to the military and General Porter."

I press my lips into a thin line.

I was wondering when we'd be hearing his name. The infamous five-star general who runs Salaryan with an iron fist. I've heard that his family has been doing so for centuries. In this land, he is judge, jury, and executioner. However, in his eyes, he's more comparable to an untouchable god.

I'm pretty sure he still bleeds. So, more of a narcissist than a god, really.

The only person worse than him whom I've been unfortunate enough to meet on several occasions is his right-hand man, Prime Minister Henderson. A greasy, scheming, and wholly untrustworthy specimen. Hopefully, we're spared from them making an appearance today. It's unlikely, as cadets at the academy fall pretty low on the priorities of high-ranking officials. *Especially* those two.

Finally, the professor turns around to address us, his face partially obscured and only the bottom half of his jawline visible. Thin lips atop a weak chin are the only indication we have of his appearance. Depending on his next actions, you can bet your ass that I'll be looking at every single one of my professor's lower jaws in the near future.

"I will call you up one by one for you to perform your blood offering. Once everyone has joined their blood into the goblet, we will move on to the next crucial step."

He steps to the side of the pillar, making room for a first-year to join.

I throw up a silent prayer of gratitude that we sat in the middle. It gives me a chance to prepare for exactly what we're offering. They haven't been very forthcoming about that part.

"We'll start in the middle and work our way down one side, then the other," he says as he points at me.

Of course we're starting in the middle.

Why wouldn't we start in the middle?

He folds his hands in front of his stomach as he waits for me to rise. I won't give him the satisfaction of hesitating.

I stand and slowly walk toward him. I don't look at my friends, though, afraid of what I'll see on their faces. My steps are deliberate as I walk and stop directly across from him on the other side of the goblet.

This is where I'll stand and bleed for tradition.

I cautiously peer down.

It's empty, and the morbid part of my brain wonders how much blood it would take to fill it. The serpent remains still, ready to strike.

I take a deep breath as he raises his hand, gesturing for mine.

Slowly, I bring it up and set it into his waiting palm. His firm, cool grip is a stark contrast to my damp, sweaty one. His other hand reaches into his deep cloak pocket and pulls out a crimson-colored dagger about the size of my forearm. The lethal tip hovers above my upturned wrist. Dark blue veins stand out against my pale skin, and I fear they act as a beacon for his weapon. It's as if they are offering themselves as tribute.

No one speaks.

The scrape of a boot against the stone floor reaches my ears, a stark contrast to the otherwise silent hall. I can feel a low, pulsing strain running through the students in the pews—part reverence, part hunger—as all eyes are fixed on me.

I bite down on the inside of my lip, forcing myself to hold still and not show any signs of the fear permeating through my entire body. I doubt anyone wants to be willingly cut open, but add an audience and it becomes exponentially more terrifying, for some reason.

It's a vulnerable feeling of being violated for entertainment.

The professor's lips pull into a sinister smile right before he starts speaking in a language I don't recognize or understand. The words are rapid and harsh. The tip of the knife presses into my wrist, but it has yet to draw any blood. He continues speaking in the foreign language, while squeezing my wrist in his beefy palm.

My breaths come out in rapid bursts as if the very air I'm breathing is painful, but I don't pull my wrist away, and I don't squirm.

My stomach churns.

A drop of sweat slides down my back.

I feel everyone staring at me.

He continues to speak in that eerie dialect, but it's starting to sound more like a chant than unknown words at this point. If evil had a sound, this would be it.

The tip of the knife presses deeper, digging into the soft flesh and bringing forth a reluctant wince from my lips. A drop of blood appears, and I know without a doubt his pupils are fully blown under his hood.

This doesn't feel like a ceremony. It feels like an execution.

Every muscle in my body tightens as I clench my teeth to keep from crying out in pain. I won't give him that. Fuck him and every single person who thought I'd never make it this far. I made it. And I'll be damned if I give them anything more to take from me.

Revulsion coats my spine as his tongue darts out to lick his bottom lip, almost as if he's getting extreme satisfaction from the pain being inflicted.

He probably is.

Sick fuck.

Without removing the pressure from his grip, he makes a long gash and swiftly flips my wrist over, allowing the blood to flow into the bottom of the basin. The drops hit the metal like a farewell to my independence.

My teeth sink into my lip as he digs his fingers into the sides of the cut, encouraging more blood to be produced. As if I'm not already giving enough.

The chanting continues as my eyes grow heavy, and dizziness washes over me. Between the loss of blood, the diminishing adrenaline rush, and the odd verbiage he's spewing, I'm feeling weak. And so, so tired. I let my eyes flutter closed. If I can just rest for a minute, the pain will subside, and I'll feel better. I can regain my bearings.

I hear the rustle of a cloak. "It's too soon for that. You'll miss what's to come," the professor whispers in a foreboding tone.

The coolness of damp fabric being draped over my fresh injury forces me to pry my eyes open, the heaviness making it difficult. Something sweet and spicy hits my nostrils.

Yarrow.

A favorite of healers to treat battle wounds.

Without further ado, he pushes me back toward my seat and calls up the next willing participant. Finnley's hood is pushed back just enough that I can see the anger marking his features as he walks by, along with something else in his stormy eyes. I'm too mentally tapped to pinpoint what, but it's there.

There's more to these unknown words being spoken than they're letting on. I feel as if I've been drugged. My head lolls for a moment, vision swimming in slow motion. It's as if I'm witnessing the remainder of the ceremony through haze-filled eyes.

I struggle to watch Finnley go through the ritual, but time isn't moving correctly anymore. One second, he's walking toward the goblet, I blink, and he's returning to his seat. I drag my uncooperative eyes to him to offer support in any way I can, even if it's an understanding look, but he's staring straight ahead.

I accept at the moment that we're all fucked. I give up on trying to communicate with him. Instead, I preserve my remaining energy.

The ritual concludes in what seems like rapid succession after everyone has provided their offering. I'm sure the goblet is now close to overflowing with our "lifeblood and consent." The robbed fiend turns back toward the audience, his form swaying in my vision. My fingers twitch uselessly, and my limbs feel boneless.

"We have our offering. Now the removals begin," he says, spreading his arms wide. "At attention!" he orders in a stern voice while clapping his hands in front of his face. "Weapons ready."

Weapons ready?

The fuck?

I vigorously rub my eyes, trying to clear them, but everything is still so fuzzy.

Finnley attempts to stand but loses his balance and crashes back into his chair. Muffled curses fly out of his mouth, but he doesn't attempt to stand again.

My eyes dart to a hooded Veil walking closer to the dais as the rest spread out through the hall in strict military formation. The Noctryns appear to walk more casually toward random places.

I follow the Veil's approach with weary eyes as he makes his way toward us. The surrounding candlelight bleeds into gold halos, and spots dance in my vision. His steps are predatory, and he's heading directly toward me. His head is bowed, and his hood is pulled low enough to maintain anonymity.

A throwing axe rests in his hand.

Without thinking, I reach for Finnley. The moment my fingers brush against the side of his palm, an axe lands directly at my feet. I jerk my hand back and look in the direction it came from. The Veil's head is tilted to the side in a menacing way as if daring me to reach for his hand again.

I reach for Finnley's hand again because *fuck him*.

One second, I have a grip on his pinky finger, and the next, I'm being hauled to my feet, spun around, and my arms pinned securely behind my back. The room immediately spins on its axis, causing my stomach to do somersaults.

Through the nausea and dizziness, my eyes land on a Noctryn directly in the back. Shadows swirl around him in violent tendrils. It appears as if he takes a step forward but halts when the professor's austere voice rings out again.

"Cadets, as the voicebounds come down the line, you will drink from their chalice. Be greedy. Don't leave a drop," he says in the same foreboding tone he's carried throughout the ceremony. The directions wash over me in their abruptness. I want to refuse, but I'm borderline delirious.

Voicebound is just a fancy word for prisoner. Their voices were robbed from them both figuratively and literally as they're imprisoned to serve for a crime they've been accused of. Accused being the main word. There is no such thing as a fair trial when the verdict has already been decided.

They trickle in one by one in a single file line, heads bowed, and hands cuffed in front of them. Each holds a small black cup in their grip. The Veil at my back presses flush up against me. I can hear his breaths and feel the rise and fall of his chest synchronizing with each intake. Could it be

Ambrose? I would know right away if it was him, wouldn't I? I can't think clearly enough to work it out.

What would generally be akin to breathing is now an impossible puzzle. I could typically pick him out of a hundred men while blindfolded, but all of my senses have been diminished to the point of being useless. My mind feels like my head is being held underwater and severely oxygen-deprived.

A voicebound stops in front of each of us, head down and hands held out.

"Drink up, cadets," the smarmy professor instructs from somewhere close by.

We're meant to reach out and take the small chalice and drink, but both of my hands are currently being held captive behind me in an unforgiving grip. A grip that screams punishment for my defiance. The captor at my back seems to realize this at the same time and moves both of my wrists into one large hand, his other taking the drink from the worn-down-looking female.

Dirty-blonde hair hangs in front of her downcast eyes. Her lips are chapped and scabbed over from extreme dehydration, and her prison uniform is threadbare.

The brute at my back holds the small cup in his large hand, tilting my chin up and gently pressing it to my lips. "Drink," he whispers.

Goose bumps race up my arms.

The thought that hits me first is how incredibly intimate the gesture is. I consider defying him for a second, but he would probably just waterboard me with it instead.

I slowly do as told and sip the warm liquid. It has a faint earthy smell and a smoky taste as it goes down. I swallow all of it and lean back into the Veil's chest.

He leans close to my ear. "Good girl," he murmurs.

I rest my entire body weight against him because at this point he's all but holding me up. Surprisingly, he doesn't say anything and just allows me to settle in.

"Battle stances," a deep voice calls out.

The Veil at my back doesn't move into a battle stance but remains standing stoically behind me. I thought Veils were sticklers for following orders, but apparently not this one.

At first, I feel nothing. Just the continued hazy feeling that portrays the room as spinning, and an overly smoky taste that lingers in my mouth. Then it slowly morphs into a rapid burn licking along my ribs. Not pain but heat—raw and palpable.

It doesn't happen quickly. It's more like a rising inferno. Slow and steady. The room gradually fractures around me, and my vision explodes into white-hot fury as the heat spreads throughout my body. I feel like I'm burning from the inside out.

I collapse to my knees, my hands clawing at the ground searching for salvation that isn't coming. My breaths come in ragged gasps between the screams that tear from my throat. The heat becomes a burn that mutates into liquid molten, replacing the blood in my veins.

Pain. Immeasurable, indescribable pain.

A scream tears from my throat.

I fall to my side in convulsions, my spine twisted. Something has begun, and I honestly don't care if I survive it.

In fact, I pray for death.

Beg for it.

Salvation. An end to the torment.

Whatever they had us drink wasn't meant to heal or enhance. It was meant to remake. I scream for what feels like hours, maybe days. My throat is raw from it. That and from begging for death to claim me. I have no idea how long the agony lasts, but eventually, it subsides enough for me to peel my eyes open.

Death didn't listen to my pleas. It typically doesn't. The ceremonial hall is still here, along with all the key players.

My world was ripped apart vessel by vessel, but nothing changed in theirs. The Veil remains standing rigidly in front of me, looking down upon my broken body, both of his hands curled into fists.

"Get ready...They're starting to emerge," a low and steady voice rings out.

The sound of weapons being drawn echoes around us. Groans of agony come from both sides of where I lie. What threat could we possibly pose? We're all indisposed at the moment, and even at our best, we couldn't compete with upperclassmen or professors.

A shrill scream pierces the air and collides with the bellows of a man in agony.

I raise my weary head to look in their direction. The student is hunched over, pulling at his hair as if he's trying to tear it from his scalp.

I blink slowly.

I must be hallucinating. His form elongates, his fingers transform into claws, and black scales emerge across his body, replacing flesh. He raises his head to roar, throwing his chair across the room in the process. I freeze at the sight of his raging red eyes darting over the heads of the upperclassmen who have their weapons drawn and ready to return any kind of attack.

The shrieking of a female, hunched over, arms cradling her stomach, draws the beast's attention. He turns and tears toward her in a full gallop, his claws shredding the wooden dais. A dagger is thrown from the left, lodging in his hind leg, but he doesn't falter. He grabs the shrieking cadet, his teeth tearing into her neck.

Blood sprays across his face. She frantically grabs his head, and ice starts to coat his entire body.

Chaos erupts all around.

Complete and utter pandemonium.

Veils are forcing cadets to the ground left and right as their powers erupt in uncontrollable anarchy. Noctryns throw daggers and unleash shadows with lethal precision. A first-year close by screams as shadows erupt from his hands, and his body contorts in an unnatural angle.

The professors linger in the back, arms folded, just watching the mayhem unfold. Sentinels relishing the unraveling order they're meant to control.

I shake my head to try to clear it.

It's absolute anarchy in here.

I call out to Mallory as she thrashes on the floor, her hands clutching her head, but my voice cracks, and sound refuses to come out. Finnley remains in his chair staring straight ahead, but his eyes are vacant. Mayline rushes over, grabbing onto Mallory's hand. Shadows ripple around her, but not in a disorderly way. She seems in control. Calm.

I try to rise on all fours, but my arms tremble, and my legs feel numb and hollow. Powers erupt and emerge around me, but the only thing I feel is my broken body. Nothing materializes from within.

I flinch and cover my head as a Noctryn tackles an initiate right next to me.

The student is bearing fangs and looking at me through bloodshot eyes like I'm their next meal. He writhes and screams beneath the dark wielder but is thoroughly subdued by the upperclassman. The Veil, standing guard over me, leans down and scoops me up in his arms. The familiar scent of a stormy tide washes over me.

Darkness coils at the edge of my vision.

The darkness isn't cruel or loud, and I gladly let it take me.

Chapter Fifteen

Expectations are high at the academy.

I've known that since before I enrolled. Yet to know it and to witness it are two different things.

Many are still nursing various injuries from the Blood Initiation Ceremony. Some from their first-year peers and others from the upperclassmen maintaining order. Even with the bodily damage and mental exhaustion, we're expected to attend our classes for the day.

First-years still have powers emerging at inconvenient times, which explains the multitude of upperclassmen pulled from their own classes to guard the hallways and lecture halls alike. Their expressions are stony and uncompromising. I still haven't figured out if they want us to succeed and join their ranks or fail so they can move on with their academic year without having to hover over us.

The chair legs wobble as I take my seat in another mixed class of both light and dark magic. This class is the one I look forward to the most. The one I know I'll excel at. It won't matter if I'm stuck between two worlds in this room. What's taught in this class has already been. The lessons learned over and over again, so they don't repeat themselves.

History.

The professor of the class walks in holding a stack of books balanced precariously under her chin. With the ease of someone who's done it a hundred times, she sets them on her desk without any falling from their designated place and moves over to the teaching podium.

She screams worn elegance. Unlike the other professors here, her robes have seen better days. Almost as if she couldn't be bothered to replace them. It doesn't seem to faze her though, as she regally pushes her slim-framed glasses up the bridge of her nose. It also doesn't escape my notice that her fingertips are ink-stained. More than likely from poring over pages of print in the archives. Her pale skin is a stark contrast to the pitch-black hair, bluntly resting on her shoulders. It's as if she has the pallor of something once buried. A mysterious aura surrounds her like a signature perfume.

I squeeze my quill and sit forward.

Every student in here is staring at her with rapt attention. I don't know anyone in here except Makon, and I made a point to sit as far from him as possible. I quickly jot down the professor's name inside my textbook as she introduces herself.

Professor Hawkins.

She looks around the class before continuing. "As you are all aware, yesterday was intense," she says in a soft but weighted tone. Agreement echoes across the rows. "I know some of you are still recovering and coming to terms with the many changes happening within your bodies." She glances over the ridge of her glasses as the faces stare back at her. "As I'm sure some of you have figured out, your birth blockers were removed once you drank from the chalices. Powers that should have gradually manifested over the past decade erupted full force within minutes. This is not only unnatural but beyond excruciating. For that, I apologize."

I put the pieces together while lying in bed last night. My body felt like it was collapsing in on itself, but my mind slowly became clearer as the effects of the drink wore off.

Our birth blockers are gone. Ripped from somewhere they never should have been. We now have full access to the powers we were assigned at birth, powers that should have begun to mature when we hit puberty. I should feel ecstatic. But I don't. I'm filled with trepidation and unease.

I'm a Liminal, and thus far, nothing has emerged. Not even a whisper of magic. It's not unheard of to have a slight delay, but there isn't much information on Liminals. What if I'm broken and have nothing to offer?

"How long until we have control over them?" a round-faced first-year asks from the front.

"That depends entirely on you," Professor Hawkins responds while pulling out a large text from under her podium. The book is so heavy that you can hear her exerted breathing while lifting it. It falls with a resounding thud against the podium as she wipes her hands on the front of her thin robes. Murmurs break out across the rows.

A hand shoots up in the air. "Are we going to be guarded like criminals until we can control them?" a girl with a tattoo covering half of her face asks.

"Possibly. That is entirely up to you as well."

The professor talks in riddles. Answering but not divulging.

I want so badly to ask about those of us who are still waiting. I don't, though. Not yet. I don't want to draw unnecessary attention to myself.

As if on cue, a book catches on fire a few rows down. The surprised first-year jumps back from his chair, desperately trying to fan it with his hands. The only thing he accomplishes is adding to its intensity. A Noctryn general, seated a few seats down from him, waves his hand without looking up from his text and diminishes the flames with his shadows.

The shaken Veil hesitantly retakes his seat, throwing cautious looks between his ruined text and the general, who's paying him no mind.

"Alright, everyone. Books out. Those who have not burned them, please flip to chapter one. We are going to start at the beginning," the professor says while opening her own text.

The first-year continues to stare at his burned text.

Her voice washes over the room as she discusses the history of Salaryan and the introduction of Kintoira Academy. I know most of everything she's reading out loud by heart, but still cling to it like a well-missed friend. We've been spoon-fed the rich history of this realm since we could walk. I've devoured everything taught with insatiable hunger.

I think, had I not chosen this path, I would have become a librarian or a historian. Instead of battlefields and weapons, it would have been quiet halls and dust-covered tomes.

Another first-year cries out in pain as his hands start to twitch with small bursts of shadows erupting. He looks around the room in panic as if someone can make it go away. Makon rolls his eyes in the seat next to him and whispers something under his breath while staring at the young man in clear agitation. One minute, the boy is in near hysterics, and the next, he's slumped over in his seat, unconscious.

I suck in a deep breath.

That easy. He rendered a man useless *that easy*.

His dark eyes meet mine from where he's sitting. He lifts a brow and blows me a kiss.

On anyone else, it would appear harmless, but between his lethal abilities and the wild appearance of war braids paired with his wicked facial scar, it comes across as menacing.

I force my gaze back down to my text.

I refuse to be baited.

Even if it was impressive as hell. I'll never admit that, though.

There aren't any more magical eruptions for the remainder of the class. Professor Hawkins thoroughly goes over every detail of the early years in the realm and the academy. When she closes her text and dismisses us, I quickly gather up my belongings and shove them in my pack. I have exactly five minutes to make it to my last class, and it's two floors up.

A looming shadow falls over my shoulder.

I should've known I couldn't escape without having to acknowledge his presence. I press my lips into a thin, tight line and peer up at him beneath my scowl.

"You're either avoiding me because my good looks intimidate you or because you still think you're not one of us," he says. "Let me guess, you still think you're a Veil."

Every syllable lands like a well-aimed smirk.

I stand to my full height and throw my pack over my shoulder. I don't have time for this. Craning my neck back, I look up to meet his eyes. "I *am* a Veil," I retort.

"Only you're not," he replies simply. I can hear the satisfaction in his voice. It's dripping with it.

"Why don't you pick on someone your own size?" a feminine voice quips from behind him.

His shoulders stiffen at the intrusion. He draws a hand across his mouth before slowly turning toward the newcomer. A silver-haired woman with a heart-shaped face and violet eyes stares back at him with a look that reeks of disdain. To say she's breathtaking would be criminally understated. To imply she is unimpressed with him would be woefully downplayed.

I don't personally know her. I've seen her a few times in passing and at meals, but she was typically by Yaretta's side. I made sure to keep my distance. I certainly didn't expect her to speak up on my behalf.

Makon circles her as a predator might when sizing up his prey. His thumb traces over his bottom lip as if he's contemplating all the ways to devour her, and none of them in the good way. "The thing is, I don't see anyone around here my size," he says in a condescending tone.

She scoffs under her breath, clearly unimpressed. "Then perhaps you should move along and look elsewhere." She raises a delicate brow at him and somehow looks down her nose at the same time. It's quite a feat, considering he's easily half a foot taller than she is.

"Perhaps you should stay out of conversations you're not invited into," he counters, his voice tight with annoyance.

I'd love to stay and see this play out, but I'm already late to class. I shuffle backward, discreetly working my way toward the door. I'm banking on the fact they're too wrapped up in their battle of wills to miss me. I hate leaving her in this predicament, but something tells me she can handle her own.

"What's your name, first-year?" he demands.

She chuckles softly. "I didn't hear you say please," she all but coos in his direction. Her lips are pulled into a contemptuous smirk aimed to antagonize and rile.

The provocateur might have met his match.

His eyes narrow slightly. "Doesn't matter. You're inconsequential."

She leans in close, invading his personal space. "Careful there, big guy, that's an awfully big word for such a small, ignorant mind."

A shadow of a smile curves over his mouth. "Was there something you wanted, or are you just naturally annoying?"

"There is definitely nothing here that I want." A small laugh breaks free from her lips before she runs her eyes down his body and up again. "Or need."

She pushes past him and toward me, throwing a wink in my direction.

His hardened eyes watch her disappear through the door. He doesn't even look at me, just continues to stare at the door she passed through.

I quickly take the opening and scurry through after her.

I make it to class with seconds to spare. Now that I'm here, I'm debating turning right around and leaving. The stale smell of sweat, old blood, and fear sinks into my bones. Padded floors, mirrored walls, and punching bags surround me. Weapons of every kind line the walls. Faint torchlight flickers from the wall sconces, casting the entire sparring room in menacing shadows. If there was any course that intimidates me, it's this one.

I rub my upper arms with a sinking feeling of trepidation.

Combat Practice.

First through fourth-years are gathered around the mats. They're dressed in varying uniforms. Some are in their standard issue, while others don their fighting leathers. A few third and fourth-years stand off to the side, wrapping their knuckles as they talk. A pair of second-years are on the center mat, throwing lethal punches. Their heavy breathing and fists meeting flesh can be heard from where I stand.

I swallow hard.

My eyes dart around the room, looking for a familiar face. Misery loves company and all that. Unfortunately, I don't recognize any faces. I don't know anyone here.

I haven't had time to compare schedules with Mallory or Finnley, and Ambrose is always MIA. It feels like I see him less now than I did in his first year at the academy, when we had literal cities separating us.

In fact, I haven't seen him since before the blood initiation took place, so I haven't been able to confirm my theory on who it was that held me while my world went dark. I'm so used to him catching me when I fall that I expect it to be him. I want it to be him. But I also don't want to set myself up for disappointment.

I glance around, not entirely sure where I'm supposed to be. Torchlight burns in wrought-iron sconces, casting shadows across the faces of the fighters. Some look nervous, others look excited. It's equal parts trial and lesson. The room thrums with barely constrained power.

Flickers of shadow emerge from the palm of a first-year standing close to me before he snuffs them out.

I step to the side a little.

I don't entirely trust him not to smother me with them by accident. Or let's be honest, on purpose. The Noctryns still aren't my number one fan.

Veils, either, for that matter.

I'm really killing it at the whole "fitting in" thing.

We stand off to the side waiting for instructions as we watch second through fourth-years battle it out. The sound of a fist meeting a jawline, followed by a grunt, reaches us from one of the sparring sessions close by.

I stand a little straighter as a handful of captains and majors walk our way, each signia standing out in stark contrast to their uniforms. A red C or M rests on each of their shoulders.

Two Veils and three Noctryns stop directly in front of us. Their eyes look us over.

Appraising.

Evaluating.

Judging.

A Veil with unruly hair and boyish features steps forward. "Hello, first-years. We'll be assigning you to your sparring partners," he says. His hands are clasped tightly behind his back while he paces in front of us. "Today is just an introduction to the course and what it has to offer. That being said, we'll be placing each of you with an upperclassman. Some will be placed with officers and others with peers."

Wonderful.

Not only am I not a strong fighter, but pair me with an experienced one and I'll be face-to-the-mat more often than not.

The major starts calling last names along with their sparring partners. "Porter with Wren." The general's son. I don't personally know him, but I've heard the rumors that he's just as slimy as his father. I wouldn't mind watching the match go down between him and Koa.

He steps forward, moving to his designated spot. He's on the shorter side with lanky limbs. Mousy blond hair and bland features make him completely forgettable.

"Vivinche with Ieilen," he calls out next.

The major continues to go down the line until it's just me and another first year.

"Caderyn and Adair," he says.

I lift my chin and step forward.

He jerks his head for me to follow a Noctryn captain standing to his left.

We pass by duos battling it out and walk around upperclassmen doling out instructions to first-years. He leads me to an area in the back, cloaked in low lighting and more secluded than the other training areas. A dark wielder rests on his knees while he wipes blood from his mouth. Another stands shirtless, his back facing us, while he quenches his thirst.

I immediately know who it is without even seeing his face.

His back ripples with muscle. Beads of sweat work their way down his trim waist. But it's the unapproachable air surrounding him that gives away the identity.

"Adair, your sparring partner is ready," the captain delivers before turning to leave.

The man on the mat rises from his knees and walks over to my new partner. They exchange a few words before he takes his leave as well.

We're all alone. Lucky me.

He tips his head back, taking another long drink before turning to face me.

Stoic.

Detached.

Indifferent.

His eyes give away nothing but take everything.

"Hello, *Heathen*," he says, walking toward me.

Kingston Adair.

Now I know his full name. I was probably better off not knowing it. Distance is safety with this one.

I stare at him defiantly. My mother didn't raise a woman who cowers. Even when defeat is the clear result, you must never show them weakness. They can take everything from you but not your pride. They can only obtain that if you willingly sacrifice it. Which I will not be doing.

He stares back without emotion. His eyes are more black than brown today. His full lips are set in a straight line devoid of any expression.

His mask of apathy is fully in place.

He's the kind of beautiful you run from without looking back.

The type that is statuesque and flawless.

The sinister and cold kind.

The kind that will leave you feeling empty as time goes on.

He lets those dark eyes roam over me, sizing me up. I feel stripped raw by a mere look. I'm not sure what it is he's searching for, but whatever it is, he seems to have found it. He turns on his heel and walks over to the corner, grabbing a black shirt and pulling it over his head and down his ripped abdomen.

Someone so cold shouldn't make me feel so warm. I instantly feel guilty. Like I committed some violation against the love I have for another.

It's just because I'm touch-starved at the moment.

It has nothing to do with the actual man.

His dark hair falls over his brow, thoroughly disheveled from his earlier fight. He walks back toward me, looking up at me from under his thick brow while he adjusts the wrappings on his hands. "Why are you here?" he demands.

I clench my fingers in annoyance. "The same reason I suspect you are. To manifest my powers and help protect Salaryan from those who wish it harm," I recite back in a clipped tone.

He crosses his arms over his chest. "Let me try again. Why are you here?" he repeats.

I square my shoulders and widen my stance. "Did I stutter?" I reply, my voice soft but cutting.

"Did I?" he retorts in a challenge, meeting my glare head-on.

"I'm here to be a soldier," I say with clear exasperation. "The same as every other student at this academy." It takes every ounce of my willpower not to break eye contact.

I get the feeling this is some kind of test, and I'm pretty sure I'm fucking it up.

Royally.

He stops directly in front of me. "That's the generic answer. I want the true answer," he says.

"Well, that's the only one I have to give."

"Your mother is a Veil," he says flatly. It's a statement, not a question.

"Yes, and your point is?" I bite out, frustration breaking through my tone.

He lifts a hand to his jaw, stroking it as if he's thinking about how to deliver the next blow. "She's made quite a reputation for herself. Created big shoes to fill. Valor, sacrifice, all of it. Tell me this, are you here to earn your own reputation or compete with hers?"

"Fuck you," I snarl.

"I thought we've established that you're not my type," he says coolly.

What an asshole.

"Are we going to spar or sit here and talk about our feelings? I can find another partner if needed."

"That won't be happening," he delivers with finality. "That easy. I got into your head that easily. The biggest aspect of being a solid fighter isn't in the physicality portion but resides in the mental part," he states, tapping the side of his head. "If you don't learn to control that facet, you will fail. Every. Single. Time."

I nod in understanding.

Point made.

Embarrassingly so.

He looks me up and down. "The first thing we're going to work on is form. Posture is the first step in being skilled at hand-to-hand combat."

I steal a glance at myself in the mirror. Immediately, I straighten my spine and pull my shoulders back.

Kingston walks closer to me until we're toe to toe, looking down at me before taking one hand and pushing my lower back in and taking the other to push my shoulders down. The skin feels burned where he touched it. Not from flames but more like frostbite.

"Balance. Without it, you'll have difficulty distributing your weight. Size doesn't matter," he adds. "All weight has to be distributed. Even when there isn't much to allocate. Now spread your feet shoulder width apart and slightly bend your knees," he orders with quiet authority.

I feel ridiculous, but do as instructed.

"Good. Now raise your hands in front of your face while making a fist with each hand," he states while walking around me in a circle. "Blocking is just as important as swinging. Potentially more so. A well-delivered punch will remove you from a fight before you even have a chance to begin."

I raise both hands in front of my face, curling them into fists.

Apparently, it's a bit too high because he grabs both in his much larger hands and slightly lowers them to nose and mouth level.

"If you put them in front of your eyes, you won't see a punch coming. The left guards your temple, and the right is for your opponent. You never lower your guard unless you're actively throwing a fist toward the enemy."

I blow a loose tendril of hair out of my face. "I know how to throw a punch. What I need to learn is how to fight."

"Hit me," he orders.

"Hit you?" I repeat back to him like a damn parrot.

"Did I stutter?" he demands, throwing my earlier jab back at me.

I don't need to be told twice.

I swing hard, putting every ounce of my weight behind the punch. My body flies forward, and I brace for impact. He sidesteps, making it look effortless like I punched him in slow motion. I stumble, catching myself just before I hit the ground and make an even bigger fool of myself.

"Dead," he delivers without an ounce of sympathy. "You'd be dead if this were real. There's more to a punch than just extending your arm. Precision, focus, control, and breathing are all factors that have to be taken into consideration before landing the hit." He shakes his head in disappointment. "You lack all of them."

Thankfully, he isn't blunt or anything.

He runs a hand through his sweaty hair. The sides are still shorter than the top, but when it's not perfectly poised and is disheveled like it is now, he looks more primal and less refined.

I hold my hands up. "Okay, so all I have to do is stand with a certain posture, maintain solid eye contact while breathing correctly with my guard up before throwing a punch with precision and control," I drawl.

"Precisely," he deadpans.

This is pointless. I'm as good as dead.

"That's impossible. How can anyone maintain all of that while in the heat of battle? I can't focus on perfect form and try to vanquish someone."

He just stares at me.

I try not to fidget under his scrutiny. He's acting as if I've said something ridiculous.

"Let's focus on throwing a punch, and then we'll get to the vanquishing part. Once you establish a fighting pattern, you won't have to think about it during battle. It will come as naturally as breathing." He steps back onto the mat. "It's as much a tether to your core as your abilities manifesting."

"If you say so—"

"I do."

"Then let's practice."

"So eager to end up on your back, I see," he taunts.

I roll my eyes and get into the fighting position. "I'm not your type, remember?" I remind him.

"Impossible to forget," he delivers without missing a beat.

It still feels ridiculous, but I go with it, shifting my weight from foot to foot like I've seen others do before they beat the shit out of each other. Kingston doesn't do any of the things he taught me. Instead, he just faces me with his arms crossed.

"Do I just try and hit you now?" I ask, my eyes flickering toward him.

He raises a brow. "That's the general idea, unless you would rather just look at me."

I step forward, throwing a punch at his jaw—more emotion than form—and am greeted with nothing but air again. He gracefully steps to the side, and before I can catch my bearings, he kicks out his leg, bringing both of mine out from under me. I land heavily on my back, the breath rushing out of my lungs in a swift exhale.

Gasping for a solid breath and coming up short, I try to roll to the side. It feels as if both lungs are filled with a thousand needles instead of oxygen. I keep trying to get a sliver of breath, begging my lungs to cooperate, but they are currently taking a hiatus.

Kingston crouches down in front of me. "When you strike, do it with resolve and purpose. Don't lash out blindly."

I raise my eyes, full of hatred, to glare at him. I can't respond because that would require being able to breathe, but I put everything I am thinking into my scowl.

"Again," he orders, rising to his feet.

I push to my knees, the breath slowly returning but not fast enough. I continue to try to gulp the air greedily, making small gasping noises as I do. The sounds of fists meeting flesh echo through the gym, filling the silence as I try to get to my feet.

"Keep that chin tucked. Don't give them an easy target," he orders while watching me regain my footing.

I step forward again, throwing another weak punch that doesn't land.

He grabs my extended arm before I can pull it back and spins me in place. My back crashes against his chest. His smell, woodsy with a hint of something spicy, maybe bergamot, wraps around me. How can he smell so alluring when he's covered in sweat and assaulting people?

"Always expect the unexpected," he breathes in my ear. "Your opponent will use any opening to bring you to your knees."

I'm not short, but I'm not tall either. Averagely average, but being held captive in his arms makes me feel incredibly feminine.

Fragile but not vulnerable.

"Okay, you can let go now." The words come out flat and controlled.

"Is that what you'll demand the enemy to do?" he asks, his voice low and mocking.

Both of my arms are pinned in front of me, rendering them useless. Throwing my head back would be ineffective because it would just hit his chest. I know nothing about evasive maneuvers to escape. His strength outmatches mine ten to one.

"Do you yield?" he asks.

"Never," I bite out.

He lets out a deep chuckle, more threat than actual laugh. "What would you're beloved Ambrose have you do?" he asks, leaning in close.

The question takes me aback because Ambrose wouldn't put me in this scenario. He wouldn't throw my lack of skill set in my face and demand I acknowledge it. No, he would teach and guide me. I'd feel safe and capable. I don't say any of this, though, because Kingston wouldn't understand. He'd just judge and mock me further for my answer.

"He'd probably recommend I get as far away from you as possible," I snap.

"Then do it," he says.

I wiggle my wrists, trying to find leverage to slip from his grasp, but it's not feasible. I kick my feet back, trying to hit a shin or ankle, but when I connect, nothing. He doesn't budge.

He's wrapped around me, cutting off any viable solution.

"There aren't any options. Your size makes it impossible." I know he won't hurt me. I don't know how, but I know it, yet being this helpless brings out a desperation in me. I need to know that I could escape if it came down to it, and it's shamefully obvious that's not the case.

"Is that what he would tell you? To just give up?" he demands. There's an underlying edge to his voice that I haven't heard before.

"Of course not," I say, my words coming out breathy and anxious. "He would teach me."

"That's what I'm trying to do. I'm showing you how to stand on your own without a crutch."

"I'm perfectly capable of standing on my own!"

"Show me, then. Get out of my grasp," he orders.

I twist my body sideways, arching my back, trying to break his grip. Pain radiates up my arms as I try to wrench my wrists from his lethal grasp, the violent and urgent need to escape sinking its claws into my skin.

I can feel moisture pooling in my eyes, and I hate it.

"Admit it, *Heathen*. You can't." He abruptly releases me from his grasp, causing me to fall forward.

I catch myself and stand on shaky legs, rubbing my wrists from where his brutal hands gripped them so roughly. I bet he gets off on his superiority over my helplessness. "You love that I can't." I put all my rage and self-doubt into the glare I direct at him. "Seeing someone so close to Ambrose fail at your feet is probably the highlight of your day. You hate me on sight just by association!" I yell.

I can feel the tremor in my lip and the tears of frustration building in the corners of my eyes. I hate that when I get mad and overstimulated, I angry-cry.

Kingston just stares at me with those dark, unreadable eyes.

It'll be a cold day in hell before I cry at his feet. I sink my teeth into the sides of my cheeks and relish in the pain.

"Watching a more than capable soldier be weakened by someone who claims to care for her is not my idea of a good time," he answers coldly.

He turns to walk away, clearly dismissing me.

I guess our little training session is done then. It's amazing how quickly he can shut it all off and disregard someone. I'm even slightly envious of it. I should just let him go. Give thanks this sparing session is over with, grab my shit, and leave. But I'm so angry that he thinks he knows me. That he summed me up and found me lacking. I've also never been good at knowing when to keep my mouth shut.

"If you were half the man Ambrose was, I wouldn't be staring at a retreating back."

One second, he's walking away, his stride composed and calm. Finished with me. The next, my hair is wrapped around his fist, head tilted to the side, his fangs sunk deep into my neck. He's dominance, and I'm submission. He doesn't remove his jaw but lingers. Rather in wrath or restraint, I'm unsure.

I can feel his breath hot against my skin. I squeeze his forearm like a lifeline. Both knees buckle beneath me, but he holds me up with one arm, his fingers digging into my ribs, while the other presses my body into his. There is no space left, no escape offered. I have no choice but to surrender to his taking.

I pushed, and he responded. I should be afraid, or at the very least, repulsed, but I'm not any of those things. I'm *intrigued*. I feel a pulse between my thighs, sharp and shameful in its timing. My body is committing the ultimate act of betrayal, and I have no control over it.

Suddenly, without warning, he releases me.

He tears himself away, fangs slipping free, causing me to flinch. Blood smears his lips and runs down his chin. His eyes are glassy as if in a blood haze. Both pupils are blown wide, drowning out any color other than black. They flick to my neck and then back to me.

Pain flares, white-hot, and I stagger to the side, grabbing the spot his mouth had been. Kingston makes no move to come near me, but his eyes track my every move. I watch in horror and captivation as he wipes the blood from his mouth with the back of his hand.

He looks dazed. Blood lusting. Ruined.

"Fuck."

I point an accusing finger at him. "You bit me!"

"It won't happen again," he says, each syllable deliberate and methodical.

I pull my hand away and stare at the blood coating my fingers.

The room slightly tilts.

He moved impossibly fast. I've never seen anything like it. I'd heard the rumors of his skill set and how he climbed the ranks quicker than those before him. To be a major in second-year, you have to be ruthless and superior to your peers, but I'm starting to think he hasn't even shown us what he's truly capable of. He's an irreplaceable tool in the realm's fighting force and hasn't even graduated from Kintoira.

The possibilities of what he will become before he leaves these walls are endless.

Endless and horrifying.

His eyes move to my hand, locked on the remnants of his bite. They rise back to mine before shuttering, locking down any kind of emotion that might have been swimming in their dark depths. Turning to leave, he grabs his bag from the floor and walks out, leaving me standing in the center of the mat with blood dripping down my neck, filled with more questions than answers.

Chapter Sixteen

What I lack in grace, I make up for in spite.

So when we're given leave for the weekend to spend it how we want, I bask in sheer joy that Yaretta can't join. Apparently, those gifted with perception are needed for a project this weekend at the academy. I'm not sure how I feel about the fact that she can determine the location and status of other people, but I hope she sees Ambrose and me walking side by side.

I also hope it eats her alive.

Tree branches, brittle and frost-covered, rustle in the frigid wind as we make our way through the Witchwood. The cold air bites into my exposed cheeks and weasels its way through the heavy layers I wrapped myself in. These woods sit slightly farther northwest than the Forsaken Forest and are not only marginally more ominous below the bruised-colored sky but also vastly more dangerous.

This is my first time experiencing their unwelcome ambience.

Since it's the only way for students to reach Moorechester, the quaint little village that is technically a part of the academy, I have no choice but to walk through its Gothic embrace. Only students, academy staff, and supposed witches have access. Since these are their woods after all.

I've heard there are a few shops, including a bakery and even a charming little pub. At this point, I'd walk through lava to experience something sweet paired with a nice cup of something frothy that doesn't come from the dining hall.

I lean over, careful my hair doesn't sway and reveal the bite marks lingering on my neck, and nudge Ambrose in the shoulder. "So, are there really witches in these woods?" I ask, only partially teasing. "Are the rumors true? Do they really despise all men?"

He turns those frosty eyes on me, and I could sink into their glacial depths. "Yes. And yes," he answers.

I frown. "Seriously? Should we be worried?" I mean, the last thing I want to do at the moment is stumble upon some highly dangerous women who hate men. Definitely not while walking next to a man I care very much about.

I've heard stories about how vicious they can be. Of course, who knows how much of it is actually true and how much is simply tales passed down as scare tactics. I've never met one. They're not exactly beach dwellers and are certainly not welcome at any of the ports.

"Some say they kidnap men and turn them into slaves," he whispers, looking down at me, his brows drawn tight. "Especially in the bedroom."

I feel my jaw drop in horror.

A smile tugs at his lips before he casually bites down on the bottom one to prevent it from spreading.

"Very funny." I shove him playfully and step back, running my fingers through the ends of my braid.

Pictures of Ambrose tied to a bed flutter through my head. How would it feel to have a man like him completely at my mercy? To be able to play out every dark fantasy I've ever had. My lips part slightly, and my eyes become unfocused, lost in the make-believe scenario.

I'm shaken from the direction my thoughts have taken by the heavy weight of his stare. I clear my throat and look over at him as casually as possible, praying the lustful thoughts aren't plastered across my face.

For a moment, his expression doesn't change, but then I see the way his jaw tenses, fingers curling into his palms, before quickly averting his gaze as if looking too long might open something in him that he isn't ready to acknowledge.

I cross my arms and move to safer territory. "Have you seen one?" I ask.

He answers, his voice rougher than before, "No, haven't had the privilege."

We walk in silence for a while through the dense trail. Ancient trees surround us, their branches clawing at the sky, black silhouettes against a gray backdrop. Mist curls along the cold, damp ground, like something sentient and patient. The air presses down upon us, thick with moisture and the faint smell of decay. Winter is but a touch away.

The trail is wide enough that we can walk side by side with room to spare. I throw an occasional glance out of the corner of my eye, but he seems to be too deep in thought to notice. Why am I being so awkward? This is *Ambrose* we're talking about. The man who has seen me at my absolute worst and still considers me a friend.

"How long until we get to Moorechester?" I ask, brushing imaginary lint from my sleeve, needing to break the tension.

"About another two miles. We just have to go a little farther before we cross the Blood River, and then we'll be at the end of the Witchwood."

I stop walking.

Ambrose stops as well, turning to face me.

"Blood River?" I ask, narrowing my eyes at him.

He gives me a sheepish smile.

"As in a river filled with blood?" I ask, dread sinking into the words. "Please tell me it's just a catchy name and not factual."

"Technically, it's a river that is mixed with blood," he answers, the arrows jostling in the quiver attached to his back.

I let out a laugh that sounds slightly hysterical.

He shrugs, then starts walking again, throwing a quick look over his shoulder to see if I'm coming. Instead, he catches me staring at the back of his head like he's lost his mind.

He smiles and turns back around again.

I wrinkle my nose in annoyance and quickly join him.

"It's unclear where it originates from, but it's definitely blood," he continues as if we're talking about the weather. "Some theorize it comes from the witch's sacrificial offerings to the woods they call home, but there's no proof to that theory."

Oh good. No proof of that theory. That makes me feel better.

I roll my eyes.

The cawing of a raven in the distance adds an eerie layer to our already portentous surroundings. I quicken my step to stay close, my boots sinking into the damp earth. I'm certainly a desirable target for anything and anyone at the moment. I still haven't manifested, and it's a constant worry and heaviness that resides in my gut.

I'm dead weight.

The academy doesn't keep dead weight around. I haven't brought it up to him yet, or the events that transpired at the blood initiation, but they've been heavy on my mind.

Ambrose hasn't approached it either.

We eventually come to a thinning in the trees that opens up to a flowing river of ruby rapids. It's roughly eighteen feet in width with large stones strategically placed throughout. There's way to get from one side to the other. Not unless we swim through the sinister-looking current.

I scratch the top of my head, trying to work out how I land in these ridiculous situations. "Where's the bridge?" I ask in a cautious tone.

He throws his head back, laughter breaking free. Thick brown waves fall to his shoulders, and his blue eyes flash like crystals. Tan skin, athletic build, perfect smile. Gods help me, he's the whole package. If he weren't so damn nice to look at, I might consider pushing him into the river.

"There isn't one, brat. Come on, it'll be like when we were kids. There wasn't any challenge we wouldn't take head-on," he says, lip curling in a half smile.

"But we're *not* kids," I remind him.

His eyes rake over me. "I'm very aware of that fact," he murmurs.

I can feel my cheeks warming under his scrutiny. "Then you're also aware this isn't my idea of a good time," I say, changing the subject. Apparently, getting his attention in a way that I've wanted for so long is causing me to squirm.

"We can hold hands if you want. If you fall, I've got you," he instructs, moving closer and grabbing one of my hands. "You're safe. I won't fall."

His hand completely engulfs mine.

I hold my breath as we take the first step, landing on a large stone at the edge of the river. The surface is slippery and unsteady from moisture and algae. I squeeze his hand in a bruising grip. He moves to the next stone, guiding us in precise movements as if he's done this a hundred times. And let's be honest, he probably has. I won't wonder who he came with all those other weekends.

I bite my lips together and focus on the task at hand. It's the safer option.

We make our way across the rapids, the sound of water smashing over boulders drowning out any possibility of conversation. When we jump and land on the other side, and I feel the soft dirt beneath my feet, I let out a long exhale.

They really need to just build a bridge and be done with it.

Snow has started to fall from the brooding skies as we enter the cobbled streets of Moorechester. Orange hues shine through the lattice windows of the shops like a warm invitation. The brutal cold is unforgiving, forcing me to burrow deep into my oversized cloak. I'll never get used to the weather here.

It doesn't seem to stop the contagious laughter of other students as they pop in and out of shops, some holding bags, others sipping hot beverages. Ambrose takes my hand, cutting through a few of the buildings, leading us to a worn-down building tucked in the corner.

A wooden sign swings on creaking hinges overhead. Faded letters spell out the name Copper Penny Pub. We duck inside, escaping the continuous snowfall and biting cold. The clatter of tankards, veracious chatter, and the scraping of chairs across the uneven floorboards greet us upon entering.

It reminds me of Brylan's port.

It's perfect. Exactly what I needed.

Ambrose leads us to a small table in the back. The air in here is warm and thick, but not in an uncomfortable way. It's a welcome reprieve from outside. I immediately start removing layers before sitting down. Ambrose follows suit, hanging his bow on the back of his chair before taking off his cloak.

I can't help but notice the way his cream-colored, long-sleeved shirt clings to his body once he removes it.

I internally sigh. My tongue feels heavy and stuck to the roof of my mouth.

He's filled out so much since joining the academy. He's now muscle and hardness where he was once youth and malleability. I watch with a level of unhealthy yearning as he flags down a server and orders each of us an ale. He sits down and leans back in his chair.

His entire focus now rests on me.

Unlike my earlier sparring partner, this look isn't cold and calculated with a side of diabolical. It's familiar, welcoming, and warm like embers burning with nostalgia. I'm not sure why *he* even entered my thoughts, except maybe to point out his shortcomings and Ambrose's attributes. A stark comparison between something good for me and something that would gleefully watch me crumble.

"Well, this is pleasant," I say, scanning the room as cheers erupt around an arm-wrestling match.

A look of affection passes over his face. "Wait until you taste their home-brewed ale. Absolute perfection," he replies, tapping his fingers along the grooved table. The steady rhythm is hypnotizing.

"I'm just glad you wanted to bring me here." A small smile pulls at my lips. "It's nice just spending time with you. I've missed you so much," I acknowledge in a soft whisper.

"I've missed you, too, Nori. I wish we could meet up more often, but being an officer with a full course load," he says, placing his palms on the table, "it's just hard."

"Oh, I completely understand." My voice comes out a little too smooth and polished. The last thing I want is to come across as demanding and needy. "How about that blood initiation, huh? Talk about intense!" I throw it out there as informally as possible to gauge his reaction without implicating the weight his answer will bring.

"You're not lying," he says. "They certainly don't do you any favors by warning you what you're walking into, do they?" His eyes dart to the bar as if he's looking for our server, but I get a feeling he just doesn't want to meet my eyes.

"Yeah, and it's all so formal and cloaked in anonymity," I venture, staring at his face for a reaction.

He nods in agreement, but continues to look toward the bar, doing everything in his powers to avoid the conversation.

I decide to take it into my own hands and cut the bullshit. "Were you there?" I ask point-blank.

He pauses, his entire demeanor seeming to freeze before finally bringing his attention back to me. "I was," he admits quietly.

His pale eyes hold me captive. Anxiousness stirs in my veins.

To suspect is one thing, but to hear the confirmation is another entirely. He saw me at a very vulnerable point and witnessed another Veil carry me from the darkness. Unless he was the one who held me while chaos ensued. I have my suspicions, but lately, he's so closed off that I could be entirely wrong.

He leans forward, his elbows resting on the table as he searches my face for the truths he thinks I should be given.

As if I'm not owed all of them.

I don't move out of fear that he'll change his mind and not want to discuss what happened. I hold his stare, but I refuse to ask more questions.

It's his turn to offer answers.

He clears his throat. "Officers are required to attend. We don't have a choice. Veils and Noctryns alike," he adds before breaking eye contact and looking around the pub. His brows are drawn tight, and his broad shoulders tense.

So it's like that.

Okay.

More secrecy, more games on who will ask the right questions to get the correct answers. I'm so tired of pulling and begging only to get half answers and partial truths. I'm exhausted from being the one who tries to keep this friendship afloat. A person can only give so much of themselves repeatedly with nothing offered in return before they burn out.

"Is this how we're playing it now, Ballard? I have to come out and demand an answer before I'm on the receiving end of honesty? Okay, fine. Let's do it your way." I lean forward, my face inches from his. "Were you or were you not the Veil who restrained me and so helpfully poured the blocker remover down my throat?" I all but hiss, blinking hard to keep my emotions in check.

He can have my anger, but he doesn't deserve my despair. That's meant just for me.

He rubs a hand down his face and leans back in his chair.

It's uncomfortable to be called out on your shit, so by all means, get as comfortable as possible.

"I would never let someone hold you in a vulnerable state if I had the opportunity to be the one doing it. I took a compromising situation and made sure you'd succeed. Just like I always do," he responds, crossing his arms in clear defense. "Yes, it was me."

The air leaks out of my lungs.

It's not a burst, like you read about, but more of a slow trickle. As if it wants to remain as long as possible to witness your pain.

He clenches his jaw, nostrils flaring. "If I'm able to prevent you from failing or being hurt, there is nothing that will stand in my way. Not even you," he warns.

The sad part is, I understand. I'd do the same thing for him, even if it meant that he hated me for it.

"Here you are," the server says as she hands us each our mugs of ale.

Ambrose tips his head toward her in thanks, but I never remove my eyes from his face. "Enjoy," she throws out, oblivious to the tension in the air before sauntering off.

He held me in his arms. He made sure I did what was needed to succeed at the academy. He whispered soft words in my ear that could easily be misconstrued for something else. I may have been out of it and incoherent, but I remember everything he said.

Everything.

The fact that he whispered *good girl* in my ear will be something I will remember on my deathbed. I know underneath his strict exterior, something is there. He's just too damn scared to act on it, which is rather ironic. He sits here spewing words of defiance in regard to allowing me not to fail when he's too scared to even try.

"I wouldn't want any other version of you than the one I remember from that day. I'd just also like the honest one who existed before becoming a Veil." I beg him not only to hear me but also to listen.

His eyes shutter momentarily before he looks down and takes a big gulp of his ale. I gingerly sip mine because, as much as I tried to be one of the boys growing up, I could never hold my weight in ale. The last thing I want to do is get tipsy during this conversation since it's the first time in a long time that he's opened up to me at all.

"Right now, I don't know what I want, Nori. I know what I need and what's expected of me, but I don't know what I want." His fingers curl around his mug. "It's not fair to you, and I know that. I know you want more than I can give right now, and it haunts me. I want to be the reason you smile and the strength you deserve, but right now, my loyalties lie in succeeding and ascending," he says with a subtle shake of his head. "Everything I have to offer someone is on a superficial level, and I would never do that to you. You mean too much to me for that."

His eyes look somber.

My soul is breaking.

It would have hurt less to be stabbed in the heart with a hot poker.

I mean too much to him but not enough to set aside his ambitions and explore what we could grow into. What happens when we've outgrown the bounds of friendship but can't move into the next dynamic? Do we wither and deteriorate to a point where our friendship can't survive?

I refuse to lose him from my life, as I couldn't survive the fallout, but I also can't remain in this stalemate where my feelings are unreciprocated. I can't watch the man I've slowly fallen in love with over the past decade lie in bed after bed of other women.

"Where does that leave me, then?" I ask quietly, afraid of the answer but needing it even more.

"In the same place you've always been, Nori. My best friend and confidant. You're my home."

I inhale softly, his words so unfair. "That's the problem, Ambrose. I don't think I can remain in the same place I've always been…" I say on a broken whisper, staring into my lap. I don't say more because I've laid myself bare enough. He doesn't offer up any words of comfort and I won't search for them.

Instead, he reaches across the table, palm up, waiting for me to take the extended olive branch. A confirmation that I'll give him space, and our friendship is solid. An agreement that I'll fall on the wayside and bide my time.

"I'm just asking you not to give up on me," he says.

Against my better judgment, I place my palm in his.

Chapter Seventeen

Night has fallen by the time we leave the pub, and the village seems to have gotten busier while we were tucked away. Students make their way through the cobbled streets. Some are covered in black, and others wear shades of brown and cream.

Separate never mingled.

"Look what the cat dragged in," a sharp voice calls.

I turn and see Finnley and Mallory making their way toward us. They squeeze through a group of Veils and laugh as Finnley almost slips on an icy patch of sidewalk. Mallory's face is partially covered behind a thick brown scarf, but Finnley's is bare and pink from the cold. A huge smile graces his face by the time he reaches us.

I melt into his open arms and squeeze.

I can't help but smile in return as we pull apart. He just has that effect on people, bringing out their genuine happiness. "Where are you two headed?" I ask, trying to ignore the way Ambrose stiffened at my side when Finnley wrapped me in his arms.

"There are a few shops we want to hit before heading back," Mallory answers in a muffled voice. Her signature cut his hidden beneath a plush beanie, and all I can see is her eyes, heavy with makeup, peering back at us.

"How's it going?" Finnley asks while reaching out to shake Ambrose's hand.

"It's going," he answers, nodding and gripping Finnley's hand harder than necessary. "I never got a chance to thank you for taking care of Nori in the final trial. It won't be forgotten."

"What are you talking about? She took care of me." Finnley laughs, removing his hand from Ambrose's rough grip.

"Ambrose is taking me to a shop. You guys should come along," I suggest, looking back and forth between Finnley and Mallory. I steal a glance at Ambrose and find his eyes narrowed in on me. Right now, I just need some breathing room, and by inviting my friends, I'm granted that. It will change the dynamic, which is exactly what I want.

"Sounds great!" Mallory exclaims as she grabs Finnley's arm. She's apparently not giving him a choice in the matter, per usual.

Finnley buttons up his cloak while shooting me a look that tells me he knows exactly what I'm doing.

I shrug my shoulders and start walking. Snow crunches beneath our boots as we make our way down the uneven, cobbled path. The town feels antique, timeless, and quiet. Little shops line the street on each side, their doors closed as the snowflakes fall lazily from the sky. The warmth and aromas wafting through when a student exits a shop greet us as we make our way down the well-worn path.

We pass shop after shop until Ambrose stops in front of one that looks older than the rest. Almost as if it wants to blend in with its surroundings and only attracts those who seek it out. Numerous books sit in the window, advertised as first editions.

A bookstore.

Excitement skirts along my insides. Maybe they have something on Liminals. The academy library didn't have much on the subject, and I'm desperate for information.

An old brass bell chimes as we enter, and the smell of musk and broken spines greets us. I inhale deeply.

"It's the oldest bookstore in the northern portion of Salaryan. Some say the entire realm, but there have been disputes on the subject," Ambrose whispers over my shoulder.

Turning, I give him a tentative smile. I know he's trying, so the least I can do is reciprocate.

Mallory and Finnley leave us to explore what the old shop has to offer. The spine of well-used titles hums beneath my fingertips, full of knowledge just waiting to be cracked open once more. A small round table wobbles as I step away, setting a book down, and walk toward a spiral staircase leading to another floor.

Everyone knows places like this keep the good stuff tucked away.

Worn and decrepit metal creaks beneath my combat boots as I ascend the stairs. The air is colder and thicker, as if it doesn't receive many visitors. The old floor groans beneath me as I step onto the worn boards of the landing. I hover on the threshold, wanting to move forward but hesitating. The entire floor looks like something long forgotten and not wanting to be disturbed. It smells of mildew, faint decay, and old parchment. Row after row of bookshelves line the floor, filled with not only books but maps, old trinkets, and a few sad-looking plants.

Me too, guys. Me too.

Firelight flickers in a small lamp that sits upon a worn-down desk in the corner of the room. I could spend all night here and not even scratch the surface. My soft footfalls are the only sounds as I push forward and make my way down the center aisle, glancing at each row as I go. Dust rests upon most of the shelves, a clear indication that people tend to favor downstairs.

I turn and walk down a random aisle just past an old grandfather clock that no longer ticks. A large tome wrapped in orange dragonhide sits haphazardly on the shelf. I carefully push it to the side to reveal an old atlas. Moving farther along, I pick up the next book and open a weary-looking spellbook, flipping through the pages. The ink shifts beneath my inspection, clearly notating the fact that I'm not a witch and therefore unworthy of its contents. I drop it back on the shelf and wipe the dust from my palms onto the sides of my cloak.

Farther down the stacks is a shelf filled with mismatched books and a small sign hanging in front. It says that the books are unreadable to anyone who desires to do so and will rearrange themselves so as not to be bothered. A few books on the bottom look to be ledgers of some sort. I crouch and flip one open to see names and places, some being crossed out violently. Cautiously, I put it back and move back to the main aisle.

The back of the second story doesn't get much light, since the lamp doesn't cast its glow this far. It's harder to make out the titles, but I'm too invested to stop now. I bend down and push a cracked hourglass out of the way to grab a book that almost seems to pulse beneath my palm. It's thick and intricate in its design. *Dark Objects and Their Origins* by Sanderson Thurboult.

The first thing that stands out as I flip through the delicate pages is the fact that the majority of the early ones are missing. Pages ripped from their roots. I'm assuming these are the parts that speak of the origins. Other pages feature images of various items, such as a dagger belonging to a past political figure and a compass belonging to a renowned alchemist. The more I flip, the more objects are discussed, including where they could now reside. Every individual in the book wears Noctryn attire issued for active military personnel.

Tucking it under my arm, I stand. This one is coming home with me.

I make my way back toward the front, grabbing a few more books along the way. *Constellations and Their Link to Manifestations,* as well as *Runes and Implications.*

I head back downstairs and find Ambrose relaxed in a chair that looks anything but, with his head leaned back and eyes closed. Deciding not to disturb him just yet, I walk over to the counter to make my purchases.

A black cat languidly stretches across the worn wood, eyeing me with wide green eyes, silently judging. The books thud against the counter as I drop them and reach into my pocket for the necessary coins. I exhale a heavy breath as I wait, coins in hand. When it doesn't appear that anyone is rushing to assist, I ring the silver little bell on the counter. The cat pads over and sits next to the chiming bell, staring at me as if I'm a nuisance.

"Hello, is anyone working?" I call out in a raised voice.

"You set the coins on the counter and leave them. The bookkeeper has never been seen, but books get shelved, and money gets deposited, so we know there's one in here somewhere," Ambrose says from his seat, head still back with both eyes closed.

Okay, then.

I leave the money and tuck my new purchases under my arm, making my way over to him. "Have you seen Finnley or Mallory?" I ask, looking down at him.

"They headed out about an hour ago. Told me to tell you they would meet up with you back at the academy."

"An hour ago?" I exclaim, kicking the leg of his chair to make him look at me. "I was only upstairs for a few moments. How did they leave an hour ago?"

"Nori, you've been up there for ages," he replies dryly, opening one eye to pin me beneath a blue stare.

Impossible.

I wasn't up there longer than a quarter of an hour, tops. He takes in my confused expression and pushes forward in his seat. "I dunno, maybe you just lost track of time." The chair squeaks across the floor as he stands and stretches. His shirt rises slightly to reveal a sharp V cut into his abdomen.

I let out a small cough and tear my eyes away, turning toward the door to leave.

"Hey," he says, grabbing my elbow to stop me. "Did you find what you were looking for?"

I blow out a breath. "Nope. But I found some other good ones."

"I never doubted you would," he says, his brows lifting in a knowing way.

He was right. I *did* love this place.

The minute we get back to the academy, it's in complete chaos.

Students assemble in the halls in various forms of undress, throwing on academy attire, sheathing weapons, and making their way down the darkened halls.

Ambrose cuts a sharp look in my direction, and I nod for him to go. I know what he's asking without him even having to voice it. He grips my shoulder reassuringly before sprinting in the same direction as the rest of the officers.

I squeeze my books close to my chest. This is my new reality.

"It's hard knowing you'll never be his first priority, isn't it?" a taunting female voice full of mocking satisfaction asks.

I turn my head and narrow my eyes on Yaretta, who has slithered up beside me. She watches Ambrose make his way through the crowd. I refuse to acknowledge her snub and grip my books tighter before walking in the direction he took off in. Maybe if I grip them tight enough, I won't smack her in the face with them.

She's persistent, though, and follows me closely. "Kintoira isn't the place you grew up in. Times are different now. He has *other things* to occupy his attention. By the way, Norissa, how's the manifestation coming along?" she quips like she actually cares. She would love nothing more than to see me tossed out or erased entirely.

I grind my teeth but keep walking.

Metal clings against armor as daggers and swords are sheathed.

I want so badly to pat the dagger strapped to my thigh just to reassure myself it's safely in place, but I won't. Not when this serpent is keeping pace beside me. I can feel her irritation at being ignored. She's practically vibrating with it.

Good.

"Do you want to know where he was the night of the final trial?" she asks, voice full of venom.

I whip my head toward her and watch her lips pull into a feral smile. After finally getting the reaction she so desperately craved, she veers off to stop next to Emory, who's talking with a group of Veils, but she doesn't take her viper glare off me.

Emory raises her eyes to meet mine before moving to Yaretta and taking in the entire situation.

I squeeze the edges of my books, knuckles turning white, and turn away. The hall is crammed as we all try to get to the same place, urgency making everyone erratic and clumsy.

"Do you have any idea what's going on?" Emory asks, coming up beside me, her violet eyes narrowed in concern.

I shake my head and shrug my shoulders. "I know just about as much as everyone else, I suppose. Which is pretty much nothing."

"They've ordered everyone to attend an assembly, I know that much. There's talk of another attack having taken place," she whispers, looking around to be sure we're not heard. "Apparently, someone heard a few professors discussing it, and it's spreading like wildfire among the student body."

Another attack. They're getting bolder.

"Well, seems you know more than I do," I reply. Not unfriendly, but not encouraging further discussion either.

"Poking your nose where it doesn't belong again, Voss?" A heavy arm is thrown over my shoulders, dragging me to his side. Makon's gaze is targeted on Emory like she's the enemy.

She rolls her eyes but continues talking to me like he isn't there. "That's all the information I was able to gather. I'll see you in there."

Before I can get a word out, Makon cuts in. "Why don't you worry about playing with your little magic abilities? You know, the things you Veils are so good at," he says, leaning in close, voice dropping, and eyes locked in on his prey. "Leave the battles and fighting to the ones more suited for it."

"The only thing you're suited for is handling your massive ego."

"It's not the only thing massive about me," he taunts.

I push his arm off my shoulders at the mental image I could have done without. "We'd better hurry, or they're going to start without us."

Grabbing Makon's wrist, I drag him behind me before there's bloodshed. If the look on Emory's face is anything to go by, I should be more worried for Makon than her.

The assembly hall is packed to the brim, voices loud with questions and accusations flying. A professor stands at the front, actively trying to get everyone to shut up.

Unsuccessfully.

The next moment, Kingston, helmet in hand, steps up beside the professor, effectively ceasing all chatter. His very presence commands absolute respect and obedience. The professor, worry lines creasing the corners of his eyes, clasps his hands behind his back before quickly acknowledging the soldier by his side and addressing us.

"I'm sure you've heard the rumors being thrown around about another attack. However, for once, the rumors are rooted in fact. An attack was carried out on Ashbarrow, and the casualties are heavy." A gasp is heard somewhere in the audience. "The majority of the small town wasn't spared. It happened quickly and in the dead of the night before our armies could respond."

There's a good chance, based on the gasp just heard, that some of us have family in that town. We were basically just told they were slaughtered.

The exhausted-looking professor takes a moment before continuing, "There's more. They didn't stop with the massacre but proceeded to raid Harkin House. A few residents were taken. At this time, none have been recovered."

I look around the room to gauge the reactions of the other cadets.

What purpose would wraiths have for taking the mentally unstable? Why not just consume them on the spot?

"We're all thinking the same thing," Makon says out of the corner of his mouth. His brows are drawn tight, and his hand rests on the lethal dagger at his waist.

I look away and bring my attention back to the front, toward Kingston. He stands stoically next to the professor. His dark eyes already aimed at me.

"I'd like to say that's all we have to worry about at the moment, but alas, there's one more thing. A dark object has been taken from the academy's catacombs... along with a professor." Murmurs and hushed whispers break out among the students. Noctryns cast accusing glances toward the Veils, and they in return offer glances of suspicion.

Kingston widens his stance, and all chatter ceases.

The professor takes a deep breath. "Professor Hunstal, a light magic instructor and expert in languages, was last seen this afternoon. Her current whereabouts are unknown, but her lodgings were found in disarray." He pauses and brings his shoulders back, resolve etched into the creases of his face. "A select few Noctryns will begin interrogations right away. The only individuals able to get through these walls unnoticed are students and professors. Someone here knows something. We will not rest until both are recovered." He adjusts his robes and briskly heads for the exit, not pausing to take any of the questions plastered to so many of our faces.

I squish my books to my chest and meet Kingston's stare unflinchingly.

Chapter Eighteen

One by one, we're pulled from our classes.

Unsurprisingly, the Noctryns target their opposers first with the interrogations. Even less shocking is the fact that they lumped me in with them. To say the Veils are pissed would be an understatement. How do we know it wasn't one of the interrogators who committed the acts in question?

I pull the cap over my ears as we enter a lower level of the academy, one that sits far below the first floor and definitely wasn't mentioned in any of the brochures. It's deep into the foreboding catacombs. If I thought the living quarters were cold and damp, I sadly overestimated the ability of the academy to surpass them.

I take slow, measured steps as I follow my guide downward, the stone stairs slick with age. Somewhere in the distance is a steady drip of water. It's musty, bleak, and the last place I want to be. Griffin had the honor of escorting me and currently leads the way. He's been quiet thus far, which is perfect for me. I have zero desire to converse with someone taking me into the depths of depravity. He carries a heavy torch that outlines his silhouette as we make our way through the long, winding passageways.

Crumbled stones and rubble are pushed off to the sides, and we pass a few empty cells that look to be forgotten. The catacombs seem endless. It's understandable why they have someone escort us. Perhaps it isn't so much a show of force as I originally thought, but more so to make sure we reach our destination. Although I'm not sure which would be worse at the moment. Becoming lost in the dark passages or having my mind manipulated and invaded.

After a few more turns, we come to a large wooden door. Griffin pivots and stops in front of it, turning to face me with a bored expression. I quirk my lips, lean against the wall, and sink to my heels, resting my head against the cold stone. Neither of us makes any effort to speak.

I close my eyes and pretend I'm alone.

I've heard firsthand what these interrogations can be like. Ambrose didn't cut corners when explaining how uncomfortable they are. How intrusive it is to have someone poke into the deep walls of your mind. While there's no way for me to mentally prepare for what's about to transpire, I can at least try to calm my thoughts beforehand. I'm obviously innocent and know nothing about either disappearance, but I'm still nervous about a stranger peering into my personal memories. I don't care for the idea of someone being in my head.

Sometimes I don't even like being in there.

The minutes slowly tick by before the door creaks open, causing me to crack my eyes slightly. A first-year walks out, eyes glossy and chin slightly trembling. She looks down at me before quickly averting her gaze and gaining her composure.

Griffin signals for me to rise before placing his hand on my back and pushing me none-too gently through the door. The minute I'm all the way in, he shuts it with a loud slam of finality.

Fuck you very much, then.

I glance around the small room as my chest rises and falls with rapid breaths. Chains hang from the ceiling with cuffs dangling at the ends, rusted and stained. The feeling of terror and unwilling confessions are etched into every corner and crevice of this interrogation room. In the center of the room sits a table bare of anything but two chairs. One of them is currently being occupied by none other than the king of interrogations.

Kingston fucking Adair.

He's leaned back completely at ease, both legs sprawled wide with his hands resting behind his head. This is just another day in the office for him.

I walk over stiffly and place both palms on the table, standing in front of the vacant seat. I never take my weary eyes off him.

"We meet again," he says in a deep, rich voice that I would recognize in my sleep. The brown hues of his eyes shine like burnt amber in the torchlight.

"Unwilling on my part, as usual. It seems we're obtaining a theme."

He inclines his head in a gesture for me to sit, ignoring my barb.

I take a seat. It's not like I have any other option at the moment.

I'm a pawn, and he's the king on the board.

In the end, we'll end up at the same place, but I have to play the game.

The muscles bunch beneath his dark, long-sleeved shirt as he sits forward and rests his elbows on his knees. His black hair is slicked back from his face, allowing every hard angle and sardonic expression to fuel the deviant aura he cloaks himself in. He's dressed in black from his shirt down to his combat boots. It's as if the moment he enters a room, you can feel the warmth leave.

It's absolutely frigid in this cell.

He gives off the distinct expression that everything around him is a nuisance and vastly beneath him. Apathy being a main weapon in his arsenal. He's beautifully detached in the most ruthless way possible. And somehow, I'm constantly on his radar.

I cross my ankles more out of the need to do something while sitting under his intense scrutiny than anything else. He's staring at me as if I've already been found guilty of a crime, and this whole charade is more of a formality than an actual interrogation. I do my best not to fidget while pinned beneath his dark glare, full of accusations.

The torches on the walls flicker in unison with my erratic heartbeat. Resignation seeps from the walls, cold and slick with age, the faint scent of iron and blood clinging to the air. This room was built to devour sound. To hide secrets and relish pain.

Kingston pushes off his knees and sits back a little, slightly crossing his arms and tapping his fingers against his lips. "Do you have anything you want to share with me before we start?" he asks, clearly knowing I won't be sharing anything with him. At least not willingly.

"You mean besides the fact that I don't want to be here?" I answer with the perpetual scowl I wear around him. "I haven't done anything wrong,"

"I'll determine that," he replies curtly while holding that unwavering eye contact he seems to favor.

Without warning, he grabs the front of my chair and pulls me toward him, the legs scraping loudly against the stone floor. I grip the edges tightly, so I don't fall right out of it. "Was that necessary?" I hiss.

"Very."

He leans toward me again, his black-rimmed eyes mesmerizing in their intensity. "I can hear your hatred loud and clear. Do me a favor and try to tone it down a bit so we can get started," he instructs, like I should have known to do this.

I forget he can dip into my head whenever the desire strikes him. I try not to think anything negative about the infuriating man sitting across from me, but it's impossible. It's like telling someone to try not to breathe.

Don't think anything bad.

Don't think anything bad.

I. Can't. Stand. You. Adair.

"So how exactly does this work? You can already just dive right in and violate my thoughts, so what's the next step in proving my innocence?"

"I can hear what *most* people are thinking, currently, depending on how loud their thoughts are. Yours are obnoxiously loud. Delving into memories is a bit more complicated," he answers. "I have to have a tether to your energy, a type of connection."

"You have to touch me," I state without premise.

"Unfortunately," he drawls, appraising me like I'm a petulant headache.

Without warning, he closes his eyes and reaches out, putting a hand on each side of my head. At first, I jolt from his hands on me, but then the pressure is immediate, as if someone is ripping out threads of my existence. I'm forced to close my eyelids from the incredible tension permeating through my head. Vivid images of the past forty-eight hours rapidly appear behind my eyelids. A bird's-eye view of my writhing form on the ground during the Blood Ritual Ceremony, being carried to my room while unconscious, and the trip to Moorechester with Ambrose.

I get to watch Ambrose's rejection play out in front of my eyes again in stark detail before I'm at the bookshop picking out a few titles. Suddenly, the books blur into the academy doors opening, and I'm walking into the chaos that's transpiring in all directions before the image abruptly vanishes, and the pressure subsides.

I carefully peel my eyes open.

Kingston stares at me, hands on his knees, but the accusation that was previously buried in those depths has lessened.

Slightly.

Checkmate, asshole.

"He's always been an idiot," he says, his tone lower than I've heard it.

I'm embarrassed but even more angry. "I'm sure you enjoyed that part the best," I seethe. "That was private and not for you to witness."

It's bad enough to live through a rejection, no matter how softly it was delivered, but to have to relive it with an audience? Sheer agony.

He doesn't laugh or mock me. But he is *tense*.

"Why the interest in dark objects?" he asks, swiftly changing the subject.

Shit.

That little tidbit certainly doesn't help me not look guilty in some regard. Thank fuck I was at Moorechester when the abductions presumably took place.

"It looked interesting," I say flatly.

He raises a dark brow.

I take a deep breath. This entire charade of being civil is exhausting. "I have no idea where I fit in the scheme of things, as a Liminal. At this point, nothing has manifested, neither light nor dark abilities, so I figured, why not look into both?"

"Curiosity is an essential aspect of wielding. It's also critical you're familiar with facets of the Noctryn ideology since we don't yet know where you fall in the scheme of things," he states, rolling his sleeves up and exposing his corded forearms. "Dark objects are crucial for Noctryns. Do you know anything about the matter?"

"Nothing."

"They are *created*. More specifically, they're made for a Noctryn who wields deep levels of dark magic with the potential to burn out. Without a way to stabilize themselves, that amount of dark power can lead to madness. An elite dark wielder paired with a dark object is a reputable force." His lower lip pulls between his teeth, just enough for the point of his left canine to show. "But a Noctryn who delves too deep without the proper tools is a hazard to themself. And everyone around them."

"How are they created?" I ask, suddenly very curious.

"By the very few who can. Unfortunately, only Noctryns have access to learning the process, and since we don't know exactly where you fall on the spectrum, we'll have to save that for another day," he answers.

Secrecy upon secrecy. The layers are abundant.

I rub my temples to try and ease some of the residual tension from the surprisingly quick interrogation. I'm thankful he only probed into the necessary timeline. He could have taken full advantage and gone back as far as he deemed necessary.

He pushes back and away from me. "It will subside as the day goes on. The human mind isn't used to being probed and dug through by intrusive hands," he assures me.

I give him a sarcastic thumbs-up.

His usual impassive face breaks into a slight smirk. It only amplifies his regal beauty. Perhaps it's a good thing he doesn't smile. It'd probably be detrimental to the female population if a mere smirk is this lethal.

I smack my thighs with both hands and stand up. If this meeting is adjourned, I'd very much like to get the hell out of here.

I glance toward the door. "Are we done here?"

"We're done here." His eyes track me as I push the chair in. "Oh, and Caderyn," he says, holding my gaze, "It would *most definitely* be detrimental to the female population."

I narrow my eyes on his smug smirk before turning on my heel and leaving.

I might be going insane because I swear I hear deep masculine laughter weave its way through the door after it shuts.

Shaking my head, I follow Griffin out of the damp catacombs.

Chapter Nineteen

The air in the halls is thick with suspicion and whispers.

Glances and tight nods are shared in passing. Silence falls when someone enters a room. Conversation feels weighted as if there's more than one meaning behind every sentence—everything feels coded.

The separation between Veils and Noctryns is at an all-time peak. Trust was thin before, but now it's nonexistent. Accusations are tossed about and insults slung. The academy felt split in half. One side thrums with barely restrained power, whereas the other is heavy and cold with simmering dark magic.

Earlier in the halls, an intense argument between a second-year Veil and a third-year Noctryn resulted in the dark wielder's cloak igniting in sparks by "accident." Training sessions during combat practice have ended with frozen limbs, mind injuries from deep mental manipulation, and broken bones. A few of the shifters have suffered extreme exhaustion from shifting too often under duress. Makon was furious during our earlier class when a dark wielder's eyes started bleeding from pushing past her limits.

It's chaos. Dangerous, catastrophic chaos.

Classes aren't going much better. Runes and Wards was a struggle for me this morning. Finnley and most of the other Veils seem to be grasping it as the class progresses, but I haven't been able to create one ruin or break a singular ward. Half of the time, I don't even know what they're talking about, and let's face it, besides Finnley, most aren't willing to help.

Ambrose tried to tutor me during our astrology class—the one class we share together—but I ended up more confused. And once again, he was the only one who acknowledged my existence.

Sometimes I think it would have been better to place as a Noctryn instead of this in-between. It was the last thing I wanted, but I promise nothing is more isolating than not being able to relate to others. Being different automatically labels you as an outsider.

Being a *Liminal* labels you as a traitorous outsider.

It's a constant tug-of-war.

The usual sounds of the sparring gym greet me as I enter. I make my way to the back, toss my bag down, and plop down beside it. I grab my wrappings out of the side pocket and bring one across the back of my hand, through my fingers, and up my wrist multiple times like Kingston taught me. By the time I finish the second hand, there's still no sight of him.

I resort to watching others perfect their techniques while I wait. Eryk is getting absolutely pummeled by a sharp uppercut from Koa. Apparently, being the general's son doesn't buy you safety. In fact, it looks detrimental. The tension between the students is bleeding over into the sparring rings if the grunts and body slams echoing through the gym are any indication.

Coincidentally, the first years are all paired with a student from the opposite regiment.

Lucky us.

They hate us and are significantly more advanced.

Eryk staggers to his feet, slightly swaying with a nasty-looking bruise already forming on his jaw. He tucks his head and charges Koa, who simply sidesteps his advance and watches him run into a hanging bag.

I let out a sharp exhale through my nose.

What an idiot.

I hear them before I see them. Heavy footsteps walk my way from the direction of a small office that sits in the opposite corner of my sparring mat. Turning my head slightly, I watch Kingston and Corrine make their way over to me. Both are deep in conversation and don't pay me any mind. Her hair is pulled up high on her head, but her curtain bangs hang flawlessly in place. I will never master that level of looking put-together.

A muscle ticks in Kingston's jaw as he listens to her speak. They're within earshot when they simultaneously realize I'm sitting here, causing both to abruptly stop talking.

The corner of my lip slightly raises. He looks anything but thrilled to see me.

"Good. You're here," he states, his eyes moving to my wrapped hands. "And ready."

"Considering it's my class schedule, where else would I be?" I shoot back.

"Nice to see she hasn't lost her redeeming personality," Corrine says, crossing her arms and spreading her feet in what I assume is supposed to be an intimidating gesture.

Fun fact—It's not.

"If she has any redeeming qualities, that's not one I would list," he responds dryly, stepping to the opposite side of the mat.

I roll my eyes. Whatever. "Are we sparring or not?"

"No," he answers.

I lean back on my palms and kick my feet out. "Then, by all means, what *are* we doing?" I ask.

"Quinn is going to strength train with you. In case you two haven't met, Quinn meet Caderyn, Caderyn meet Quinn."

"You can call me Nori," I say, looking up at her. No need for the formality of last names.

"You can call me Quinn," she says flatly.

I ignore her and turn back to Kingston. "Why are we not working on combat techniques?"

His gaze falls on me completely. My fingers twitch against the mat. I feel unnerved. "You currently don't have the strength to be efficient in any kind of battle," he answers bluntly. Okay, no need to sugarcoat it.

"I've never heard him speak quite so eloquently. To be a bit more precise, he's saying you're soft. You'd be more of a hindrance in battle than a help," Corrine casually flings in my direction.

Someone decided to wake up and be a rude bitch today.

Two can play that game.

And I play it better.

"Trust me, I read between the lines just fine," I state, disdain dripping from my words.

"We're going to start with bodyweight exercises," Kingston informs me, his tone cool as he offers me his hand to help me up. "Pull-ups, push-ups, you get the idea, and then move into combat conditioning. Once we get you where you need to be physically, we'll move to weapons-based training and grappling." He drops my hand and steps back. "Then, when I think you're ready, and only when I think you're ready, we'll transition into magic resistance training, as that's all mental defense, which is infinitely harder than physical."

I bite my lip in hesitation, but give him a firm nod.

The following two hours are grueling. I feel like I'm going to vomit or pass out. Possibly both at the same time. My cheeks are flushed, and my long waves hang in limp disarray. Corrine pushed me past the limits I thought possible. It's like she has a personal vendetta against me and didn't waste a precious second using it. Every muscle and ligament in my exhausted body is currently screaming and thrashing in anguish.

Kingston paced the side of the mat the entire session, calling out weaknesses and pointing out places that needed improvement. He was brutally honest and effortlessly efficient. He wasn't unkind, though. He didn't set out to make me feel less than. It was more about utilizing my full potential and becoming a formidable opponent. It's almost as if he knows I'm capable but sheltered.

Today, I was forced to be self-reliant and succeed on my own, or fail.

I rose to every challenge, even if I didn't necessarily achieve what they asked of me. I still gave it my all, and now my soft, untrained muscles are thoroughly pissed.

Kingston stands over me, looking down at my exhausted form as I lie stretched out on the mat like a starfish. "We'll continue this during every session, and you'll meet with Quinn twice a week in the training field for additional practice," he orders, his tone leaving no room for discussion.

Corinne scoffs. "At this rate, she should be in a desirable position by next year. If she's lucky."

Kingston tilts his head in her direction, and she immediately looks away.

I slowly sit up and rise to my feet, limping over to grab my bag. I quickly remove my wrappings and shove them in the side pocket. Gripping the edge of my shirt, I bring it up to wipe the sweat from my brow. As I turn to leave, I catch Kingston watching me. His eyes lift just enough to meet mine—quick and deliberate— before he averts his gaze and walks over to speak with Corinne and another Noctryn who joined them.

I don't take offense to his curt dismissals anymore. He does what needs to be done, accomplishes the task, and moves on. It's efficient and oddly works for me.

All action and less talk.

It's just who he is.

Soft chatter and the clinking of silverware greet me as I meet Finnley and Mallory in the dining hall. Exhausted, sore, sweating, and starving, I force my broken body to grab a lunch tray and overload it with fruits, sweets, and a full entrée. I limp through the crowded tables, heading toward my friends.

I plop down in an open seat and immediately groan. Mallory's eyes widen, and Finnley lets out a low whistle. I raise my shoulder in a half shrug. I'm not the least bit embarrassed about my appetite. "Hush," I mutter. "I feel like death and still have three more classes to attend."

"You smell like death, too," Finnley supplies.

"How's the class load coming along?" Mallory asks, shooting Finnley a murderous look as she moves her salad around with her fork.

"It's not. I'm struggling in every Veil class, and I'm getting my ass handed to me in the Noctryn ones," I answer monotonously. I'm too tired to even add inflection to my voice.

"It'll get easier," she offers, her tone softening.

Finnley nods in agreement. "If it makes you feel any better, I wouldn't mess with you right now," he says around a mouthful of food.

"It doesn't," I say in a defeated voice, although I give him a small smile because I can only imagine how I look.

I dig in while they continue to chat. The hunger in me is voracious. I've completely checked out and am in my own little world when I hear the word *dark object* mentioned. I swallow my food half-chewed and sit forward a little. "Have they found it?" I quickly ask.

"Nope," Finnley answers simply. "They also haven't found the missing professor."

Mallory sets her fork down. "I do find it odd that the professor who disappeared last year was also a Veil, and his room was in complete disarray as well. Almost as if someone was looking for something." She quirks her lip to the side, drumming her fingertips along the table. "Just a little convenient that both were instructors of light magic."

"Was anything missing from their rooms?" I ask.

She shakes her head. "Not that I've heard. It was mentioned that Professor Huntsal was seen talking to Eryk Porter shortly before she was reported missing. From what I've heard the conversation looked a little tense before Eryk stormed off."

"She was the language professor, right?" I ask.

"Yep, she was. I had her second period," Finnley chimes in.

I take a large bite of my cookie, pondering why a professor of languages and a dark object would go missing at the same time. "What did the professor teach that went missing last year?" I ask around the mouthful of cookie.

"A guy in my ethics class, Murphy, told me he taught alchemy before Professor Lyric took over," Mallory answers.

Language and alchemy are vastly different. Why would both go missing nearly a year apart? Even more confounding is that both occurred at the same time that a dark object went missing.

What are we overlooking?

"Has the academy let anyone in the student body know exactly what dark objects were taken?"

"Nope. Evidently, that's classified." Finnley sits back in his chair and rubs his stomach.

The corners of Mallory's mouth turn down as she lets out an exaggerated sigh. "In other news, my manifestation is royally pissing me off," she whines.

"Wait, what? You fully manifested?" I shriek. "Tell me everything!"

She blushes and looks around before breaking into a wide smile. "I did."

I motion for her to continue, needing all the details.

"Apparently, it's a foreseeing ability. However, at the moment, everything is as clear as mud. I can see different probable outcomes, but not why they change, and let me tell you, they alter vastly," she groans as she rubs the back of her neck. "Thus far, even with practice, nothing has panned out the way I predicted it would happen." Her brows dip and her lips thin, causing her face to morph into a crestfallen appearance.

"Mallory, that's invaluable... You'll be incredibly sought after when we graduate. You could sway the outcomes of battles and negotiations, and save lives. That's beyond powerful," I tell her. Her manifestation is incredibly respected in the army. I've even heard my mother talk about it in high regard, and that's saying something.

"It's all a bit overbearing at the moment."

Finnley is suddenly quiet and staring at his plate.

"What about you, Finnley?" I ask, wiggling my brows at him. "Have you...?" I trail off at the blank expression on his face.

"It's too soon to know where it's headed. Best to hold off talking about it until I'm sure," he evades.

I kick his foot playfully under the table. "I'm sure whatever it is will be just as impressive as Mallory's," I offer, taking the hint that he doesn't want to talk about it. "I mean, at least you both are manifesting, regardless of how murky it all is right now. So many already did during the blood initiation, and then others are slowly coming into their powers like you both. And then there's me." I pat my chest. "I haven't shown anything," I say, hoping to boost their morale a bit with self-deprecation.

"You will, Nori. Give yourself time. There haven't been many Liminals before you. To be part of each regiment is impressive enough in itself," Finnley offers with his usual customary support.

"I don't know about impressive, but it sure is isolating," I whisper.

Chapter Twenty

After lunch, I head out to the training field to meet Ambrose before my next class.

Snow crunches under my boots as I step into the clearing and walk across the field. The mazes are long gone, as if they never existed. It's now a frozen expanse of white under the gray winter sky. Wooden dummies and practice weapons are scattered among the fresh powder. The far edges of the perimeter blur in a haze of frost and fog, making the area feel mysterious and beautiful. This is where cadets have their endurance, skills, and resolve tested.

Right now, it's just vast fields of fallen snow and Ambrose up ahead.

A soft gasp leaves me as he raises his hands, fire shooting out with deadly accuracy, hitting target after target. The flames are a sentinel being, moving like a living thing. Angry, ancient, and powerful. It behaves like a caged beast finally freed.

His hood is lowered, the wind tugging at his unbound hair, whipping it across his face as he concentrates. His shoulders tense as he puts all his effort into controlling the unpredictable flames. It's magnificent to witness. I carefully make my way to his side, clearing my throat so he knows I'm here. He shoots a quick look in my direction before closing both fists, extinguishing the fire immediately.

I slowly clap my hands. "Impressive."

"It's a great party trick," he teases, a quiet smile tugging at his lips.

"I still can't believe you're a fire wielder," I admit, shaking my head in disbelief.

"You and me both." He quietly laughs and rubs his hands on his thighs.

He approaches the targets, inspecting the first as he runs a hand over the burnt bull's-eye. His broad frame causes him to sink in the snow as he makes his rounds to the other three. He's a perfectionist, and nothing less than excellence will pass his scrutiny. He must be satisfied with what he sees because he turns and walks directly back toward me.

I wrap my arms around myself, as if the gesture will protect me from the elements. He throws a heavy arm over my shoulder and looks down at me, his lips pulling into a full-blown smile, highlighting his straight white teeth. "It *was* pretty cool, huh?" he asks.

The corners of my mouth lift. "Very badass," I confirm.

I scan the area as we walk back toward Kintoira. The training field is empty except for the two of us. Soon, lunch will be over, and it will once again be filled with students practicing their craft, but for the moment, it's quiet and peaceful.

"How did they remove the mazes so quickly? The walls were enormous."

"They didn't actually remove anything," he answers, taking in our surroundings.

I keep walking, waiting for him to answer because it's too cold to stop and talk. "Well, they didn't grow legs and walk away."

He tugs me in close to him and ruffles my hair.

I swat him away.

"It was an illusion, brat. A hell specifically crafted for you by the upper-level Noctryns. Nothing you saw, feared, and escaped from within that maze was real."

I can feel my jaw drop on its own accord. Ambrose takes a finger and pushes it closed.

"You're kidding," I choke out.

"Nope, I'm not," he answers simply, like it's obvious that we weren't truly fighting for our lives within those passageways. "You were never in any real danger, Nori. The final trial is created to weed out the mentally weak, more so than to weed out prospects by death. Although that is certainly a probability."

"So that's why I couldn't see what Finnley was seeing unless I touched his face," I whisper.

He pulls his bottom lip between his teeth, debating on how much knowledge to leak. "Correct. They took each of your biggest fears, as well as a combined fear, and brought them to life. As an officer, I was able to get all the details from your maze run." His eyes cut to me, but he looks completely unapologetic. "Seems like your little friend doesn't care for wraiths, hence his battle with one. The thing that keeps you up at night…" he trails off, hesitation smeared across his face.

I bite my lip. Hard. "Keep going."

"Your biggest weakness is yourself and losing those you care about. That's why the mirrors were incorporated. You were forced to face your reflection and lose your friend in the same way."

I don't say anything. I just let him continue.

"And last but not least, you both hate spiders."

I brush a small strand of hair behind my ear and give him a subtle nod. I don't disagree with him. "So Finnley never really got pulled into the mirror? It was all in my head?"

"He stepped through an archway you couldn't see. Something called him through so that you could live out your own horror, so to speak. But all in all, he was never technically inside a mirror."

"Although something did call him through the archway?" I repeat, stopping to face Ambrose.

He slips his arm off my shoulders, allowing it to fall to his side. "Correct, but only the Noctryns know what it was. They pick and choose the information they share with the Veil officers." His brows furrow in an angry pinch.

I'm both annoyed and impressed at the dark wielders' tenacity.

I can feel Ambrose's heavy stare on me as I replay everything in my head from that day. I know he's trying to decide whether he wants to ask something or not.

"Go ahead, I can see the wheels spinning," I tell him, stopping to fully face him.

He clears his throat and rubs the back of his neck with his hand, his bicep flexing with the motion. "Have you had any dark manifestations?"

"I haven't had any manifestations, period. Light or dark."

His tongue pokes the inside of his cheek. "No shadows or mind manipulation abilities making themselves known? No success with their blood magic?" he asks, his gaze sharpening on me.

"Nothing," I confirm. At this point, I'm not sure how upset I'd be if a shadow emerged. At least it would be *something*.

"Thank the gods."

"Should I be thankful, though, Ambrose? I've shown nothing. Nada. Zip. I'm literally one of the last who have yet to manifest, and I'm starting to really doubt the outcome here while you're dancing around in gratitude."

He blinks. "It'll happen, Nori. You're just a late bloomer," he assures me, his eyes hardening like there isn't another option or explanation.

I kick the snow and start walking again. "Have you heard any updates on Professor Huntsal? I wasn't sure if they shared anything in your officer's class that the rest of us aren't privy to?"

He pulls his gaze away before throwing his head back and sighing. "No. They haven't shared much except updated orders. We've been assigned the task of investigating her disappearance, while the Noctryns have been assigned to look into the missing dark object. At this point, we've both come up short. Whoever took them had complete access to the academy and a big enough reason to risk taking them."

What kind of reason would someone have to risk something so big? The ramifications of doing so would be astronomical.

"They'd have to be very familiar with the academy layout as well as where dark objects were being kept," I murmur more to myself. "Or know someone else who has this information."

"Nothing for you to worry that pretty little head about," he assures me, scooping up a ball of snow and chucking it across the field. "From what I understand, you passed that *dickhead's* interrogation with flying colors." He puts extra emphasis on the word dickhead.

"Well, it is something for me to worry about, Ambrose," I correct him. "And honestly, the interrogation wasn't as bad as I imagined it would be."

He stops and looks at me as if I've lost my mind. I shrug and pull my hood up. The snow has started to fall again.

He jogs to catch up with me, gripping me by the shoulder, stopping me and spinning me toward him. "Don't trust him. Any of them, but *especially* him. He always has some kind of trick tucked up his sleeve," he states. "I mean it, Nori. Don't mistake what you think is kindness for anything other than it is. A means to an end."

"And here I was thinking you two were becoming friends," I reply sarcastically.

He yanks on my braid gently and shoots me one of his devastating smiles.

The kind he used to get out of trouble with.

Only now, it's me who feels like they're in trouble.

Chapter Twenty-One

The desk shakes as I drop my head.

A groan escapes.

We've been practicing shadow craft for over an hour, and if failure were a currency, I'd be rich. When Professor Rinkin informed us we'd be at our most vulnerable when learning to wield, she wasn't kidding. I've tried everything from intense concentration to ridiculous hand movements. I even resorted to the deepest pits of depravity and asked Kingston for advice. He not only gave it, but also poured himself into the explanation, as if his own success were on the line. Sometimes I think he wants me to succeed in the dark classes just to be able to rub Ambrose's face in it. Other times, I'm not so sure of his motivations.

At times, I think he despises me. But then I'm not so sure.

He's a walking contradiction that I can't figure out.

Shadows swirl in every direction in the class. Some small, like smoke erupting from students' fingertips, and others dark and volatile, like death on swift wings. Laughter erupts from someone close by as they grasp the concept of control. It's one thing to cast a shadow, but another entirely to control them. At least from what I've been told. It really is beauty in the most brutal form. Something so ethereal and mysterious, yet also full of potential to decimate someone.

As most beautiful things are.

"I've yet to see casting accomplished with one's head on a desk, but I'm open to trying," Kingston drawls.

Without lifting my head, I give him the middle finger.

It's like our signature greeting at this point.

A deep and sinister laugh comes from above me, practically causing me to have whiplash as I sit up. "Excuse me, good sir, but did you just laugh?" I ask in an incredulous tone.

"Believe it or not, it does happen on rare occasions," he replies straight-faced, like it, in fact, never happened.

I narrow my eyes at him. "Prove it. Do it again," I order.

"The probability of me laughing on command is the same as you wielding on command."

I pause. "Geeze, you don't have to be an ass."

"And you don't have to pout."

"I'm not pouting. I'm simply giving up. There's a difference." I drop my head back on the desk.

"Then you are definitely not a Noctryn. Glad we got that sorted," he states with apathy.

I raise my head slightly. "I never wanted to be," I remind him, giving him a sharp look.

A dark chuckle slips free. "Let me guess. You still bleed the colors of a Veil, holding onto that false sense of righteousness," he mocks. "*Veil.* It really is a fitting name. Lift it and you might not like what you see."

I hold his gaze in challenge. "Are you insinuating that abandoning my birth magic only to engulf myself in dark arts is more genuine and pure? More righteous?"

"At this point, you haven't manifested either, so it's a moot point," he responds flatly.

Ouch. Someone woke up and chose violence today.

"When my powers decide to finally make themselves known, they will without a doubt be on the light spectrum. So don't bother getting your hopes up."

A smile curves along his lips. "Trust me, if this class is any indication, they were never up."

I scrunch my nose and tilt my head. "Well, unfortunately for me, I didn't have a choice in who my partner was, so it seems we both got the short end of the stick."

"You wound me, *Heathen*."

He doesn't look wounded in the slightest.

In fact, he looks bored.

"I could be so lucky."

He gives me a stare that could bury me and appraises me with those black-rimmed eyes. Unnatural, otherworldly and mysterious. It'd be so easy to squirm under his assessment, but I won't. For some reason, I don't like the idea of him thinking of me as timid. I'm better than that.

"Like what you see?" I ask in a dry tone.

"It's more about what I don't see, Caderyn. There's zero grit, effort or determination on your part." His words are sharp and cutting.

"Are you kidding me right now? I am trying! I'm doing my best to pull something that's not there from an empty well. I am not a Noctryn!," I repeat for the hundredth time. "The sooner you and I both accept that, the better. Then I can get out of these classes and focus on the ones that really matter."

He shakes his head. "With that projection, you'll never wield. As a Liminal, you have dark abilities, whether you like it or not. They may be subtle, but they're there. It could be in just your thought process and not necessarily in magic, but it's there." His lips pull up in a snarl. "If it wasn't there, you wouldn't be a Liminal. You would have tested inconclusive by not placing in *either* and swiftly executed." He softly laughs. It doesn't sound friendly. "You, however, placed in *both*. Get up, straighten your spine, and try again. And again, if needed. You don't get to quit while at this academy and certainly not while under my mentorship," he bites out.

"I never asked for your mentorship," I remind him.

He just looks at me with disappointment, which is worse than anger.

If this man, who doesn't even like me, isn't giving up on me, then I certainly won't give up on myself. Whether I like him or not, he's spitting facts. Even if they are a bit hard to swallow.

I close my eyes, place my palms up, and focus everything I have on bringing forth some kind of shadow. Professor Rinkin said it comes from our core. It's like taking a deep breath and exhaling the shadows out into the world. They're an extension of ourselves, a small fraction of our very essence being released to protect and defend. I'm not sure what to do when my core keeps coming up empty. No matter how long I focus and will it to cooperate, nothing happens.

"It's better to fail than not try," Kingston says quietly.

I peel my eyes open to meet his satisfied stare.

Perhaps it's not so much that he wants me to show the darker qualities, but more so that he doesn't want to see me give up on myself. I honestly cannot figure out this perplexing man. There are so many layers to him, so much more than the surface level of indifference he shows the world.

The professor claps loudly, signaling the end of class.

His satisfied expression dissolves as he reaches a hand toward me. "Walk with me?"

I stare at his hand with suspicion. "Why, are you planning on taking me somewhere isolated to get rid of me once and for all?"

"And allow my ego to get out of hand without someone to insult me routinely?"

A reluctant smile dances across my lips as I grab my pack, take his hand against my better judgment, and stand.

We make our way down the noisy halls, preventing any real conversation. Heading down the dimly lit corridor, he leads the way and cuts through the crowd with ease. To my surprise, he veers right instead of toward the entrance and heads up a winding staircase.

I follow closely behind as students pass us by, throwing curious glances our way.

The Liminal clothed in gray on the heels of a man cloaked in the same color as his soul. One ostracized and the other feared.

We make a striking pair.

He pushes a heavy door open at the end of a narrow passageway, and we exit onto the battlements. I pull my sleeves down over my hands and step out onto the cold, worn stones. It's freezing, and the snow keeps falling. I take in my surroundings of snowcapped mountains and glistening pines as far as the eye can see. Tendrils of crimson hair blow around my face as I tilt my head back, catching a few snowflakes on my tongue.

I hope I never stop being in awe of the beauty of snow. It coats everything in a blanket of silence, allowing me to shut off the noise in my head. Endless white powder on every surface, makes everything seem untouched by man. Pure and pristine. It's a reminder that magic is all around us, appearing in the most inconspicuous ways.

A reminder I certainly needed.

"You were made to live somewhere it snows," Kingston says, watching me catch the snowflakes. His rich baritone washes over me.

"Oh yeah? And why's that?" I ask, wiping a few flakes off the tip of my nose.

His eyes linger on me longer than necessary. "Besides being a pale red-head that should probably avoid the sun?"

I level him with a flat stare.

He leans closer, voice low. "Because you appreciate the beauty in cold things. Things that can be deadly and harsh but treat the right person with reverence."

Pulling back, he walks over to the battlement wall.

I swallow.

Well, that was poetic and unexpected. "And here I was thinking you brought me up here just to push me over," I say to his back.

The black fabric of his uniform hugs his form. His hair, dark as midnight and slicked back flawlessly, is dusted with fresh snowflakes. "Careful, you almost sounded grateful," he replies over his shoulder, his lips curling into a smirk.

"If I didn't know better, I'd almost say you like having me around."

He turns toward me, his body rigid. "I brought you up here to talk freely, without prying ears."

I scrunch my brow in confusion at the turn of the conversation.

"Are you familiar with the history between the Noctryns and the Veils?"

I give a slight nod in response. "History happens to be a favorite subject of mine."

His jaw tenses. "That's not history, that's what they teach you. What they want you to know," he replies in a low tone.

"Are they not one and the same?"

"Hardly."

"By all means, indulge me, then."

He runs a hand slowly down his face and over the short stubble. "Salaryan is an oligarchy. Power lies with a few egotistical men who control it by placing their personal endeavors at the forefront. They decide where soldiers are stationed, which cities deserve protection, and which information the general population should be made aware of. It's self-preservation at its finest, and transparency at its worst," he says, giving me his undivided attention. "The underprivileged and those with less to offer feel the brunt of it," he finishes, something deeper lacing every word.

This is all common knowledge, but to speak it aloud is heresy. I cast a glance around to be sure we're alone. "This is dangerous territory, Adair," I whisper.

"Which is why I brought you up here, where we're alone."

I huff out a laugh. "And you trust me not to repeat any of this?"

"Yes," he answers without hesitation, inclining his head. "This information is important and not something you're going to learn in any classroom," he states. "The realm used to be run by those who were taught the responsibilities and sacrifices needed to rule a kingdom from their very birth. It was granted to men and women through hereditary succession. Those who had an entire upbringing of duties and obligations thrust upon their shoulders." His words are heavy, but his deliverance is executed with passion. "They bore the weight of an entire kingdom with the well-being of their citizens at the forefront. Their crowns were crushing, but they wore them with resolve, and the kingdom prospered because of it."

My mouth opens and then closes.

For a second, I say nothing, just stare at his warm brown eyes that watch me with an unreadable expression. "Are you telling me that Salaryan used to be run by *royals*?" I question, full of incredulity.

"That's just the tip of the iceberg."

I pace back and forth in front of him, my boots wearing a thin trail in the freshly fallen snow. He patiently waits for me to absorb what he's telling me. His broody form is now resting against the wall, his legs crossed in front of him and arms folded.

I stop and face him, nodding once for him to continue.

He indulges me. "Members of the royal family, whether immediate or extended, were classified as Noctryns."

The breath lodges in my throat. There's no fucking way.

"It was a right bestowed at birth and not by a military academy," he continues, like he didn't just rob me of my breath. "Their dark manifestations were revered, not feared. And they were manifestations, not something given because they sacrificed abilities to wield darkness. It's all propaganda shoved down our throats, and we chew and swallow without questioning it," he says, disgust evident in his tone. "They protected their people from outside forces of any kind, even building walls to keep the enemy out and performing blood magic to keep the wraiths at bay. The Noctryns were respected and loved by their people. Their armies were feared across the domains." His eyes bore into mine. "The most elite and powerful stood guard at the royal's side."

"And who were they?"

He clenches and unclenches his fists at his sides. "Veils," he reveals.

A shiver runs down my spine.

Impossible. This is all impossible.

"Nothing is impossible, Caderyn."

"No," I breathe, "this isn't true. You're lying. Why are you telling me this?" I demand, walking up and poking a finger in his chest. The red M at his shoulder stands out like a mockery among the lies he's spewing. "The Veils never served the Noctryns. We detest everything you stand for!"

He looks down at me through his lashes. "I'm telling you this, *Heathen*, because you deserve to know. You're half Noctryn, whether you want to admit it or not. This may help you see us in a different light." His face is stoic, but his eyes are filled with something I can't quite put my finger on. "What you do with this information is entirely up to you. However,

I highly recommend keeping it disclosed. Not everyone is privy to it, not even all of the dark regiment at this academy."

I walk to stand beside him and clutch the edge of the battlement walls, knuckles turning white as I stare at nothing and everything. All the lessons I was raised upon are carefully crafted lies? Why? Why would the divide between the two powerhouses be encouraged?

Is Kingston being honest, or is this some sort of devious plot to bury me?

I don't doubt he has something up his sleeve, just like Ambrose said.

"What happened to these so-called royals?" I ask, trying to find holes in his story.

"Glad you asked," he answers, stepping a little too close and invading my space. "Assassinated. Picked off one by one, and those who they couldn't get to were targets of a smear campaign, turning the Veils against them," he says, his breath falling over my ear. "Their most trusted soldiers became their most determined hunters. The immediate royal line was wiped out, and the remaining Noctryns were enlisted as mere foot soldiers."

The gray stones of Kintoira Academy sit in front of us. An academy built on deceit and sinister plots, if what Kingston is saying is true.

His eyes take on a faraway look as he leans back and keeps talking. "A lethal army of both light and dark magic was put together to protect a small group of weak-minded men. Men who ran the kingdom into the ground. An academy was created for future generations to be classified into the categories they deemed appropriate." A dark laugh slips free. "The very same academy you're currently enrolled in."

I watch him start to pace the battlement, his face drawn into harsh lines while he talks. I stay quiet, letting him tell me everything. "They made a mistake, though. They didn't count on the surviving original Noctryns refusing to forget and not letting the grudge die. The blood magic woven into Salaryan's walls, the ones that kept the abnormalities out, eventually failed, and the casting needed to resurrect it died with the royals," he says. "A separation between the magic was created, and simultaneously, Salaryan was opened up to be preyed upon by forces darker than they could have imagined."

If this is true, which I'm not saying it is, but if it is, at one point in time, there was no mistrust and hatred between the two powerhouses. They fought side by side and trusted each other before turning on one another.

I blow out a breath and stare at the cold man before me. Timeless, distant, and full of things still left unsaid. His mask never fell, but it shifted, showing something raw and real. Perhaps his silence isn't detachment but protection.

I have a million things on my plate and a hundred places I'm supposed to be, but first, I'm visiting the library.

Chapter Twenty-Two

I stare at the three large piles of timeworn texts in front of me with annoyance.

I grabbed every history book I could find, returned to retrieve more, and still came up empty-handed. There hasn't been a single mention of royals in Salaryan's history.

Trust me, I checked and then double-checked.

The foundation of the wraith attacks, the evolution of prosperous cities within the realm, and an abundance of information on Veils and Noctryns all reside within the rough-edged pages. But nothing that ever links them to a monarch. Definitely nothing that correlated a camaraderie between the two. I went back hundreds of years, and not one king, queen, or even a princeling was mentioned.

Moonlight spills through the arched windows, and a few remaining lamps that haven't burned out cast a warm glow on the large stained-glass window. The library is all but abandoned at this hour. The thick carpet beneath my feet masks the insistent tapping of my foot, my anxiety rushing to the forefront and telling me that I'm missing something.

Something right in front of my face.

My fingers drum across the hardcover of a tome, bound in cracked leather, the cover lacking a title but bearing the crest of Kintoira. I scan the isolated library, my mind searching for a loophole or overlooked factor. In the corner, a lone student sits hunched over a table, half covered in shadows as he pores over a manuscript. Apparently, we both had the same idea. Look for answers while the rest of the world sleeps.

I reach down into my bag, sorting through the contents for the quill that I tossed in the bottom earlier. My fingers graze the edges of what feels like a book.

That's odd...

I haven't checked out any books, and the ones I bought are currently sitting beneath my bed.

Carefully, I pull a small, palm-sized book out from the bottom of my bag. I turn it in my hands, but don't recognize it. The cover is silver, like moonlight, and shimmers as I look it over. The corners are slightly bent, as if it's cherished and has been read many times.

I slowly open the cover, and a recognizable scent assaults my nostrils, but I can't pinpoint where I've smelled it before.

It's just *familiar*.

The first page is blank, with no author's name or title. I flip to the next page, and it's also blank. I go through page by page, expecting something, but each one is the same as before. Empty, except for small dark red marks on random pages. Regardless of how many pages I turn or how closely I look, each one remains the same. However, they don't *feel* empty. They call to me with a heavy weight. There's a strain to the pages as if they want to be read.

To be understood.

As if they will reveal their contents once they choose to.

Or it's earned.

A clock chimes somewhere in the distance, alerting me to the midnight hour. I've been at this all night without success. I now know exactly what I did at the start of the day. Unless every book in Kintoira's archives has been purposely edited to exclude the royals and their affiliations with the Veils, this has been a complete waste of my time.

Closing the odd little book, I tuck it back in my bag, push a few volumes on the table out of the way, and close my eyes for a moment. I rest my cheek against the cool, worn-down wood. Exhaustion weighs heavily in my limbs, and my eyes are so tired they hurt. The sounds and smells of the library quiet my mind, offering a sense of respite. Delicate pages being turned in the corner, like a soothing hymn. The steady yet soft tick of a nearby clock, and the fragrance of old parchment and dry ink. It all creates the perfect symphony for rest.

Until it doesn't.

Slowly, the air becomes heavy with the coppery scent of blood and something far more nefarious. A dense forest gradually begins to surround me, one that's been turned into a battlefield. Shouts arise in all directions, orders are barked, and war cries bellow. The sound of armor rushing through the trees and the vibrations of hooves shake the ground as the horses' charge fall upon me. An arrow hisses by, narrowly missing my head.

I duck and hide behind the thick trunk of a tree.

No one ever mentions how loud war is.

If it's not the clash of metal or the screaming, it's your own heartbeat. I can feel it thudding against my ribs.

Veils wield alongside the Noctryns.

Fire and ice, steel and shadows.

Black blood drips from the tips of swords, and daggers embed into their enemies with calculated coldness. There's no room for emotions or fear as the threat to a kingdom is demolished. Electric currents fly from the palms of a nearby Veil, and another shifts into an indigo-hued harpy, her mouth open on a punishing screech as she rips out the throat of a wraith. A dark wielder has another wrapped in obsidian shadows, the tendrils tightening around its throat before effectively snapping the decaying head from its shoulders.

It's absolute madness in every direction.

The Veils alongside the Noctryns are taking no fucking prisoners. They're extremely outnumbered and still come out swinging.

I grind my teeth as my gaze darts around the battle taking place. I'm in the middle of an all-out clash like a sitting duck.

The sudden smell of decay and sulfur permeates the air, making me try to breathe through my nose instead of my mouth. I tear my eyes to the side, trying to find where the smell is coming from, when they land on the biggest wraith I've ever seen in any textbook. It's facing a Noctryn, also one of the largest I've seen, but compared to the wraith, he doesn't stand a chance.

I hold my breath, preparing to see the soldier decimated and feasted upon.

There's absolutely nothing I can do to help. But I'm not going to just sit here. I pat my thigh, looking for my hidden dagger, but it's gone. I wouldn't have forgotten it. Something isn't right here.

Without hesitation, the cloaked abomination charges and lunges for the warrior, but the Noctryn is faster than I anticipate. He lands a hit with the hilt of his sword to the back of the wraith's head. Regaining its footing, it turns around slowly, the hood falling back to reveal rotting skin and hollow eyes. It whips its head to the side before opening its razor-filled mouth and screaming in fury.

I instinctively move backward. It's a living nightmare in the flesh.

The Noctryn tightens the grip on his sword, using the other gloved hand to wave the decaying monster on. Taunting it. Pissing it off. The wraith descends on the soldier full of rage and force, the ground shaking beneath its charge, cloak snapping behind it in synchronized ferocity. Without hesitation, the soldier pulls the other sword from his back, raises both as he shifts his weight, and digs his heels into the ground.

I bite my lip and pray harder than I've ever prayed before.

It doesn't escape me that I'm praying for a dark wielder, but between him and the wraith, it's going to be him.

Every single time.

The moment the wraith is close enough that his mouth is opening to retrieve the soul he thinks he's owed, the soldier brings down both swords in a brutal, two-handed strike, severing the decomposing head from its body. My gaze drops as the head slides from its body, rolls across the ground, and stops inches from my feet.

I look back toward the Noctryn.

Dual swords drip black gore as he stands there, watching the decapitated head before raising his helm to stare directly at me. I can't see anything behind the obsidian visor, but I know without a doubt, regardless of the battle ensuing all around us, his entire focus is now on me.

"Nori... Nori, get up," a delicate voice says, gently shaking my shoulders. "C'mon... that can't be comfortable."

I slowly peel my heavy eyelids open and use the back of my hand to wipe the drool that's pooled in the corner of my mouth. Mallory is watching me with a concerned expression in her wide eyes. Her pale-blue hair is spiked in various directions. "I know you have a full class load, but this is a bit much," she whispers, looking around at all the history books surrounding me.

I stretch both arms above my head, my lips parting in a long yawn. "What time is it?" I ask.

"Half past ten."

"In the morning?" I croak.

She nods like it's obvious. "Yeah."

Fuuuck.

I stand so fast the chair falls over, earning me a few glares from nearby students. "She's going to kill me," I panic-whisper as I bend down to pick it up.

"Who's going to kill you?" Mallory's eyebrows knit together, creating a furrow between her eyes.

I want to give her more of my time, but at the moment, I don't have any. "I gotta go, but I'll catch up with you later," I toss over my shoulder, exiting the library as if my ass is on fire.

Pebbles fly up from under my boots as I run with everything in me toward the practice field. The gate leading out to it swings on its hinges, smacking the small stone wall as I run through, my steps faltering as I rush down the stairs slick with ice.

I tumble into the field with absolutely no grace.

A few isolated groups are practicing their craft, but I don't see Corinne right away. I scan the area looking for her, afraid I won't find her, but also dreading the fact that I might. Stepping forward, I'm careful to give the wielders a wide berth. A third-year Veil with a braided crown and a look of fierce concentration on her face is encased in an electrical sphere, with bursts of currents spidering out around her.

Quickly moving past, I pass by a handful of Noctryns attacking each other with swords in lethal combinations, their shadows withering around them, seeking out any weaknesses in their opponent. Farther down, another Veil is shifting, and an unimpressed fourth-year Noctryn is leaning against a large boulder, his nose scrunched, and eyes filled with disgust as he watches.

My steps become faster and my shoulders tense as each scan comes up empty. I'm about to give up and accept the fact that I blew it when I finally see them. Corrine stands behind Makon, a large dagger pressed to his throat, whispering something in his ear with a smug look on her face.

His answering grin is pure menace.

He grips her forearms and presses his throat into the blade, causing droplets of blood to drip down his neck. Her brows sink, and she goes to pull back, but the next moment, he has her flipped over his shoulder. She lands soundly on her back with his knee pinning her chest down and his Damascus dagger at her throat.

I can see her lips from here, pulling into a snarl and cursing him.

His face breaks out in a deep, rich laugh. Standing, he offers her his hand, which she smacks away. Her fighting leathers look damp and uncomfortable, leading me to wonder just how many times Makon has landed her in the snow.

I take a deep breath and reluctantly step toward them.

I fear my leathers are about to be even more uncomfortable. I awkwardly clear my throat. "Sorry, I'm late."

Makon's head swivels toward me. "Well, hello, little Caderyn, how nice of you to join us." A cruel smile creeps over his face.

"You're late," Corrine huffs, tucking her dagger back in its sheath.

"I know," I admit, "I got caught up in the library. I'm sorry."

"Come on now, Quinn, cut her some slack. *She was in the library*," Makon says, adding air quotations around the word library.

"I was—" I start.

"I don't care if you were protecting the general himself—"

"In the library, you can check for yourself."

"When I tell you to be here at ten sharp, you're here ten minutes before," Corinne snaps, her high black ponytail swishing as she walks toward me.

I bite my tongue and give a stiff nod.

At this point, any argument I have is weak, and regardless of how bad I want to bark back, it's not worth it. I'll grin and take it on the chin. She grabs one of my wrists, her pinched features clearly painting her unhappiness with me, turns it over, and slaps a small dagger in my palm.

I look at it, then at her, hesitation clearly written all over my face. We're supposed to be working on strength training, not battle tactics. According to Kingston, I'm not ready for that yet. She looks at me like I'm stupid.

"Congrats, first-year. Today is your lucky day," she insists, malice coating her words.

"I seriously doubt that," I retort blandly. "Luck and I aren't exactly on a first-name basis."

"You're going hand-to-hand with one of the best," she says, her lips pulling into a sardonic sneer. I'm starting to wonder if this is the only expression she knows how to make.

I look around us. "Are you seeing someone that I'm not?"

Makon laughs, drawing my attention back to him. "I see someone woke up and chose to be a brat." He walks over and stops directly in front of me. His long black hair is partially bound in a warrior's knot at his crown, and the rest hangs loosely over his shoulders. His eyes are a deeper brown than his brother's and lack the onyx ring. The scar running down his temple to his mouth makes the smirk he's throwing in my direction seem downright hazardous.

I take a slight step back, then curse myself for doing so.

"A lot of women would love to be in your shoes right now and have the opportunity to have their hands all over me," he says, his voice low and thick.

"Rest assured, I am not one of those women."

He steps closer. "Yet," he purrs, circling me.

He's the predator, and I'm the prey.

Story of my life.

Corrine crawls up on one of the boulders and kicks her legs out in front of her. "The goal is to draw first blood. The smallest drop and you're victorious. Loser runs four laps around the training field," she says, waving her hands dismissively.

Four laps? I'll die before I reach one.

I can't run thirty seconds without being winded. I hate cardio more than I hate trying to wield shadows.

I exhale heavily and grip my dagger, stepping toward Makon.

This day fucking sucks.

He tilts his head, his tongue running over his teeth. Fucker looks like he's measuring my worth or something.

I swing out blindly, and he knocks the blade out of my hand into the snow.

He bears his teeth in an antagonizing smile. "Pathetic," he says, each syllable dipped in poisonous mockery.

I keep my eyes on him while I bend down to retrieve the blade.

Tossing my long ponytail over my shoulder, I stand and point the dagger at his annoying face. All I need is one small nick. Just one. The snow makes any sudden movement difficult, causing my boots to sink into the powder, throwing off any speed or precision I might have.

I lunge forward again, and Makon swats me to the side like an annoying gnat. Both of my hands and knees sink into the fallen snow.

I was right, wet leather is extremely uncomfortable.

"Is this seriously the best you've got? The academy fucked up in your assessment, Caderyn," he spits in my direction. "You're definitely 100 percent Veil."

"Finally, something we agree on," I growl from the ground.

I'm tired of being shoved into the snow, and even more tired of being fucking awful at sparring. This extra training isn't helpful either. It's just making a joke of me. "I think it's quite obvious to everyone that I don't have any Noctryn in me!"

His lips tug in amusement. "Would you like to?" he asks, his voice dripping with innuendo.

Ugh. Just no.

I stand and jab my wrist out, aiming for his throat, but I end up being thrown onto my back instead. He lands firmly on top of me, his thigh shoved between my legs, effectively ceasing any movement on my part. "Tap out, little Caderyn," he orders, his face inches from mine.

I raise my face as close as possible to his and growl, "Never."

One minute he's on top of me, and the next, he's four feet away on his back.

Kingston stands above me, shadows swirling around him in violent tendrils. His lips are pulled into a vicious snarl, and his canines are on full display. He looks like he'd like nothing more than to tear his brother apart, slowly and violently. "That's enough training for today," he says in a low voice.

He's talking to me, but his glare is on Makon.

"Thank fuck," Corrine replies, inspecting her nails from her perch.

Makon props himself up on his elbows, a slow, mocking smirk already in place. "Little touchy today, aren't we, big bro?" he asks. "Looks like that'll be four laps, little Caderyn," he throws in my direction, as he rises to his feet.

I close my eyes and let my head fall back into the snow.

"The victor doesn't run," Kingston declares.

"Which is why I, the victor, won't be running," Makon replies slowly.

I can hear Kingston's dark chuckle above me, and it sends shivers over my skin. "She drew blood," he says.

My eyes pop open, and I lift my head to look. Sure as shit, Makon holds up his hand inspecting it, and there's a small line of crimson. The dagger must have grazed him when Kingston threw him off me.

"You gotta be shitting me," Makon mutters.

Kingston crosses his arms. "That'll be four laps, little bro," he orders.

Chapter Twenty-Three

"So let me get this straight, you're telling me that big, brooding specimen of a man threw Makon off you?"

I roll my eyes rather dramatically. "It's really not that big of a deal. I think he was just pissed they didn't follow his instructions and started weapons training. Something *he* clearly thinks I'm not ready for." Mallory looks at me like she disagrees, but doesn't say anything further on the matter. With another history class finished, we stuff our texts into our packs.

I look over at her. "If you don't mind, I'm going to stay after for a minute to speak with the professor."

She throws me an easy smile. "Sure thing. I'll see you this afternoon."

I throw my pack over my shoulder and make my way down to the dais. Professor Hawkins is shoving loose pieces of parchment into the front of a roughly bound text, pushing her glasses up the bridge of her nose repeatedly and muttering under her breath.

I open my mouth to speak and then close it. I'm not even sure how to approach this. Gripping the strap of my pack, I step forward. "Sorry to bother you—" I start.

"Oh. Hello, Norissa," Professor Hawkins interrupts without looking up. She looks as discombobulated as usual.

Her sharp, birdlike eyes dart around her desk.

I clear my throat and try again. "Sorry to bother you. I was hoping I could steal a few moments of your time."

"Of course, what can I do for you?" she asks, clearly distracted.

A flicker of apprehension washes over me. This could be a colossal mistake, but there are no rewards without risks. I'm just not sure this one is worth the reward. "I know this is going to sound...crazy, but I've been playing around with a theory and am practically treading water at this point. I'm conducting some research on Salaryan's history," I inform her, trying to get to the point but also not sure I want to.

She pauses, looking through the clutter on top of her desk, then stands completely straight, her entire focus now resting on me.

I adjust my collar, the fabric suddenly confining. "I'm trying to determine whether the realm, at any point in time, had an affiliation with a monarchy. I know this is a far-fetched theory," I say, but stop when her eyes widen briefly before she quickly masks it.

She forces a smile, too tight to be natural. "That is quite the theory," she says with a soft laugh.

I fidget with the strap of my pack. She's hiding something. "I know,"—I laugh nervously—"like I said, far-fetched. I just have way too much time on my hands, apparently."

"I find that hard to believe with your current class load."

"Trouble sleeping. Frees up some extra hours for me," I say, clearly trying to evade. I'm not sure I like the intense scrutiny I'm suddenly under. This wasn't a good idea.

She sits down in the wooden chair at her desk. "Listen, Norissa, you're incredibly bright. The entire faculty is very interested in your path as a Liminal. There hasn't been one for a very long time," she states, placing her hands on top of her desk. "That being said, you're watched more than the typical student at Kintoira. Be very careful what you dig into or ask about," she warns.

"Okay," I quickly agree.

The tapping of her fingers along her desk makes me want to jump out of my skin. "The major and his staff are notorious for taking offense at the slightest indiscretion. The last thing you want to be labeled as is treasonous or draw their ire," she says quietly.

That is definitely not on my bucket list. Traitors are banished. Banishment is being sent to the other side of the wall. A place of ruin and murder. Everything wants to kill you, especially the biggest threat of all.

Wraiths.

I gulp and nod. All at the same time. "Understood."

I turn to leave, tucking my curiosity right back where it belongs.

"Norissa," she calls, stopping me in my tracks.

I look over my shoulder.

Her translucent complexion appears paler than usual. "Your answers will come in due time. Sometimes the resolution we seek is that much sweeter when flavored with patience."

I furrow my brows in confusion.

"Enjoy the rest of your day, Ms. Caderyn." She returns her attention to her desk, her dark, severely cut hair partially covering her face. I'm very clearly being dismissed.

I head straight to my room, skipping astrology class altogether. Dropping my bag, I bend down, and pull out *Dark Objects and Their Origins* from under my bed. The book is heavy in my lap. The worn black leather cover is smooth from age and soft beneath my touch. The pages are delicate from use and faded with time. The text inside is blunt with short sentences and few adjectives, much like a typical Noctryn.

The book pulses beneath my fingertips, just like it did in the old book-shop. I flip through the pages. Some of the chapters are written in what I think is Casacian, the native language of Casacia, but I can't read it, so I skip over those. I'm not even sure how many from Casacia can still speak the language. Solarish became the predominant dialect throughout the realm, and since then, many languages have disappeared. Casacian is now pretty much a dead language. Somewhere around the midsection, the language changes to the common tongue, and the author starts discussing the process of creating dark objects.

Ha! I don't need you to teach me, Kingston. I have it all right here.

The text says that they're primarily used for stabilizing. They are created when a Noctryn combines their blood, melted iron, and the desired object. The ritual is finalized with an oath, which they sadly didn't include. Once the dark object has been created, only the individual or a blood relative can use it to stabilize their powers. The text says that not having a stabilizer is to welcome madness for those powerful enough.

I find it ironic that only the dark ones have the ability to create a stabilizer. They give up their birth-given abilities to be able to wield dark magic, but are given the ability to create. It proceeds to say that if a Veil attempts to possess a dark object, it would be catastrophic to the user, and the object would be rendered useless. A light wielder cannot perform dark magic, as light and dark cancel each other out. This applies to all wielders except Liminals.

Oh my gods.

It's discussing Liminals!

I hunch over the book, my nose so close it's almost touching the pages. The page states that the only time the cancelation process has been known to fail is during the phenomenon known as *Liminals*. Instead of revo-cation, these individuals gain both attributes. Light and dark. They're incredibly rare and appear only every four to five generations. Their powers have been known to be monumental but closely guarded.

That's it.

There's nothing else on the subject.

I rapidly turn the pages, and there is no further mention of them. Tapping my fingers against the spine of the book, I try to figure out why this subject is so taboo. It's like they are deliberately making this difficult for me. I flip to the back of the book. There's a lot of information about predominant figures throughout history and the dark objects they created. A spear, a dagger, and a ring, among others, decorate the pages.

My fingers halt over one of the names. *Sanderson Thurboult.*

The same name as the author.

An older man with wiry white hair and stern eyes looks back at me. He has a quiet but powerful aura. Dangling from his neck is a black locket. I squint my eyes. On the front, a crown is etched into the delicate metal, with twin swords crossing behind it. It doesn't say much about him except that he was a Noctryn who specialized in blood magic and lived a few centuries ago. The exact date isn't listed.

I release a loud, drawn-out sigh.

Tossing the text to the side, I reach under my bed for one of the others. I scan the cover, but it's the astrology book. Flinging it away, I blindly reach under again for my other Moorechester purchase, but my fingers land on something smaller. I pull it out. It's the little silver book from my bag. I'd tossed it under the bed with the others and forgotten all about it. Full of nothing, yet it feels heavy.

There's always some kind of mystery shrouding everything I touch these days. Nothing is just given freely. Not even information. The night I found this little sucker in my bag, I tried everything to see if words would appear.

I looked at it under the faint glow of moonlight and sang to it. I even tried to negotiate with it.

Silence.

I crack the spine open, even though I know the pages are still blank. I'm careful not to touch any of the rust-colored stains throughout. I'm not sure, but I suspect those stains are dried blood. It's slightly disturbing that someone just kept handling the book while bleeding on the pages. Luckily, the majority seems to have buried into the spine.

I scoff.

Always something bleeding or demanding blood around here.

Always something bleeding...

My hand freezes over the parchment.

Always something demanding blood.

No fucking way.

I reach up in the drawer of my nightstand and pull out the dagger Ambrose gave me. I quickly make a small cut along my fingertip and flip back to the first page. Blood drips onto the blank sheet. *Drip. Drip. Drip.* The majority of it runs off into the crevasse, sinking deep into the spine. An audible gasp flies from my lips. A bit absorbs into the page itself, disappearing.

Words faintly appear, curling across the page like a wisp of fog, before becoming darker the longer the blood soaks.

Hello, Liminal.

My mouth falls slightly open, lips parted in shock. I don't even breathe afraid the words will disappear. The candle on my dresser sputters faintly. The writing vanishes. The silence feels deliberate. I debate squeezing more blood into the book, but quickly think better of it. Instead, I reach out and run my fingers along the edge of the page.

Words start flowing across the page again.

You're thoughts are loud.

I internally roll my eyes. *So I've been told.*

"Sorry, I haven't exactly conversed with a book before," I reply carefully. "I'm not sure of the proper protocol."

The words disappear again. Another pause.

Knowledge is patient. It does not rush. It waits. Assesses.

I lean forward. "What are you?" I whisper.

The cover vibrates faintly beneath my fingertips.

I am infinite. An abyss. What are you?

"Lost," I answer honestly.

You seek answers as armor. That is not learning. That is fear masked as interest.

I pull back. The words hit like an arrow. Precise and painful. "What am I supposed to do? I've been here for weeks and haven't manifested. In fact, I'm not even doing great at my academics, either."

Unlearn what you have been taught. Knowledge is not given freely.

Riddles.

That's what this book speaks in. Just like everything else. "Where did you come from? How'd you even end up in my bag?"

The spine bends in my palm. The pages delicately turn on their own.

I am where I should be. I am a reflection. A collection of information too dangerous to be written into common texts.

The words shimmer and disappear. I stare at the blank page. It hums with weighted expectancy. My pulse quickens. "Are you familiar with Liminals?" I ask.

Letters dance across the page.

Vastly.

"Tell me." As soon as they're spoken, I want to take the words back. What if I don't like what it has to say?

Sentences swirl across the page regardless of my feelings.

Those that are neither here nor there. A key that fits into only one lock. A heartbeat that is out of rhythm. Light and dark cannot touch what is ambiguous.

I narrow my eyes. "That's about as clear as mud."

The air pulses around me, candles flicker, and the curtains billow in angry waves. The page snaps out of my hand, turning to the next.

If I must spell it out for you to make you understand, then you are not ready. Turning pages is not character development. You act like a mere student.

"I am a student!"

You are so much more.

I try a different approach. "Do you know anything about the disappearances?" I ask, raising my eyebrows in a silent challenge.

It hums almost as if it's preening.

You look for answers embedded within my pages. I cannot answer what you're not yet willing to acknowledge.

I frown at the now blank page. "That's not an answer."

Precisely.

I give a slow, deliberate blink.

"Do you know where they are? Are they alive?"

The question isn't where they are but who took them to where they are.

I pinch the bridge of my nose. I'm not typically known for an abundance of patience, and the little I do have is running thin. I'm also conversing with a book, so my sanity is clearly in question here. "Fine. *Who* took them?" I put extra emphasis on the word who.

Finally, a question worth acknowledging.

Blank page again.

"Are you going to tell me?"

No.

I clench my jaw and resist the urge to throw the book against the wall. "Why not?"

The ink fades and comes back bolder. Swifter. As if written in anger.

You demand yet you do not give.

"What am I supposed to give?" I ask, completely bewildered. I already gave this thing my freakin blood.

You seek validation. Return when you are willing to listen. Or simply do not return.

The writing disappears, and the book slams closed on its own accord. Full of contempt. I scrunch my nose and toss it away from me.

Cryptic bitch.

The candle flickers bright again, and the air is once again still. A harsh pounding on my door shakes me from my annoyance. I quickly shove all the books, including the little asshole one, under my bed and rise to my feet. I stretch out my legs as I walk, knees stiff and sore from sitting so long.

The incessant pounding gets louder.

"I'm coming. Hold your horses," I yell and yank the door open. Ambrose stands there, fist midair to knock again. His thick eyebrows are drawn slightly inward, and he's holding my gaze as if he didn't think I'd actually answer. I cross my arms. "Is there a reason you're beating down my door?"

"Where were you?" he demands.

"You'll have to be a bit more specific."

He pushes past me into the room.

"Sure, come on in," I drawl, spreading my arms wide.

"You missed astrology. I thought something happened to you," he says in a clipped tone, turning toward me, his shoulders squared, and eyes narrowed.

"I was reading," I reply, as I walk over to my dresser and shut a few drawers I forgot to close earlier.

"Reading?" he repeats, looking around my room in a suspicious manner. His brown hair falls over his shoulder, disheveled like he's been running his hands through it.

"Yes. Reading. Did you need something?" I ask.

He scoffs and removes his longbow, throwing it on my bed. "Ugh, yeah, I do, Nori. I need for you to not miss class."

I snort, picking up his bow and setting it on the floor. "Ambrose, you're not responsible for me, nor do I owe you an explanation on where I am."

He walks toward me with measured, deliberate steps.

I choose the wrong moment and let out a little laugh at his audacity.

His head tilts. "Is this funny to you, Norissa?" he asks, continuing to stalk toward me. He called me by my full first name.

Yep, he's pissed.

"I'm just saying it's not that big of a deal. I'm fine." I gesture to myself, indicating I'm whole and hearty.

He clicks his tongue, stopping directly in front of me. His glacial eyes hold me prisoner. "You see, that's the problem, Norissa. It *is* a big deal. Plenty of people at Kintoira would like to see you fall. In fact, they wouldn't mind being the reason you do," he says, looking down at me. "So when you suddenly stop showing up to classes, it's a problem for me."

I toss my hair over my shoulder in irritation as I look up at him. "Okay. Fine. Noted. Inform Ambrose when I'm playing hooky," I say, waving my hand dismissively.

He bends down, his face now so close that I can feel his breath. "Glad we understand each other."

"Same," I mock.

His eyes move to my mouth. I go utterly still. He brings them back to my eyes. "If anything happened to you…" He trails off, his voice suddenly rough.

Okay, now I kind of feel bad. "I'm fine, Ambrose. I didn't mean to worry you or disappoint you."

His jaw flexes once before speaking. "You could never disappoint me, Nori. You're my constant. The adamantine thread that holds everything good in my world together."

I stare at him for a heartbeat before throwing myself forward and wrapping my arms around his back. He gives the best bear hugs, and I desperately need one. I never really knew what a home felt like, but I imagine it would feel exactly like this.

"I promise, I'll do my best not to worry you anymore. I should have said something before bailing on you," I say into his chest.

A long history stretches between us. Bruised knees, hushed dares under the Brylan sky, stolen moments of mischief. He looked at me differently then. Now he's looking at me with something a lot like reverence. Something he cherishes.

He reaches up and tucks a loose strand of fiery hair behind my ear, his fingers brushing against the side of my face. The same thing he did as a child when I would be upset or hurt. His hands were clumsy back then. They aren't anymore.

I lift my face, questions lingering in my eyes. Candlelight flickers between us, casting the sharp angles of his face in burnished warmth. His gaze drops to my lips, then rises back to my eyes. His jaw clenches, like he's fighting the desires racing through his head. The breath hitches in my lungs as one of his hands presses gently to my waist, pulling me closer. A flicker of something passes over his eyes, but he doesn't retreat.

"You'll hate me for this," he whispers.

I keep my mouth firmly shut.

Fear presses into my bones that I'll ruin the moment. I tilt my chin up in pure defiance. Daring and begging him all at the same time. I've waited years for this. He looks like the boy I ran through fields with, but different. Bigger. Harder. Ruthless. My past and future all combined in one man. My chest tightens as I think of how much he means to me.

He breaks first as his lips crash over mine.

It's not gentle and soft. It's years in the making.

His hand slides to the back of my head, cradling it and pulling me in, kissing me hard. I grip onto his forearms, praying my knees won't give out. He kisses like someone who's starving. Like he's afraid he's never going to get another chance. I've stubbornly waited for this man. Years of stolen glances and buried feelings. A half-moan, half-plea slips out as he grips my hair in his fist. He swallows the sound and growls low in his throat, deepening the kiss.

This is a pure *claiming*.

I sink my fingers into his shirt, trying to get closer. He pushes me backward causing my back to slam into the nearest wall. His mouth moves across my jaw and then lower, continuing down my neck. His tongue licks over the pulse beating there before he gently bites down. I inhale sharply at the sudden intrusion. My core throbs with need. My skin is burning hot, and I feel like I'm going to burst into flames all at the same time.

His mouth moves back to mine with raw hunger. I slip my hands beneath his shirt, needing more contact. I just need to touch him. I'm desperate and brazen in my touch. Every nerve ending feels like it's about to combust. Calloused fingertips work their way up, pulling my shirt from my shoulder. Cold air touches my bare skin, causing the exposed area to erupt in goose bumps. He pulls the fabric farther down, and I arch into him, begging for something I don't understand.

But he does.

His eyes meet mine. "Nori," he rasps, saying my name like a prayer. Like he's full of devotion, and I'm the only one he wants to give it to. He bends his head, lips running over the curve of my shoulder before moving to my collarbone, and then lower. My head falls back against the wall, breath coming out in rapid bursts. His mouth moves over my breast, worshipping it as if he's waited years to give in to the temptation. His teeth gently bite down on my nipple before he pulls it back into his mouth. When I feel like I'm going to collapse, he moves his mouth back to mine. It's rougher, more desperate.

A clearing of a throat douses me like ice water.

Ambrose pulls back, breaking the kiss, his breath broken and ragged. He moves to stand in front of me, blocking me from view.

I pull my shirt back in place just as the intruder speaks.

"As an officer, I would assume the rules were clear to you. No fornication with first-years," a deep, all-too-familiar voice states.

Chapter Twenty-Four

I want to die. On the spot.

Mortification blossoms in my chest. Anger not too far behind. The person it's directed at is none other than myself. How could I forget to close the fucking door? One of the best moments of my life becomes a blatant display of voyeurism.

I slowly peek my head around Ambrose's shoulder and see Kingston leaning up against the doorframe, both hands resting in his pockets. His face is a mask of indifference, and his dark eyes are unreadable.

"How about you get out and close the fucking door?" Ambrose grinds out between his teeth.

"Why?" Kingston replies, raising a dark brow. "It was just getting good."

"Fuck off, Adair," Ambrose growls.

A cruel smile creeps over Kingston's face. "As I previously mentioned, *Captain*, there will be no fucking of any kind today."

Ambrose's fists curl at his side. Anger vibrates off him in waves. I gently rest my hand in the crook of his arm, trying to defuse the situation.

Kingston's eyes narrow at my touch. His jaw flexes tightly. "All officers are to report to the briefing room," he says coldly, moving his glare to Ambrose. He then turns on his heel and leaves without a backward glance, shadows swirling around him in controlled chaos.

I lift my eyes to Ambrose as worry washes over me.

Briefing room? Whatever they're calling all the officers in for on such short notice can't be good.

"Fuck," Ambrose mutters under his breath.

I move to stand in front of him, pulling his face down to look at me. "What? What's wrong?"

"I'm sorry, Nori. I don't know what the hell I was thinking," he says in a strained voice.

I pull back like he slapped me. If he's regretting what we just did, I will burn this entire place down. "Don't you dare apologize," I warn. "Don't act like this was a mistake. You don't get to do that!"

A look of regret flickers in his eyes.

For a second, we just stand there. Sorrow etched in his features, anger pulsating in mine. This has been his tactic since the moment I stepped foot in this academy. He gives an inch and takes two back. I might have blinders on when it comes to him, but I'm not an idiot. I do not appreciate being treated like one. It feels like he's purposely creating distance between us, something he's never done before.

"It wasn't a mistake," he finally says, running a finger down my cheek. "Just bad timing. You're a first-year, and I'm one of your captains. It shouldn't have happened this way."

I stare into his beautiful blue eyes, the same ones I've looked into countless times.

I'd give up everything. Everything. Just to live with this man by my side, no restrictions. And it seems like he's pulling away, slipping between my fingers.

He leans down, gently placing a kiss on my forehead.

I close my eyes, bracing for the crushing blow I know is coming. A lump forms in my throat when he pulls back and retreats through the door, closing it on his way out. He doesn't say anything. Just leaves.

Sorrow flows freely through my veins. To know what it feels like to be held in his arms and ravaged by his mouth only makes the cut that much deeper. I swallow the pain down and grab my cloak.

I need fresh air.

Frigid December air whips my hair around my face. I pull the cloak tighter around my shoulder and breathe in deeply through my nostrils. The urge to find somewhere secluded and just scream is overwhelming. Purge every emotion to the wind.

The gate creaks on its hinges as I push through. I cut through the training field and slip into the Witchwood. The damp ground is soft beneath my feet. Thick evergreen branches cluster together so tightly overhead that the sky disappears. The natural light dims as if a curtain has been drawn around me. The woods are offering me the solace I so desperately crave.

I'm not fooled, though. It's always a give-and-take. These woods are no different.

I know they are perilous at best and can't be trusted. I simply do not care at the moment. I want to forget. Forget how much I love a man who doesn't want to be loved. I want to ignore the fact that I haven't manifested. Disregard how awful I am in every single class. Dismiss the fact that a very broody Noctryn major despises me. I want to pretend that coming to Kintoira Academy wasn't one big mistake.

The problem is, I've never been very good at pretending.

The forest is quiet. No wind, no rustle of branches. The only sounds are the random cawing of a raven in the distance and the soft crunch of my boots walking through the snow. This place devours all the noise in my head as well.

It's beautiful and abysmal at the same time.

This kind of silence shatters your thoughts and amplifies your regrets.

A walking contradiction, just like me.

Pushing a low-hanging branch out of the way, I step off the beaten path through the foliage and walk through the undisturbed snow. I plop down on a fallen log, the wool of my cloak protecting me from the dampness.

Ambrose always says that when I get overwhelmed or angry, I hide. He often joked that's why I was so introverted, because I'm usually overstimulated somehow. He isn't wrong. Not really. Sometimes everything is just too... everything. Something is so liberating about just being alone. No judgment. No repercussions. Only redemptive isolation.

It's certainly easy to do that here when everyone avoids me.

I kick the snow with my boot and tilt my head back. I scan the tree line for even a sliver of muted sky. Small patches break through the canopy like gray freckles coating the branches. I drum my fingers on the rough bark as I close my eyes.

One second, I'm enjoying the silence, and the next, hushed voices cause my ears to perk up. Seriously? I can't even mope in peace?

I snap my head down and scan the surrounding area. The thick foliage hides me from view but also blocks whoever is walking this way. As the voices draw closer, I slip off the wet log, sliding into the snow. I try to make myself as small as possible. I don't feel like dealing with conversation or explaining why I'm frolicking among the sticks. There's also a very strong possibility that whoever it is doesn't care for me very much, and I'm out here all alone.

"That's what I've been trying to tell you," a male voice insists, urgency laced through each word.

A stick snaps in half. "I heard you. All *three* times," another male replies. The second speaker sounds calm and collected, unlike the first. I don't recognize either voice, but they're speaking in hushed tones. It makes it hard to identify them.

"But you're not taking this seriously," the first one says, his voice dripping with disdain.

A loud sigh comes from the other side of the underbrush. "I am taking it seriously, Rhett. What do you want me to do? Hmm? We didn't find it, and the other option just isn't feasible at the moment."

"Because you're working with morons."

They must have stopped walking just past my hiding place. I remain as still as possible. I don't know of anyone named Rhett, but that isn't saying much.

"Sure thing, *brother*," the second speaker replies, his voice low.

Someone sighs, the sound short and irritated. "Did you know there have been reports that Adair was in Casacia recently?"

"Which Adair? There are two."

"Both," Rhett answers.

The reply comes back low and cold. "When? They've been here every single day. I have eyes on them within the academy at all times."

Rhett chuckles softly. "During your Asylamation week. It was brought to my attention that there was a reported wraith attack within the city that hasn't been made public."

An attack on Casacia? So that's where Kingston was coming back from that first day.

"That doesn't make any sense. Students don't report to active duty until they've graduated," the second speaker says, clearly bewildered.

I hold my breath and slide out from behind the log. Slinking across the ground, I move closer, hanging onto every word. Snow sloshes into my boots as I crawl through the wet powder.

"That's the interesting part... why would the military remove a handful of Noctryns from Kintoira to assist during an attack? Not to mention, why would the wraiths be so bold as to attack a heavily guarded city? What are they after?" A few seconds pass before he speaks again. "The whole purpose of sending you here was to finish what I started. But I'm thinkin' you're becoming a tad bit too comfortable in that uniform," he points out, a soft thud following his words as if he's tapping the other man's chest.

"It'll get done, Rhett. Just like I said it would."

"Good. I'll be in touch."

His footsteps trail off, leaving me once again in silence. After a few moments, the second speaker quietly follows him.

I stand and move toward the thick branches that were shielding me from their view. As carefully as possible, I peel back the overgrown bush and poke my head out. His steps are quick, and the distance between us is vast enough that I can only make out the back of his drawn hood. Any kind of identification is impossible.

I wait a few minutes before pushing all the way through and following the trail back to the academy. I head straight to Finnley's room. I need to talk to someone I trust. I have a sinking feeling this has something to do with the missing professor. Maybe even the dark object that was stolen.

The door shakes beneath my heavy knocks.

Silence answers.

Come on. Come on. Please be in there.

"You looking for Finnley?" a voice asks from behind, startling me.

I spin around, my gaze falling on the girl from the bonfire. Ambrose's little messenger. She's propped against her doorframe, both arms crossed over her chest. Her mahogany hair is pulled up in her signature tight ponytail. She watches me with a silent question.

"No," I drawl. "I'm knocking for the fun of it."

She shrugs, turning to go back to her room.

Dammit. "Wait," I call out, pushing all my pride aside.

She turns back around, her sharp gaze falling on me.

"Do you know where he is?" I ask begrudgingly.

She flicks her head in the direction I just came from. "Saw him in the study hall a few minutes ago," she says simply.

I give her a short nod of thanks and head that way. I can feel her eyes on me the entire length of the hall. As soon as I round the corner, I practically break out in a sprint. The moment my feet hit the landing, a large hand shoots out, wrapping tightly around my wrist.

"Hello, *little Caderyn.*"

Motherfucker. Today is not my day.

"What do you want, Makon?" I ask in clear exasperation.

He doesn't take the hint and proceeds to hold my wrist. "What's the rush? Didn't anyone ever tell you running indoors is ill-advised?" His large frame blocks any escape, and he's clearly not in a hurry to release my wrist.

I glance down at his hand before bringing my attention swiftly back to him.

A sharp glint appears in his eyes. "It's starting to make sense. I'll admit I didn't get it at first, but I'm starting to understand," he says in a dark undertone.

I roll my eyes. I have no idea what he's talking about, nor do I care. "Awesome. Now let go of me," I order.

He shrugs. "I don't think I will."

"Makon, I really don't have time for this today."

"Make time."

This man is insufferable.

I mentally pray for patience and physically yank my wrist in a downward motion.

His lips pull into a grin, full of mirth and malice as his grip tightens.

"What do you want?" I grunt, flicking my eyes to his darker ones.

He's dressed head to toe in black fighting leathers, with a dagger at his hip and a long sword at his back. He looks like a warrior god seeking vengeance. And death. Somehow, I landed in his grasp instead.

He lifts a shoulder. "Everyone's in a bad mood today. Tell me, why is that, little Caderyn?"

"Stop calling me that. And how would I know?" I hiss.

"I think you're the only one who would know," he answers cryptically.

"Well, I don't. So kindly fuck off and let go."

A soft chuckle slips past his lips. "Your presence is requested in the training field."

"What? Why? I don't have practice today."

"You do now." A corner of his mouth lifts into a vicious smirk.

"You—"

"Careful, you don't want to hurt my feelings now, do you?" he asks, a hand over his heart in mock hurt. He keeps a hold of my wrist as he turns, clearly not trusting me to get to our destination on my own.

The moment his back is turned, I stick out my tongue. "Jackass," I mutter.

"I heard that."

I'm pulled through the barbican, past the courtyard, down the stone steps, and onto the training field. All against my will, I might add. The moment our feet cross the threshold to the field, he drops my wrist as if he never wanted to hold it in the first place. I massage the red mark from his manhandling and step in front of him to tell him exactly where he can go.

His eyes dart over my head, directly behind me.

I turn to follow his gaze, and a borderline hysterical laugh breaks free. Unbelievable. Just when I thought today couldn't get any worse. Not one, not two, but four Noctryns in full battle gear stand at attention. Each face is obscured by a darkened helmet, staring straight at us. I've got four bodies of muscle in front of me and a wall of muscle behind me.

Not going to lie, my chances aren't looking too good right now.

I spin around, lunge sideways, and attempt to sidestep Makon. I barely make it five steps before I'm immediately wrapped in shadows. The cold tendrils render any movement impossible. This is the first time I've actually felt a shadow—the frigidity comes as a surprise.

"That was dumb," Makon says in a low, disappointed voice, shaking his head as he steps in front of me. He drags me back to the waiting upperclassmen, depositing me directly in front of the tallest. The shadows recede.

It's now just me and a possible expiration date.

The Noctryn tilts his dark head slowly. A predator studying his unwilling prey.

I cross my arms and push my chin up. I won't make it easy on him, and I certainly won't beg. If I'm to go up against a handful of dark wielders, I'll do it on my feet.

He doesn't speak. It's as if he's purposely making this uncomfortable.

I feel like a rabbit caught in a snare. Silence surrounds me, and my instinct is telling me to run. Fast.

He stands unnervingly still, just staring at me.

I draw in a long breath and exhale. The angry slant of my eyes reflects me in his visor. I look pissed off. I *am* pissed off.

"So," I say, "to what do I owe the pleasure?"

He steps forward. Each movement is sudden and precise. The other three hang back. Well, that's informative. Now I know who the leader of the group is. As if I had any doubt to begin with.

I throw the other three a mocking smile and a little wave. Unfortunately, I don't get any reaction from the trio.

The leader places a gloved hand under my chin, tilting my head back and forcing me to look at him. His masked face hides whatever emotion lies underneath. Twin swords gleam at his back as they do with many of the dark wielders, as well as daggers tucked in various places along his armor. He looks as if his sole purpose is to destroy.

Kingston fucking Adair.

He drops his hand and adjusts his gloves. "Your survival skills are seriously lacking," the dark voice says behind the helmet.

An undignified huff slips past my lips. Out of all the scenarios I played out in my head, this one's the worst. I say absolutely nothing.

He continues to stare at me, in no apparent hurry to alleviate my discomfort.

"Evidently, my luck is too," I finally admit, under my breath.

His cold laugh sends shivers down my spine and red flags in every direction. "Today, practice will be a little bit different from what you're used to. We're running a drill." I can feel his eyes taking me in from head to toe. "Your ability to blend into your surroundings will be tested since you're fighting skills are obviously not up to par," he says dryly.

"Sounds fun," I reply sarcastically. "And let me guess, you guys have to find me?"

"Not find you. Hunt you," he delivers coldly.

Come again?

I cock my head to the side. "Hunt me?" I repeat.

"You'll have a ten-minute head start." He lifts a gloved hand, pointing toward the Witchwood. "And then we hunt."

"And if I refuse?"

He fully faces me. "I would not recommend that, Heathen."

I flick my eyes toward the woods. "What are the stakes?" I ask. There are always stakes.

"If you remain hidden for one hour, you get two weeks off field practice," he says, keeping his head toward me.

"And if you find me?" The apprehension on my face is reflected in his visor.

"If we find you—" He steps closer, wrapping a loose strand of my hair around a gloved finger. "We fuck you."

I rear back. "Excuse me? That will certainly not be happening," I declare. Hell would freeze over before I let this man touch me.

He lifts a shoulder. "Then don't get caught."

"And all that shit you threw at Ambrose earlier? About me being a first-year?" I throw right back in his face.

"I've changed my mind." He drops his hand and leans close to my face. "*Run.*"

I do what any reasonable person would do.

I run.

CHAPTER TWENTY-FIVE

I wince as another branch smacks me in the face.

Twigs and leaves are tangled in my hair. Cuts line my cheeks, and my lungs are waving the white flag. Each breath I take makes my chest heave, and the air burns as it goes down.

It's been ten minutes, or close to, and I'm running like my life depends on it. Because it does. Not only are they twice my size and lethally skilled, but they also have dark magic on their side. The only thing I have is sheer desperation. With limited options, I keep pushing forward. Hopefully, I can get far enough away that they lose interest. Unlikely, I know. But it's all I have to cling to. The only other option I have is to find a good hiding spot and hope they suck at hide-and-seek.

I keep thinking of the most random things to try to throw Kingston off. There's no doubt in my mind he's eavesdropping this very second.

Bread pudding. Dirty socks. Shadow-Wielding class sucks. So do shadow wielders.

There's another big problem.

Snow.

Every single step I take is a flashing beacon to my location. I have to get out of the snow. My boots sink into the well-worn path as I advance. The earth is soft and damp beneath my feet. Sweat beads across my forehead, causing loose tendrils to stick to the moisture along my hairline. The rough cotton shirt clings to my back.

I slip my arms out of my heavy cloak and toss it behind a large pine without breaking my stride. Stopping is not an option. Every second can be the difference between victory and defeat. In this case, defeat would likely break every piece of my soul. There'd be no coming back from what he said they'd do.

Up ahead, I hear the sound I've been praying for. I stumble over a root protruding from the dirt and nearly fall forward. My hands shoot out, grabbing onto a tree to right myself. A grunt flies from my mouth, the sting of the bark digging into my flesh. I quickly wipe my palms on my shirt and bend down to roll up both pant legs.

This is absolutely going to suck.

I bite my lower lip and step into the Blood River. The shock is immediate. Cold, unlike anything I've ever felt, radiates up my legs and steals my breath. Precious seconds tick by as I stand in the freezing rapids, the rush overtaking my system. The intense feeling quickly turns into a numbing sensation, and I wade farther in.

Once I'm thigh level with the rapids, I turn and make my way upriver, against the current. They'll think I went east, and I followed the downward current, as any sane person would do, considering it'd be so much easier. Each step is treacherous and exhausting. The current makes any progress painstakingly slow, and my entire lower half is starting to lose feeling.

"Shit!" I yell as my boot slips along a rock. Both arms fly out to balance myself and slip into the freezing water instead. I quickly yank them out and stand, bringing my hands in front of my face. Crimson water droplets race down my wrist. I can't let my mind go there. Not when this river is my salvation.

It's not real blood. It's not real blood. SHIT. Rancid bathwater. Sloppy kisses. Monsoons.

The only problem is, I'm pretty sure it is real blood.

I walk for what feels like another fifteen minutes before I drag myself out of the red tinted water and onto the riverbank. I roll on my back and close my eyes. Pebbles dig into the soggy fabric of my shirt, and sand buries itself in my hair. Both of my hands and feet tingle, and a trail of blood trickles down my shin from one of the many falls I took in the currents. If there wasn't so much on the line right now, I think I might give up. I'm tired. So. So. Tired.

Caderyn women do not show weakness.

The words echo in my head like a horrifying symphony.

Even in near death, I can't escape my mother's judgment.

Shivers wrack my body as I lie on the pebbled bank. I can feel my breath coming out more shallow than it should be. I wave my fingers in front of my face. Relief hits me that they haven't yet taken on a blueish hue. Clenching my teeth, I roll to my side and push myself up. I need to move. Staying in one place is the worst thing a person can do when trying to survive. To be stagnant is to be dead.

Ignoring the way my legs tremble, I push through the thick trees, wandering farther into the dense woods. If I've counted correctly, which is a gamble with how sluggish my mind feels, I should only have about thirty minutes or less left on the clock. I just need to remain under the radar for a little bit longer.

Treading as quietly as possible, I keep moving. Sound echoes here and carries far. I'm all but dragging my legs at this point, demanding they cooperate. Everything hurts. Physically and mentally. I am literally one big ball of hurt right now. It would be easy to just rest for another moment, but instead, I push aside a large branch and step under it.

A hand covers my mouth from behind.

Not hurried. Not agitated. Measured.

As if he'd been silently waiting for me. The scream pulled from my throat is effectively muffled by leather and armor. I desperately pull at his forearm, only for his other gloved hand to wrap around my midsection, holding me firmly in place.

I know exactly which Noctryn found me.

He moves like the shadows he controls, silent and with purpose. I didn't hear the metallic clinking of his armor or anything. A silent tear slips down my cheek. There's nowhere to go from here.

He brings his helmet closer to my ear. "Still can't follow directions, I see. I thought I told you not to get caught," he says, a warning note to his voice as he pulls his hand away from my mouth slightly.

"F-fuck off," I say, shivers now wracking my entire body.

He makes a tsking sound with his tongue. "It wasn't a bad idea. Upstream through a river to prevent tracks. Thinking like a soldier," he advises. "The only issue is how you're thinking, it's so fucking loud you give away everything."

FUCK YOU! I think as loudly as possible.

"That's the general idea," he says in my ear with a chilling, taunting calm.

Despite my shitty circumstances, I throw my head back as hard as I can into the center of his helmet. Pain immediately erupts across the back of my skull. He releases me and takes a step back. I'm in no shape to run, and to attempt it would be a waste of time.

Instead, I slowly turn around, wincing from the radiating pain.

He reaches up and pulls off his helmet, throwing it to the side. He spits blood from a split lip and looks at me, a menacing grin appearing across his face.

I smirk, unable to help myself.

"I like a little fight in my women. Even if they do look like a frozen, drowned rat," he says icily.

His words are sharper and crueler than any weapon.

"Where are all your little friends?" I ask, purposely ignoring him. I'm shivering so hard that my teeth are clanking together

"Why? Were you looking forward to more than just one of us?" he asks, flashing me a cold smile.

Bile rises in my throat. This can't be happening. Things like this don't happen to me. I'm looked after, protected. Ambrose would kill someone for just thinking of touching me.

Ambrose. Gods, how I wish he were here.

One moment I'm contemplating my life, and the next, I'm slammed into a tree mid-thought, my back pressing into the rough bark. There's a crack in his icy facade as his black-rimmed eyes are filled with something other than indifference. He runs a thumb along the side of my neck. The same place he bit me. His lips pull into a snarl. "It's ill-advised to think of another man when you're about to be fucked by the one standing in front of you," he says while dragging his dark eyes across my face.

I let out a mocking laugh. "He'll kill you."

"He can try."

I turn my face away, refusing to look at him a second longer.

His rough hands grab my leg, lifting it and wrapping it around his waist. I squeeze my eyes shut. goose bumps scatter across my exposed calf as he pushes the wet fabric up. My breath hitches when he starts rubbing small circles along the back of my leg.

I whip my head back toward him, ready to plead for the insanity to stop. Instead, I'm met with an unflinching stare. It holds my internal plea hostage with unforgiving eyes. "Why do you hate me?" I ask in a broken tone.

His dark hair, wet from sweat, hangs loosely over his brow, giving him an effortlessly defiant look. "Hate isn't the word I would use," he says, while using his other hand to rub his fingers over the side of my neck. His eyes linger on the spot he's rubbing. "He kissed you," he says coldly. "Here."

His thumb hovers over the exact spot Ambrose kissed.

I press my lips together and don't move.

His hand slides higher up my leg, toward my thigh. I can feel my throat thicken. No one, not even Ambrose, has dared to touch me this familiarly. He's taking things I haven't offered to give. Unfortunately, that's not even the most unhinged thing happening. No, that would be my traitorous body. Shallow breaths. Racing pulse. I've never had control taken from me. To lose it would cause a level of anxiety that isn't healthy. Right now, nothing is in my control.

And I like it. Some sick part of me actually likes it.

Norissa, get your shit together. Stop this before it goes too far.

The problem is, I can't stop this. And to be honest, I'm not sure I even want to at this point. Blame it on the sluggish feeling from the cold or the fact that, for once in my life, I don't have to consider repercussions. I'm no longer at the helm, and it's the most freeing feeling in the world.

"You let him kiss the exact spot I sank my teeth into?" he asks in a low, dark voice.

His words are cold and measured.

I narrow my eyes on him before turning my head to stare into the dark forest. I can feel his eyes locked on me. His hand moves higher up my leg. I press my lips together, refusing to let one sound slip past.

"Your silence is hurtful, *Heathen*. I was just becoming fond of your cruelty."

I squint my eyes shut, begging my body not to betray me any further.

His hand moves from the pulse point in my neck to grip my chin, forcing my face back toward him. "Eyes on me," he commands.

"Adair, just let me go," I plead. "You've proven your point."

He grips my thigh, his fingers digging into the soft flesh, tugging me toward him. The juncture of my thighs now sits firmly against him. His lips pull up in a smirk as I throw my head back against the tree bark.

This isn't happening.

He leans in slowly, and I quickly turn my face away. His breath is hot against my ear. "Remind me again how much you hate me."

His hand slides higher still, and I stop breathing altogether.

Just when I think my time is up, his hand stops moving and instead wraps around the hilt of my dagger, removing it from its hidden sheath. He abruptly drops my leg and steps back. "I'm sure, as your major, I don't need to remind you that weapons are off-limits for first-years," he says, throwing the dagger into the woods.

I grip the tree for balance. I'm speechless. Instead of violating me, he robbed me.

I could have stabbed him. Instead, I forgot that I had a weapon attached to my thigh. No, I was too focused on his adept fingers on my skin. The thrill of having someone want me in such a way that they took the choice from me.

"Don't flatter yourself, Caderyn," he says, reading my thoughts effortlessly. "I meant we'd fuck you metaphorically, not physically." He turns his back toward me as he walks a short distance away. "Although during practice the next few weeks you'll wish it was the other way around," he says over his shoulder.

I clench my jaw and bite my tongue.

He reaches behind a tree, grabbing a blanket out of a pack that I didn't even see. His eyes land on mine as he throws it over my shoulders. "Do me a favor and don't die out here. I'd hate to have to carry you all the way back," he says coldly.

His brows pull down, and his upper lip lifts in distaste as he looks me over.

I can't figure him out. One second, I think he truly despises me, and the next, I suspect he's just really good at hiding the fact that he doesn't. Then we start all over again.

"I'd hate to be a burden," I say sarcastically, my pride oddly bruised. "And stay out of my head!"

"Then learn to block me," he says simply.

Block him? How do you block someone from your thoughts when you can't even control your thoughts?

His eyes dart to the right, and his head slowly follows. He lets out a long exhale and rubs the bridge of his nose. "Fuck."

A slight rustle of branches is the only indication I have before one of the most beautiful women I've ever seen steps through.

Chapter Twenty-Six

Beauty and cruelty often go hand in hand.

At least that's the way it seems to go.

The woman walking toward us with the grace of a hunter is stunning beyond mere words. But not in the quiet, subtle way. Not in the beauty that grows on you over time. No, she's beautiful in the way that screams for you to acknowledge it. To bow down and obey. The kind that causes men to go to war.

But the malevolence is in the eyes.

They never lie.

There's a lingering brutality among hers. The crimson-colored orbs sweep over us, taking in the scene before her. A half-frozen woman hugging a tree for support and a perpetually stoic Noctryn in full battle gear.

She stops a few feet away, her red dress flowing around her sinuous form. The deep color is a stark contrast to the straight white hair falling to her waist. Her full lips pull into a saccharin grin as she looks from Kingston to me and back again.

"Hello, King," she says in a velvety voice.

He dips his head. "Constance." His body is rigid, and shadows hover along his fingers.

With raised eyebrows, I look back and forth between the two. They clearly know each other. I just haven't figured out on what terms.

Her eyes remain on Kingston as she moves toward him, slowly circling his much larger frame. She reaches out and runs her fingers down the length of his arm.

My fingers curl slightly at my sides.

"It's been a while," she says, stopping in front of him.

He lowers his head to look directly at her. "It has," he replies in a flat voice.

"One would think you haven't missed me," she comments, a lethal edge to her tone. Her crimson eyes are locked on his face.

I snort under my breath.

Kingston raises his eyes to look directly at me, a warning lingering in the amber depths. He turns his attention back to the woman in front of him. "What are you doing so far east?" he asks, his dark voice surrounding us in the quiet forest.

"Foraging. Why do you ask?" she taunts, moving her hand to his armored chest.

His dark eyes follow the movement before his gloved hand captures hers. His glare is sharp and fixed. "What do you want, Constance?"

"Were you going to fuck her?" she asks bluntly.

I bristle behind her. I knew from the moment I saw her that she was trouble, but now she's just pissing me off.

Kingston casually dismisses her. "That's none of your business."

"So you're done with me, and you've moved on to—" she begins, turning and roaming her eyes over me. Eyes that clearly want to hurt me. "Lesser quality."

I'm about to show her exactly what kind of *quality* I am.

I push off the tree, but before I even take one step forward, a dark voice echoes through my skull.

Do not fucking move from that spot.

I whip my eyes toward Kingston. But his eyes remain on the woman who's now looking up at him. Did he just telepathically order me around?

Okay then. Let's have a conversation, asshole.

Stay out of my head!

Also, how about you wrap this little reunion up? I'm a freakin' icicle over here!

A muscle jumps in the corner of his jaw.

Working on it.

"We agreed it was casual," he says tightly.

"Ah, we did." She inclines her head in mock agreement. "Pity."

"We were also just leaving." His hands flex at his sides, betraying both unease and agitation.

She gives him a smile with too many teeth to be considered warm. It's more like a challenge. "Were you now?"

Can you just tell this bitch to skedaddle?

Be the asshole I know you're capable of being. The one you save just for me.

I'm going to be frozen to this tree if we stay much longer.

You don't tell a witch to skedaddle.

Oh shit.

Yes. Oh shit is correct.

He keeps his eyes on her, but I can see the tension in his stance. His shoulders are still, and his posture is calm, but it's there. It's in the tightness of his jaw, the way his fingers clench tightly at his sides, and his breath coming out too measured. The kind of stillness that occurs when someone is holding back their demons.

A witch.

Apparently, there *are* actual witches in the Witchwoods. I knew something was off about her. Wait until I tell Ambrose.

Kingston's eyes cut toward me, narrowed in a silent warning.

I shrug.

I'm too cold to raise my arm and give him the finger.

"We'll be on our way now," he says in a tone that clearly shows the conversation is done. He walks over to me and grabs my hand. Wisps of onyx shadows follow in his wake. He's pretty brave turning his back on the woman whose eyes are currently promising pain.

"King," she calls in a smooth voice.

He stops walking, his back still toward her. "Should your bed ever get lonely again, you know where to find me."

Without answering her, he reaches down and grabs his helmet, then proceeds to pull us through the woods, back toward the academy.

I scoff.

Seriously, Adair? With a witch?

He looks at me out of the corner of his eye. "Jealous?" he asks, a sexual undertone lacing his words.

"Ugh, clearly not," I remind him, staring at my hand gripped in his. "Here against my will, remember?"

"You seemed willing enough back in the clearing."

I look at him like he's crazy. "You are out of your mind. Has anyone ever told you that?"

"You're in denial. Has anyone ever told you that?"

I stop walking, pull my hand from his, and cross my arms. "Explain."

He fully faces me. "You're not what you thought you were, yet you refuse to accept what you can be. You view this world in black and white when it's so much more than that." His lip curls. "Perhaps you should pull your head out of the sand, actually start trying in your dark studies and stop focusing so much on a man who clearly has no clue what he wants."

His words sting. "You don't know what you're talking about."

"Caderyn, if there's one thing I understand, it's this. It's okay not to fit inside the mold that was created for you. You're entitled to be exactly what you were made to be," he states, his words coming out direct and unapologetic. "Don't let anyone steal that from you. Not even yourself." His eyes hold me rooted to the spot. The gold is diminishing, and the black ring seems larger.

He is a walking enigma. Cold and detached, but sees things others choose not to. He's dark in the most delicious ways—dark hair, dark eyes, and dark tendencies. But he's also the only one who shines a light on me and pushes me to accept all aspects of myself. Even the uglier ones.

He never judges me for not being perfect, just for trying to be.

"I do accept what I am. What I can be. It's just at the moment it seems that the only thing I am good at is not being good at anything."

"False." He shakes his head at me. "Low confidence isn't a good look on you."

Frustration bubbles below my skin. "You can't just say something and make it so. Maybe this isn't what I was meant to do. Maybe I'm needed elsewhere."

"You're needed here. The sooner you accept that, the better off you'll be. No one is going to do it for you. There is no hand-holding in this academy." His fingers flex over the helmet in his hand.

"I know that," I counter. "I just don't know what I need to do to manifest. I'm a Liminal," I remind him. "I have no instruction manual on the steps needed to be taken. But thank you for reminding me I'm on my own," I seethe, turning on my heel, the blanket snapping as I walk away.

Kingston's fingers close over my wrist, stopping me mid-stride. "We are born alone, and we die alone. We're all on our own. It's not just you, Heathen."

I'm feeling irritable and annoyed at the fact that he's making sense. Reckless and defiant enough to push him. "Technically, I'm not alone. I have Ambrose in my corner and hopefully sooner rather than later, in my bed."

His eyes meet mine, and a chill sweeps through the air.

His sharp jaw ticks, and his canines flash.

I can bite, too. "And we all know where you can go if yours gets too cold." I cross my arms and raise a brow.

"Where do you think I'll be tonight?"

I want to punch him right in the face, and I'm not sure what bothers me more. What he said, or the fact that I want to hit him because of it.

The rest of the walk back is in silence. I feel Kingston watching me out of the corner of his eye. I think he's trying to determine whether he should just carry me the rest of the way to speed the journey up, but he knows that it'll probably irritate me more.

The moment our feet step onto the training field, I push past him. Makon and the three Noctryns from earlier swivel their heads in our direction. Makon's face breaks out in a wide grin. The bastards never even joined the hunt. It was a scare tactic. An efficient one, though, I'll give him that.

"Looks like there won't be a training break for you," Makon hollers between his hands.

I pull the damp blanket tighter around my shoulders and ignore him.

We cross the field, our path back to the academy bringing us closer to them. "That didn't take as long as I thought it would," one of them says. His helmet masks his identity. He reaches out and touches the soggy blanket resting around my rigid frame. "Geeze King, what'd you do? Try to drown her?"

"She decided a swim was in order," he answers dryly.

"Does she know *how* to swim?" one of the other helmeted men asks.

I'm pretty sure I recognize the second speaker as Koa, but at this point, I don't care who they are. They're all my enemies.

"A-assholes," I mutter under my breath, shivering.

Kingston grabs my elbow and starts pulling me toward the academy. I'm so exhausted, I just let him.

"WHAT THE FUCK IS GOING ON HERE?" an angry voice thunders across the field. I turn my head to find Ambrose stalking our way.

His face is a mask of fury.

I close my eyes and exhale. He's here. Everything will be okay.

His shoulders are rigid, and both nostrils are flaring. His large strides eat up the space between us in no time. The second he reaches me, he grips both shoulders and lets his eyes run over my frozen body. A tendon in his neck stands out from suppressed anger.

Without warning, he turns and punches Kingston right in the jaw.

Kingston's head whips to the side. My eyes widen, going back and forth between the two. A fight between two heavyweights. This will end in death. There isn't another plausible conclusion.

"Did you do this?" Ambrose grinds out through clenched teeth, pointing at my frozen form.

Kingston uses the back of his forearm to wipe the blood from his already split lip. "That was your one free hit, Ballard," he says in a low tone.

Ambrose steps up to Kingston, his eyes hard. Chest to chest, they stare at each other with pure hatred. "You leave her out of this. We can settle our score whenever you're ready," Ambrose snarls.

Kingston's lips draw tight, pulling into a sneer. "Are you so eager to die, Captain?"

Ambrose laughs, low and mirthless. The Noctryns surrounding us step back, giving the two men a wide berth. They'd never insult their major by interfering. Kingston stares at Ambrose with a gaze so cold it could give frostbite.

Speaking of frostbite, I'm pretty sure I might have it. I try to pull my blanket tighter around me, but my fingers fumble. They're clumsy and won't cooperate. I blink my eyes slowly, trying to focus on what's about to unfold, but my eyes are heavy. I'm struggling to keep them open. I can feel my body sway slightly, and black dots dance along my vision.

"You always want what isn't yours to have," Ambrose taunts. "This is no different."

Kingston flashes his canines. "Rich, coming from you of all people," he growls.

I blink my eyes rapidly, trying to clear my vision and keep up with the insults being thrown back and forth. Shit's about to go down. I try to focus, but my knees lock up right as Kingston steps up to Ambrose. I reach out to stop him.

I see Ambrose whip his head toward me, his brows pulled down in concern.

Then I collapse.

Chapter Twenty-Seven

I open my eyes to the light pouring through my window. I'm in my room. There's no cold forest or turbulent rivers filled with red tides. A fluffy comforter is pulled up to my chin, and I'm burrowed into a couple of pillows.

A movement in the corner of the room draws my attention. Ambrose is hunched over in a chair next to my dresser, elbows on his knees, staring at the floor. Scarred knuckles push back the thick strands always falling into his eyes. He looks as if he has the weight of the world on his broad shoulders.

I take a moment to stare at him, unabashedly.

Stubbles shadows his strong jaw. His mouth is set in a grim straight line, and his long legs are spread out in front of him. Both of his sleeves are rolled to the elbows, revealing forearms traced with thick veins and muscle.

He's a masterpiece.

"It seems we've come full circle, ending up back in my room," I say softly. I'm extremely parched, so the words come out a little scratchier than usual.

He drops his hands and jumps to his feet. "Nori," he says, eyes widening. "You're awake. You scared the shit out of me!" he adds in a rough voice, advancing on me.

I lick my lips. "What happened?"

"You passed out."

"For how long?"

The bed dips as he sits on the edge. "Almost a full day. You're lucky you didn't get hypothermia. It was close," he rasps, two lines forming between his brows.

"Have you been in that chair the entire time?" I ask.

"Where else would I be?" His eyes are bloodshot, and his hair looks like he's been pulling at it all night.

I grab his hand and squeeze.

He brings it to his mouth, gently kissing my knuckles.

I sit further up.

"You should rest," he orders, helping me adjust the pillows at my back.

"I think I've rested enough."

He skims his hand down the side of my face, as if he's reassuring himself I'm awake. That I'm okay. "Is there anything I can get you? Water? Another pair of socks?"

I wiggle my toes in the comfy socks and shake my head. I run my eyes over his body, the shirt pulling tightly at his muscular chest. "No, but I can think of something else," I mutter softly. I'm either delirious or grew a backbone in that river.

"Nori..." he warns.

But for once, I don't listen. I'm tired of playing it safe. Kingston was right. I'm entitled to be exactly what I was made to be. And currently, if all goes according to my plan, that's underneath Ambrose.

Without allowing myself time to second-guess this, I reach up and pull his face down to mine, crushing my lips into his. He doesn't pull away, but he also doesn't deepen the kiss. I slide my tongue along the edges of his lips, teasing and tasting. He lets out a low moan but holds steady in not reciprocating. The need to feel his weight on top of me is overbearing.

Suffocating in its intensity. I grip the front of his shirt and pull him down on the bed with me. He braces an arm on the side of my head, holding himself up so he doesn't crush me with his full weight. I want it, though. I want to be pressed into this mattress under him.

My fingers sink into his shoulder, urging him closer. His other hand sinks into my hair, and his knee goes between my thighs. His restraint is slipping.

I arch up, begging for more. He growls low in his throat and finally, finally deepens the kiss. My fingers curl into the sheets. Our tongues worship each other. The warmth of his hand settles over my stomach as he slowly works his way up, pushing my shirt up and over my breasts. Cold air caresses the peaks before he drags his mouth from mine and works his way down my neck toward my chest. His lips sink over my nipple, pulling it into his mouth. I grip his hair and cry out as he bites down. He quickly licks and sucks it, soothing the sting.

The balance between pleasure and pain is exquisite. I can feel the moisture gathering between my legs. I want more. I want Ambrose to show me everything I've been missing all these years while I've been waiting. For him. Show me the things he's learned and save it all for me from now on.

He raises his head and moves to the other breast, giving it equal attention. Slowly, while continuing to lavish my nipple, he slides a calloused hand up my thigh. His deft fingers leave a trail of fire in their wake. The sensations are too much and not enough. A moan tears from my lips when he bites down before flicking his tongue over the peak. I tilt his head slightly and press him down harder.

I need *more*.

His hand reaches my panties, his fingers trailing over the simple cotton. I know they are soaked. Embarrassingly so. The palm of his hand presses into my mound, rubbing the fabric through the moisture.

A breath whooshes out of me.

Oh my god. Oh my god.

Ambrose Ballard is touching me.

His hand is right there.

I could break just from the thought alone.

The skies darken and lightning cracks outside the window, but it's nothing compared to the untamed electricity in this room.

I raise my hips, asking for more. I need this like I need the breath in my lungs. Cold air caresses the puckered peak where his mouth just was as Ambrose crashes his mouth over mine. The kiss is laced with urgency and years of restraint. Our tongues dominate each other. I press my knees together, seeking some kind of release as his hand continues to rub over my wet entrance.

He removes his hand from between my thighs and pushes my legs back open. Moving back to my panties, he pushes them to the side and slides a finger through the slick folds.

I moan into his mouth, my fingers digging into his arms.

"Fuck, Nori," he rasps into my mouth.

His mouth lowers to my shoulder, biting down—hard. Without warning, he sinks a long finger into my entrance. I throw my head back and cry out as he gently moves it back and forth, giving me time to get used to the invasion. "You're so tight—fuck," he growls into my skin. "Tell me I'm your first," he says, low in his throat.

I whimper. "You're my first."

"No one's ever touched you like this?"

I shake my head. Words evade me.

He pumps his finger in and out of me, increasing the speed. He pulls it out and thrusts it all the way back in. He brings me to the brink before pulling back again.

"Please, Ambrose," I beg.

"Say you're mine," he orders, his glacial eyes staring into mine.

I'm on the edge, so close.

"I'm yours, Ambrose. I've always only ever been yours," I sob, thrashing my head into the pillow.

He curls his finger, and I come undone.

"Oh my God," I cry out.

"That's it, baby. Give me everything."

I ride out the rest of the orgasm with his hand buried between my thighs.

"That was the hottest thing I've ever seen," he breathes, his face hovering above mine.

I reach up and run my tongue along his lips. "We have to do that again."

He laughs and rises from the bed, pulling the cover back up to my chin. "We're just getting started."

My lips turn down in a pout. "You're leaving?"

Leaning down, he plants a soft kiss on my forehead. "I have to go, and you need to rest. But I'll see you this evening at dinner."

"Okay."

The room already feels empty as I watch him walk to the door. He looks over his shoulder, a smirk playing along his lips before he brings his finger, the one that was just buried between my thighs, to his mouth. I hold his stare and can feel my jaw slightly drop open as he pushes it between his lips, sucking off all my juices.

"Delicious," he says, before opening the door and walking out.

Holy shit.

A squeal breaks free as I jump out of the bed.

Dancing around the room, excitement over taking me, I feel lighter than I have in ages. Things are finally starting to look up. I feel invincible. The floor is cold on my knees as I reach under my bed and pull out the little silver book. It fits perfectly in my hand as I crack it open.

I jump back on my bed, reaching over to retrieve my dagger from the nightstand, before I remember that Kingston threw it in the woods.

Prick.

I need something to slice my finger with. Without an offering, these pages will remain blank. With a glance around the room, I don't see many options. Using my fingernails, I chip off a small piece of a wood splinter from the bed frame and press it into the tip of my finger. Hard. Blood drips onto the parchment, sinking into the spine.

Hello, Liminal.

The dark letters float across the page.

I shift back in the bed, putting the book in my lap. "Hello...I don't really know what to call you. Silver? Unless you have another name?"

The letters retreat before reappearing.

The name I have is not part of your language. You can refer to me with your chosen name.

Okay. Silver it is. "Tell me something I don't know, Silver. Something I don't but should." I'm feeling so happy right now that I'm just in the mood to talk. I can't help but smile when I think of what just happened. For some reason, I don't feel I can discuss this with Mallory or Finnley. It's as if speaking it aloud with a real person will dim the magic.

The words drift from the page as if caught on a warm summer breeze.

You should not be broken.

You are made to mend.

The things you should know but do not would decimate you.

I frown and sit up a little straighter. "Okay. That's only slightly ominous," I mumble sarcastically. "Tell me what I should know, and I'll worry about it breaking me."

Words claw their way across the page.

Things that have long been buried. Secrets stowed beneath layers of false-hood.

The edge of the page crinkles beneath my fingers. Frustration builds within my chest at the never-ending puzzles and partial answers this book gives me. "I have an idea. Let's try a different approach, shall we?" I say. "You answer in layman's terms and stop speaking in riddles, we'll keep it simple. Now, who buried these secrets?"

You did.

I stare at the words.

"What secret did I bury?" I ask, hesitation making the words come out soft. I've yet to be decimated, but my good mood certainly has been.

The page stays blank for a minute or so. Words begin drifting across in deep ink, almost as if they're being etched into the pages.

The answer is not what you buried. But who you buried.

I lean in close to the pages, my heart palpitating. "Are you insinuating that I killed someone and don't remember? And then buried them?" I laugh a bit hysterically.

This time, the page doesn't wipe itself clean. It just continues in large, loopy script.

The mirror will give you the answer you seek. You are so much more.

"I don't have a magical mirror, Silver! I also didn't kill anyone! What is even going on right now?" I ask, frustration obliterating my earlier mood. "Why are you saying these things to me? Is this what you do? Just create chaos and watch the world burn around you. You're not being very helpful." The words come out rushed and annoyed.

You didn't ask for help. You asked for truth.

The writing sinks into the pages, disappearing from view.

I look toward the ceiling and pray for patience.

Elegant scrawl writhes under my fingertips.

You demand, yet you do not give.

"WHAT DO YOU WANT?" I scream at the book. So much for patience.

Angry letters dig into the parchment.

HONESTY.

That's it. Just the one word.

If it's just one simple ask, why does it send chills up my spine? "Ask me anything and I'll answer. Unlike you," I snap, hunched over the book and waiting.

Are you ready to be a Liminal? To lift the veil and see what truly lies beneath?

"Yes," I answer without hesitation.

You are more than a manifestation. You are a vessel. A give and a take. A corrector of invisible threads. A weaver.

There's a pause, and then more words appear.

Find your lock. It will undo you.

Then underneath, in sharper scrawl—*Seek it anyway.*

I stare at the words scribbled in red ink. Appearing like a prophecy disguised as a blood omen. The pages wait with a humming pulse as if they want me to deny them. My fingers hover above the angry red letters. Maybe if I smear it, the book will take it back. "Would Ambrose know anything about this key?" I ask in a cautious tone. It'd be nice to have someone at my side, someone to help me unravel the shit show going on all around.

Without hesitation, red splashes across the page.

No.

"Is he part of my destiny?" I ask, waiting with bated breath.

You are asking the wrong questions.

The words disappear, and the book firmly shuts on its own accord.

I exhale and lean back, tossing it to the end of the bed.

A vessel. A weaver. I'm a soldier, not a seamstress. Besides being a moody bitch, the book at my feet hasn't done anything but leave me more confused each time I converse with it.

I throw off the covers, dress quickly, and head out. I need answers, not rest.

The study hall is empty when I poke my head inside. All except for a headful of curls bent over a book in the back. I figured he'd be here. I shut the door firmly, and his head whips up, hazel eyes wide. The moment they rest on me, they relax, and a lopsided grin appears.

"Well, well. Look what the cat dragged in," Finnley says, his eyes twinkling with mirth in the glow of the hanging lanterns.

I roll my eyes and walk over to him. "Taking this studying thing a bit seriously, huh?" I ask, turning his book toward me. Paragraphs about the intricate layers of alchemy cover each page.

"Well, these looks only go so far," he says with a wink, closing the book and leaning back in his chair.

I plop down in the chair next to him and kick my feet up on the table. "Huh, I didn't know you were taking alchemy. Care to study for us both? I'm only drowning in defeat in most of my classes."

"I don't take half of your classes, Nori. Not sure I'm going to be much help in that department."

"Lucky you," I say on a sigh.

"Where have ya been? I feel like we never see each other anymore with classes and"—he gulps dramatically—"*responsibilities.*"

The chair creaks beneath me as I shake my head. "You're ridiculous. And as far as where I've been—I've been around. Just busy, you know."

He pins me with an understanding look. "Yeah, I get it. Double the class load, double the work. Doesn't leave much time to get out," he acknowledges.

"It doesn't," I agree. "Hey, speaking of getting out, I was in the Witchwood the other day." I won't mention I was hiding in the sticks and eavesdropping on someone. "I stumbled across a couple of people who were discussing something about an attack on Casacia. You haven't heard anything, have you? I don't know why, but I feel like maybe it's all linked to what's going on here, with the missing object and professor."

"I haven't heard anything," he says without missing a beat. "But I'm sure if something like that happened, the academy would alert us. That'd be a pretty big breach of the walls."

I tap my fingers along the table. I could have asked Kingston directly, but I have zero expectations that he would confide in me. "You're probably right." I blow out a breath, changing the subject. "How's the manifestation coming along? You haven't filled me in yet. Did you get something really cool? Ice wielder or maybe a shape shifter—"

"I'm still working out the kinks. We'll revisit this later." He laughs under his breath. The laughter doesn't meet his eyes.

"Oh. Okay, yeah, sure." I'm not going to press him, but I'm starting to get worried. He's holding something back, and from the dark circles under his eyes, it's taking a toll on him.

He scans the room before he leans in. "Nori, there was something I wanted to talk to you about, though. I didn't want to say anything earlier, but it seemed odd to me, and I think you should know."

I lean forward. "Yeah?" I ask, focusing all my attention on him.

"It's probably nothing," he counters in an even tone.

"Tell me anyway."

"It's just the other night I was walking back to my room, and the door to Professor Tainey's room was slightly cracked. I didn't think much of it and was going to just walk past, but I heard a familiar voice that sounded angry." He rubs the back of his neck. "I stopped to listen, and someone was demanding to know why the test he was smuggled was useless and nothing like the test used for the Asylamation assessment—"

I gulp. *Ambrose.*

"Which I thought was an odd thing to say, but not my problem, you know? Anyway, I was going to leave, but stopped when I heard your name. It was Ambrose speaking." He pauses before continuing. "He was telling the professor that because of his mistake, you didn't place Veil and ended up as a Liminal. That you were going to find out the truth because of Tainey's carelessness. I pressed my ear to the door, and the professor was apologizing and saying he did his best," he says. "Something was thrown across the room, and Ambrose practically growled that if you find out about your father, he'll come back and personally cut Tainey's throat."

Time ceases to move.

It slows to a pace where I can see the particles in the air.

I don't speak. I can't manage to form a coherent thought, let alone an intelligible sentence. Ambrose never even met my father. The written assessment was never going to be enough to land me in that Veil uniform.

Something I now understand but refused to acknowledge then.

"Nori," Finnley calls. His hand lands on my arm, and I raise my eyes to meet his.

"What else did he say?" I ask, my voice slightly breaking.

Finnley sighs. "Not much. It sounded like Tainey was on the verge of tears, and Ambrose told him he'd better pray he doesn't have to come back."

No one but my mother knows who my father is. She never even told me. Regardless of how many times I asked, she never told me. The only information I could peel out of her was that he was a fellow soldier, whom she mistakenly gave her heart to, and he broke it. It's been a massive void in my life—the feeling that a part of my identity has always been missing—and it's my fault. I'm the reason he left. I've been reminded of the fact numerous times throughout my life. But why would Ambrose say these things to the professor—especially behind my back?

I feel like I'm going to puke.

"Are you okay? You look a little pale," he says through the pressure in my skull.

I slowly nod.

Am I okay? No. Definitely the opposite of okay, but I'm not putting that on him.

A slight frown appears on his lips, and concern swims in his eyes.

Breathe, Heathen.

I inhale sharply.

"What's wrong?" Finnley asks, leaning in.

I shake my head. "Nothing," I answer. "Nothing, I'm fine."

Get out of my head, Henchman!

A dark laugh vibrates through my skull. *Henchman? I like it. How adorable that you've given me a nickname. And one so fitting.*

I squeeze my eyes shut. *Shadows. Burning candles. Blood.*

A little blood never scared me, he says in a low, throaty hum.

Ugh.

At least you're breathing again.

GO AWAY!

A dark laugh resonates before I'm left to my own thoughts again.

Finnley grabs my hand. "Nori, you good?" he asks with a worried look on his face.

"All good," I reply quickly. Too quickly. "I hate to leave, but I've got something I have to do." I stand quickly, push the chair in, and head for the door.

"No worries," he calls after me. "Catch you later?"

"Absolutely," I answer, turning to look at him.

Our eyes meet for a second. There's something in his gaze—soft, quiet, almost resolute. Not an apology, not exactly. But something. I'm not sure what I see in those turbulent eyes, but I turn and leave. I don't have the luxury of dissecting another mystery at the moment.

The stone walls of the dimly lit hall feel like they're closing in around me. I stare at the flicker of flames in the candelabras along the passageway, wishing I could snuff them out and sink into the floor. The sound of my heavy footsteps vibrates through the walkway. I came here to become the best version of myself I could. A Veil to rival my mother's expectations. To fight in the same regiment as her and finally showcase my worth.

Instead, I'm stuck somewhere in between. Failing at both. Teachers and dark objects are missing, and I've had my brain prodded to prove my innocence. A book cryptically insults me each time we converse. I have a Noctryn major who has an agenda for me. And my best friend is speaking in puzzles behind my back about haunting subjects of my past.

I curl my fingers and close my eyes.

Everything's fine. Everything's fine. Everything. Is. Fine.

I open my eyes and wince. Everything is so far from fine that it's laughable at this point. The long hall ends, and I push through the heavy wooden door. A few Veils pass me as I slip into the main hall and head toward the officer's class that Ambrose is currently taking. It's on the far south end of the academy and tucked in the corner of the turret.

A door opens up ahead, and two people step out deep in conversation. An unlikely duo to say the least.

"Of course I was with him," Yaretta seethes, throwing her hands in the air.

"Did he say anything? Have there been any updates?"

"Listen, Eryk, the last thing that we talk about when we're together is missing professors or those dirty blood leeches losing one of their precious objects."

What is Eryk Porter doing with Yaretta? They have about as much in common as oil and water. "I don't think you understand the significance of what's happening," he barks, causing Yaretta to stop and really look at him.

"I'm not sure who you think you're talking to, Porter, but I'm not the one. The only reason we're on the same side here is because we each have end goals that complement each other. That's it. So watch your tone when you speak to me."

I plaster my back against the wall and peek around the column that blocks me from view.

Eryk bounces on the heels of his feet. His mousy eyes are hard and directed at Yaretta. "I don't need to remind you who my father is."

Figured that one was coming. Surprised it took so long.

Yaretta throws her head back, a shrill laugh breaking free. "Please, save the theatrics. Your father hasn't shown his face in this academy since he took reign," she hisses. "Face it, Eryk, you're an afterthought. And always will be." She spins on her heel and marches off without giving him a chance to even respond.

He fists his hands at his side. "Bitch," he mutters, walking in the same direction she took off in.

I step out from my hiding space and look around.

Clear.

There's an awareness in the air. I don't like it. I'm not a witch, but I am a woman, and we're intuitive. I've learned to trust my gut. It hasn't steered me wrong yet.

I open the door they just came through and poke my head inside. The harsh smell of chemicals mixed with stale ingredients permeates my nostrils. I pinch my nose and cross the threshold. It's an alchemy lab of some sort, with tabletops lined with various beakers, petri dishes, and scales. A few mismatched microscopes sit on the back counters.

My eyes drift to the shelves along the walls. Hundreds of preserved specimens sit along them. What looks to be a human heart, various insects, and small rodents sloshing in colored liquids, among other things. Small colored glass jars labeled with ingredients such as salt, Phoenix ash, crushed bone, and random gemstones sit on numerous bookshelves.

I walk over to the wall closest to me and run my fingers along a faded anatomical chart and a sparkling celestial chart. I'm not sure if the room is interesting or something out of a nightmare.

I back up a step and look around.

What were they doing in here? This classroom looks like it hasn't been used in ages, dust coats most of the lab equipment, and there's a staleness to the air. Stepping around a few stacks of books and old journals, I walk along the tables looking for anything they could have left behind, but everything looks undisturbed. Perhaps they just ducked in here to talk in private. I'd give anything to have been able to hear that conversation. What could two notoriously selfish people have in common that they're conspiring about?

Stepping back into the hallway, I push the door shut.

I shake my head and decide I can only handle one mystery at a time.

Chapter Twenty-Eight

I don't make it to the officer's class before the bell tolls. I lost track of time in my snooping. I quickly turn around, cursing under my breath, and head toward Professor Rinkin's class instead. I can't afford to miss another class.

Her long blonde braid swishes across her back as she writes on the board. All I have left on the schedule for today is two classes. Shadow Craft and Blood Magic.

I scrunch my nose. I'm not looking forward to the last class. Professor Moravek creeps me out, and the entire taboo subject does as well.

Plopping down in my seat, I crack my knuckles one by one. My partner in crime hasn't arrived yet, so I'm saved from that. I crack my book open to the page written on the board and pull out my quills, lining them up neatly on my desk. The sound of books being tossed onto desks, pages being turned, and chatter throughout the rows almost drowns out the tardy bell.

Kingston's seat remains empty.

I turn and look at the door, but it's firmly shut. No one is coming through at the last minute. I'm not worried, per se, just confused as to why an officer is missing one of the most crucial classes for dark wielders.

You're late, I sing in my head.

Nothing. Crickets.

I furrow my brows and decide I don't exactly like being ignored by him.

"Turn to page one hundred and fifty-three," the professor says loudly.

I'm already on the page and decide I'll try one more time.

Not very majorish of you to play hooky.

I swear I can hear a scoff through the mental bond or whatever it is that Kingston does.

Are you coming or not? I think irritably.

Not.

Seriously?

I roll my eyes and grab my quill to take notes.

The rest of class goes by in a blur between the three sheets of notes and the half hour of Shadow-Wielding. Shadows from light gray to obsidian black swirl around the room. A slate-gray shadow grabs the wrist of a second-year, pulling her toward the wielder. She digs her heels in and casts a rebuke, but her shadow is smothered beneath his stronger one. Another fourth-year has shadows, the color of coal, wrapped around a first-year's neck. His almost translucent shadow is no match and is quickly snuffed out.

My partner is nowhere to be found, nor are my shadows. I slouch in my seat and watch the other Noctryns try to kill each other.

This is such a waste of my time.

Finally, the bell chimes, and I jump up and exit through the door. I shoulder through the throng of other students, head down, teeth clenched. I'm not in the mood for the noise and chaos of the halls today. I pull my replacement cloak up around my neck, the original still sitting in the Witchwood. The chill is at an all-time peak, and snow falls heavily outside the domed windows.

I climb the stairs and head for the second floor. Taking a deep breath, I open the door and enter Professor Moravek's class. I take my usual seat in the back corner. There's no text for this class. Everything needed stays locked up in his classroom. Secrecy upon secrecy per usual. Darkness and evil doings toiled together.

The chair next to me squeaks along the stone floor as it's pulled back, and a hulking frame sits beside me. I'm so deep in my thoughts, that I don't even bother looking over until I can feel someone staring at the side of my head.

I exhale loudly and turn, giving them the attention they so desperately want.

"Hello, little Caderyn."

Makon leans forward, elbows on the long table and dark eyes pinning me to the spot. His brow is furrowed, his long hair pulled back from his face, and his scar is reflected in the flickers of the torch directly behind us.

I purse my lips and look back toward the front of the class. He never sits next to me, and now here he is, taking up all the space. He's handsome in the untamed way. Wild and reckless with a side of rogue.

And right now, I'm about sick of handsome men.

"One of these days, you're going to succeed in hurting my feelings," he says, his thick brow raising.

"I very much doubt your feelings have enough depth to be hurt," I retort, staring straight ahead. I can see him out of my peripheral vision, much to my dismay.

His lip pulls up in a smirk. "I'm one of the few people you haven't pissed off lately. Might not wanna burn this bridge."

"Some bridges are beautiful when they burn," I say coldly. "There's a peace in knowing it can't be undone."

"Rough morning?" he asks, amusement apparent in his voice.

I turn and look at him. "You have no idea." It's only when the flames hit his face just right that I see the black eye forming. "Speaking of a bad morning, who'd you piss off?"

He laughs. "More like who did *you* piss off?"

I shift my weight in my seat and turn toward him more. "What are you talking about?"

"I'd rather not have both eyes match. I think I'll sit this one out," he says.

I stare at him, hoping to pressure him into talking. He stares back, clearly not backing down. "Hmm."

"Hmm, what?" he asks

"Just didn't take you for the timid type."

He tilts his head to the side as if my words entertain him. "Not timid, little Caderyn. But also, not stupid."

The tables fill up around us, and Professor Moravek walks in, his black robes billowing behind his hurried footsteps. Long, bony fingers steeple in front of him as he turns and faces us. His face is a mosh of unbalance—a large, crooked nose, thin lips pulled to the side, and deep-set, sunken eyes that regard us with borderline animosity. There's a tic in the left one.

Maylin's mink-brown eyes meet mine from across the room. She gives me a small smile in clear understanding and agreement that he gives us the creeps.

"Everyone, open the drawer in front of you and remove the small knives that have been sterilized and readied for your use," the professor instructs us, his shrill voice like nails on a chalkboard.

Makon pulls the drawer out on our table, and we each remove a small knife, the tip pointed and stained from repeated use. "What's with the dreary expressions today?" he asks under his breath.

"Life," I answer simply, as I prick the tip of my finger and squeeze the blood into an empty vial.

Makon makes a long gash across his palm and lets it drip into his. "That's a cop-out. We're soldiers. Life is always going to be hard. I have a feeling you're used to its harsh blows, so what's really eating at you?" He's oddly perceptive. Not something you would assume on first impressions. I'm starting to think Makon has layers that he doesn't show many people.

"I don't know who to trust, what's real, and what's not. Nothing is really black and white, is it?" I continue squeezing the blood out of my finger.

Drip. Drip. Drip.

Out of the corner of my eye, I see him watching me. I pull my eyes from the vial and give him my attention.

"Finally catching on, are we?" he asks, a serious look leveled at me.

His vial is already filled with blood, considering he made a much larger gash in his hand. "Your blood, my blood, and I bet even one of those useless Veils if I cut them open. It all flows red."

I chuckle. "Couldn't resist throwing an insult in their direction, could you?"

"Never," he deadpans.

I don't miss the way I referred to them as "their" and not "our."

One by one, we pour our vials filled with blood into the large dish sitting atop each of our tables and whisper the incantation written on the blackboard. The blood from my finger and Makon's palm swirls together, becoming a combination of him and me. A unification of power and the possibility of.

We dip our fingers into the mixed blood and draw the symbol on the blackboard on each other's wrists, each repeating the same incantation. Makon pupils are blown wide, and I know without a doubt mine match.

He runs his tongue over his teeth, and I bite down on my lip.

A rush of adrenaline courses through the veins when blood magic is performed. The feeling can be highly addictive, which is why this particular magic is dangerous for a Noctryn. Too much use, especially without the necessary skills and a reliable dark object to ground them, can lead to incurable madness. A certifiable way to earn yourself a room at Harkin House, where padded walls and insanity are the only company offered.

I latch onto the edge of the table, my fingers curling around it. Makon rotates his neck, the corded veins popping out as he does so. The professor doesn't tell us what this exact hex does, so we wait and ride out the high.

A dark cloud washes over my eyes. A murky memory, one not of my own, floats to the surface. Regardless of how firmly I try to lock it in its Cimmerian cave, it drifts to the forefront like a tendril of fog. Onyx marble floors gleam beneath my bare feet as I walk through the halls of a luxurious structure. The cathedral ceilings are carved from stone, intricate runes etched into their hard surface. Arched windows are open, allowing the winter breeze to float through the passageway, causing the candles in the hanging chandeliers to flicker.

The soft sound of my breath is my only companion as I make my way through the grand halls of what looks to be a castle. The dark colors and gold-rimmed portraits lining the walls speak of wealth and expensive taste. Snow blows in through an open set of doors, falling across the shiny marble floor. I leave footprints in it as I push forward, opening another large set of doors to my right.

The high-pitched laughter of a small child draws my attention to the center of the room. He's lounged in a throne, hands over his eyes as he speaks a language I don't understand. Possibly Casacian, but I can't be sure. It seems as if he's counting. His dark hair sticks up in disarray, and his little feet are kicking back and forth as they hang over the armrest.

I step farther into the empty room. It's large, with a domed ceiling and dark marble floors. A crimson runner stretches all the way to twin thrones and is soft and plush beneath my bare feet. One throne is larger than the other. Behind them is a large tapestry backdrop that hangs from the ceiling, featuring a familiar crest. An obsidian crown with twin swords is crossed behind it. The same crest that Sanderson Thurboult had on the locket that was draped around his neck in his portrait.

The little boy stops speaking, drops his hands, and looks around the room. His eyes glaze right over me, as if he can't see me standing here. He gets up and runs behind the throne chairs, lifting the tapestry to look behind it. His infectious laughter follows him around the room.

"Hello?" I call. But he continues looking for something or someone, oblivious to the stranger standing in the room with him.

The room that looks very much like a royal hall.

Another child's laughter rings out from behind the second chair, but he doesn't come out. The first little boy runs in that direction, his small face breaking out in a huge smile.

"I've been looking for you."

I quickly turn and face the woman who spoke. Dark hair so black it almost appears blue is regally styled atop her head with a dainty gold crown seated upon it. Walnut-colored eyes narrow in frustration, and her thin lips pull into a line of disappointment as she stares back at me.

I raise my hands and step back. "I'm sorry, I didn't mean to intrude. I don't know where I am—" I start, but she walks through me.

THROUGH ME.

I jump back and quickly turn to face the direction she went. The little boy stops laughing and raises his wide eyes to stare up at the woman. "Hello, Your Majesty," he says in a small, frail voice.

"Come. Your father is awaiting us in the dining hall," she orders in a sharp tone, grabbing the little boy's hand. "The king is not to be kept waiting."

He drops his head and walks beside her.

When they're halfway to me, his steps falter, and he looks over his shoulder in the direction the other child's laughter came from. The royal woman stops and throws a sharp look over her shoulder just as the tapestry slightly moves. She pulls her shrewd eyes down and says in a regal voice, "How many times must I tell you not to play with the dirty-blood?"

He wipes his nose with the back of his hand and drops his head again. I watch as they exit through the grand doors, and the room begins to grow fuzzy around the edges. It tilts on its axis, causing the contents of my stomach to feel as if they're going to rejoin my mouth. The pressure in my skull intensifies.

I close my eyes, rub them with the base of my palm, and reopen them.

I'm back in the classroom, staring at a pissed-off Makon. His eyes are pulled into slits, and his mouth is firm. The usual smirk or taunting grin he wears has been completely erased.

I sit up a little straighter. "I think I just visited someone else's memory," I say, breathless, gripping the edge of the table for balance.

Makon doesn't seem surprised. "Did you, now?" His voice is inflection-less. Flat.

"You good?"

A fake smile flickers across his face, not reaching his eyes. "Impeccable," he answers, turning away from me and toward the professor.

Moravek claps his hands loudly. Once. Twice. "Welcome back, everyone. I hope the little trip down memory lane wasn't too eventful. This was an exercise in mind manipulation, something that blood magic can be quite beneficial for," he advises. "Not everyone is skilled enough and has the ability to dip into the crevasses of the brain without it, which makes this incantation priceless. The only downside is that you have to experience the memory in first person, which, depending on the circumstance, isn't always pleasant." His thin lips pull up at the corners.

It's a safe assumption that the idea of anyone experiencing discomfort is incredibly appetizing to him.

I know his kind. I grew up around them.

I look back over at Makon, who now has his back turned to me as he talks with another upperclassman. The professor erases the blackboard and waves his hand, indicating we're dismissed before the bell has even rung.

He doesn't have to tell me twice.

I grab my pack, sling it over my shoulder and look at the back of Makon's head. The Noctryn he's speaking to raises his eyes to mine and says something to Makon, causing him to partially turn in his seat.

I keep my expression neutral. "You coming?" I ask.

"Nah, I'll catch you later," he says, without fully facing me, and turns back to his conversation.

Okay then.

I grip the strap of my bag and throw one last glance toward him before turning and leaving.

CHAPTER TWENTY-NINE

The chatter is loud.

I should have waited a bit and not eaten at peak hour, but I need to see Ambrose. I dropped my bag in my room, took a quick shower in the communal bathrooms, and donned a fresh pair of gray… everything. Every article of clothing I now own is some shade of dull gray.

Bleak and monotonous.

With frantic steps, I headed straight here. He isn't slipping through my fingers again.

I spot Finnley, Mallory, and a few other Veils I recognize sitting in the center of the dining hall. The long wooden tables are crammed with students and their vivacious appetites. I squeeze through a table of rambunctious third-years and slide into an open seat directly in front of Mallory. Her wide smile greets me, and her large moss-colored eyes crinkle at the edges. "Aren't you going to eat?" she asks around a mouthful of sandwich.

I give her a quiet shake of my head. "Nah, don't really have an appetite right now."

I feel eyes on me and look a few seats down past Finnley. The second-year captain from the bonfire is pinning me beneath her scrutiny. I give her a little mock wave to let her know I see her and don't give a shit what her problem is, then turn back to Mallory.

"Who's the ball of sunshine skewering me with her eyes?" I ask, tilting my head in the girl's direction.

Mallory, without an ounce of discretion, leans her peacock-blue head over her tray before bringing her attention back to me. "Willa Hinx. She's a second-year and a bit glacial, but other than that, pretty cool."

I somehow seriously doubt that, but don't voice my opinion. I'm here for something else. I scan the hall for Ambrose.

"Not here yet," Mallory says, studying me.

Either it's obvious who I'm looking for, or she's dipping into her manifestation. Finnley finally notices I'm here and leans across the table, offering up a fist bump. I tap it lightly with my knuckles, and he sits back down, his eyes smiling before his mouth can catch up. "You're finally joining us for a meal. Thought you only slunk in to get food when everyone left," he teases.

I give him a tired smile. "I just need to talk to someone today. I'm not actually here to eat."

He closes his eyes briefly before opening them and giving me a nod of understanding. He knows why I'm here. He also knows exactly how much his earlier words impacted me.

He angles his head, gesturing behind me. "Incoming," he mouths.

I twist in my seat, and my gut follows suit.

Ambrose is walking in, head down, with Yaretta at his side. They're not touching but walking close enough together that my stomach roils, and I'm glad I haven't eaten anything yet.

I take a deep breath. I'm going to need it.

Standing without so much as a fare thee well to my friends, I walk toward the duo. Ambrose looks up at my approaching footsteps right before a tender grin appears. Yaretta raises her head to see what he's looking at, when I stop in front of them, and her sneering gaze falls on me.

I raise my fist back and smash it into her face.

She huddles over, gripping her nose, blood flowing through her fingers. "WHAT THE FUCK?" she screams, her voice garbled from the gushing blood.

Ambrose grabs her shoulders, turning her toward him, attempting to assess the damage. "What the hell, Norissa. What was that for?" he demands in a harsh tone. The tone of a captain, not my best friend.

Better yet, the tone of a disloyal best friend.

Before I can reply, Yaretta pushes past Ambrose and comes for me. The lower part of her face is covered in blood, which is dripping onto the floor. Her eyes promise retribution, but I'm beyond the point of rational thought. As her bloody fingers sink into my hair, I grab the back of her head and push it toward the floor. She tugs the hair clutched in her fist, causing water to pool in my eyes. She's bent over, face downward from my grip. I don't even think. I pull my fist back and thrust it upward.

The uppercut isn't clean and definitely not skilled, but it's enough to cause her head to fly backward and her grasp to loosen on my hair. *Thank you, Corinne.* Those endless drills that I bitched about the entire time came in handy. I'm not as soft as I was when I entered the academy. I have a long way to go, but I can feel strength in areas that weren't there before. Endless hours under Corinne's drills and Kingston's watchful glare have honed my body slightly.

But that's all I need.

A *slight* upper hand.

In this case, directly to her jaw.

She screeches and lunges for my hair again, but I continue to throw punches, determined to stay out of her bloody grip.

Ambrose grabs her around her waist, and a pair of strong arms wrap around mine. I'm pulled off my feet, arms still thrown out in an arc, trying to land a hit. Ambrose is ordering Yaretta to cease, his face a mask of fury at the entire ordeal.

I angrily push the loose hair out of my face. I can feel blood smeared along my cheeks and forehead, courtesy of her bloody nose. I'm practically vibrating with hatred as she squirms in his hands, throwing all kinds of curses my way.

Too bad she's a fucking Veil and doesn't have the ability to follow through.

"Careful, Heathen, you might want to tuck that darkness back in," Kingston whispers in my ear.

I'm still so fired up that I don't even care he has his arms wrapped around me, one right below my breasts and the other tightly around my midsection, effectively keeping me stationary.

"This isn't over, you bitch," I warn her, my nose scrunching in fury.

Her broken face contorts in rage.

A dark chuckle trickles over my ear. "*That's my girl,*" Kingston breathes.

Ambrose's glacial eyes rise over the top of Yaretta's head to land on the arms wrapped around my midsection. They narrow, and his lips pull up in a snarl. Unfortunately, he can't do much about it because if he lets go of the banshee in his arms, this whole charade is going to continue.

I sure as shit wish he would. I'd love nothing more than to land a few more hits.

I pull at Kingston's fingers, fighting to get loose. Red clouds my vision, and I want to tear her from Ambrose's arms. Those same hands that were on me not that long ago are currently wrapped around her.

His eyes fall to my face, disappointment etched in every single line.

Well, you know what? Screw you, Ambrose!

It's because of him we're in this mess. Maybe if he had thought about how walking into a dining hall full of students with a past lover might make me feel, we wouldn't all be covered in her blood.

The dining hall is completely silent now except for the insults thrown back and forth between Yaretta and me, and the occasional harsh explicative Ambrose throws at the ceiling. Kingston is quiet behind me, his arms holding me in place, but he's not trying to subdue my words. He's just keeping me stationary. He's letting me get it all out verbally.

Finally, when Ambrose hands Yaretta off to another high-ranking Veil who carries her out of the dining hall, kicking and screaming, the fight leaves my body. I all but go limp in Kingston's arms.

Ambrose storms over, fury overtaking his features. "What the hell was that all about, Nori?" he seethes, leaning in close to my face.

"Why don't you tell me?" I snap back.

He exhales loudly and raises his harsh glare to the man standing behind me. "You can let her go now, Adair," he orders.

Kingston stiffens behind me. "Careful, Ballard. I don't follow your orders. I outrank you in more ways than one," he says in a quiet, lethal tone.

Ambrose grinds his teeth and steps forward.

I tap Kingston's thigh. "I'm good. You can let go of me now," I say. The last thing we need is another fight breaking out. This one would make mine with Yaretta look like child's play.

His arms slip from my waist, and he steps back.

I turn to look at him to say something. I don't know if I should thank him or yell at him for pulling me off her.

His bronze eyes are unreadable as usual, the obsidian ring adding a touch of forbidden to his stoic exterior. His hair is slicked back, the top slightly longer than it was when I first met him, although the sides are still just as short. His lips lift in a smirk, and he tilts his head at me in a silent acknowledgment. He raises his head and throws one last glare at Ambrose, before heading toward a table full of Noctryns who are watching the ordeal like their favorite pastime. I can't look away as he sinks into a chair, the aura of a predator coming off him in waves.

Koa throws him some kind of fruit, which Kingston catches with one hand before sinking his teeth into it. Koa must feel me staring because his ash-colored eyes fall on me, his braids tumbling over his eyes as he grins in my direction.

"Have you lost your mind?" Ambrose voices, full of reproach.

I swivel my head back to him, my fingers itching to smack him across the face. I'm not sure where this violence is coming from, but I won't lie and say it doesn't feel good to just let it out. All of it. To not be a doormat for once.

I move closer to him. "Well, Ambrose, where do you think it's coming from?" I ask, dissent lacing my words. I have to raise my head to glare at him, which loses some effectiveness, but standing on a chair would look ridiculous.

"I don't know, Nori. You tell me," he growls.

"Oh, now I'm Nori. What happened to Norissa?"

"You're unbelievable. What's gotten into you?"

I laugh darkly. "If I have to tell you why I'm absolutely seething right now, then it's not worth my time to explain."

He narrows his eyes at me. "Are you jealous?"

I throw my hands in the air. "It isn't about jealousy, Ambrose! It's about respect. Which you clearly don't have for me," I finish.

He looks around the dining hall, suddenly aware that we're still the center of attention. Grabbing my elbow, he pulls me into the hall, away from prying eyes. "What are you going on about?" he demands, his glare trained on me.

I roll my eyes and look away. I know this man isn't this obtuse.

He grips my chin, turning my head back toward him. "Don't do that. Don't shut me out."

"You disrespected me," I whisper. "Where was the loyalty? Hmm?" The words are laced with more hurt than anger.

He sighs deeply. "I'm assuming you feel like I betrayed you?" he asks, furrowing his forehead.

I move my mouth to the side, refusing to say any more.

"You've never done well with betrayal," he says simply.

No shit.

"Nori, look at me." He tilts my head back so that I'm forced to look in those bottomless pools of promise. "I didn't betray you. We were going over scenarios relating to the professor's disappearance. As second-years, we have a bit more responsibility on our shoulders regarding the disappearance. More than first-years. I'd never do anything to be disloyal to you," he promises, staring into my eyes. "I'm sorry Yaretta and I have history. I didn't even think of her in that way when walking together, which is why I could have never imagined you'd feel any kind of way."

I believe him, but at this point, it doesn't even matter. We can't change what happened and it wasn't even the reason I was seeking him out to begin with. I've been completely sidetracked. The real reason I was looking for him comes rushing back like a punch to the gut. "Did you meet with Professor Tainey the other night?"

He drops his hand from my chin and blinks a few times. Slower than normal. His lips part like he's going to say something but decides against it.

I cross my arms, step back, and wait for my world to shatter.

Please deny it, Ambrose. Let it just be a big misunderstanding.

He steps forward like he's going to touch me, but I move out of his grasp. "Ambrose, now is not the time to be evasive." There's a hardness to my tone that I don't use with him. Ever. But at this moment, too much is on the line. A lifelong friendship, a future with the man I love, and buried family secrets that I know nothing about.

"Why?" he asks in a raw voice.

There's so much emotion packed into the one little word. Fear. Regret. Longing.

There's just as much emotion in my eyes. Pleading. Dread. Hope.

"Nori…" he whispers.

"No," I respond, holding up my hand. "Did you or did you not meet with him?"

He lowers his head. "Yes." It's so quiet I almost don't hear him.

I feel like I've been punched in the heart before it was roughly removed from my chest. If that part is true, more than likely the rest of everything else Finnley said is as well. And Ambrose knows it. He knows why I'm asking.

"Tell me," I command, proud that my voice isn't breaking. "Everything."

He raises his head, his eyes begging me to let it go. To stop this before there's no turning back. Students pass by us, unaware that my entire life is on the cusp of shattering. Their chatter and laughter are a macabre backdrop to my demise.

His Adam's apple moves as he swallows. He closes his eyes before opening them again. Hardened resolve now lingers in their depths. "I did it to protect you," he says in an unapologetic tone. "And I'd do it again."

My breath is coming out in sharp rasps. I want to run from this, but I can't. The feeling that everything is about to change washes over me.

Everything I thought I knew is about to be demolished. The one constant that I had in my life just stabbed me in the heart and is standing over my bleeding corpse, telling me he'd do it all over again, given the chance.

His hands clench at his sides. "Our mothers have been best friends since childhood, Nori. I've been in your life since the moment you were born, friendship thrust upon us, whether we wanted it or not. Lucky for us, we were inseparable from the start." He swallows. "You were the little sister I never asked for but absolutely fucking adored. There isn't anything I wouldn't have done for you," he says, running his hands through his dark waves. He licks his lips and keeps talking. "Which is why, when our mothers approached me at a young age and asked me to be your shadow, I never even hesitated. Why would I? I didn't think anything of it until we were a little older and your mother approached me again. Alone this time."

My stomach does the kind of flip that happens right before you puke.

He continues talking as if I'm not crumbling from the inside out. "She asked me if I could keep a secret if it meant protecting someone I loved. I said yes without hesitation. I'll never forget the way her lips curled in satisfaction at that moment," he says, his eyes hardening and his voice lowering. "Like you, every family member of mine through the generations that entered the military has tested as Veils. Our mothers were already making a name for themselves in their Salaryan unit, and as most narcissists do, they wanted to be sure their legacy continued."

He shakes his head. "They knew, without a doubt, one day we'd follow in their footsteps and enter Kintoira Academy. Your mother told me there wasn't a sliver of worry that I would test as anything but light. It was in my very DNA," he says before pausing. "But you were another story."

I watch as he sinks onto the hard stone bench beside us. He drops his head down, supporting it in his hands, with both elbows on his knees.

I remain standing. Silent.

"I didn't understand she meant literally," he whispers. He takes a deep breath and continues. "She said that you had dark roots, so dark they could shade out the sun and turn your light into full shadows. Being only eight years old, I couldn't grasp what she was confiding in me, but I listened with rapt attention," he says. "Her tone hardened, and her lips pulled up in distaste as she kept talking, moving onto your lineage. She mentioned that at one time, a man in her life took everything from her." He looks at me full of hesitation. "Your father."

I press my hand into my stomach, trying to steady myself.

His eyes are full of sadness. "Your mother told me he left when she was pregnant with you. That she could feel his darkness flowing in your tiny body while she carried you. She knew that you wouldn't place as a Veil, so I was instructed to do anything and everything to make it happen. I was to guide you throughout childhood to think and react like a Veil." He laughs under his breath but keeps talking. "To rationalize as one with light magic would. To smother out any darkness residing in your soul."

A silent tear runs down my cheek.

"You pretended to be my friend," I say in a broken whisper.

"NO!" Ambrose shouts, jumping up from the bench. "I was—*am* your best friend."

Years of childhood memories flash through my mind. Ambrose preventing me from punching a local boy in the nose when he took my last penny pie. Ambrose teaching me about the stars and how they correlate with our birth-given abilities, and the importance of never, ever sacrificing them for anything. The way we would lie on our backs in the fields of barley and dream about the manifestations we would inherit one day. The slurs he taught me to say about Noctryns and how they were the cesspool of the world.

It was all staged.

I was dressed as the villain and didn't even know it.

"I paid Professor Tainey handsomely to obtain a copy of the written assessment. I figured if you had a chance to be prepared for what the academy was going to ask, you would have a better chance of answering them as a Veil might. I feared…" He looks down at his hands, sorrow etched into his features. "I feared if you had to answer on the spot without time to prepare, you would answer the way a future Noctryn might."

He rubs a scarred hand down his face. "Obviously, it didn't work because the test was completely different. Someone must have gotten wind of my deal and orchestrated a new test being issued. Hence, my conversation with Tainey that night. To say I was livid would have been an understatement." He laughs harshly. "All the years I tried to protect you came to a screeching halt. It was out of my hands, and I didn't miss the way Adair looked at you. Like a personal vendetta to take out his deviant tastes on."

The one person who I felt understood me was bribed to be my friend. The friendship I held on to to get me through some of the roughest days of my life was fabricated. For years.

"What darkness did I have in me, Ambrose?" I ask. "Tell me. What was so bad about me that my mother had to order you to shape me into the person she thought I should be?" My voice comes out unsteady.

His eyes search mine. Sadness and regret shine back at me. "Your father was a Noctryn."

I stop breathing.

The world stops spinning.

My blood turns to ice.

"Impossible," I breathe, my eyes searching his for some kind of denial. "Veils and Noctryns can't procreate. You know this!" I dig my fingers into my scalp, the pain being the only thing to keep me present. "Once a Noctryn sacrifices their manifestations to be able to wield dark magic, it cancels out their light magic. Light and dark always cancel each other out, which makes procreation between the two impossible."

A dark chuckle leaves his lips. "That's the way it's *supposed* to work. However, sometimes fate has other plans."

"This is why my mother never talks about him." The words slip out, quiet and devastated.

He nods. "That and I'm sure the fact that he left you both doesn't help matters. She didn't confirm what he was until I was a grown man, but I had my suspicions."

I bite down on my thumbnail, gnawing lightly at the corner. "How could she be with a Noctryn soldier while enlisted as a Veil in the military? They would have discharged her, or worse."

"Which is why our mothers swore me to secrecy."

I walk in circles, trying to work it all out in my head. "It still doesn't make sense. How a Veil and a Noctryn created life."

Ambrose grabs my hand, stopping me from pacing back and forth.

I quickly yank it out of his grip.

"You're a Liminal," he says in a soft tone.

Light and dark cannot touch what is ambiguous.

Silver's words come back in stark clarity.

I'm not light, but I'm also not dark. I'm the in-between.

The result of a Veil mother and a Noctryn father. Something that shouldn't exist.

I stop pacing. "If that were the case, the regiment would have figured out that my mother shacked up with a dark wielder the minute my results came out after the trial. They'd have already arrested her."

"It's one of the ways a Liminal can be created, but not the only way," he informs me. "Being the decorated officer she is, I very much doubt any suspicion will be cast in her direction on that front."

I stop and stare at my best friend.

It's slightly confounding how my heart can be so resolutely frigid while my blood burns like the firepits of hell. Betrayal sits heavy in my gut. Regret mixes with the stark blue irises of the eyes I've dreamed about most of my life. I'm an idiot. To think I was ever enough for him by just being myself.

"You kept this from me for years," I accuse, stepping back. I need distance between us.

The shadows dance in the dark corners of the alcoves, and the tapestry closest to us moves as if there is a breeze. The temperature feels like it's dropped ten degrees in the last few minutes. I wrap my arms around myself, seeking warmth from the frigid hall and even colder betrayal settling into my bones.

Ambrose just stares at me. As if he's trying to memorize the lines and curvatures of my face. He doesn't, however, disagree.

"Stay the fuck away from me," I seethe, pointing my finger in his direction.

I am coming undone.

A lifetime of crafting myself to their standards, of repressing little wants and desires that scared me in their depths. I always feared something was off about myself. The love of solitude, the violent tendencies when my anger became too much, and the feeling of always wanting more than what was being offered. Turns out I had a reason to be suspicious of it all.

"Nori... please," he begs, extending his arm toward me.

"Stop." I hold my hand up. "Everything you say to me is a lie. Stay away from me, Ambrose, and forget I even exist," I order, retreating backward.

I angrily wipe the tears streaming down my face with the back of my hand.

He doesn't get to see them. He's taken enough.

I spin on my heel and flee down the corridor, leaving my heart shattered at his feet.

Chapter Thirty

The dark classroom hugs me like a desperate gulp of air. I didn't want to stay in my room, afraid he'd seek me out again. I can't face Ambrose right now. I'm still so raw and fragile that I feel like one wrong word, and I'll splinter.

The empty Apothecary class is my current refuge. The faint smell of herbs and potions floats through the air. There are numerous bookshelves stacked with old tomes that are filled with recipes. Some for healing, others for mayhem.

Depends on your mood, I guess.

A few of the walls have smoke stains from the centuries of alchemy performed in this room. There are a few cauldrons across from me, filled with a foul-smelling substance. Every so often, a bubble will form and pop within the concoction, breaking the silence that's keeping me company.

I trace my finger over the carving that's etched deep into the old table I'm sitting at. Sleep has eluded me for the past few weeks, and I've been in a constant lull of mediocracy. I'm passing classes, but just barely. I haven't died in the practice drills with Corinne yet, but I've also made very little improvement. I've had absolutely nothing in the manifestation department occur. I'm just surviving at this point.

Barely.

And most definitely not thriving.

Ambrose has tried to corner me any chance he gets, but by sheer willpower, I keep evading him. Finnley and Mallory are concerned, but they give me the space I so desperately need. Kingston has been oddly absent during most of our shared classes and from my combat training sessions. I've been sitting in Shadowcraft, watching others hone their skills and being tossed around like a rag doll in battle defense tactics by Corinne. Or whoever she chooses to accompany her during the training.

It's been an absolute grand time, let me tell you.

I watch two drops of condensation race down the opaque window. The one I've been secretly cheering for is in the lead. They look like two teardrops falling in tandem, one slightly more broken and eager to reach its destination. It breaks itself onto the window ledge, its sad song finished in such an anticlimactic way.

Twisting my unruly hair into a messy bun, I grab a quill out of my bag and secure it in place. I rest uneasy eyes on the book in front of me. The silver cover shimmers in the glow of the candle that's sitting atop the table. I guess I'm a masochist because I flip the cover open and flatten out the blank page. I reach behind me and stab the tip of my finger with the quill wrapped up in my hair. I don't even feel the sting. As if it's a perfectly normal thing to do, I squeeze drops of blood onto the pages and wait.

The response is almost immediate. Red ink splotches beneath my watchful gaze.

Hello, Weaver.

I arch a delicate red brow. Hmph. Well, that's new. "Tired of calling me Liminal?" I ask blandly.

Delicate curves splash across the page.

A thread has more than one name.

I'm not sure I care to have more than one. Life is already complicated enough.

"Right now, I just need a friend, Silver. Not a puzzle to be worked out." I close my eyes and squeeze the sides of the book. "I'm not positive, but I think I might be at rock bottom."

I reluctantly peel my eyes back open to read the response. The letters sink into the pages before being replaced with new words.

Rock bottom is never really the bottom. They'll just bring a shovel.

I raise one corner of my mouth in a half-smile. Apparently, Silver has a sense of humor. Who knew. "Helpful as always," I mutter, my voice lacking any real anger.

The page flips on its own accord.

Sometimes, things done with the best of intentions cut the deepest. Only those who care deeply enough have the ability to break the skin.

There's a pause, but the page hums beneath my fingertips like it's not quite through. Slowly, it finishes its thought.

They also have the ability to decimate us beyond rationality.

"Isn't that the truth?" I rub the page between my fingers. "Silver, what's my place in all of this? What's the endgame for me? Do I belong here? Is leaving even an option at this point?"

The page flips again but remains empty, as if it's weighing its words carefully. Finally, when I'm not sure I can't wait much longer, the letters spiral across the parchment.

Don your mask with reverence. Covertness is key. The ending is yours, what kind shall it be?

I toss my head back and stare at the ceiling.

Without thinking, I lean forward, close the book, and toss it in my bag. I've had just about all I can handle from everyone at this point, including the odd little book.

Every once in a while, footfall passes by the door, a student on their way to or from class. I'm surrounded by more people than I've ever been surrounded by in my entire life, yet I feel more alone than ever. There are hundreds of students here, not to mention the professors, medical staff, dining personnel, and even the voicebounds forced to serve their sentence within these walls. Yet I am unequivocally alone.

Funny, how I used to think that was such a luxury.

I craved time carved out by myself, thrived on it in fact. Yet here I am, sitting in this darkened classroom, basking in the realization that it's lonely. Truly isolating to not have a singular person in your corner that you can trust to catch you.

A trust fall.

Yeah, I don't have one of those.

Not anymore. Potentially never had one in the first place.

And to be honest, I'm not sure I'll ever open myself up to having one again. To be this bitter at such a young age is not only unhealthy but heartbreaking. I never want to feel that hollow feeling again that I felt that day in the hall. To feel like my insides are being dug out with a dull spoon while I desperately try to stay conscious, to wrap my hands around my still beating heart and protect it the best I can. To only realize that while I was so busy trying to protect it, it was turning to ash in my palms.

I'd cry right now if I had any tears left. However, my pillow has absorbed every single one that I had bottled up over the years. I gave them all away. I have no more left to give.

Trust is an easy thing to give someone, especially when you love them. But once broken, it's never fully put together again. Even if I do trust someone in the future, the edges will be cracked and pieces missing. It will never have that same smooth finish it had at the beginning. Broken people are never fully repaired. We just exist because we have no other choice.

And that's exactly what Ambrose did. He broke me. He reached so far inside and twisted. Cruelly. He knew how important finding my father was to me, how daunting it was to think it might never happen. I trailed after Ambrose my entire life like a lost pup, scooping up whatever crumbs he dropped along the way. I thrived on his attention, blossomed under his friendship, and relied on him for my happiness. That was my first mistake. Relying on someone to be happy.

The second was trusting that he would never use that undisputed loyalty against me. And yet, here we are. A nineteen-year-old girl hiding in the shadows of an empty classroom, wondering if the pain will ever stop.

I *loved* him. And right now, I am grieving that loss.

It doesn't mean I instantly don't love him anymore, but I know it will never be as intense as it was before. Nothing will ever be the same, and the notion of that is giving full-blown grief.

A tear slips down, falling onto my lip, the salty taste a direct reflection of the state of my heart. Apparently, I do have a few tears left after all. Nineteen years of lies. I wonder if any of it was real or just fulfilling an oath to my mother. I've been shaped and molded to be exactly who she thinks I should be.

I laugh bitterly.

I don't even know who I truly am.

I'm so lost and have no sense of direction.

I lay my wet cheek onto the smooth wooden table and close my eyes. I have a while before I need to be somewhere.

The door creaks on its hinges behind me as it slowly opens.

Grinding my teeth, I don't even open my eyes. I don't have enough fucking strength to do this right now. It was only a matter of time before he found me. I just thought I had more of it. I'm sure he's going to try to reason with me, to assure me that everything he did and lied about was for my own good. It's ironic how everyone thinks they know what's best for you, but they are the ones who end up driving you to the brink.

"Please," I mutter, digging my nails into the table, "just go away."

I can hear him walking closer.

It takes me a second, but I realize the footsteps aren't as heavy as Ambrose's. I raise my head and open my eyes at the same time, right before a rag is pressed firmly over my mouth from behind. I jerk forward, trying to pull out of the firm grip. The rag muffles my screams as I blindly reach over my head. I sink my nails into the attacker's hand, but I can feel the ferocity of my escape fading.

Quickly.

The classroom is starting to blur, and my movements become jerkier. Slower. Blinking rapidly, I try to clear the spots from my vision.

I can't lose consciousness.

Focus! Focus! FOCU...

The moment I feel my grasp loosen and fall completely, I know I'm in deep shit. Every breath that slips through my lips into the cloth is now erratic and shallow. With one last effort, I twitch my fingers and attempt to muffle out a curse before my body falls limp and the room darkens completely.

CHAPTER THIRTY-ONE

AMBROSE

The pressure behind my eyes is excruciating.

Instead of sitting in Copper Penny Pub, I'm now sitting in the library hoping Nori comes through.

This place even smells like her—vanilla, cinnamon and solitude.

I rub a hand down my face.

I'm such a fucking idiot.

I should have told her. I never meant for any of this to hurt her. Just the opposite.

I was protecting her.

When Maeve cornered me as a child, I thought I was helping Nori. She was like a little sister to me, and I would have done anything for her. The feelings I had for her were bottomless. As time went on, those feelings included fear. Not of her, but for her. I saw flashes of characteristics that made me wonder. She had an edge, a defiance that stood out among the other girls. I figured she'd outgrow it, and it was just her lashing out from the lack of a father figure. So I stepped into that role, protected her, and chased away unwanted attention.

I gave more than one bloody nose over that girl.

As the years passed, so did the way I saw her. She wasn't just a tag-along or someone I saw with sibling affection. It went deeper.

I let out a low, humorless laugh under my breath.

She burrowed beneath my skin, regardless of how hard I fought it. She wasn't a gangly little tomboy anymore. She was changing, and I wasn't the only one to notice. With her long red hair and vibrant green eyes always wide with wonder, she was stunning.

Add in the freckles scattered across the bridge of her nose, and she was ethereal.

Her friendship was my lifeline, and I wouldn't risk it for anything. I didn't want to lose her, and I was afraid that if I let her know how she was changing in my eyes, that's exactly what would happen. So I kept my mouth shut. And the other boys away.

The real danger was in the way her body was changing, though. She was growing into her long, skinny limbs. She no longer resembled one of the lads, even when she tried to discreetly hide her new curves behind baggy clothes.

She was fucking beautiful.

Dangerously so.

Now, she's fucking lethal.

She could bring any man she wanted to their knees, and they'd thank her for it. I hate it. I have to share her with the world now. A small part of me wishes she had stayed tucked away in Brylan. Away from these unsatiable soldiers' lingering looks.

Especially that bastard, Kingston.

I don't trust him, and I don't like the way he watches her.

I rub my temples, wishing I could rub away the last twenty-four hours.

Maeve had to throw a wrench in everything. I shouldn't have been drinking that night on the beach, but I was, and she caught me in a vulnerable state. She said I wasn't doing enough to keep her daughter pure, that she was slipping through our fingers. I wanted so bad to tell her there was no "our," and she was solely mine.

Maeve never deserved Nori. She was always cruel and cold to her.

I didn't tell her that. Like the coward I was, I just watched through my hangover as her devious mouth formed the words that would all but bring my world crashing down around me. "You have to try harder, Ambrose. Because there's a darkness in Nori," she said, her sharp eyes boring into mine. "Her legacy demands her light be forsaken. Her father was a Noctryn."

And that was when I knew I'd watch the world burn just to protect her.

I'd light the match.

Suddenly, everything made sense. All the years of defiance and angry outbursts. It was her very core rebelling at the idea of her mother's ideologies being shoved down her throat. And right then and there, I knew I never wanted her to feel how I felt at that moment. I wanted to shield her. If she thought for one second that she had dark lineage running through her veins, it would skew her results at the academy, and she wouldn't place as a Veil.

Or worse, she wouldn't place at all.

A death sentence.

They'd have to dig two graves because I wouldn't go down without a fight.

That was before the results came out after Asylamation, and I learned about Liminals. I'd never even heard of them up until that point. How something like this was kept from us in our education is still beyond comprehension. I never gave it much thought on *how* Nori had come to be because I was too focused on keeping her alive.

Maeve had to have known. And she decided to keep that information to herself.

General Porter and his forefathers before him went to great lengths to keep any and all information on the subject buried. Just like he does with anything that stands in his way, people included. I wouldn't even begin to guess how many graves have been dug because of his family.

When Nori arrived at the academy, I was too far buried in the secrets forced upon me that I couldn't tell her at that point. She'd hate me. So instead, I kept my distance. I didn't know how to look her in the eyes and keep the lies from coming out.

She'd know.

I drop my head into my hands. Defeat presses down harshly on my shoulders.

Look at me now. Pathetically sitting in a library, praying for a glimpse of that red hair. I'd give anything to see her look at me with something other than disgust.

My hands slide down my face before clawing their way back through my hair.

Who am I kidding? At this point, I'd sever a limb just to have her look at me.

Dammit. Everything is fucked.

The chair moves back, scraping along the floor as I push up. I'm not going to just sit here and wait. We have way too much history between us to throw it away. We'll figure it out. We always figure it out.

I make my way up to the hall where her room is, and rap my knuckles on her door. There's no movement from the other side. I twist the knob and push. It opens easily. Her bed is made and the room tidy. The books she bought from Moorechester sit on her nightstand, and a few notebooks for class rest on the end of her bed. Nori, however, is nowhere to be found. Not surprising, though. She's doing a remarkable job of avoiding me.

I glance at the bed one more time. The memory of her writhing beneath me comes to the forefront. Her tiny moans and pleas not to stop ring through my ears. I firmly shut the door and head back to the first floor, wanting to get out of the Noctryn wing as quickly as possible.

The air is palpable with dirty magic.

"Ballard," a feminine voice calls from up ahead. A first-year Noctryn, according to the marks on her uniform, skips down the steps toward me. "Hey," she says out of breath, stopping a few steps above me.

I nod in acknowledgment, not in the mood to talk.

She tucks her black hair behind her ear and doesn't retreat from my callous greeting. "Have you seen Nori? We were supposed to meet to study for an upcoming test for our Blood Magic class."

An icy feeling works its way down my spine.

"When?" I ask sharply, forcing myself not to jump to any conclusions.

"About an hour ago, but she didn't show."

I can feel my shoulders stiffen, but I keep my composure. "Your name?" I demand.

She reaches her hand out to shake mine. "Mayline Zhou. Nice to meet you."

I quickly shake it and start walking down the steps. "Where were you scheduled to meet?" I need details, and I need them quickly. It's not like Nori to bail on someone, not even when her own world falls around her feet.

"The study hall. I waited well past our meeting time, but she just never showed."

I push past classrooms and down corridors, not bothering to see if she's keeping up.

I finally reach the study hall and throw the doors open.

Empty.

Racing back toward the main floor, Mayline at my heels, a foreboding feeling rises, heavy in my chest. I pick up the speed, almost at a full-blown run. The sound of armor greets my ears as I skid into the foyer. Kingston and a handful of others are suited up, weapons strapped to every inch of their armor.

"What's going on?" I order, my voice carrying over the clinking of weapons.

Kingston turns his head toward me, his eyes full of hatred.

"Wraith attack," he answers, sliding his helmet on.

Mayline's worried eyes meet mine.

And then all hell breaks loose.

Chapter Thirty-Two

The throbbing in my head finally wakes me up.

Each breath I take feels like a mouthful of gravel sliding down my parched throat. A chemical residue lingers on my tongue, and the taste of it heightens the nauseous feeling pinging around my stomach. Sand crunches beneath my face, sticking to my cheek as I slowly try to lift my head. The air is stifling and thick with the smell of rotting meat, iron, and sweat.

I gag and swallow down the will to vomit.

Pushing myself up on an elbow, I slowly take in my surroundings. Sandstone walls surround me on three sides. No windows. The only source of light is coming through the bars, toward the front of the crude cell. Claustrophobia claws at my skin. This prison wasn't built but carved. Created to keep things from ever leaving.

The uneven floor digs into my side as I shift my weight and try to sit up.

Dizziness comes in heavy waves. I decide to pace myself and try something different. I crawl over to the metal bars and place my face between them, peering out through the openings. The sun beats down in the center of a pit-like room, shining through a large opening over a hundred feet up. The sky is clear and bright. I'm no longer anywhere near Kintoira. That much I'm positive of.

Numerous cells line the outer edges of the circular pit, but if anyone's inside any of them, there isn't any movement.

"Hello," I call out, voice cracking over the words.

The rustle of robes comes from the shadows of a cell a few rows down.

I press my face farther into the bars. "Hello, is anyone out there. I need help," I whisper through the pain in my throat.

The scent of decay hits me in the face as the figure glides closer.

I push back and fall on my ass, scooting farther back. It stops directly in front of the bars—the same ones that my face was just pressed into—and grips the metal with both hands. Fingers with flesh hanging from the bone wrap around the bars, and black liquid seeps down the metal.

I don't move. I don't even blink.

It drops one of its hands and pushes the decrepit-looking hood back from its face. The face of a man, or what was once a man, looks back at me. Dead skin hangs in ribbons along his jaw and cheeks. His eyes are sunken and void of color. They haven't completely rotted yet, but they look like they're on the cusp of it. His lips, thin and covered in the thick black liquid, pull back to reveal sharpened teeth, yellow and decayed.

And then he smiles.

The sand flies up as I scramble as far back as possible. I tuck my feet under me and press my back into the jagged rocks.

"So glad you could join us," it rasps in a voice that sounds like it's choking on blood.

It spoke.

Wraiths do not speak.

Holy shit.

What in the fuck is going on? What drugs did they give me? Wraiths don't think except for the sole purpose of feeding. Yet this one not only tried to communicate, it's now staring at me expectantly like it would like a response.

I shake my head back and forth. "This isn't real," I whisper. "This is just a nightmare."

I'm still drugged and unconscious. This is just my mind playing tricks on me.

I need to wake up.

"I'll agree, you *are* in a nightmare," it chuckles darkly, before coughing and gurgling. "Although you're wide awake, I'm afraid." It pushes its face into the bars, flesh sticking to the metal and tearing. The smell is overpowering, and I swear I can taste it on my tongue.

"Where am I?" I ask against my better judgment.

The wraith grips the bars tighter. "In hell," it says through a sardonic smile.

The loud slam of a door makes me jump. The wraith doesn't turn around to look, though. His gaze is on my mouth. He's practically salivating. Without a doubt, he's envisioning how my soul will taste when he places his rancid mouth over mine. When he feasts on my tongue before tearing my existence from my body and then moving onto my flesh.

Another figure draped in heavy robes comes into view to stand a few feet behind the monster in front of me. I'm not sure why, but for some reason, I have a feeling the monster in the back is ten times worse. They're of a smaller stature, and their robes are newer and brighter. The red fabric hangs loose on their frame and covers their shoes.

"Come now, Frederick. You're scaring the poor girl."

I know that voice. I recognize it, but I'm not sure *where* I know it from. It's young, boyish even. And Frederick? Who the hell is Frederick?

Sharp rocks continue to dig into my back. I've pushed so far back that there isn't anywhere else for me to go. My limbs still feel heavy and sluggish, making any kind of escape attempt impossible.

The man in the red robes steps forward, directly next to the wraith. Neither the smell nor the threat of the monstrosity at his side seems to bother him. He makes a gesture with his hands, and the wraith backs off, but not before looking down at the man.

Disdain, if a wraith can even have that, flitters across its decaying face. He moves back to the shadows from which he came from.

"Welcome, Norissa. We're so happy to have you," the man says in a smarmy voice.

Despite the heat in the air, I shiver. "Who are you? What do you want with me?"

"It figures you wouldn't even recognize my voice. Always so much better than the rest of us, weren't you? Important, right?" His tone went from cocky to downright hateful.

Small fingers reach up and pull his hood back.

I close my eyes, a weak chuckle slipping through my lips. I should have seen this coming.

"Disappointed?" he mocks, stepping closer to my cell.

"You would know, wouldn't you? I'm sure that's the general consensus where you're concerned," I reply in a raspy voice.

The bars shake as he jumps forward, gripping them and rattling them in anger. "Watch your fucking mouth," he says, spit flying from his face into the sand below his feet.

I bite my tongue. I need time to regain my strength and can't do that if I push him too far.

He steps back, seemingly appeased at what he observes as obedience. "Finally, seems you're learning your place."

I grind my teeth but don't answer. It fucking kills me not to, but I don't.

He rubs his chin with his small, childlike fingers. "Do you know how hard it was to get you alone? Away from the watchful eyes of your guard dogs?" he asks me calmly. "I've been waiting weeks for the perfect opportunity, and finally one presented itself. I won't lie, I was a little disappointed by how easy it was in the end. It was almost like you gave up."

I bring both hands in front of me, raising my middle fingers.

A sharp laugh leaves him. "Thank goodness. I was worried there was nothing left for us to break."

I keep my face neutral, but inside, I'm panicking. This does not sound promising. I'll die before I beg, but that doesn't mean I'm eager to be tortured. In fact, I'd like to skip that step altogether if possible.

The air hangs thick and unmoving between us. Sweat beads along my neck and temples, trickling down into my torn shirt. Each breath I take feels labored, as if the putrid air itself doesn't want to be drawn in.

"I've worked so hard behind the scenes, and you didn't even know. Couldn't even appreciate the amount of effort I put in." He walks back and forth in front of the rusty iron bars, seemingly content to just hear himself talk. I let him. It will buy me some time for these drugs to work their way out of my system. Giving me some kind of chance to fight back. "I mean, c'mon." He chuckles, throwing his hands in the air. "How do you think you became a lieutenant the night you arrived?"

He looks at me expectantly, like he wants me to join in on this game.

Scoffing, when I just stare at him, he continues talking as if he never stopped. "I needed you to step up and fail miserably in front of your classmates and professors. I needed to add a little extra pressure during Asylamation week for you to crumble. To lose all credibility." He licks his thin lips. "With any luck, you wouldn't survive the trials. So"—he sighs for extra emphasis—"I put a little whisper in dear ole' Father's ear to make it happen."

He tilts his head and raises his palms like it's the most obvious answer in the world as he keeps pacing.

I snort under my breath.

His head whips in my direction, eyes narrowed, but he continues as if I didn't interrupt. "Unfortunately, you didn't fail, which put a kink in my plans. Have to say, Pops wasn't too happy with you," he snarls. "Or me."

I blow out an exaggerated breath. "I'm sure it's not the first time the general was disappointed in his son," I respond dryly.

Eryk Porter stares at me for a solid thirty seconds before throwing his head back and laughing.

It crosses my mind that he might actually be crazy. Nothing like the way he portrayed himself during our time together at Kintoira. He was as bland and forgettable as humanly possible. But maybe that was more strategic than genetic.

"Feisty. I like it," he answers. "Can't wait to bleed it out of you." His eyes have taken on a maniacal appearance, and I fear that my time is running out.

I wiggle my toes and curl my fingers in the sand. The feeling is coming back, making it easier to control them. As much as I don't want to, I have to keep him talking.

I clear my throat. "Why all the interest in me? Who cares if I survived the first week or died trying?"

"Nori, Nori, Nori. You really don't know anything, do you?" He makes a tsking sound with his tongue against the back of his teeth. "You don't honestly believe that your mother was the only one who knew your father was a Noctryn, do you? You see, it's my family's responsibility to know everything that goes on within this realm, anything that may cause hiccups in the way we run it." The fabric of his cloak rustles as he walks in front of me. "Your mother was better off alive to us than dead." He stops and looks directly at me. "For the time being," he says, while smirking. "So when a fellow student who just so happens to have owed me a favor was doing some research of his own to help a family member in need, your name came up in his findings."

He offers me a condescending smile.

I'm grinding my teeth so hard they actually hurt.

But I don't reply to him. I let him just keep on talking.

"Turns out the thing he needed most was one of the rarest objects in the realm. A *Liminal*," he breathes, his eyes wide with excitement. "However, there's not much information on how a Liminal comes to be. There are rumors of certain black magic that can assist, but that's heresy and unpredictable. As most dark magic is," he says with obvious distaste.

I shift my weight and rotate my wrists as discreetly as possible. The side effects of whatever they drugged me with is slowly leaving my limbs. The heavy weight is becoming lighter the longer Eryk drones on.

"How did he find out about me?" I ask, participating merely to keep the conversation going.

He nods once, like he's impressed with my question. "He knew your father," he says simply. "He had his own reasons for digging into your father's past, and imagine his shock when he discovered his prior lover was a Veil. And not just any Veil, but a very pregnant one."

He claps his hands in front of him in glee.

I nod like I'm actively invested in his words. "And let me guess—He put two and two together, figured out I was that child, born from impossible odds, and the Liminal he needed?"

"Look, Frederick! She is sharper than a marble," Eryk says in a delighted tone while looking over at the sulking wraith in the corner.

Frederick is the fucking wraith.

"Okay, so, why am I here with you and not in your friend's cell?"

"Because he slipped up and mentioned you one night over drinks. How he was coming to the academy under false pretenses, but honestly just needed to collect one thing before he was on his way," he says, pressing his face back into the bars. "*You.*"

I tilt my head and keep pushing. "Once again, why am I here and not in his possession? What could you possibly need with me?"

His mouth flattens like my question was dense. "I'm a Porter," he answers, as if that's the obvious answer. "Our desires always come first. As soon as my father found out about you through me, he agreed to put in the recommendation for you to be a lieutenant, in hopes you'd take care of the dirty work for us and succumb to the trials."

I rotate my ankles and dig my fingers into the sand.

"Having so many cadets look to you for leadership always adds a layer of pressure that not many survive. It would save us from getting our hands dirty. Again."

Again?

"What do you have against Liminals?"

He presses his face further into the bars, his cheeks appearing squished. "They can be our undoing," he whispers, his eyes looking completely unhinged.

I move my fingers through the sand, never taking my eyes off him. "And the wraiths? How do they fit into all of this?"

"You mean our personal army? Honestly, I'm surprised your mother never joined their ranks."

I sit forward, my fists now curling in my lap.

"What is that supposed to mean?" I ask, sweat beading over my lip.

He leans forward and lowers his voice, as if sharing a delicious secret. "They're *Veils*, Norissa."

The blood drains from my face.

I blink hard.

Once. Twice. Three times.

I shake my head in refusal.

"No," I deny.

"Yes," he answers, a cruel smile pulling at the corner of his mouth. "Veils who were power hungry. Who wanted their manifestations without limits. Light wielders who dabbled in dark magic, attempting to create a dark object for their personal use." He nods his head at my horrified expression. "They wanted a way to prevent burnout and have the ability to wield their gods-given manifestation without restraint."

I drop my gaze to the floor.

"That's impossible. Veils can't create or use dark objects," I mutter, more to myself than Eryk.

"Well, technically, they can," he answers cryptically. "With consequences."

I shake my head again in denial. This isn't plausible.

He sighs like he's disappointed with me. "Why do you think Casacia kept getting attacked? Yes, we tried to keep it from the general population, but evidently, it's impossible to keep things completely under wraps. The iron. The wraiths want iron, Nori."

He claps his hands together to get my attention. I raise my eyes to meet his manic ones. "The city is rich in minerals, *especially* iron. Lacking Noctryn blood for the process, they double up on the iron, add their own blood to create the dark object, and use a malediction they create. But as you can see by Frederick's appearance, it comes with slight disadvantages." He looks over at the wraith and winces.

The wraith bristles in the corner, clearly not liking being the topic of our conversation.

"Why would they do this, knowing the consequences?" I ask, lifting my chin and holding his stare.

"Because each one believes that they're the exception. Their thirst for power blinds them, and we use that to our advantage. They become the general's personal army to annihilate the threat of powerful Noctryns from the realm," he says, his boots dragging small trenches in the sand. "The dark wielders that want to dethrone the Porters from running Salaryan. Keeping order and preventing chaos. We've used them for centuries throughout my family's rule," he adds, glancing at the wraith again. "We allow them to target particular cities to get the needed ingredients," he supplies, a smug smile resting on his lips. "And they're too dumb to realize it."

"Why would they do anything for the general if they already have a death sentence?"

The dark chuckle that escapes him raises the hair on my arms. "Because, dear Norissa, we've been working for centuries to find the cure, and we're close. So, so close. Once we can cure them, we can control them, and they'll last longer than they do in the forms of wraiths."

"People would notice loved ones missing. They wouldn't just disappear without someone noticing."

"The general is good at fabricating deceit and false charges. They simply disappear to serve a life sentence," he gloats, like it's the most brilliant plan ever thought of.

I bite my lip and tilt my head. "Why are you telling me all of this?"

His smile slowly spreads, and his empty eyes narrow in satisfaction.

I laugh softly, nodding my head in clear understanding.

He doesn't plan for me to ever leave this pit.

"You see, Nori, the Noctryns are a defiant lot. They buck against authority and don't particularly like being told what to do. The insolence never left their blood."

My ears perk up at his last sentence, but before I can focus on it, the door opens again.

Two more cloaked figures, hoods pulled back, walk quickly in our direction, boots loud on the hard stone of the doorway. I recognize one instantly by the hatred shining in her eyes, but the other I've never seen before.

The air shifts as they walk up to Eryk, his attention thankfully moving from me to them.

The approaching man pats Eryk on the shoulder. "Eryk, don't be so humble. You forgot to mention the blood of the Liminals on your family's hands throughout the centuries," he says, his voice cheery and loud throughout the open area.

"That's confidential, you imbecile," Eryk replies angrily.

The man just responds by squeezing Eryk's shoulders in a condescending way. "Relax, it's not like it's going to leave this pit." He laughs under his breath. "Say, how many Liminals has your family murdered over the past seven hundred years?"

Eryk grips the front of the man's shirt. "That's enough," he growls.

The man, taller than Eryk and thicker, steps back, raising both hands in mock defeat.

I stare at Yaretta, and she stares back. She hasn't stopped staring since she first entered.

Eryk shoves the man away and turns his full attention back to me. "Now, where were we?" he asks, rubbing his hands together. "Ah, yes," he bursts out, unable to contain his excitement. "Time to play."

He walks up to the bars, whistling under his breath while he removes a key from his pocket, and quickly unlocks the cell. Hard, jagged rocks dig into the back of my skull as I hug the wall. It's three against one. Four, if you count Frederick. I'm starting to accept the chance of ever leaving this cell is slim to none, but I'll go down fighting. I won't make it easy on them.

My fingers brush over the sand-caked wall as I shuffle toward the corner. A sliver of some kind of sharp rock scratches against my palm. Small but piercing. As discreetly as possible, I curl my fingers around it and gently pull it from its resting place. It pops out easily, thankfully falling into my upturned palm. I keep it behind my back, running my fingers over the rough edges.

Eryk lifts the hem of his slightly too-large robe out of the sand before stepping into the confines of my prison. His wide nose crinkles in disgust as he looks around. "Pity, I might be doing you a favor by removing you from this filthy cell," he mutters, looking around where I've been held. Eryk isn't a big man by any means, slightly on the short side and lanky, but I know the mistake in underestimating someone. I need to aim for the eyes, throat, or the weak spot between his legs.

He holds his hand out to me like I'm a rabid dog he's trying to earn the trust of.

I run my tongue over my teeth. This man is stupider than I thought.

"If you think I'm grabbing your hand on my own free will, you're out of your mind," I say, snorting under my breath.

He sighs and steps farther into the cell. "Very well, we'll do this your way then." He looks over his shoulder. "Frederick, would you mind coming in here?"

Fuck.

I'm out of time. I should have known he wouldn't do the grunt work himself. That was a slight mistake on my part.

He doesn't even notice the shift in my weight as I make my move.

I jump up, lunge forward, the rock firmly gripped in my hand as I aim for his throat. He moves quicker than I anticipate, and my movements are clumsy and miscalculated. The rock slices across the edge of his cheek in a jagged, shallow cut. He hisses and grabs at his face with his right hand, his eyes going wide before he uses the other hand to backhand me hard enough that I fall to my knees.

The drugs linger in my system, causing my reflexes to be delayed. A sharp sting radiates across my face, but I can't focus on it before I'm roughly pulled to my feet again. The smell hits me first, and then the realization that my sleeves feel wet.

I look down, and decomposing flesh, moist with rot, holds each of my arms in its surprisingly firm grip. My back is flush with the tattered robes of what was once a Veil.

"That was unwise," Eryk says, walking closer to me.

His beady eyes run up and down my body. It feels as if the torture has already begun. I need to find a safe place in my mind and go there. Lock myself away and disassociate. There's nothing I can do to protect my body, but I can try to protect my mind. At least until it's over and I slip into the next life. Because I have no doubt that their nefarious plans do not include me leaving this pit in one piece.

He trails a finger over the welt that I know iS already forming from his hit, and licks the top of his thin lip. This sick bastard is getting off on my pain.

I lift my chin higher.

Fuck him.

"Are we going to stand here and look at her all day, or cut her open and drain her?" Yaretta asks, hatred seeping into each syllable that passes through her callous lips.

Eryk tsks in her direction. "Patience is key, Yaretta. I've waited so long for this," he coos, running his hand along my jaw. "Don't rush me."

She arches a thin brow, heavy with makeup, but remains silent.

Adrenaline runs rampant through my veins. Everything is heightened. Except time. That has slowed down to an insufferable rate. I can hear the erratic thuds of my heartbeat in my ears. But I'm not scared.

I'm angry.

I'm also surprised.

I thought I'd be frantic, doing anything and everything in my power to stay alive. But I'm not. I'm resolute in the acceptance of it. Calm even. Unwavering. But very, very angry. This wasn't the way I was supposed to go. Inconsequential in the big scheme of things. Simply being murdered for who I am. Something completely out of my control.

Eryk turns suddenly on his heel and exits the cell. I'm shoved roughly from behind, the wraith no longer holding me. The only saving grace in this nightmare at the moment. He gestures with his hands, and I'm pushed unceremoniously into the sand. I land on my knees, hard, and catch myself with my hands.

A devious laugh comes from above me as Yaretta looks down, her brunette hair perfectly styled, and makeup expertly applied. She looks as if she is attending a nice dinner, not my execution.

Bending down to my level, she pins me beneath her cold stare. "Beg."

I spit at her feet.

She stands and kicks sand right in my face. The granules stick to my damp skin. I use my sleeve to wipe it from my eyes and mouth as best as I can.

I'm going to kill this bitch.

"Can we get on with it? I have places to be," the man who entered with Yaretta says in a bored tone.

"Shut up, Rhett. I want to enjoy this!" Yaretta snaps.

Rhett...

"Here's how it's going to go," Eryk says, moving to stand beside Yaretta. "We're going to break you." He grins. "Then, when we've had our fill, we're going to drain you of most of your blood because"—he bends down, gripping my hair and pulling my head back—"it turns out, Liminal blood might just be the last ingredient needed to heal the wraiths." A malicious smile plays along his lips. "And then, I'm going to let Frederick here, finally, eat."

"He's going to kill you. You know that, right?" I ask, my lips curling back.

Yaretta laughs. "Who, Ambrose? He's at Kintoira right now as we speak, enjoying a nice dinner in the dining hall," she says, full of venom. "No one's coming to save you, Norissa."

I close my eyes as the last hope I had bleeds out into the sand. I completely forgot that Yaretta was a perceiver. She can pinpoint a person to their exact location at any given time. Of course Eryk would utilize her. Despair coils around my throat. No one's coming for me. I'm going to die alone in this hellhole with a group of people who hate me.

For some reason, the idea of dying surrounded by hate instead of love is the most tragic part of this whole ordeal.

"Yep. There it is," she breathes, her eyes lighting with glee. "The moment she's accepted defeat."

"Rhett, will you fetch us the chair?" Eryk asks casually over his shoulder.

Rhett mumbles something under his breath, tosses his hood back, and walks into an empty cell before coming back out with a rusty metal chair. I look from the chair to Rhett's face. For some reason I'll probably never understand, I want to memorize the face of each of my captors.

His hair is a dark blond, almost brown, with shrewd light-green eyes. Both ears are pierced, and various tattoos run up his neck. He's built like someone who takes pride in their appearance. Either that or his career choice is responsible for his physique.

He drops the chair unceremoniously at Eryk's feet.

"Much appreciated," Eryk replies dryly.

"Up, bitch. We're ready to play," Yaretta says, bouncing on her feet. She doesn't make a move to put her hands on me, though.

Hmph, not as dumb as she looks after all.

Eryk looks behind me and nods.

Frederick grabs my arms, hoisting me up and roughly deposits me on the metal chair. Rhett walks around him with ropes in each hand and starts wrapping my ankles to the legs of the chair and binding my wrists tightly together.

I pull on the bindings, but they don't budge.

He knows what he's doing. He's done this before.

"This is going to hurt." The heat of his breath skims my neck. "And I'm going to enjoy every second of it." His tone completely changes when he whispers it. It's no longer bored and compliant, but filled with fury and hate.

I turn as much as the ropes will allow and look at him. So much hostility swims in his eyes that it almost takes my breath away.

Yaretta steps up in front of me, bringing my attention back to her. She lifts two of my fingers and snaps them backward. I lurch forward but refuse to scream. My throat feels thick, and it's hard to swallow.

Rhett grabs a fistful of my hair and sharply yanks my head back. "You'll watch as we break you," he says harshly.

Eryk walks up to me, pulls his fist back, and slams it into my jaw.

My head flies backward, and dots dance in my vision.

Unfortunately, I don't pass out. I'm coherent much longer than I antic-ipate or want during the hits, breaks, and cuts.

Chapter Thirty-Three

Sticky strands of hair caked with dried blood stick to my forehead. I have no idea how long I've been in this pit or strapped to this chair. It could be hours or days. I'm delirious from the pain and exhaustion. The moment I feel death beckoning me, it slips through my fingers. I'm eager to greet it past the point of sanity. But before I can slip into the next life, I'm ripped from its clutches and brought back to this hell made of sand and sweat.

They break me repeatedly, but not enough for death to claim me.

Yaretta rests against the bars of an empty cell, while Rhett and Eryk discuss the next steps. Frederick paces behind me, his hunger becoming insatiable. I think he's worried they're going to kill me, and my soul will escape before he gets to feed.

Blood trickles into my mouth from the cracks in my lips. I can't remember the last time I've had anything to drink, and the heat is stifling. My shirt clings to my back, damp from perspiration and fear. Both of my bare feet are resting on top of the hot sand, and I can feel the blisters forming. The metal from the chair feels like it's melting my skin off.

I welcome death with open arms. Pray for it. I've reached the point where I might even beg for it.

The sand around me is no longer golden, but now a muted crimson. A testament to the pain that has passed. The sun beats down on my broken form, causing the dried blood covering me to become itchy and unbearable.

For a glorious second, a shadow falls across the sky, blocking out the sun entirely. If I weren't so delirious, I might look up out of curiosity. However, I can barely lift my head enough to look in front of me, let alone look upward.

Instead, I bask in the precious seconds I'm given a reprieve from the sweltering rays.

I used to enjoy days filled with sunshine and surf. I'd walk through the broken tides, let my hair hang loose and become tangled from the sea breeze while catching sand crabs. The warmth would tuck away the darkness I felt swimming beneath my flesh, if only for a moment. It was my little secret. But in those stolen moments, it was everything. Now, I'm not sure I'll ever love sunshine the same way. Not after baking in it for who knows how long, while they broke me piece by piece.

It will never again feel safe. I will never again feel warmth as a welcome reprieve.

I spit into the stifling sand, blood mixing with the saliva. The movement causes me to inhale sharply, pain lancing through my jaw and up toward my ear. I'm pretty sure it's dislocated.

The ground shakes beneath my feet.

Screams tear from Yaretta and shouts from the men.

I manage to lift my head just enough.

Death.

Death has come for its dues.

Death has arrived on waves of shadow and demands retribution.

Darkness surrounds us, and in the middle of it all is a Noctryn, shadows pouring out of each hand and a promise of reckoning in his dark eyes.

Kingston.

I can't explain it, but I suddenly feel peace. Vengeance will be served. Even if I'm not the one able to do so, I know my debts will be collected.

He takes one look at me, and his eyes turn black.

Eryk screams out orders, his arms flailing in panic, and a door opens from the side. The blood curdles in my veins as wraith after wraith enters, their hoods hiding their decomposing faces but not the stench or the palpable thirst they bring with them.

Kingston's shadows wrap around their throats, before going through their mouth and nose, cutting off all oxygen. He pulls both swords from his back, one in each hand, and starts cutting through the rotting army. He fights like he lives. Every step is measured, every strike an answer. Steel cuts through the air as wraiths fall at his feet, heads removed from their bodies. Some scream as they collapse while others never have a chance to make a sound.

There are no evasive moves.

He simply disappears and reappears like a reaper demanding vengeance.

I suck in a broken breath.

The simple gesture causes a sharp pain to knife through my side.

They just keep coming. For every wraith he cuts down, three more enter through the door.

Two ropes fall down the opening of the pit.

I slowly tilt my head back, pain radiating down my spine as I look up. I watch through swollen eyes as two soldiers make short work of the climb, landing heavily in the middle of the chaos. One in a ballistic vest, gauntlets on his wrists and forearms. An assassin ready to strike. The other is wearing the same uniform as I am, just not gray.

The look on his face is another story altogether.

Ambrose looks at my injured state and lets out a roar that shakes the walls.

He cuts down a wraith without taking his eyes off me and starts in my direction. He sheathes his weapon, raises his hands, fires burning in each palm, and throws them with lethal precision. The abominations fall at his feet. Ashes mixing with sand.

Yaretta leaps away from the metal bars she's been holding onto and runs behind me. She grabs my hair in a painful grip and thrusts a knife under my chin.

Finnley takes measured steps in my direction, his arms held out, not even looking at the death and destruction happening around him. His focus is entirely on me.

Fear and hesitation are pooled in his eyes.

"Yaretta, don't do this. You're better than this," he pleads, slowly walking toward us.

She digs the tip of the knife into my lower jaw, as blood trickles onto my lap. "Stop right there or I swear to the gods I'll skewer her head on this blade," she screams over the sound of battle taking place all around us.

Finnley ducks as a wraith grabs for him, quickly standing and driving his elbow into its face. A shadow slithers around its neck before it even hits the ground, squeezing until the head falls forward and rolls across the sand, landing at my feet.

Ambrose drives his knee into the face of another, as he spins and throws his sword, landing deep in the chest of one coming at me from the side. He's resorted to hand-to-hand combat now. He won't use his fire this close to me. Not with it being so unpredictable.

My gaze swings between Kingston and Ambrose. Darkness spills from Kingston as he dispatches two at the same time.

We're outnumbered, and they just keep coming.

Finnley is mere steps away. I turn my broken gaze on him.

"Hi again," he mouths, but I can read his lips perfectly. He turns his worried eyes to the person behind me. "Yaretta, please."

She laughs cruelly. "See, Norissa, that's how you beg. It's not so hard, is it?" she taunts, digging the tip in even farther.

I wince and hold as still as possible.

"Hello, brother," a deep voice says from the inside of a cell.

Finnley's head whips in the direction it came from. "Rhett?" he asks, confusion coating his words.

"The one and only," Rhett answers, stepping out from his hiding place, his arms spread wide.

Finnley's eyes move from his brother to my broken face, and back again. "What are you doing here? What the fuck is going on?" he demands, his brows pulled down with a solid mixture of turmoil and fear etched across his face.

"What you should have done from the beginning, but apparently I can't count on you," he answers in a deranged voice. He points at me while looking at Finnley, a satisfied glint appearing in his eyes. "We got her, Finnley."

I slice my eyes to Finnley's face.

I have no idea what's going on. I can barely see out of the swelling in my eyes. Yaretta has my head pulled back at an unnatural angle, and every breath vibrates against what I'm convinced are multiple broken ribs. One wrong move and I'm going to end up with a punctured lung or a dagger through my jaw. I'm doing my best to put the pieces of the puzzle together, but it's almost impossible to concentrate with my body deteriorating by the second.

He doesn't look at me, just keeps his narrowed eyes on Rhett. "This wasn't a part of the plan," he replies, his tone turning icy.

"I came up with a better one, Finnley. Look," he says before disappearing into the cell directly in front of me. He opens an adjacent door and shuffles through. A few seconds later, he walks back out, pushing two people who are bound and gagged.

Finnley's eyes widen. "What are *they* doing here?" he demands, his voice rising above the fighting.

I shoot my eyes toward Finnley. Confusion and denial are painted across my features.

Rhett pushes the two prisoners into the chaos. A man and woman in tattered professor robes, faces hollow and emaciated. Their eyes dart around the pit filled with dozens of wraiths. They glaze over the Noctryn surrounded by shadows cutting wraiths down one by one, and the Veil dispatching them where they stand.

The woman screams behind her gag, and the man shakes his head in denial. I wasn't in her class, but I vaguely recognize the woman as Professor Hunstal. A starved version of her.

I can only assume that the man is the missing alchemy professor from last year.

His cheeks are sunken in, and bruises cover his temple area.

"We no longer need them, do we? I mean, now that we have the Liminal and the book," Rhett remarks, walking back into the cell and coming out with my bag. "See," he says, smiling as he opens my bag and shows Finnley Silver resting at the bottom of it.

I tear my gaze away from my bag. From my secret little book.

"Finnley, what's he talking about?" I ask through my teeth, trying not to move my mouth too much since the dagger is resting directly under it.

Yaretta grips my hair tighter. "Shut up, bitch," she seethes.

Finnley tears his eyes away from his brother and looks at me. Fear shines in his eyes, along with something else that makes me want to puke.

Regret.

Gods no. Please, no, not again.

I can't take one more ounce of treachery.

"Tell her. Go on then," Rhett encourages, gripping the back of the professors' necks and moving toward us.

Finnley turns fully toward him, his arms outstretched. "Stop it, Rhett. Please. It's not too late to undo all of this," he pleads, desperation making his movements jerky.

Rhett shakes his head in disappointment. "How are we even blood related?" he asks on a shallow sigh. "Allow me, then."

Finnley steps toward his brother.

"You move, and I'll kill her," Yaretta warns him.

He stops and looks into my eyes, full of remorse, as his brother continues talking.

"You see, dear Norissa, your father ruined our family. Tore us apart from the bottom and watched us crumble. All because he was a selfish bastard. *Our father*," he growls, rubbing his chest where his heart should be, "loved our mother fiercely, but died protecting the realm from the very monsters in this room." He points to the battle erupting around us. "He gave his life to keep the wraiths at bay. And for what? The general to use them behind the people's backs?" he demands in anger. "You see, there are monsters everywhere, Norissa. Different kinds hiding among us."

He tucks a few strands of hair behind Professor Hunstal's ear, causing her to whimper behind her gag. He pats her cheek in a condescending way. "After his death, she did her best to raise me on her own, but she was pregnant with Finnley, and the loneliness was creeping into her bones. I wasn't enough." He stares off for a second as if he's in a different place and time. The bellow of a wraith being torn in half by shadows causes him to remember where he is.

He starts talking again as if it isn't madness to be having this conversation with pandemonium erupting around us. "After her grieving period was over and she returned to active duty, she met your father." He rubs his chin thoughtfully. "Do you even know his name?" he asks, dipping his chin with a knowing smirk.

I bite the side of my cheek and continue to meet his stare. I won't play his games, but a small part of me, the little girl who still wants a father, is hanging onto his every word, praying he tells me.

He drops his hand and starts pacing in front of the professors. "Well, his name was Solomon. Solomon Vynchael."

I exhale sharply.

And for the first time since the torture started, a tear escapes.

"Our mother, Sierra, met your father during a breach of the wall. Their units were ordered to contain it. He decided that day that she was his mate." He chuckles darkly. "If you buy into that bullshit. Anyway, she fell desperately in love with him too, explaining it as a love they had no choice but to follow through on. A fierce, ferocious kind of attachment."

The salt from my tears burns the various cuts on my face, but I'm thankful for the sting. Anything to balance out the way my heart is being eviscerated.

He looks at me, smiling low and cold. "The kind where he can leave his pregnant lover without a backward glance."

The heart I protected for so long, fragments in my chest.

He doesn't pause for my pain. "They were inseparable. To the point that nothing else mattered. Not even me. I was still young, young enough to need my mother. But I just needed to bide my time. You see, everything was about to change." He ducks as a knife soars past his head. "Solomon fell in battle, a conflict with an opposing kingdom, a misunderstanding, and our mother lost her mind with grief. She couldn't accept that her mate was no longer in this life. To put it mildly, she went mad," he says. "Ended up at Harkin House, where Finnley was born, and we were taken from her and raised in the broken homes of people desperate enough for coin to take in a pair of orphans."

"Rhett, that's enough," Finnley says, inching closer.

Rhett ignores his brother. "Your mother, of course, found out about her ex-lover's death, and his mate's new home of padded walls and syringes. As a high-ranking officer, she made sure we were never allowed to visit our mother." His angry eyes hold me captive. "She threatened every family we landed with."

I swallow the bile coming up my throat.

A soft cry drags my attention to the professors. "Leave them out of this. They have nothing to do with our past. *We* have nothing to do with our past."

Rhett shakes his head in denial. "Go ahead, Finnley, it's your turn," he orders. "Or Yaretta here will carve out your little friend's jugular."

To drive the point home, she digs the blade deeper, causing me to cry out.

Kingston's head whips in my direction at the sound, shadows rushing toward me as he rips the heart out of a wraith's chest with his bare hands.

He's surrounded.

"You do that, and she'll die before they reach me," Yaretta screams at him.

Kingston grinds his teeth, swiftly decapitates another wraith coming at him and points his sword at Yaretta. Fury and the promise of pain reflect back.

The shadows stop right before they reach us.

His fully black eyes meet mine.

Hang on, Norissa.

I'm coming.

I can't help the small tilt of my lip. This is the first time he's ever called me by my first name.

"Okay," Finnley says, holding up his hands. "Okay, I'll tell her." He looks up at the sky, then at the ground. He doesn't meet my eyes as he speaks. "We needed to fix her."

I silently beg him with my eyes to stop talking. If he would just look at me, he'd see I just want him to stop.

He clenches and unclenches his fists at his sides. "To get her out of the continuous hell she lives in. There were rumors of a way to fix the mind, regardless of how broken it is. We spent years researching it, but we needed experts, which we clearly weren't," he says. "We needed a dark object and an incantation for it to work. Rhett stole a dark object last year while he was at Kintoira, but being a Veil, he obviously couldn't use it, so he kidnapped the alchemy professor." His jaw tightens and a muscle jumps as he speaks. "We thought, with someone who knew about metals, we could find a way for the incantation and dark object to be used by a Veil. We couldn't get it right, though, the research we were finding was in too many different dead languages. We decided I would enroll in the academy to finish what Rhett started before he graduated," he says, finally lifting his sorrow-filled eyes to meet mine. "Which is when I met you."

I shake my head for him to stop. I don't want to hear anymore.

Please just stop.

He runs a hand through his limp curls and stares at me with so much raw vulnerability. His ashy brows furrow as my eyes widen in alarm. A wraith is approaching him from behind, and there isn't enough time for him to react.

I watch in slow motion as its rotten fingers reach out for Finnley's hair. It's the maze all over again. Only it's not.

This time will change everything.

My mouth is open on a silent scream, a refusal filled with fury and regret. When I think I'm about to fragment on the pain I'm having to bear witness to, an arrow pierces its throat, and the wraith crumples at Finnley's feet.

I drag my eyes up to Ambrose, who's fighting his way through a horde, trying to get to me. He throws his bow down, flames rising from his palms as he starts burning through the abominations again.

There's a desperation to his movements.

His skin is pale and soaked with sweat. He's going to burn out. And when he does, they'll descend on him like the plague they are and take the last thing I have worth living for.

I can't let that happen.

I won't let that happen.

Finnley steps away from the dead wraith and walks closer to me, staring at his feet as he does so. "We didn't know about Liminals yet. They were wiped from our texts as you now know." He smiles sadly. "I was working on finding another dark object for Rhett to give the professor to work with. But then you placed as a Liminal. Both Veil and Noctryn." He looks at me as if I'm something precious. "It was like you fell in my lap," he says, hanging his head. "You already considered me a friend. I knew I could use you to help us."

"Look at me when you speak of betraying me," I say in a soft, broken whisper, as blood drips down my chest. The gray shirt is brittle with dried blood. It's now a mesh of rust-colored stains co-mingling with the vibrant crimson of fresh blood.

He raises his head. "I didn't want to use you, Nori. I couldn't. Which is why I kidnapped Professor Hunstal and stole another dark object instead."

Rhett clears his throat. "That's close enough. She can hear you from where you stand."

The sound of Kingston and Ambrose fighting their way through the endless army is a chaotic symphony of violence surrounding us.

Finnley stops approaching and doesn't even look at his brother. "I figured with an expert in language and an expert in alchemy, we could use the old texts to figure out an incantation to create our own dark object. But..." He rubs his face with both hands, clearly agitated by the turn of events. "I'm sure you put two and two together that we ended up needing a Noctryn after all. What dark wielder is going to help a light wielder, though?" He laughs darkly. "Unlikely."

Rhett claps his hands together in quick succession. "Which is why we needed *you*. Because you are not only Noctryn, but a Liminal. End of story," he says with finality. "Thank you, Finnley."

Finnley turns to reprimand his brother, but Rhett shakes his finger back and forth. He grabs both professors and pushes them. The alchemy professor's wide eyes are going back and forth between the two men. Sweat trickles down his brow, and the vein in his forehead is popping out. Professor Huntsal is screaming behind her gag and digging her heels in the sand.

"Come on now, don't be shy," Rhett says in a cheerful voice as he puts them directly in front of my eyes. "The party is just starting."

"Whatever you're thinking about doing, please don't—" I start.

Rhett quickly grabs Hunstal's head, twisting violently before she crumples to the sand. The alchemy professor tries to run but doesn't make it far. Rhett throws a dagger, hitting him directly in the back of the skull. He's dead before he hits the ground.

"WHAT THE FUCK, RHETT?" Finnley screams, walking over and punching his brother in the face. "What is fucking wrong with you?" He stares at his brother as if he doesn't really know him.

I look at the dead professors. The sand around them is changing from amber crystals to crimson shards. "You're both monsters," I whisper, bringing my eyes back to them.

"I'm not, Nori. You know I'm not," Finnley pleads, shaking his head in refusal. "It was us who took our mother, Nori, not the wraiths, from Harkin House. I had no other choice. She grabbed onto a fellow resident and wouldn't let go, so we ended up having to take both," he says. "I swear to you, I didn't know Rhett was going to kidnap you. I was finding another way!" he declares, dropping to his knees in front of me.

Yaretta pulls my head back.

Another friendship built on lies. An abundance of death lingers in the air.

Today would have been a good day to stay in bed.

Ambrose walks up behind Finnley, blood dripping down the side of his temple. He runs his eyes over me, taking in each wound. He looks up at Yaretta before moving over to Rhett and Eryk, who are both watching him with wary expressions.

"You're dead. You're all dead," he says in a lethally calm voice.

There's a trail of decapitated monsters in his wake.

A scoff comes from above. "How are you even here? I saw you at the academy," Yaretta flings at Ambrose, her grip tightening in my hair.

His lips curl. "You don't think Kingston and I knew we were being watched?" he growls. "You and Eryk make piss-poor spies. What you didn't count on was the fact we had a siphoner in our midst."

"Lies!" she screams, yanking my head farther back. "The academy alerts the students when one manifests!"

"Not if it's kept hidden"—He grins—"Suppressed."

I can feel her sharp fingernails digging into the tender skin of my scalp.

"All he needed was something of yours," Ambrose says. "A hair, finger-nail, anything that matches your genetic makeup to cancel or sway your manifestation." He shakes his head at her in mock disappointment. "It was easy enough to find in your room."

I internally flinch at the thought of what Ambrose was doing in her room. Even if it was with ulterior motives, the method was the same.

"You asshole," she hisses. "I would have given you everything!" she screams, cutting deeper into my flesh.

His eyes narrow in on the blood dripping freely down my shirt. His jaw ticks, but he stops talking.

Rhett steps up beside Finnley, who has distanced himself from Ambrose as nonchalantly as possible. His glare drops to me. "To be fair, my brother didn't want you to die, Nori. He's weak in that regard," he says, turning to look at Finnley. "We learned of an ancient book through our research on Liminals after we found out about you. A book that could converse with a Liminal through a blood offering, one that knew endless information of the dark arts. The problem was," he explains, rubbing his bottom lip, "we couldn't touch it to open it, even if we had your blood. Only certain dark wielders or a Liminal can touch it. Only the Liminal can converse with it. Which is why"—he dangles my bag in the air—"I brought it to you."

He dumps out my bag, and Silver falls into the sand. "You can share all of its secrets with us before you die."

Ambrose's pale face narrows in on Rhett. I can see him open and close his palms, itching to incinerate the man.

Out of the corner of my eye, I see the last wraith crumble to the ground.

Kingston walks over, his hair dripping with sweat. His sword hangs loose in his grip, bloody gore and bits of decayed flesh hanging from the blade. He's now shoulder to shoulder with Ambrose. Two soldiers who hate each other, but with fury in their eyes for the same enemy.

Kingston's eyes fall to the dagger under my chin.

His lips pull up, and his canines flash in the sun.

"Well, this little reunion has been fun and all, but we should really be going," Eryk says, nervously looking around at his dead army. He was content to stay in the background until now. "It seems this was just one big misunderstanding."

He looks around for Frederick.

Kingston throws what looks to be a piece of an arm at his chest. It rolls down and sticks to the sand. I can only assume it's the only part of Frederick that's left.

"Unfortunate," Eryk says nervously under his breath, staring at the severed limb.

One minute, he's speaking, and the next, Kingston is standing behind him, dragging a dagger across his throat. His dark, rimmed eyes never leave mine as he cuts into the flesh and bone.

Ambrose pulls a dagger from its sheath, throwing it with deadly precision.

It comes so close I can feel it slice along my cheek as it lands in the center of Yaretta's throat. My hair slips through her fingers, and the thud of her body echoes across the pit.

Rhett raises his hands in the air. "Okay, let's slow down a minute and talk about this." He backs up, hands raised, until he hits the metal bars of a cell.

Ambrose runs over to me, removing the bindings.

I fall forward, my fingers digging into his shoulders.

"Shh, I've got you. I've got you," he whispers in my ear.

Everything in me feels broken. My bones, my will, and my heart all shattered.

Kingston steps toward Rhett. "Fix her," he demands, venom in his tone.

That fucker isn't coming near me.

Kingston's attention slides back to me.

He makes one wrong move, and he's a dead man.

"He's a healer. He'll make this right," Finnley says, taking in the terrified way I'm looking at his brother. "I promise."

"He's the one who fucking did this," I answer back, fury and pain saturating my words.

Rhett gulps and walks back over to me. His eyes are pinned to the dark wielder, the one whose eyes are burning with the need for vengeance.

Ambrose stands and hovers at Rhett's back. A promise of retribution follows in his wake.

Kingston's eyes track every movement, shadows stirring in his palm, waiting for his command.

Rhett places his hands on my back, causing me to jump and shiver uncontrollably. His touch is associated with pain in my brain, and I can't undo it. Ambrose watches him with barely contained fury.

Warmth seeps through my limbs. Broken bones mend themselves, and torn ligaments fuse back together. The dull throb of pain throughout every vessel slowly starts to dissipate. I finally take a deep breath, void of discomfort for the first time in hours.

Ambrose pulls another dagger from a sheath at his thigh.

"Whoa, whoa," Rhett says, holding up both hands as he shuffles back. "I fixed her!" he yells, stumbling over his feet as he retreats.

"Stop." Finnley steps toward Ambrose. "Please, stop. He's my brother. He's all I have left."

"I'm his brother," Rhett says, frantically nodding in agreement. "He needs me."

He doesn't care about Finnley, though, just his own hide. I'm pretty sure deep down Finnley knows it as well. He looks at his brother with such disappointment. But through that lingering void is love. Unconditional. I know, at this moment, if it's between Rhett and me, he's choosing his brother.

I also know Rhett isn't making it out of here alive. I'm pretty sure he knows it, too. He may be a Veil, a soldier, but even after graduating and enlisting, he's no match for the two students standing in front of him.

Finnley looks at me with a small, sad smile on his lips. "Remember, Nori, we'll die one day, but today is not that day," he whispers to me as if we're the only ones in this pit.

He walks over and joins his brother.

We're all standing within arm's reach of each other. The best friend and man I grew to love who broke my heart, the dark major who never stopped believing in me, and the friend whom I instantly bonded with. If someone had told me yesterday that this is where I'd be today, I'd never have believed them.

Finnley drops his head before raising it back up and looking at me. There is so much sorrow and regret in his eyes, but I can't find it in me to feel any kind of forgiveness toward him.

He knew what he was doing, and he proceeded to do it anyway. He knew the cost.

Rhett reaches into his cloak, quick and deliberate, like a man filled with desperation.

Ambrose sees exactly what's happening and lunges toward him. It's all happening so fast that I can't even shout a warning.

Finnley slams the hilt of a weapon into the back of his skull with a heavy thud.

Ambrose's body folds forward, slumping in my lap before I can even get out a full breath. A scream tears from my throat as blood drips from the back of his head onto my legs. I grip the sides of his face, trying to lift his head, demanding he wake up.

Kingston's shadows swirl around us as he heads straight for me.

One second, I'm cradling Ambrose's head. I'm screaming, but I don't know if it's in my head or out loud. The next, the ground shakes with the force of a giant falling. I reluctantly pull my tear-filled eyes from the man I'm cradling in my lap.

Finnley stands behind Kingston, his hands on both shoulders, pushing him to his knees.

My jaw drops slightly.

Kingston isn't moving. Finnley's fingers are digging into his shoulders.

There can only be one reason Kingston isn't moving.

Finnley is siphoning.

Holy shit. He's the siphoner.

Kingston won't be able to move. Not as long as Finnley maintains direct contact. He'll render Kingston helpless, and if it goes on for too long, he'll render him unconscious.

Kingston's jaw clenches, and pure hell rages in his eyes as they meet mine.

Rhett punches the air with his fist. "Yes, I knew you had it in you! You should have told me you manifested!" he yells, jumping up and down like a child. He reaches into his cloak for the dagger he was trying to retrieve. "Now's the fun part," he singsongs, walking up to Kingston.

"Fuck you," Kingston growls, looking up at him.

He punches Kingston hard, causing his head to whip to the side.

He spits blood into the sand and glares at Rhett. "You're a dead man."

While Rhett's distracted, I slowly push Ambrose to the sand, gently laying his head down and stand. Finnley is too focused on draining Kingston, his eyes closed with the need for concentration. I slip behind Rhett and punch him in the back of the head as hard as I can. He curls inward, giving me just enough time to jump on his back and try to wrestle the dagger from his grip.

Kingston thrashes under Finnley's grip.

His shadows start to emerge from his hands regardless of the siphoner at his back. They're dark as midnight and angry. The temperature drops drastically around us, and the sky above darkens like death on swift wings.

I can hear Finnley yelling at me to stop, but I don't let go. I release Rhett's hands just long enough to dig my fingers into his eyes instead. He grunts in frustration before throwing me over his shoulder, causing me to land on my back and knocking the air from my lungs before kicking me multiple times.

I can hear Kingston roaring through the haze of trying to catch my breath.

It's freezing in this pit. Shivers wrack my body as I roll to my knees and push myself up, gulping for air.

Rhett walks over to Kingston and brings his fist back, punching him. Again and again. When he's almost out of breath, he strides over and pulls the dagger from Yaretta's throat before returning to stand in front of Kingston.

Kingston looks up at him, disheveled and bloody.

His lips pull into a sinister smile, his canines on full display.

He's kneeling with the blade pointed under his chin. But the only thing on his face is the promise of what's to come.

"Why are you smiling?" Rhett demands.

"Killing you is going to be the highlight of my entire existence," he answers through bloody teeth.

Rhett pulls the dagger back, and a scream tears through the air.

It's coming from me.

Time slows.

Slender lines of starlight and shadow wrap around me like the webs of a spider. Some are warm, vibrating softly like the promise of a new dawn. Others are dark, so dark they almost appear blue. Cold and void. Both kinds pulse with purpose. Memories. I'm surrounded by a kind of magic that doesn't manifest into powers but undoes them.

A soft voice echoes around me.

Norissa, weaver of threads, it whispers like the delicate wings of a butterfly. *We've been waiting for you. The one that does not control fate but repairs it. Light and dark. Not one but both.* The voice is comforting. Familiar. *Only a weaver can repair the invisible threads of fate. Or undo them altogether. Few are trusted with such a responsibility. To do so incorrectly results in chaos. War. Famine. Destruction.*

A breeze wraps around me, blowing my hair in an arch of crimson.

You can correct what was woven in error. Unravel fates, undo wrong pairings, reinstate legacies.

A thread appears in front of me—frayed, dull and coming apart at the edges. It shimmers in onyx shades, blowing in the breeze as if it's lost its purpose. It calls to me. It vibrates with urgency.

I brush my fingertips around the thread, and the room *tilts.*

I'm thrust back into the throne room, where the little boy looked so sad. An obsidian crown lies in shattered remnants upon the velvet cushion. There is grief in the room, too old to be mine. The little boy stands beside the throne. Shadows swirl around him, and anger burns in his eyes.

Wrong cannot rest, nor ill deed stand. When it is corrected, a crown will be restored, a legacy will be returned. The soft voice wraps around me. *The Arcane Heir will be found. He was meant to rule, and you were meant to find him.*

The thread hangs low in front of me. Waiting for me to choose.

There are pivotal moments in our lives that shape the legacy we leave behind.

This is one of those moments. A choice.

I reach out and hesitantly touch the pulsing thread again. The breeze stops, and the thread vibrates beneath my hand. Fury and revenge.

His.

Somehow, I know without a doubt that it belongs to him.

There's a price to be paid. Although the voice is delicate the words are not. *One must give to take. To repair the bridge between what is and what should have been. The weaver must become part of the fate. Forever tied to the thread restored.*

I should turn back and go the way I came. But I can't resist the pull the same way my lungs can't resist the urge to breathe.

A gold thread, shimmering like stardust and embers, floats toward my hand.

I must pay the price.

I take the light and dark threads and twist them together. I've made my choice.

Power radiates up my arm and through my chest. Light erupts all around, and shadows coil over my skin. The wind thrashes across my face and through my hair.

Then silence.

The threads woven together pulsate in front of me—a living thing.

I reach my hand out to trace the threads. Instead, I'm yanked from the throne room and thrown back to the present.

I fall to my knees in the frigid pit.

I raise my head and look up at Kingston, who's standing above me. Rhett's head dangles from his clenched fist. Finnley is missing.

A black locket hangs from Kingston's neck.

A crown the color of obsidian sits on his head.

A sinister smile pulls at his lips. "They forgot to kill a prince, Heathen," he growls softly.

Kingston is royalty.

Immortal.

Vengeful.

And now our fates are intertwined.

Alisha Korvane is a fantasy author who weaves tales of dark academia, slow-burn romance, and stories of redemption steeped in betrayal and heavy with secrets. Her writing is for those who find comfort in candlelight and chaos, and who believe that beauty and ruin often walk hand in hand.

Her stories are for readers that are drawn to tales that are a haunting blend of quiet rage and aching devotion. She writes for those who never stopped believing in the beauty of the broken.

She lives in rural Kentucky on a small farm with her husband and three sons. When not building worlds or creating turmoil on the page, she can be found curled up with a good book, overanalyzing something, or starting new home projects that she'll probably regret the next day.